UNEARTHING DAY

THE LONELY HUNTER SERIES
BOOK 1

S.K. KARLSSON

Published by:
S.K. Karlsson Publishing, LLC
Austin, TX

Edited by Mindy Reed, Danylle Salinas-McCord, Danielle H. Acee

Cover by Tim Barber

Interior Design by Danielle H. Acee

Paperback ISBN: 979-8-9884619-0-6

eBook ISBN: 979-8-9884619-1-3

Trigger Warning: This novel contains explicit and sensitive content related to human trafficking. The story explores themes of violence, exploitation, sexual abuse, and psychological trauma. It portrays the experiences and struggles of individuals caught in the web of human trafficking, including both adults and minors. Reader discretion is advised, as the content may be distressing or triggering for some individuals. Please take care of your well-being and seek support if needed while engaging with this book.

DOWNLOAD A FREE SAMPLE

WEAVING FATE: THE LONELY HUNTER SERIES PREQUEL

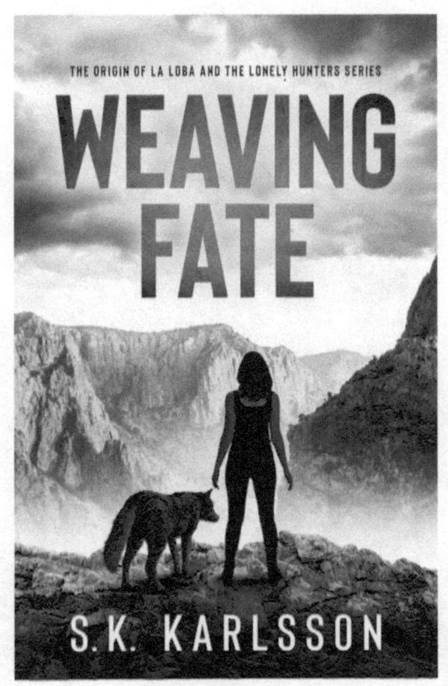

Download here:

https://BookHip.com/ZDCGMSK

"AMONG ANIMALS, there is said to be a mysterious psychic dance between predator and prey. It is said, if the prey gives a certain kind of servile eye contact, and a certain kind of shiver that causes a faint rippling of the skin over its muscles, that the prey acknowledges its weakness to the predator and agrees to become the predator's victim."

—*Women Who Run with the Wolves*

"Stalking the Intruder: The Beginning Initiation" chapter

PROLOGUE

SATURDAY, DECEMBER 27, 2003

ASH-GRAY FUR COVERED La Loba's lycanthrope form as she cast her gaze from 734 miles away toward Austin. She transitioned into her human self as snow gathered in clumps upon New Mexico's Gila Mountain conifers. With her far-seeing left eye, she observed Dia under a familiar man's stare.

La Loba's prognosticative abilities were her strength—and her curse. She sat motionless on her snowy perch. Her first encounter with an almost five-year-old Dia in the spring of 1993 was not unlike the other people whose futures she gleaned upon contact. The difference this time had boiled down to someone with whom the child's future would ultimately collide. She'd be unable to prevent their meeting, but that didn't preclude her from wanting to intercede via one of her homemade dolls.

Lucy sat among scores of other toys collecting dust on a shelf in Dia's room more than ten years later, but she'd accompanied her little human on countless outings in their early days together. She had provided her everything La Loba had intended following their brief encounter in Terlingua: peace, comfort, intuition. Then life happened. The girl's transition into adolescence punctuated a life fraught with loss and eroded her connection to her soul. Her relationship with herself shrank each year, supplanted by compliance and a desire to fit in and not be seen.

La Loba shifted her weight from her left foot to her right. Time was running out. She couldn't alter Dia's life nor force her young friend to listen to her once-trusted inner voice. There were small ways to intervene, perhaps by triggering the unintentional delivery of a protective charm from their soon-to-be mutual acquaintance. She might even be able to summon enough psychic energy to influence the teen to take a stand and assert herself when the time was appropriate. If all else failed, La Loba could at least be there for her if her journey ever drew to an end.

Restorative skills complemented La Loba's forecasting abilities. If any attempts to help Dia were dashed, she planned to intervene with a supernatural act her elders forbade. La Loba rose and transitioned back to her canine form then took one last look toward Austin. The days of tribulation the teenager faced gave the older woman pause. She sighed as she turned to retreat to her cave and prepare for the day their paths would intersect once more.

PART ONE

"Developing a relationship with the wildish nature is an essential part of women's individuation. In order to execute this, a woman must go into the dark, but at the same time she must not be irreparably trapped, captured, or killed on her way there or back."

—*Women Who Run with the Wolves*
"Stalking the Intruder: The Beginning Initiation" chapter

ONE

THURSDAY, FEBRUARY 19 – SATURDAY, FEBRUARY 21, 2004

MACY'S ONE-DAY sale loomed less than two days away, and Dia Remington bustled from one clothing rack to the next, setting clothes hangers an equal distance apart. Armed with scores of placards, coworkers Gina and Anita serpentined their way around stands of Nine West, Calvin Klein, and New York Collection dresses, affixing announcements of thirty to fifty percent off already-reduced prices.

"Looking good in here, ladies!" their manager yelled from across the floor. She pulled a cart loaded with unopened boxes behind her.

"Do you need us to unpack those?" Anita asked.

"I'll have tomorrow's crew take care of these," Lonnie said. "Why don't you all wrap it up? You can head out early if you like, Dia. Shoppers seem to be staying home to wait for Saturday."

"Awesome! Thanks, Lonnie," Dia said.

"Maybe you'll pass your test now. What was it again? Calculus?"

"Spanish, actually, and I think what you meant to say is that I'll ace it."

Lonnie gave her a high five. "Go, lady. We'll take care of it from here. Good luck tomorrow."

"See ya." Dia retrieved her purse from below the register and headed to the escalator.

"You're not going to say goodbye to us?" Gina asked.

Dia turned. "Hey, that 'see ya' was for all of y'all."

Gina laughed. "Okay, just making sure. See ya Saturday. Bring cash so we can all go out after our shift."

"Will do. Bye, you two!" She waved at Gina, who stood six inches above Anita, then descended downstairs to level one. Reddish-blond hair caught Dia's attention as she approached the men's department. Todd, Macy's hottest security guard, walked through the suits and ties section in his crimson sports jacket, serving as a deterrent to would-be shoplifters and as eye candy to female store clerks everywhere.

"Headed out early?" Todd asked.

Dia smiled, pulling her lips in to make them appear thinner. "Yeah...I mean, well, if Brogan can leave, too. He's my ride home."

"Slow enough tonight, eh?" Todd stared at Dia with a playful smile as he studied her mouth. He did this with some frequency, making her warm and uncomfortable all at the same time as she tried to read his mind. He was eight years her senior, and his flawless skin, golden brown eyes, and sharp jawline drove her to distraction. He cleared his throat. "It looked like your, um...your department was ready for Saturday."

"Well, you know Lonnie. She lives and breathes this place," she said, wishing he'd ask her out. Who cared if he was older? It wasn't like her parents would notice, anyway.

"You don't?" Todd winked.

Dia blushed. *Is he flirting?*

"Hey, my boss just told me I can leave early," Brogan said as he bounded up to them. Any possible flirtation evaporated into mist as Brogan started directing Dia to their break room lockers to clock out. "I'm so glad I don't need to cram for Carver's Spanish quiz now."

"Me, too." Dia peered back at Todd. *Is he as disappointed as I am?*

"See you Saturday," he said.

"You too, bro," Brogan said for both of them. "Come on, D."

Todd winked at her again, his affectionate smile signaling something more than amicable friendship. She gave an apologetic wave and followed her driving companion through an employee-only door. Brogan Bubenik was Dia's weeknight transportation until she could pass the test for her provisional license and save enough money for the down payment on a car of her own. They worked at Baskin-Robbins before he helped her get hired at Macy's the previous fall. It was a step up from serving ice cream, and they'd started before Thanksgiving as malls everywhere geared up for retail's most profitable time of year.

With dark brown hair and greenish-brown eyes, Brogan bore a slight resemblance to Tom Brady and had similar confidence. Last October, their mutual friend, Alison, hosted a Halloween party that included endless rounds of spin-the-bottle, which gave Dia one rare opportunity to make out with her classmate-turned-chauffeur.

"Oh, yeah! Go for it, bro," one of his friends had cheered that night.

Dia knew better than to mistake two minutes of French kissing for a long-term romance, but he crossed her mind every so often as she contemplated what dating someone must feel like. The only person aware of her feelings was her best friend, Samantha.

"I thought he and Lilly were together. Have I missed something?" she asked the last time Dia brought him up.

"They are," Dia said. "A girl can hope, though."

Lilly was captain of their high school volleyball team. Like

Brogan, she had a smile that endeared her to groups and cliques across the entire school's social strata. When Brogan fractured his leg skiing over spring break during their freshman year, she'd pushed his wheelchair between classes, leaving Dia locked in The Friend Zone unless recent rumors of a possible schism carried any weight.

Brogan darted in and out of traffic, jostling Dia to and fro and making her reach for the passenger-side safety handle. "Jesus! What's your hurry?" Her knuckles turned white as he crossed three lanes to make a right turn. "I would think leaving early from work would give you plenty of time to study tonight without endangering our lives to get home."

He operated his mother's Lexus SC 430 as if he owned the car himself, and she worried about him getting in an accident someday or causing someone else to swerve and lose control. The car's speedometer climbed toward 90 mph as Brogan raced his way to their suburban homes.

"Oh, relax," he retorted. "I'm not in a hurry to crack open my Spanish book. I just like the rush."

"Yeah? Well, your need for speed makes me want to break into my parents' supply of Xanax."

He laughed out loud. "That's why I like you, D. You say super-bizarre things."

Dia pressed herself back into her seat with both feet pushed against a make-believe brake pedal the rest of the way home.

"Pick you up on Saturday?" Brogan asked as he pulled into her driveway.

"Mmm, not sure. Maybe if my dad has to work this weekend."

"Okay, just let me know."

"Thanks, Brogan." Dia closed the door and made her way inside, where she found her parents sitting in front of the TV. "Anything good on?"

"*I* think so," Susan said. "But your dad's threatening to go to bed."

"I don't even understand how people can watch this crap," he said. "I lose brain cells every time this program comes on."

"Honey, you know how much I love *The Bachelor*. An attack on the show is an attack on me." Susan turned back to Dia with a wink.

What's up with the winking? Dia wondered. Then she reminded herself how her stepmother always put on a show for the benefit of her dad.

"You know what I mean. How was work, Dia?" her dad asked. "You're home a bit early, aren't you?"

"Things were super-slow, so Lonnie let me come home to study for tomorrow's big Spanish test."

"Ah," he said.

"What's the work schedule like this weekend, Dad? Are you on call?"

"Not this weekend, why? Do you need a ride?"

"If you don't mind. Some of the gals want to go out for dinner after the sale on Saturday, and Brogan won't want to stick around for that."

"It's fine by me if Susan's okay with it," he said, turning his attention back to the TV.

"Susan?" she asked.

"Sure, Dia. Though I can't see why one of your other coworkers can't drive you home."

Dia glared at her stepmother, the woman who'd insisted she get a job in the first place. "Um, okay. Yeah let me see what they say. I'm heading up. Goodnight."

"Night," her dad said.

Dia climbed the stairs two at a time and walked the length of the hallway to her room. She passed her stepbrother's room on her right and peeked inside to find Jackson sprawled across his bed, sound asleep. He was funny and energetic—the best part of her dad's marriage to Susan. And unlike his mom, he never had a bad thing to say about his stepsister.

"Good night, sweet boy," Dia whispered as she pulled the sheets up under his chin.

Dia joined Anita and Gina an hour before opening on Saturday to once again space dresses, blouses, and slacks hanging from sparkling-clean store racks. Todd unlocked the doors at ten a.m., and customers—many of whom had lined up at the entrances before sunrise—filed inside and kept everyone busy until their afternoon breaks.

With a backpack over one shoulder, Dia walked to the food court and was pleased to find the shortest line at Panda Express. She withdrew notes from her bag for an upcoming chemistry test while she waited to order her Kung Pao chicken. A Panda Express trainee made one mistake after another while entering orders from the hungry customers in front of her. Dia checked her wristwatch. *Is this why the line is so short?* she wondered. She'd be lucky to have fifteen minutes to inhale her lunch before rushing back to her department.

"How hard is it?"

She turned around and connected with a set of light gray eyes belonging to a young man she'd seen once or twice before. "I mean, don't they make the register simple enough a ten-year-old can operate it?" he asked. The stranger was dressed head to toe in black. Even his hair was black.

"I guess." Dia broke eye contact as her neck and cheeks started to flush. She turned back around, impatient for the line to move faster. A Panda Express supervisor came from the back to help his struggling trainee and hasten the fulfillment of food orders.

When she was finally able to procure her food, Dia turned to scan the food court for an empty booth and found the man in black standing next to her, smiling. The all-too-familiar heat of social awkwardness crept up her neck again, and she opted for an escape. She tossed her tray on top of a trash bin, made a quick exit from the food court, and hustled to the safety of the Macy's employee break room to eat alone.

Dia planned to tell Anita and Gina about the guy in the food court, but everyone was so busy when she got back to the department, they barely had time to make eye contact, let alone talk.

TWO

SATURDAY, FEBRUARY 28, 2004

HER COLLEAGUES LISTENED as Dia divulged rumors of a breakup between Brogan and Lilly. "Can you believe it? I mean, I just figured they'd last forever."

"Who's Lilly again?" Gina asked.

Anita rolled her eyes. "She's been Brogan's girlfriend for more than a year now—head cheerleader or something like that."

"Captain of the volleyball team," Dia said. "And I don't know for certain they're broken up. I overhead some girls talking about it in geometry yesterday."

"Is Brogan okay?" Anita asked.

"I dunno. He avoided the topic during our rides to work on Tuesday and Thursday night. It's either a bunch of gossip, or he's doing that guy thing and acting like it's no big deal."

"Let's say it *is* true. Didn't you say there was a dance coming up this spring?" Gina asked.

"The Sadie Hawkins."

"Yeah, what if you asked him? You're friends and all. Maybe this could be your chance, you know, to take things to the next level?" Anita winked at Gina.

Dia scoffed at the idea of Brogan ever saying yes as Todd

sashayed through their department en route to a call in housewares. "What about our lovely security guard instead?" she asked.

"Uh, no. Todd's like a full-grown man!" Gina said.

"Exactly! Besides, I doubt your folks would approve," Anita said.

Why did I even bring it up? Dia wondered. "You assume my parents pay that much attention to me."

"Is there anyone else you can invite?" Anita asked.

"God, all this talk about boys and high school makes my stomach turn. So glad I don't have to deal with stuff like this anymore," Gina said.

Lonnie walked up. "Dia, lunchtime. We'll see you in thirty."

Dia grabbed her backpack from a breakroom locker, stamped her timecard, and left for the food court. With a slice of cheese pizza and a Dr Pepper, she sat reading *Wuthering Heights* and taking notes when black shoes materialized in her peripheral vision. She raised her eyes and found a familiar face smiling down at her.

"Hi, I'm Baco." He extended his hand. "I'm sorry to bug you. I saw you here a week ago and didn't want to miss another chance to introduce myself properly and to tell you how beautiful you are."

Seriously? She lowered her gaze. "I think you're confusing me with someone else."

"Not at all. Weren't you over at Panda Express last Saturday when that trainee was having so much difficulty with the register?"

"Possibly," she said, maintaining attention on her book.

"May I sit?"

A quick glance at her wristwatch confirmed she had twelve minutes left on her break. "Okay…I guess."

The man slid into the seat opposite her. He wore black jeans and a button-down shirt similar to what she'd seen him in previously. His jet-black hair shone blue under the food court's fluorescent light as he took a seat across from her. Baco's natural curls were cut below his ears and framed his rectangular face, but a cowlick over his right eyebrow lent a certain playfulness to his style.

Dia had assumed him to be of Latin descent from their brief encounter last week, but upon closer inspection, his skin possessed a translucency. The bluish hue of veins beneath his pale complexion gave him a ghostlike quality. His gray eyes were stunning and penetrating, as if able to peer inside her soul.

His stare made her uneasy. *I should go*, she thought.

"You're gorgeous." He leaned forward. "Has anyone ever told you that you look like Cameron Diaz?"

Dia shifted in her seat. His repeated compliments on her looks contrasted to what the boys in school had said some years back.

"I apologize. I don't mean to make you uncomfortable."

"You're okay." She flipped the book over in her hands. Baco held his hand out for it.

"Have you read *Wuthering Heights*?" she asked.

"Comic books are more up my alley, but I recall seeing this on TV. It's been turned into a film, right?"

"Many times, actually. Laurence Olivier…do you know him?"

Baco shook his head.

"Well, Olivier portrayed Heathcliff most famously, I suppose. Heathcliff's one of like three or four main characters. My favorite portrayal is by Ralph Fiennes, though."

Baco's brow furrowed.

I'm talking too much. Can I be less of a nerd? "So, you like movies?"

"Definitely." The crease above his eyes smoothed back down.

"Cool. You mentioned comic books. Does that mean you're into superheroes?"

"Sure, you know, X-Men or Spiderman. Those *Matrix* films weren't bad. Did you see those?" he asked.

"'There is no spoon.'"

"Come again? Oh, wait. You're quoting Neo."

Dia smiled at her pop culture reference. "Close. It was one of the kids in the first movie who said the line. Remember? One of the other potential candidates?"

Baco stared back at her looking a bit lost and the crease above his eyes returned.

"Never mind," she said.

"And you? Any stand-out movies on your list?" Baco asked.

"*Lord of the Rings* has to be my current favorite. I can watch Frodo and Sam once a month or more! Of course, my younger brother and stepmom pretty much control the TV, so it's either *Love Actually* or some other chick flick for Susan while Jackson is like you. He's a huge fan of *X-Men*. Did you catch *Return of the King*?"

"No, I missed that one. I caught *Mystic River*, though. Boy, talk about being creeped out!"

"Right? Creepy is accurate."

"Um, I don't think I got your name."

"Oh, sorry. I'm Dia."

"Is that short for Claudia or something?"

"My mom named me after my maternal grandmother, whose name was Diana, but Dia is pronounced like Dee-a."

"Gotcha. And what do your friends call you?"

"Dia usually, but my best friend calls me by first initial, D."

"Like D-E-E?"

"You got it. She's the only one who's allowed to call me that." Brogan's image popped to mind. "Well, maybe more than one. She uses it most, though. We've known each other since we were little."

"Hmm." He handed her book back, brushing her hand with his index finger. "So, do you go to school around here?"

Hasn't Susan warned me more than once not to talk to strangers? Dia searched for a response that would allow her to answer without sounding evasive. "Yes, a few blocks away from here." *Not a hundred percent true, but close enough.* "And you? Do you take classes nearby?"

"I moved here eight or so weeks ago for work. I'm in sales, and my territory's been expanded to include all of Texas."

"So, a promotion?"

"How do you mean?"

"You've been promoted, it sounds like. I heard you say your territory had been expanded."

"Oh, sorry. Yeah, I guess you can say they advanced me up the old totem pole."

Dia broke eye contact to look at the time, knowing she'd hear one of Lonnie's lectures if she stayed much longer.

"Do you need to leave?"

"I'm going to be late if I don't." She preferred to stick around and learn more about her new friend. She guessed him to be older than her, though she hoped only as old as a freshman at UT.

"I can walk with you."

"I'd like that." They stood and walked away from the food court. "So where were you living before moving to Austin?"

"Dallas is home. My manager lives there, too. I could probably stay in the DFW area and manage my territory, but with my *promotion*, he thought it best I come here for a while until I hire staff. Then, I'll do something similar in Houston and El Paso, too."

"What do you sell?"

"Software."

Dia struggled to pin down his age, but he struck her as too

young to have so much responsibility already. If he was growing a team, she wondered how much he made and if working for him would earn her more income than what she did in retail. Earning minimum wage made saving up for her own car next to impossible.

Walking side by side, Baco's hand brushed hers as he moved close to avoid bumping into passing shoppers. He was tall. Since she was 5'9", she guessed him to be 6'2" or 6'3". For a brief moment, she considered the possibility of taking Baco to the spring dance. *Who am I kidding? He's got business things like hiring and sales quotas to worry about.*

"So how long do you expect to stay in Austin?" Dia paused at a gift shop two doors down from Macy's.

"I get such a kick out of this territory—Texas in general." Baco pointed at the display case filled with pennants, bumper stickers, and scorpions encased in resin. "Our state sure likes to celebrate itself, doesn't it?"

"Other states don't?" She'd never been beyond Texas' borders.

"Not like this." He pointed to a poster that stated, *I'm not from Texas, but I got here as fast as I could* between an array of stuffed armadillos, jalapeño jelly jars, and T-shirts emblazoned with the state flag. "Oh, and I'm sure Texas is the only place with state-edition trucks."

"I never gave it much thought, but you never see *Missouri*-edition Chevys, do you?"

"Exactly. Right? So, are you a senior? What are your plans after graduation?"

"College, but I have two more years to go still. I'm a sophomore." She darted her eyes away from him as he smiled at her. "I might go premed so that I can go on to medical school like my dad. Journalism sounds interesting, though. I'd like to travel across the country and even around Europe and Asia, reporting on history as it unfolds."

"Is traveling what appeals to you, or writing?"

"Hmm. I'm not sure, to tell you the truth."

"Well, when you mentioned traveling, your eyes sparkled, and your face brightened."

This weird guy in the goth-like clothes was flattering her as he stared as if looking straight through her. Baco paid more attention to what she said than anyone else had in a long time.

"So, what do you do for a good time, Miss Dia?"

She peered up at him. "Sorry?"

"For fun? In your free time?"

"Free time? Right. I don't get much time for anything after classes, studying, and work. I babysit some. Does watching someone else's kids count as entertainment?"

"Um, no."

"I guess I'd go to more movies, but sunset walks give me peace of mind when I'm stressed," she said. *God, can I sound any lamer?*

"Lake Travis is nearby. Do you ever go swimming?"

"My dad's friend has a yacht near Volente Beach."

"A yacht? Are you rich or something?"

"Ha! If we were, then *we* would have a houseboat. I wouldn't work twenty hours a week, either. No, he's a surgeon. My stepmom thinks he lives beyond his means."

"Funny."

"So, no, I don't spend a lot of time on the water, or any of Austin's lakes for that matter, although it sounds tempting. I'm curious about Barton Springs."

"What if we went out some time to grab a pizza or something?"

She rolled Baco's invitation around in her mind. *Why would he invite me? What could someone like him see in me?*

"I, um." she cleared her throat as he leaned closer. No one had ever asked her out unless she counted nerdy Eric's invite to play D&D back in ninth-grade physical science class. "I would like that very much."

"Great! When?"

Is this how boys ask girls out? "Well, I should probably check with my family first and make sure we don't have anything going on."

"What's your number?"

"I'm sorry?"

"Your phone number?" Baco jutted his head a few degrees forward and squinted his eyes. "Is it okay if I call you sometime?"

"Oh, sorry!" *He must think I'm an idiot.* She dug in her backpack for a sheet of notebook paper as Baco waited. The process took way longer than she would have liked. Thirty seconds had passed like slow-moving primordial goo by the time she'd finally written her cell number down. "Here you go."

Dia spotted Lonnie just beyond the Macy's entrance looking at her wristwatch. Tension shot up her spine. "I'd better go. My boss is pacing over there, and I'm guessing she's wondering why I'm late."

"I'm sorry. Tell her to blame me."

"No, the fault's all mine. I just stopped paying attention to the time."

"You'll answer when I call this? You didn't give me the digits for some cranky old woman, did you?"

"No, I promise you'll reach me," Dia said.

"I'm teasing. You're super literal."

"Beats being gullible, I guess, which is how my stepmom describes me."

"I think you're perfect." Baco stretched out his hand.

Blood rushed to the surface of Dia's skin as she shook it, this time returning his squeeze.

"Enjoy the rest of your shift." He turned and sauntered back toward the food court.

"Thanks." She spun around with a pep in her step and walked up to Lonnie as she entered Macy's. "I'm sorry it took so long to get back from lunch. Would it help if I said I may have just met someone who is boyfriend material?"

"All right; calm down," Lonnie said. "You're more than just a minute tardy, though. You're closer to five minutes late."

"Yes, I understand."

"You remember I don't have patience for behavior like this, right?"

"Yes ma'am, I hear you."

"Are you going to keep agreeing with everything I say?"

"Yep." Dia grinned from ear to ear.

"Oh, brother. Just punch back in and get back out here ASAP, will you?"

"Yes, ma'am," Dia said.

She scurried to Macy's employee lounge to clock in then almost knocked a young child over as she skipped back to the women's dress department. Four hours struck her as an unbearably long time to endure talking with customers, but talk she did, outselling all the other associates combined for a record performance.

"You should flirt with boys more often," Gina said.

"Ha-ha," Dia said. "I'm going to miss our group at dinner tonight, FYI."

"Really? Why?"

"Hey, I made it last week and I promise to go next time, but I've gotta get home and visit with my dad."

"Lame...so lame," Anita said. "We're going to gossip about you behind your back if you don't meet us."

"Yes, but you'll do it with love." Dia made a kissy face at her. "Wow, 9:35 already. I'll catch up with y'all on Tuesday."

Gina rolled her eyes. "Oh, fine. Go do what you must do."

"Night, night, chicas." Dia floated on air as she exited the store. A note with her name on it peeked out from Brogan's passenger-side wiper blade, and she grabbed it before he noticed anything.

Dia,

It was such a pleasant surprise meeting you today. I hope I'll get to see you again real soon.

Baco

Her first date, perhaps her first boyfriend, and now her first love letter. Dia thought it was really cool that he knew which car belonged to Brogan. She barely remembered the drive home from work as she entertained varying dating scenarios with her new, handsome friend.

THREE

SUNDAY, FEBRUARY 29 – MONDAY, MARCH 1, 2004

HOMEWORK BECKONED the morning after Dia's shift, but focusing remained next to impossible. Baco's invitation for a date spun around her head. She pondered how best to bring it up with her dad, but she had missed him the night before when an eight-car pileup on I-35 required him to work.

Downstairs, Susan whistled and hummed as she fried bacon in her favorite iron skillet. At some point, she would shout upstairs her intentions to pour pancake batter and invite Dia to join them for Sunday brunch. Dia crossed her fingers that her stepmom remembered to add blueberries this week.

Concentrating on her studies continued to prove difficult between wafts of fried pork and memories of her encounter with the cute boy from the food court. No one had ever called her beautiful before. *Was he for real? Why would someone as handsome as Baco want to talk to me?*

Wuthering Heights and her Spanish homework were no closer to getting done as she lay there daydreaming. She hated how procrastination made her feel and knew her paper—while not due until Thursday—required the most effort.

"Just do your work!" She picked up Brontë's novel and penned an eight-point outline in less than ten minutes. With any luck, she'd get a rough draft of her essay written in time to catch *America's Funniest Home Videos* at 6:00 p.m. Spanish would have to wait.

"Dia, five-minute warning!" Susan called from downstairs.

"*Dia, five-minute warning*," her stepbrother echoed two rooms down from hers. Dia rolled her eyes before jotting down some final thoughts on Catherine's choice of Linton over Heathcliff.

Jackson burst into her bedroom. "*Five-minute warning!*" he mimicked once more. Privacy was next to impossible with her nearly thirteen-year-old stepbrother. She turned to scold him but found disciplining someone as cute as him far too difficult. Jackson's missing father still remained a mystery after a decade, but she guessed him to be a blond surfer. Jackson's swimmer's hair hung in front of his pale blue eyes. Dimples framed his smile as he threw himself on her unmade bed.

"Scram, silly boy!"

"Never! What are you working on, anyway? It's Sunday morning."

"Homework. Familiar with the concept?" Dia tossed a pillow at him.

"Nope, but I think it's something you nerdy kids do for fun," he said.

"Aren't you a smart kid?"

"Yeah, not like you, though."

"Whatever."

"Whatevs... Mom says you have five minutes like *now*," Jackson said as he left her room, throwing a stuffed animal at her head.

Dia turned back to her desk, smiling. She went to pick up the British classic, but Baco's note sticking out of her purse caught her eye. She retrieved it and reread and obsessed over his words before returning it to her bag.

Her new friend stood out from other guys. His dark features and monochromatic wardrobe gave him a European vibe, quite different from Brogan's all-American looks. Compared to Todd, Baco was less handsome, but they shared something in common. She struggled to put her finger on it. Perhaps it was because neither of them was from Cedar Park High. They had experience and independence, but something else separated Baco from the boys she normally encountered.

The word "sophisticated" came to mind when she thought of him. Even if they were all black, his clothes reminded her of male models in magazines. All he needed was a day's growth of facial hair, and she imagined he could adorn a Calvin Klein billboard. Unlike Todd, this new, dark stranger projected a combined mix of mystery and confidence. She didn't have to struggle to read his mind like she often did with her security-guard admirer. In some way, her friend struck her as more mature even, which stopped her for a moment as she contemplated his age. *Still not sure...* She'd have a hard time persuading her family to let her go out with him if he was much older than her. Or would she? For all the attention they paid, she could accept an invitation from the crown prince of England and her parents would be none the wiser.

Dia played yesterday's conversation back in her mind. Baco said he managed a team or intended to put a group together of some sort...something to do with software. He said he planned to set everything up here in Austin before going to Houston or El Paso. The details were blurry. She didn't recall any mention of college. Perhaps he was one of those lucky folks whose talent and connections enabled him to create a career straight out of high school.

"Breakfast is ready!" Susan called.

Dia jumped up and changed into a pair of sweatpants and a T-shirt. She dropped her pajamas in her laundry basket as she made her way out of her room and downstairs. On the way to the kitchen, she searched for a smart approach to discussing Baco without mentioning his occupation. She didn't want to make it an issue if there was no reason to.

Over the years, her father had grown distant from her. He parented by absentee ballot most of the time and left the heavy lifting to his second wife. Dia had come to accept that, but now she worried her first invitation to go on a legitimate date might reactivate his involvement in her life.

Still, I'm going to need permission from one of them. She rounded the pony wall into the kitchen. "Hey, everyone."

"Morning, sweetie." Kyle Remington tipped the corner down on the Sunday paper, peering over his readers at his daughter.

Dad it is! It had to be him, regardless of how much time they spent—or didn't spend—together these days. Besides, the idea of discussing boys with the woman who fought to maintain her position in their house as an alpha female soured her otherwise bubbly mood. Dia plopped down next to Jackson, who sat with his fork and knife in hand. Sunlight filled their spacious breakfast nook as it reflected off their backyard pool. She had to squint to adjust her eyes. To her left, PGA announcers prepped for their final day of the weekend tournament. Jim Nantz led the effort and recapped three days of play for home viewers.

Her dad would absorb Nantz's analysis for several hours to come from one of many TVs in their kitchen, family room, or upstairs media room. He mainly concentrated on two things in his life: work and golf. Everything else competed for his attention. If Dia opened up the discussion about Baco by bringing up her dad's favorite pastime, then she might increase her chances of going out with him.

Tiger Woods' face graced Sunday's sports section. His contribution to the game had piqued everyone's interest over recent years. "How's it looking for Tiger, Dad? This will be his fourth win at the Masters later this year, right?"

"Tiger's not been doing too well lately. My money is on Mickelson."

"Who?"

"Phil Mickelson."

"Has he ever won?"

"No, not yet."

Susan rounded the kitchen island with a plate stacked high with six-inch pancakes—none of them with blueberries.

"About time!" Jackson snatched three pancakes before his mom set them down on the table.

"Jackson, calm down!" Susan's face contorted in disapproval.

"Sorry," he said, spitting out crumbs.

"Mickelson's won on the tour for years," her dad said. "But no majors. I hate to jinx him, but this will potentially be his first...especially considering Tiger's slump."

"Gotcha." Dia shook her head. *Just bring it up, will you?* "So...I met someone at lunch yesterday. He's kind, respectful even, and I think y'all would like him."

Her dad's eyebrows edged upward while he cut his food.

Laughing out loud, Susan peered at Dia through narrowed eyes. "How would you know all that about him if he's some boy you *just* met?"

"I guess what I'm trying to say, or ask, is whether I might be able to see him sometime."

"You mean a date, then?" Susan asked.

Jackson chimed in. "Sister has a boyfriend."

Dia's ears grew warm, and she knew her skin was turning red as she sat there. "Dad, what do you think?"

He washed his pancakes down with a gulp of coffee before looking at his daughter. She sensed him wanting to say something. He looked down and resumed eating instead.

"Dia, you're not even fifteen yet," Susan said.

"I turn *sixteen* in May!" Dia picked her plate up and stood. Her appetite was gone.

"Where are you going, young lady?" Susan asked. "You haven't been excused."

You horrible, unbearable bitch. "I'm not hungry." Dia took her dishes to the sink.

She left the kitchen and returned to her room where she crumbled down on an unmade bed, pounding a fist into the nearest pillow. *Why does that woman always have to stick her nose in?* Time could not pass fast enough until high school graduation to create some much-needed space from her dad's house. God, how she missed her real mom at times like these.

Dia stood up and searched her bookshelves for her oldest, most treasured possession: a wooden doll a woman gave her during a trip to Big Bend as a young child. It had painted eyes and lips and horsehair fashioned into braids. Named Lucy, it always seemed to connect Dia to the woman who loved her more than anything in the world. She cradled Lucy to her heart and closed her eyes, imagining how the conversation might have gone if her mom had still been alive. *Darling, he sounds charming. Tell me more about him.*

Just then, the floorboard creaked outside her room. There was a knock on her door. Half expecting her dad to enter, she raised her eyes to find Jackson instead.

"Hey, D. Sorry for poking fun a little while ago."

She studied her stepbrother's face as he sat on the edge of the bed. "Thanks, Jack." *How could someone so sweet come from such a spiteful a-hole?*

"They'll come around after they've thought about it some," he said.

"Unlikely, but I appreciate you trying to make me feel better. Why does your mom have to be so mean, anyway?"

"You got me. Maybe she's jealous. That doesn't really make sense to me, but that's what I heard one of the characters say to another girl on TV the other night."

"Good grief! What were you watching, and what did you do with my little brother?"

"I'm not a total idiot."

"Just a partial?"

"Hey, now!"

"Teasing. I love you, little man." She ruffled the top of his head.

"Love you, too." He left and closed the door behind him.

If her dad wasn't going to give her the green light on seeing Baco, then she'd have to figure something else out. Dia sat at her desk to resume her *Wuthering Heights* assignment as an idea took shape in her head.

A day later, Brogan stood at his locker, chatting with his fellow soccer teammates before lunch. Dia studied him from several feet away. He commanded attention from his friends while flirting with any girl brave enough to pass the testosterone-charged athletic squad. To Dia, he came across as trying a little too hard to be cool. *Why do boys act that way?*

The question was answered as she closed her locker and turned to walk to Language Arts. She passed Lilly on her right and saw mascara smeared under her eyes. *Has their breakup become official?* she wondered. Dia would have to wait until tomorrow's ride to work for Brogan to offer up a more specific answer. She had prayed for this golden opportunity barely a week ago but could not care less now.

High school seemed beneath her all of a sudden. A text from her best friend the night before had cemented Dia's plans for Friday night's date with Baco, parental approval be damned. Her classmates' failed romance struck Dia as theatrical in light of her pending date and potential relationship. She ignored the drama while others gossiped about how it ended and who would work harder to move on. There'd be vigorous attempts by both Lilly and Brogan to make each other jealous at the upcoming dance. For this reason, Dia felt grateful to be standing on the outside looking in, observing, rather than being used as a possible pawn.

Tuesday couldn't arrive fast enough. The drive with Brogan would fill in the gaps on his breakup, but with any luck, it would bring another face-to-face encounter with Baco. Dia floated through the rest of her day, encouraged by the fact that she'd soon go on her very first date.

FOUR

TUESDAY, MARCH 2 – FRIDAY, MARCH 5, 2004

TUESDAY'S SHIFT at Macy's allowed for little socializing as Dia replenished empty racks with new dresses.

"So, are you going to invite Brogan to the dance now or what?" Anita asked.

"Mmm, I don't think so. He kept pretty mum about things on our way here tonight. He acts so tough in front of his friends, but something tells me he and Lilly won't be apart for long. I mean, what other reason would he have for being so quiet?"

"God alone knows the mysteries of what men think, I guess, but then who else is there for you to ask?"

"Oh, you never know." Dia's cheeks flushed with color.

"Tell us!" Gina said.

"No, I want to wait just a bit before I say anything. If all goes well this Friday, then I'll let you in on my secret."

"So mysterious," Anita said.

"What's 'mysterious?'" Todd asked from behind them.

"Geez! Creep much?" Gina asked.

"Hey, there. What's up?" Dia asked as her friends searched for more inventory to unpack.

"You gotta date this weekend?" he asked.

"Yeah, I do actually." She caught him staring at her lips again. "Surprised?"

"Not at all. I guess I just didn't realize you were old enough."

"What is it with everyone thinking I'm too young to go out with a guy?"

Todd corkscrewed his mouth to the left. "Who's 'everyone?'"

"Never mind. Um, look, I'm going to pop over to the food court real quick for a soda. Can you tell the others? I'll be back in five."

"Yeah, sure. I suppose."

Dia skipped out of the store, eager to make the most of her time away. A moment later, she met Baco at the Panda Express, and he handed her a drink.

"Hi, beautiful. Here's your Dr Pepper."

"Thank you." Dia took the drink from Baco's hands. "Listen, um…I only have a second, but it turns out I'm going to be spending the night with my best friend on Friday," she said as she sipped her soda. Her stomach flip-flopped under the weight of his stare.

"Really? Okay. So, pick you up at her place? Or are you trying to wriggle out of seeing me?" Baco winked as she returned the cup to him.

"Are you kidding? No, it's just going to be easier this way. And I can meet you at the restaurant."

"Whatever you say, babe."

"K, I gotta hurry back. Thanks for the DP."

"Sure thing. I'll text you tomorrow, and we can firm up where we want to eat."

Three days later, time dragged slower than snails traveling on the shell of a tortoise as Dia anticipated her upcoming rendezvous. Butterflies swirled around in her belly and up to her chest. *Will he hold my hand, open doors for me, or kiss me goodnight?* Buoyed by excitement, her world came into crisp focus pondering how her evening might end.

She could not recall ever feeling this alive and found it difficult to express herself to her best friend. "Thanks again for helping me out with this tonight, Sam."

"I'm excited for you. Maybe I'm a little jealous, too. I wish I had someone to go out with." Petite and attractive Samantha sat on her bed. She had sapphire eyes and silky, cascading black hair. It was difficult to think she'd ever have a hard time finding a date. Samantha attended Westwood High School, though. Their national ranking in academics fueled students' pressure to succeed. It struck Dia as odd to hear her best friend lament over a lack of romantic prospects in light of her scholastic goals.

The girls had lived only blocks from each other in Athens, Texas, then moved to Austin within six months of one another. Their busy schedules precluded them from spending much time together, so they always had a lot to update the other on when they did hang out.

"Baco does sound mysterious...." Samantha trailed off as she studied Dia's face.

Dia raised an eyebrow. "What?"

"Don't take this the wrong way. I'm sure he's great...."

How did I know she would act like this? "But?"

"You're really *into* him. I've never seen you like this, is all. I hope it doesn't distract you from everything you have going on."

Dia let out a long sigh. "What's that supposed to mean?"

"You're so caught up in this guy."

"Sam, don't be ridiculous. I'm not like one of *those* girls."

One of Sam's eyebrows arched higher than the other.

"Don't look at me like I'm pathetic, either. Can't I be a little enthusiastic?"

"You haven't had your first date yet!"

Dia sighed again. She didn't want a fight. "Fine. You're right. I'll dial it down."

"You should. Besides, you don't want to come across as too eager."

"Seriously?"

"I'm afraid you'll end up hurt, is all." Even though she was younger by six months, her best friend acted years wiser at times. She carried herself with a level of confidence most teenagers didn't have, which simultaneously attracted and annoyed Dia. Sam reminded her of Lilly. She was intelligent, driven, athletic, and personable and projected maturity well beyond her years. *Qualities I will never have.*

Sam's mom opened her bedroom door without knocking, carrying a laundry basket under her arm. "You girls want anything? I'm about to start making dinner but can bring you a snack if you don't want to wait."

"Sorry, Mom. I forgot to tell you. Dia and I are heading out for pizza in a little bit."

"Oh, okay. Do you need money?"

"Sure."

"I'll leave it on the table in the foyer," she said walking out.

"Thanks, Mrs. Bell." Dia turned to Sam with wide eyes as she mouthed a silent *thank you* to her friend.

"Of course. That's what friends are for. So, you're going to wear something cute, right? Not your normal black pants with a blouse? Show me what you stuffed in that backpack of yours. Do I have to get an iron?"

"Ha, no!" Dia's excitement returned as she pulled out a couple of options to choose from.

"Love it. Go with this one. I've always loved how this

jumper's sequined collar makes your eyes sparkle." Sam rattled on about hair and makeup next, helping ease the tension from moments earlier.

"What are you going to do while I'm with Baco?"

"Nothing too crazy. I'll hole up at Summer Moon to study."

"Seriously, on a Friday night?"

"No better time than the present to prep for the PSAT. That's something you may want to consider, too, girlie girl. Might win a National Merit Scholarship if you do."

"You're the smart one in our duo."

"Don't sell yourself short, D. You're one of the smartest people I know." Sam gave her friend a side hug. "Okay, let's get going on you, blondie!"

Aromas of fresh oregano, stewing tomatoes, and baking dough greeted them as Baco asked for a table for two at Brooklyn Heights Pizza.

Dia felt like a grown-up instead of the tagalong child, like when she went out with her father, Susan, and Jackson. Baco squeezed her hand, and she looked up to find him smiling down at her.

Insecurity washed over her like a wave as he stared. His dark hair and gray eyes contrasted beautifully against his pale skin. She couldn't see them as well in the dimly lit pizza parlor as she could in the mall's fluorescent food court. Regardless, Baco met every definition of gorgeous Dia was familiar with. She imagined Sam whispering in her ear, *He's still just a guy. He's no more special than you are.*

Dia stopped slouching to try and look less awkward, but still, a question nagged. *What does he see in me?* Girls like Lilly made dating look so effortless. Romance was not in Dia's wheelhouse; then again, here she stood on her first date with someone who looked like he'd stepped out of a magazine. *I must be doing something right.*

Fuchsia bougainvillea hung from eight-foot-tall iron posts that surrounded the outdoor patio. Their hostess walked them past two outside bars to a table for two.

"How is this?" the woman asked.

Dia deferred to Baco.

"Perfect." He moved around Dia to pull out her chair.

"Thank you," she said as she took her seat.

"My pleasure."

The sun set over the River Place golf course, and its rays refracted off western clouds and colored heaven above with varying hues of orange and purple. Strings of lights hung between lanterns, slowly replacing the evening sunlight with their warm glow.

Gazing from across their table, Baco gave a slight smile. He retrieved his menu to scan Little Brooklyn's extensive list of pizzas. *Maybe he'll try to order wine.* That would make for a curious evening that her best friend would chastise her over should she end up drunk.

Dia thought her date looked nervous as she glanced at him. "Everything okay?"

He tipped his menu down, "Excuse me?"

What made me ask that? "I was wondering what you think of their pizza choices," Dia said as heat crawled up her neck.

"I'm considering their meat lover's pizza. Unless you're a vegetarian."

"Oh, no. We're fine. I like veggies, but not over sausage and pepperoni."

"Are you ready to order?" their waiter asked, appearing out of nowhere. His nametag said *Ned.*

"Sure." Baco took one more glance at the menu in his hands. "Your large Sicilian with a bottle of your house red...two glasses." He made direct eye contact as he spoke.

"Do you have ID?"

"Yep, here you go." Baco handed over his driver's license.

"Thanks," Ned said with a frown, then he walked away.

"Europe is so much more at ease with underage drinking; they don't even question it," Baco scoffed. "You don't mind, do you? No one will ever know."

One glass couldn't hurt. "I have an occasional sip when my stepmom's parents come over for dinner."

"I promise I won't get you drunk and take advantage of you."

A blush crept up Dia's neck again. On some level, she welcomed him making such a move. Her first and last experience with kissing at age thirteen had traumatized her. She'd gone to the movies with her eighth-grade friends back in Athens. She sat next to Ryan Wilson from neighboring Corsicana, and they experienced their first French kiss during *Harry Potter*. Everyone had met outside after the movie, and Ryan's facial expression revealed a vague unpleasantness as he studied her under the theater marquee lights. His interest waned visibly, and Dia watched his smile fade while he stood in front of her. *Was it something I said?* she had wondered. Days later, a mutual friend tried explaining why Ryan was no longer interested in her. When she pushed for an explanation, the girl said, "Ryan decided he wasn't into you after he got a better look at you outside." Ryan's comment still stung, but she forced it out of her mind with the hopes of forming new memories. She never knew what Brogan thought about their spin-the-bottle experience, but she doubted he would have agreed to kiss her if he found her too repulsive.

Maybe there would be a different outcome this time.

"You've been to Europe?" Dia shifted gears to a more comfortable and safer topic.

"I have. To Greece, mostly, but also Italy and France. Have you?"

"No, I've just traveled around Texas. Pretty boring compared to what you've seen, I suppose."

"I bet you're more interesting than you think," Baco said. He reached across their table to lay his hand on hers, turning her palm to face his. They held hands throughout dinner, discussing European cities he'd once visited and the perception of Americans now that there was a war in the Middle East. They finished most of their pizza and half their bottle of wine, then packed up the leftovers.

"Am I driving you home or back to your friend's place?" he asked. They stood out front of the pizzeria next to Baco's silver Honda Civic.

"I'm meeting Sam up at the coffee shop. She's there studying."

Baco dropped off their leftover pizza and wine in his car. "On a Friday night?"

"That what I said! But she really needs a full scholarship if she's going to college."

"What about you?"

Dia shrugged her shoulders. "Too soon to know." She hated discussing her dad's job or the lifestyle it afforded them, even if the man wasn't attentive when it came to parenting. She kept her answers purposely vague.

Baco escorted her past the handful of retail stores between the restaurant and Summer Moon. "I guess this is where I leave you."

Will Baco kiss me? She hoped he wouldn't be too disappointed like Ryan after he got a better look at her. What did that even mean, anyway? *It's not like I had warts, green skin, or pimples!*

"Forget that loser," Sam had said back then.

Dia silently repeated Sam's words and turned her face up to Baco's, certain kissing him would provide a different experience this time around.

"I am so happy you came out with me tonight," he said in a near whisper. No one talked to her the way Baco did. "I'm sorry if I weirded you out during our first meeting at Panda

Express, but I... Well, I liked you the first time I saw you, and..." He leaned forward ever so slightly and kissed her, parting her lips with his tongue as he pulled her closer to his chest.

FIVE

SATURDAY, MARCH 6 – THURSDAY, MARCH 18, 2004

PAPERWORK LAID STREWN across their dining room table where Susan toggled back and forth between brochures and her laptop. Jackson's participation on the swim team kept his mom busy most of the time. His growing excellence in the water suggested a future in the Olympics, and the surest way to Beijing in 2008 was to secure a new coach.

"Did you have a fun time last night?" Susan asked without looking up from her notes.

"I did. Thanks."

Dia had no memory of her stepmom ever caring this much about anything she did unless it involved finding an after-school job. She understood how important it was for Jackson, though, and left her to her task. She rounded her dad's oversized recliner and found him with his head leaning on his right hand and his mouth hanging open halfway. "Hey, Dad."

"Oh, wait. If you could let him sleep some. Kyle ended up working late last night," Susan said from the dining room.

"Ah. Okay." Dia tiptoed back behind his chair.

"What time do you have to be at work today?" she asked.

"I'm closing, so I have to be there by one p.m. Can you take me, or should I ask Brogan?"

"Might be best to ask Brogan. There's leftover pizza in the fridge, by the way, if you want to eat something before you go."

"Pizza?"

"Yeah, we picked it up from Brooklyn Height's last night. Funniest thing… Jackson could have *sworn* he saw you there." Susan sat up and looked her stepdaughter straight in the face.

Shit. Dia swallowed the lump in her throat. "That *is* funny. It'd be a little hard seeing I was at Summer Moon with Sam."

"That's what I told him. Besides, I know there's no way you'd ever lie to us and do something you weren't supposed to. It's curious, though, right?"

Sure, it's hilarious. "Sounds like I have a twin. Thanks for the head's up on the pizza. I'll try to grab a slice before I head out." Dia slithered behind the dining room wall and climbed the stairs two at a time, eager not only to shower, but to escape any more questions. Had only Jackson seen her? Or had Susan come in to see for herself? Getting caught in a lie like that would make coordinating future rendezvous more difficult. She would have to be more careful. Dia dropped her backpack on the bed and returned her clothes back to the closet in the event her stepmom came sniffing around later.

Dia glanced at her desk clock. If she hurried, she'd be able to spill the details of last night to her coworkers and—better yet—see Baco. A quick check of her dishwater blonde hair confirmed she needed only a shake or two of baby powder to freshen it up, reducing her normal routine by twenty minutes. She left the house in under an hour and made it to the mall by noon.

"Sounds to me like you have a boyfriend," Anita said.

"Does going out for a single dinner automatically mean you're in a relationship?" Dia asked. Despite countless crushes over the years, she had no clue what went into dating and what classified it as *serious*.

"Only in Anita's world does one date signify commitment!" Gina poked her friend and roommate in the ribs.

"Hey, now. Be nice," Anita said.

"I have no idea what going out once means. All I know is that I like him."

"What do your dad and Susan say?" Gina asked.

Dia occupied herself with straightening the area surrounding their cash register.

"Hello? Your parents?" Gina asked.

"Technically, they don't know."

"What? Why not? You went out, drank wine even, and didn't tell them?" Anita asked.

"Look, I know y'all have more than a decade on me when it comes to this dating stuff—"

"Did she just call us 'old?'" Gina asked.

"I'm being serious. I meant to tell them," Dia said. "I *tried* to get their permission. My dad looked at me like I was some kind of alien. Susan talked to me like I was an idiot—as if someone like me didn't have what it takes to attract a guy."

"We all know that's because she's the pro in that department!" Gina snorted.

"I hear a lot of talking over here, and it's not with customers." Lonnie's sudden interjection into their group brought their conversation to a grinding halt. "Do you need my assistance?"

"Sorry! We're on it." Gina made a beeline for an elderly woman while Anita left for the dressing room to retrieve unused items to take back to the racks.

"Dia? Will you go help that woman over there?" Lonnie pointed to a woman flipping through suit jackets.

"Yep, I'm on it."

"And one more thing."

"Yes?"

"Let's try to leave the boyfriend chit-chat for after work, okay?"

"Sure, boss." Not talking about Baco was easy enough, but pushing all thoughts of him completely out of her mind? Not even remotely possible. She replayed last night's kiss as she made her way across the dress department, focused less on making a sale than on catching up with her new love. *Only a few more hours*, she thought. *A little bit longer, and I'll feel his lips on mine again.*

Days passed, and with Samantha's help, Dia found more chances to meet with Baco outside of the mall. They took lengthy strolls along Austin's northern greenbelts in the days leading up to spring break, holding hands and getting to know one another. He never questioned her about being introduced to her parents or picking her up at their house, as long as they could spend time together. Thankful for cooperative weather, Dia packed a blanket on their walks to make stopping for a rest—and kissing—more comfortable.

In between make-out sessions, her new boyfriend shared stories from some anthropologist his uncle turned him on to. His ideas weren't exactly romantic, but they gave her something to think about. According to *The Sex Contract*, the evolution from ape to man led to shorter gestation cycles for offspring and more dependence on moms for longer periods of time as early man moved out of the jungles and into the open savannas.

Mating had once been a free-for-all for both sexes but walking upright on two feet—*bipedalism* Baco called it—forced some sort of contractual arrangement between them where sex became the currency for survival. That made females more dependent on their male partners to find food. Males didn't want to provide for offspring resulting from unions with other males, though, sowing the early seeds for monogamy.

In its modern-day application, relationships boiled down to two things: men wanted sex and women wanted money. What any of it had to do with Baco's software business was a mystery. Dia found him fascinating, nevertheless.

"Attention counts, too. I mean obviously everyone wants that," he said one afternoon. "At our cores, though, sex compels men to do what they do, while money motivates women. The obvious problem about this is that men need women if they're going to get laid...well, straight men, I guess. As for women, the surest way to provide for their children is through a man."

"You seriously think that? I mean, what you're saying sounds old-fashioned, don't you think? It's 2004, not 1954."

"I hear you, and believe me, I can imagine how sexist this may sound. Maybe 'security' is a better word than 'money.' I'm telling the truth, though. Think about your stepmom. Women want security—or resources—to ensure their children's future, and men want sex, and they can only truly get what they want from each other, yet they prevent one another from getting what they want." Baco moved from lying beside Dia and gently rolled on top to push her deeper into the earth below her. He shimmied her legs apart to rest between them. "You believe me, don't you?"

"I do," she said, tilting her pelvis to better meet his. She felt him respond to her as he remained focused on their conversation.

"Dominic's been coaching me on this topic for a while now."

Dominic, Baco's uncle, mentor, and boss, had almost completed post-doctorate work in psychology before abandoning academia to go into business for himself. It was curious how someone would come so close to the finish line and not follow through with their education, but Dia wondered what difference it made if the man found success doing something else for a living.

Maybe I shouldn't be so judgmental. Dia listened as her boyfriend shared more about what motivated the sexes. Perhaps Susan's books comparing men and women to planets carried some weight, after all.

"Men are brilliant and creative and women nurturing and receptive," Baco said.

"Nurturing and receptive?"

"If women want to experience true joy in their relationships, then they will need to accept this for themselves and any man who's their partner. They have to be there to support a man to such the degree he's able to reach his fullest potential."

Do men want a partner or a parent? And why do guys get to be brilliant while us ladies have to be nurturing? Dia wanted to believe it, but it sounded like fellas had a lot more to gain than girls. She imagined Sam calling out, "BS!" but she refrained from expressing too negative a sentiment herself.

"What? Do you doubt me?" He was more observant than she cared for sometimes.

"Well, again, it sounds...kind of old-fashioned." She cringed, fearful of sounding critical.

"Babe, I'm just telling you what Dominic has learned after years of working with people. You don't *have* to be nurturing and receptive, but you'll probably struggle to find peace and satisfaction in your relationships if you're not. I hope you'll accept what I'm saying...for our sake."

Baco looked at her, his expression shifting back and forth between soft puppy dog and laser-intense samurai. "Men and women can help each other to reach their highest potential or they can withhold what the other wants. When women withhold sex, their partner's instinct or reaction is to withhold money. Dominic says the opposite is true as well."

Dia needed time to digest everything Baco said. His ideas

were so different from what boys her age talked about, and it reminded her of what Sam said following their first date.

"Is something wrong?" Baco asked.

"Well, my best friend…"

"Samantha?"

"Yeah. She had a question about your...um, I don't recall a hundred percent how she said it." Dia turned her head away from him. Sam had not officially met Baco that night, but she'd spotted him from inside Summer Moon as he kissed Dia goodnight. "Maybe it was your style of dress or something. She thought you were different compared to the guys from around here. You *do* come across as more advanced than a lot of them. You even seem more mature than Gina and Anita, and they're creeping up on thirty." Baco had met Dia's coworkers during their Saturday shift following their first date.

"How old does Sam think I am?"

"She said twenty-three, give or take a year or two…and you did have ID to get the wine on our first date"

Baco put his hand on her chin to adjust her gaze back on him. "How old do *you* think I am?"

"I was hoping no more than nineteen. That way, I'll be able to introduce you to my dad one day."

"Hmm. I see." He rolled to his back and sat up. Joggers ran past them on the trail, indifferent to the couple. "I have a secret. Can you give me your word not to tell anyone if I share it with you?"

Dia couldn't imagine what his secret was but was confident nothing would be large enough to undermine her growing fondness for him. "Yes, I promise."

"Your friend is right. I am older than you."

"How old?" Dia stared at him from behind.

Baco hesitated, but Dia swore she saw his gray eyes sparkle as he turned back and gazed down at her.

"Sam's observant, I gotta tell you. I'm twenty-six. I'll turn twenty-seven late October."

Dia's eyes popped out of her head. "You look so much younger!" Eleven years her senior. Her stomach tightened imagining how her dad would react if he knew. *He'd try and stop me from ever seeing Baco again. That's what he'd do.*

"People tell me that a lot. You won't tell anyone, will you? I don't want anything to separate us, and I know how weird people can get when there's such a huge age difference between two people who…two people who really care for each other."

Did he almost say love? Dia looked into Baco's eyes wanting to be the nurturing and receptive woman he described earlier —a woman he'd deliver the moon to if she submitted to him. "Yes, it'll be our little secret." Her phone beeped with a voicemail from Susan. "Duty calls. I need to get home for dinner."

She tried sitting up, but Baco pinned her down on the blanket and pressed his lips to hers, kissing her deeply. He grew hard lying on top of her, triggering Dia's own desire. He rubbed slowly against her, plunging his tongue deeper into her mouth. She wished she could lie there all night with him above her like that and opened her legs to bring him closer.

"Okay," Dia mumbled between kisses. "I need to get going…please, before Susan loses her shit." Sitting up, she ran her fingers through her hair then stood and straightened her clothes. Red heat exuded from her neck and cheeks, reflecting the passion from mere moments ago.

"Can I drive you home?"

"What if you drop me off on the side street instead?"

"Works for me. Do you think you might introduce me to your folks someday?"

"Now that I know how old you are? They'll never allow it."

"I look young for my age. You said so yourself."

"Yeah, but if Sam can pick up on it, I know my parents will." They walked hand in hand back to Baco's car. "You know, with everyone out of school next week, my family will be heading out to the lake at some point. Maybe you can come over and we can hang at my place after they're gone."

"Are you sure that's okay? I don't want to get you in trouble."

"You can always park down the street or something." She squeezed his hand.

"Okay, babe. Anything you say."

Work was sluggish with most of Austin's shoppers away for spring break. Slow foot traffic provided Dia time to update her Macy's colleagues on her blooming romance. Gina referred to him as "Mr. Mediterranean" while Anita invoked images of sweets by calling him "honey bun" or "baby cakes." Dia suspected their comments were a sign of jealousy, yet both women also doubted whether Baco was all she thought he was cracked up to be.

"Be careful."

"Are you sure he's single?"

"How does he have a full-time job but still make time to meet you after classes?"

"He looks older than eighteen to me. Are you positive he's not closer to our age?"

Their questions resonated in Dia's ears as Brogan drove her home that night. She had mentioned Baco to him and he commented about seeing him from time to time at the food court.

He shared her colleagues' points of view. "Rushing things, a little, aren't you? Have you ever gone on a date that's *not* been at the park or food court?"

The growing scrutiny of her relationship wore her down. She worried how everyone would react if they learned the truth about his age. She'd have to eliminate any chance of them finding out. Of that she was certain.

Dia struggled to remain calm as Brogan continued. "D, we're friends, and I have no agenda here. I'm not trying to derail what you've got going, but I've *seen* him. I can't put my finger on it, but I don't like him." He raced his mom's Lexus down Lakeline Boulevard, dodging in and out of traffic.

The guy who's never said a single word about his breakup with Lilly wants to coach me on romance now, she fumed, folding her arms across her chest. If he had been willing to talk weeks earlier, she might be dating him instead.

She was eager to exit his car and the accompanying lecture and sighed in relief when her house came into view as he turned on her street. Dia reached into her purse for keys, ready for the night to end. She was looking forward to calling Baco. *Will he take my invitation to the dance seriously?* she wondered. It had been all she could think about following their time together that afternoon. Dia grew nervous at the prospect, and she'd momentarily forgotten where she was when Brogan said her name.

"Dia, are you listening?"

"Yes, Brogan, I got it. 'Go slow. Don't do anything stupid.' Did I catch it all, or do you have more to say?"

"I just don't want you hurt is all," he said solemnly. His concern caught her off guard. She reached out to lay her hand on his arm.

"I'm being careful, Brogan, but I really appreciate you watching out for me." She leaned over and kissed his cheek. "I'll see you next week."

"Later."

Dia entered the house and went straight to her room. Everyone else was in their rooms, allowing her space to decompress from an evening full of comments, judgments, and opinions. If her closest friends viewed Baco negatively, then how would others react when she brought him to a school dance?

She retrieved her phone from her purse to call him, knowing his commitment to her was real no matter what everyone said. The attraction to him and craving for his affection was something she'd never experienced before. He'd activated something in her over recent weeks she never thought existed within her, and she wanted more of it—*more of him.* She was convinced he desired her as well—another new development in her life. *Baco would never hurt me or make me doubt myself like my friends are trying to do,* she thought. She dialed his number.

"Hello?" he answered.

His voice made her heart skip a beat. "Hi, it's me."

"Hey, there, 'me.'"

"Hi."

"How was work tonight?"

"Eh, slow," Dia said, omitting her discussions with Gina, Anita, and Brogan. "I was thinking, and I kinda said something about this before, but, well, I was wondering...and you can say no..." she took a deep breath, then exhaled louder than she intended. "Would you like to go with me to the Sadie Hawkins dance?" The words tumbled out of her mouth, and for a moment, all she heard was his breathing. *Oh, God. He's going to say no.*

"Are you sure your father will be okay with me escorting you to something so official?"

"He will once he sees how much we care for one another," Dia said. "Wait. Did you say yes?" If he was agreeing, she was certain she could persuade her dad to allow it.

"I would like nothing more than to be your date. I want you to believe me when I say it. My feelings for you are very strong. I want to take you to your dance, but beyond that, I want to take our relationship up a notch. I've been reflecting on us a lot, and…well…"

Dia sat up on her bed. "What are you saying?"

"I want to make love to you. You're everything I've ever wanted in a woman, and I want to show you how I feel because...because... Words fail me, to be honest."

"When were you thinking? After the dance?"

"Yes, but not if you need more time. I understand this is a big step, and I assume..."

"Are you asking if I'm a virgin?"

"Are you?"

"Of course!"

"We can talk more later, but I *do* love you, Dia, and I see no reason to wait."

"I love you too, Baco." She paused for a moment, Brogan's warnings to slow things down echoed in her ears.

"Are you still there?" Baco snapped her back to attention.

"Yes, I'm here."

"Phew, just making sure I hadn't lost you after putting myself out there like that."

"No, I'm here. I want this, too, and the dance isn't until after spring break."

Baco released his breath. "Okay, good. That gives us plenty of time to talk. I want you to think it over, but I promise you..."

"Promise me what?"

"I'll take care of you. Goodnight, Dia."

"Goodnight."

SIX

SUNDAY, MARCH 21 – MONDAY, MARCH 22, 2004

SPRING HAD ARRIVED in Central Texas. Bluebonnets peppered Austin roadways and greenbelts in dazzling displays of violet, blue, and white. All traces of wet and dreary weather evaporated as the sun warmed the hill country. Dia was spending Sunday with Baco on her last day of the break following an exhausting week of extra shifts at Macy's.

They walked hand in hand along River Place Nature Trail. A light breeze blew through Dia's hair. She squeezed Baco's hand, and joy filled her heart when she turned her head up to meet his gaze. His attention initially unnerved her when they'd first met at the mall, but now seeing him was what she yearned for every day.

"Should we head to your house?" Baco asked.

"Why not? I'm thirsty, anyway." They found a path up to her subdivision and were at Dia's house less than five minutes later.

"You're sure your parents are out for the rest of the day?"

"They're at the lake and hardly ever get home before six when they go." Dia withdrew two glasses from a kitchen cabinet.

"So, they're on your dad's friend's yacht?"

"Look at you. You remembered."

"Yes, if memory serves, you said something about Susan thinking he 'lives beyond his means.'"

"Yeah, he has a son the same age as Jackson, so it works for everyone. Lucky them, huh?" Dia filled their glasses with ice.

"I don't know. I'd say, 'lucky us.'" Baco walked across to Dia and pinned her against the island counter. "Does your dad keep any vodka here?"

"I think so."

"Would it raise any alarms if we had some?"

"What do you mean? Like, does he record measurements on the side of the bottle?"

"Well, it sounds funny when you put it like that, but yeah. Will he notice if the level drops?"

"Hmm, hard to say. You'll find it in our butler pantry if you want to check it out." Dia's stomach twisted into a mild knot as Baco moved around the corner. Her dad drank on rare occasions, mostly when entertaining. *Will he be able to tell we snuck some next time he makes martinis for company?* she wondered.

"Found it!" He sat it beside their ice-filled glasses. "Let's mix it with something. Juice maybe? What's wrong?"

"I just don't normally drink."

"You'll be fine. Think of it as Sunday-Funday! We're not driving anywhere, and your folks are out all afternoon. We have this whole place to ourselves." Baco approached her from around the island. "Breathe, babe. I'm joking. I don't need a cocktail if you're uncomfortable."

What would a little vodka hurt? "Okay. I just needed a second to think it through. Here, take our glasses. I'll look for a mixer of some sort."

The cranberry and orange juice sat behind the milk, creamers, and soda in the fridge. "We have two juices. Which works better?" she asked, holding half-gallon jugs.

"Maybe both. Let me check it out." Baco took both juices and mixed their drinks like a pro. "Here, try it."

Dia took a sip. His sugary-sweet concoction flowed down her throat. "Wow, delicious!" she said. "Who knew these two tasted so good together?"

"Not bad at all! I'm going to leave this stuff out in case we want another. Want to head upstairs?"

"Sure." She took another gulp from her glass.

"Thirsty? You may want to slow down a little."

"Yeah, I guess I am." She took Baco's hand and followed him to the second floor.

"The dance is less than two weeks away now," Dia reminded him as they entered her room. It seemed a million miles away considering she still needed her parents' approval. She'd begun searching for dresses over her Saturday lunch break on her boyfriend's insistence she find something sexy, and it begged the question: If she still required her father's permission to go with Baco, how would she ever walk out the front door in a potentially provocative dress?

"How jazzed do you feel about going on a scale of one to ten?" Baco lay back on her bed without spilling his drink. He beckoned Dia to lie next to him.

Crawling over her comforter to join him, Dia smiled. "A solid ten!"

"Wow! That high," he said winking. "How's your cocktail?"

Dia gulped down the cold, sugary drink. "Delicious," she managed to say before being met with a shower of ice. "Oops." She laughed and flopped down beside him.

"You *were* thirsty. Ready for another?" Dia nodded and handed him her glass. Her eyes trailed after him as he left to fill it. Images of them dancing filled her head as she listened to him moving around downstairs. Her thoughts drifted to his request for sex while alcohol coursed its way through her bloodstream, warming Dia up and lending color to her imagination.

"I've been thinking," he said, entering her room with another round of drinks. "You know what I'd like?"

"What would you like?" Dia opened her eyes from her daydream.

"I'd like to take a gander at your naked body." He waited for Dia to speak.

Dia held her breath. *What do I say?*

"Breathe, babe."

She wanted to please him but more on her own terms. *Am I ready for this? What about waiting until the night of the dance?*

Baco handed Dia's cocktail across the bed with half-closed eyes and a playful smile that encouraged her to drink. "What if we started by taking some photos if you're unsure? We can use my cell phone and pretend we're doing a professional photoshoot. I'll be your personal photographer."

Dia sat up and swirled her ice, trying to buy some time.

"I know. How about some tunes?" Baco walked over to her stereo and pressed the power button, adjusting the radio dial to 96.7 where "Let's Get It Started" by The Black Eyed Peas was playing. A digital camera on a shelf above caught his attention. He checked for battery life and spun around with a grin when he found it working. He returned his Nokia to his back pocket, cranked up the music volume, and then turned to Dia.

"Take another sip, babe." She did as she was told. "Another one." She took two more gulps. Her second cocktail was more than half gone, and Baco took her glass and directed her to lie down on her stomach.

Dia offered a slight, tentative smile.

Baco snapped a dozen photos as she mulled over his request. "Girl, you are so beautiful. Prop yourself up on your elbows. There, that's it. Gaze into this camera. Penetrate me with your stare through this lens. Now, I'd like you to part your lips just a little. Yeah, like that. Perfect." He took several more pictures before sauntering over and bending down to kiss Dia on her mouth. She savored the sweetness of juice on his tongue and rose up in response. Her body oozed warmth, making her question if it was the alcohol or something else causing her temperature to rise.

"You are sexy hot! Why don't we take this off?" Baco brought his hands to her shirt's hem. He put the camera down but kept eye contact as he lifted Dia's shirt up and over her head and then reached his hands behind her back to unhook her bra. He pulled the straps up and away from her shoulders, removing it. He stared at her intensely. She waited for his instructions as he resumed snapping pictures.

"Your boobs are gorgeous. Sit up, like this, and hold this between your legs." He positioned a pillow so her breasts were perched on top it. He reached out and released her hair from its ponytail then tussled it. She let him maneuver her into position. "This is what I want. Tell me you want me with your eyes, darlin'. Seduce me through the lens."

Dia performed as she was directed despite her lack of experience in *seduction*. It wasn't hard. She wanted so desperately to please her boyfriend. She'd do everything he asked, but he took only a few more photos before asking her to dress.

Baco waited patiently in her chair as Dia put her bra and shirt back on. "I am so excited to know you're a virgin. I want to explore every inch of your body and help you discover what turns you on. Have you ever done *anything*?" Baco's tone lulled her into a desire to submit to him.

"Sexually?"

"Yeah."

She looked up at him through her lowered lashes. "No."

He rose and walked up to her. "You are so perfect for me. I can't wait for the chance when we can be one."

Dia quivered at any prospect of taking their next step together. Until a few weeks ago, her predominant thoughts revolved around school and work. She occasionally daydreamed about Todd or Brogan. Now she stood on the precipice of becoming a woman.

Her future lover had undoubtedly been with multiple women. She toyed with asking him to share his sexual history and used this moment of vodka-infused vulnerability to ask. "And you? I'm guessing you're not a virgin. How many girlfriends have you had?"

"Two."

Two? No way has a man as handsome and sexy as him only had two lovers.

"My first girlfriend more or less dumped me for my best friend," Baco said. "We were young, but she still broke my heart. It took a few years before I opened myself up to trust again. I dated a girl in Houston last year, but it ended a month or so prior to moving here."

Dia listened as he spoke so matter of factly. *Is it a "defense mechanism?"* The term had come up when Gina and Anita described one of their friends. "I'm sorry. I would never do that to you." Tears filled her eyes, set off by the vodka or memories from her past. Either way, she hated that someone hurt him once. "I will love you forever, as long as you'll let me."

"Me too, Dia. I want this so much for us. I hope we'll be able to be together soon. Your words will mean even more to me then." He kissed her sweetly, softly. It was all she could do to refrain from having sex right then, but an ascending garage door startled her to attention.

"Oh, crap. My folks are home!" They rushed down the stairs. Baco bolted to the kitchen to return their cocktail ingredients to their rightful places while Dia rinsed out the glasses. Luckily, her parents had paused to talk to the next-door neighbors. When they did enter the house, Dia sat in her dad's recliner watching a movie as her future lover slipped out the front.

"How was the lake?" she asked.

"Awesome!" Jackson ran to the fridge for a coke.

"A little too cold for me still," Susan said.

"Guess that's why you're back earlier than usual then, huh?"

"What do you mean?" Susan asked.

"Nothing, just that I don't normally see you until after six."

"I have to prepare for a meeting tomorrow morning, otherwise, we'd still be out," her dad said. "One of these days, we have to get our own boat, eh hon?"

"It's your money, honey."

Sure, it is, Dia thought. "I'm going to head upstairs for a bit. Got some homework to wrap up before dinner. Let me know if I can help in the kitchen." She sped up the stairs and retreated into her room.

"Is Samantha still planning to join us tonight?"

She had forgotten all about her best friend in the afterglow of her photo session. "I'll call and find out."

Dia's optimism and buzz diminished with each second she spent defending her earlier actions.

Sam's questions echoed those from Brogan, Gina, and Anita. "Why are you rushing things?"

Dozens of thoughts raced through Dia's mind. *How are we rushing things? Is there some standard for romantic relationships? How long should someone wait between their first date and having sex? Three dates? Six dates? Six months? Two years? The wedding night?*

She'd already decided to take this next step with her boyfriend, but Sam's lack of support was now beginning to undermine her confidence. She wished she could convince Sam and others that things with Baco were real.

"All I'm saying is sex is huge, D. You've only been seeing him for a few weeks," Sam said.

"Sam, you've been my best friend since we were kids. Your opinion matters to me, but so does his. Yes, our relationship is new, but I believe in him. I trust myself. I'm almost sixteen. I wasn't born yesterday. I may not be as smart as you, but I'm smarter than most. I don't wonder where I stand with Baco. He looks out for me. I *want* this."

"I've never doubted your intelligence," Sam said. "If you're determined to do this, then I hope you're considering steps to at least avoid getting pregnant. Have you thought about what might happen if you got knocked up?"

"You're talking birth control?" Dia didn't appreciate much of what her bestie had to share, but the girl had a point. An unwanted pregnancy would bring her romance—her life—to a crashing halt.

"Of course. You don't want to end up like Becky, do you?"

A mutual friend of theirs in Athens had conceived a child early in the ninth grade. Dia cringed, reflecting on her comment moments earlier insisting she was "smarter than most." *Maybe I'm not as smart as I thought.*

"Why don't you ask Susan what to do?"

"Right. I'm sure that'd go over well. 'Hey folks, not only am I dating someone you won't approve of, but I want to go on birth control too!'" Dia rolled her eyes. "Can't *you* suggest something?"

"I propose using condoms, but Susan could take you to a doctor for a prescription. The pill is supposed to be even more effective."

"Girls, dinner's ready!" her dad called from downstairs.

"Perfect timing," Sam said.

"You're hilarious. Please don't bring it up, though, okay? I'll take care of it one way or another, I promise."

"Mum's the word." She pulled an imaginary zipper across her lips.

The following afternoon, Susan checked final preparations for her son's upcoming birthday party. "I just had the vanilla here a second ago," she said to no one in particular, banging cupboard doors in search of her missing ingredient and causing Dia to question whether the woman stood on the brink of a nervous breakdown. *If only I could be that lucky.*

It was as if Jackson's turning thirteen carried more weight than any other kid becoming a teenager—certainly more than when Dia had become one three years prior. Susan's family was coming in from every corner of Texas as well as a swim team coach who had recently emerged from the woman's exhaustive list of Olympic coaching candidates.

Presents were stacked against their dining room wall, and her dad's wife mumbled nonstop under her breath as she baked cakes, cookies, and casseroles. "Where did I put the damn flour?"

Dia listened from their staircase, gauging an opportunity to broach the subject of birth control with Susan following yesterday evening's lecture from Sam. *Jackson won't be the only one passing a milestone this spring.* She gathered up her nerve and walked in where her stepmom stood amid growing columns of batter-coated bowls and baking pans.

Susan scanned the kitchen, in search of something among her recent grocery purchases. "Do you need something?" she asked after turning to find her stepdaughter standing in the kitchen.

"Want some help?"

"What?" Her stepmom choked down a laugh. "No, I've got this." She put her hands in a bowl of raw eggs and flour mixture, avoiding eye contact.

Dia opened her mouth to say something, then closed it. *How do I say this?* Her nemesis may have had her back up against a wall preparing food for Saturday's celebration, but she was on a mission of her own. She walked to the opposite side of the kitchen island.

Buying condoms has to be easier than this! Dia had always sensed her stepmom didn't care much for her, and the woman certainly didn't treat Dia the way someone *should* treat a daughter—or a stepdaughter, for that matter. *She'd probably like it if I* did *end up pregnant.*

Dia chose her words carefully to steer clear from a conversation about sex itself. "I've been experiencing some, uh, challenges...down there...in my body. The thing is, I can't really predict when my period will start. Sam suggested going on the pill to control it." Not a total lie...Dia's period had started two years earlier, a month before her fourteenth birthday. Its unpredictability and heavy flow continued to wreak havoc on her life and warranted keeping an abundance of feminine supplies on hand at all times. She waited for a response from her stepmom.

Susan withdrew her hands from her batter and reached for a towel, but she stopped and turned, realizing she'd forgotten something. She scanned her kitchen counters for her missing ingredient.

"Susan?"

"*What* Dia? Seriously! I don't have time for this right now. Can't you see how busy I am getting ready for your brother's party?"

Stepbrother, you mean.

"I don't need you standing there pressuring me."

"I offered to help, is all." Dia's voice dropped several decibels to a whisper.

Susan retrieved the cinnamon from behind cans of sweetened condensed milk. She squinted her eyes together to measure out a teaspoon of McCormick's finest. Their conversation was over, so Dia retreated upstairs where Baco lie waiting after sneaking inside earlier. She closed the door behind her and locked it.

Dia stood in front of her dresser mirror and looked at her boyfriend's reflection.

"I heard everything," he said. "Don't worry about it. She's super stressed it seems, so don't take it personally. Besides, we can take precautions."

"We can?" Her disappointment dissolved as she looked into his eyes. He came to the edge of her bed. Dia backed up to him, and Baco moved his hand past her waistband to rest on her bottom beneath her shorts and undies.

"I want you."

Dia held her breath as Baco moved his right hand around to her front. She watched him watching her desiring his touch. With his right foot, he separated her legs as he reached his hand down her front. Baco brought his left hand up under her shirt and bra. He squeezed her breasts and brought his right hand to rest upon the apex between her legs.

"We're going to get caught." The words fell from her mouth in a husky whisper.

"Not with your brother at swim practice, we're not." Baco slid his hand up inside her. "Oh, baby, you are so wet right now." Her knees grew weak, and he supported her with his strength from behind. She felt two fingers sliding forward and back, then resting on one small piece of her anatomy she never knew existed until that very moment.

His left hand massaged her breasts and Dia dipped beneath the view of her dresser's mirror to grant him deeper access with his hands. He withdrew his left hand from her chest and brought it around to cup her buttocks while continuing to massage what she assumed was her clitoris. She was overcome by a strong desire to remove her clothes and stand naked before him. Dia grabbed her dresser and Baco lowered her shorts and underwear.

"Oh, your body turns me on so much. It's perfect in every way...tight and smooth, yet full and round. Very hot."

Dia's breathing deepened as he moved his left hand

between her legs. His middle fingers found her vagina and he teased her, circling it. She raised her head to see herself in her mirror again and to look into Baco's eyes to implore him to keep going. As if reading her mind, he inserted his middle finger. Dia beared down against his hand, and he accepted her invitation, plunging another finger inside her. He moved them up and down, back, and forth, pushing something deep within her she could not define. She teetered side to side, bearing down as he thrust his fingers upward. She was startled to feel something running down her leg and glanced up into Baco's eyes.

"Whoa, I am one lucky man! I want you so *badly*."

Dia wasn't sure what happened, but if it meant always feeling this good, then she wanted him too. She longed to have sex all night long and abandon everything else in pursuit of pleasure with her boyfriend.

"Promise me one thing," he said.

Dia squirmed in his grasp. She'd need another pair of shorts and underwear. "Yes, anything."

"That I can always do this to you."

"I promise."

Baco withdrew his hands, placed them on Dia's hips and turning her to face him as he sat back on her bed. "You are what every man wants, but you belong to me...always."

She stared into Baco's eyes and in her mind decided to forever be what he wanted.

"Now get dressed before we both get in trouble." He spanked her lightly on the bottom. She turned around to her dresser to retrieve fresh clothes as he followed her with his eyes.

SEVEN

SATURDAY, MARCH 27, 2004

OBLIVIOUS TO SOUNDS of birthday activity downstairs, Dia lay on her bed reflecting on everything she had experienced thus far with Baco. She could only imagine how giving herself completely to him would increase her affection, but recent developments pulled at her attention like a loose thread. *What would happen if I yanked it?*

Sunday's photoshoot had provided her the most erotic experience of her life until Monday afternoon, and those five minutes still made her blush. Baco's picture taking, though, had ushered in a wave of sensations that intrigued her and gave her an unparalleled sense of excitement. She recalled watching him, waiting in anticipation for his instructions.

He was commanding, controlling...sexy. His dark, tousled hair framed his face as his long slender fingers cradled her camera in front of his pale gray eyes. His prowess behind its lens reminded her of a New York fashion photographer, and she perceived herself as attractive for the first time in her life. Baco wanted her to experience life unlike anyone else. He appreciated her beauty and craving for adventure and brought both of them out in her.

She could practically feel his desire through the phone when he'd called her Tuesday.

"I've been looking at your pictures from Sunday. You're so pretty." His baritone voice reverberated in her ear, pulling her into a mild trance.

Then, he hesitated. Dia couldn't imagine what would give him pause, and she found herself holding her own breath as she waited for him to say more.

"I realize we're only a few weeks into what I believe will be forever, and I don't want to say something that could alarm you," he said. "We've talked a lot about taking our next step together. I find myself fantasizing over it quite a bit, honestly. I want to explore all the things people talk about when it comes to sex with you—from positions to role playing, you name it!"

Role playing? "I'll do whatever you want."

"You will?"

"Of course."

"It thrills me you're saying this, babe. I'm confident I can now ask you to help me fulfill my greatest fantasy."

She heard him smiling through his words. "Anything...I'll do anything for you."

"Well, maybe not for our first time together—probably not our second or our third time, either, but soon. You are everything I want in a woman. You're perfect, but even women who are total knockouts can't give us guys what we truly crave."

Wait. If a woman was amazing in every way, if she were smart, funny, successful, and beautiful, then what more could a man want or crave? "What is it, Baco?"

"Variety."

"Say again?"

"Yeah, it may not make sense what I'm saying. I'm sharing something with you most dudes don't normally talk about. I trust you though, Dia. I care about you for so many reasons but mostly for your intelligence. You're intelligent and *you get me.* I've never been so understood by someone until now, which is why I believe you'll do this for me too...when you're ready."

"Do what?" She was still unsure what he meant by variety.

"Don't worry, babe. I'll explain next time we're together. Hey, I've been thinking, I can't remember the last time I took a trip, like a mini holiday. My mom always called them 'mental-health retreats.' What do you say? It'll be hot before long. We can rent a condo down in South Padre or Port Aransas."

Baco changed the subject so abruptly it left Dia's head spinning. Now he wanted to go on vacation to the coast? Is that what he meant by "variety?"

"Anyway, I see how late it is, and you have classes tomorrow. Can you meet afterward?"

"I can't. I'm meeting Sam, and then I have a chemistry exam to study for after dinner."

"Thursday then?"

"I work, but I'm off on Saturday. Can you come over? I've been thinking of finally introducing you to my parents."

"Wait, what? I wasn't expecting that. Are you sure? I mean, didn't you say something about them having a problem with our age difference?"

"Well, you do look young, and this sneaking around is starting to stress me out. All of the family will be here for Jackson's birthday, and I'm thinking everyone will be too preoccupied to pay a whole lot of attention to us. Besides, I want you to officially meet Sam, and she'll be here, too."

Baco took a deep breath and released it louder than normal. "Okay, Saturday it is, I guess, but I can't come over until late afternoon. I hate to go so many days without seeing you, but, hey, you're my girl. Right?"

"I am...and you're my man."

On Wednesday, Dia met Samantha for a Frappuccino at Starbucks to fortify herself for a long night of homework and test preparation. She filled her in on her latest sexual encounter but avoided mention of Baco's requests for variety and a mini vacation.

Her best friend sat with her mouth agape, listening to Dia's story. She knew Sam had never come close to something as provocative. She was holding out for marriage and wouldn't even think about going to second base, let alone losing her virginity. Despite Sunday night's warning to go slow three days ago, she stared wide-eyed with curiosity and enthusiasm as Dia spoke.

"Oh, my goodness! So, you didn't have actual sex?"

Dia shook her head as a vertical crease appeared between Sam's eyebrows. "I wonder if you had an orgasm...you know, with *stuff* running down your leg and all? Did you talk with Susan about birth control?"

"Mm, it didn't go so well, but Baco says we can take precautions."

"'*Baco says.*'" Samantha drank from her cup before continuing. "D, I don't want to nag, but if you're going to do this, you gotta lock it down. Trust me when I say you don't want a baby at this point in your life."

Dia replayed Monday afternoon in her head instead of listening to her friend. Sam didn't get it. All she thought about was school, anyway. Being in a committed relationship meant going with the flow of things and trusting, didn't it? This was the power of love her favorite artists sang and wrote about in books. It was what they preached at church back in Athens.

"Hello? Anyone home?" Sam kicked her lightly on her foot. "I think you need to give your stepmom another chance and get on the pill."

Susan had been busy for days, and there'd not been another opportunity to discuss a doctor's appointment with her. The dance was a week away, and she figured it would be too late to meet with a doctor for a prescription. Wasn't there a waiting period before they took full effect anyway? Condoms might be required their first time together, after all.

Don't the guys normally take care of that? she thought. She had brought the topic up with Anita and Gina Thursday night at work, hoping to gain clarity, but that conversation ended up frustrating her more.

Anita made a funny face when she divulged what she and Baco had done earlier in the week. She immediately regretted her decision to share as her friend's face morphed into a grimace. *Why can't people be excited for me?* Even Gina, who was no stranger to intriguing encounters with men, gave her a somewhat maternal look of disapproval as the corners of her mouth pulled down.

"Honey," Gina began, "Anita thinks...."

Anita coughed.

"*We* think you ought to know something about Baco."

Dia shifted her eyes blankly from Gina to Anita. "What?"

"He spent the better part of thirty minutes talking to another girl at Sbarro last Saturday," Anita blurted out.

"Now, we can't state for certain he did anything wrong just because he was seen talking to someone else," Gina said.

Dia appreciated Gina's attempt to soften Anita's news, but it still provoked an emotion she couldn't quite name. Shock? Jealousy? Disbelief? Her stomach flip-flopped.

"Baco is a player, and you know it, Gina!" Anita pivoted from Gina to Dia. "I'm sorry, but I think you have bigger problems to solve before you start shopping for birth control. If I were you, I'd run as fast as you can from this guy. I mean, frankly, I sensed something was way off when I first met him. Gina did, too."

Dia shot a glance over to Gina, who smiled tensely.

Anita continued. "When I saw him at the food court last week, well, he kept scanning the room, like he was paranoid."

"Was he aware you were spying on him?" Gina asked.

"You don't have to take criminology classes at ACC to pick up on suspicious behavior, and no, he was too absorbed talking with that girl to notice me," Anita said. "You know how men don't see us full-figured gals…."

Less than forty-eight hours later, Dia had her first Saturday off from Macy's in months because of Jackson's birthday party, but memories of that talk with her coworkers lingered. She was more than willing to pull herself back to the present moment when company arrived.

"Hey, Chica!" Sam said, walking into her room. "Susan let me in. Your house sure is bumping with activity downstairs. Jackson must be high as a kite." She plopped down in Dia's papasan chair. "What's wrong? Did someone punch you in your stomach?"

Dia wavered, wanting her best friend's advice but suspecting her opinion would only reinforce Gina's and Anita's. These three people she trusted most, whose opinions she normally relied upon, seemed aligned in thwarting her relationship with the man she loved. *Or are they protecting me?* she wondered.

Sam snapped her fingers. "Daydreaming again? Where were you just now?"

Dia shook her head, loosening her cobwebs as she wrestled with how to begin.

"What's going with you?"

"Anita says she saw Baco talking to some girl at the mall earlier this week."

"So? Guys talk to girls all the time. What does Anita think it means?"

"She's thinks it means that he's a 'player,' and *I'm* the one getting played."

"See? This is what happens when you start having sex too soon," Sam said.

"We haven't done it yet!"

Sam let out a sigh of relief and grabbed Dia's hands. "Honey, *you* may not call what happened Monday sex, but that's what it was. I don't know what your girlfriend from work saw, but you haven't known Baco long enough to *not* suspect him of anything. Why not ask him about it?"

The doorbell rang. "Dia, there's someone here for you," Susan called up.

"Okay! Can you send him on up?" Dia looked at Sam, panicked. "I got it. He's here. Can we change topics?"

"Of course," she smiled. "I'm excited to finally meet this guy. I want to return to this conversation, though. It's no accident you're choosing to talk to me about this. Don't you think?"

Samantha offered one of her bear hugs, and Dia stood a little taller. When Baco walked into her bedroom, the excitement of his arrival chased all other feelings away.

"You must be Samantha," Baco reached his hand out to shake Samantha's.

"The one and only," Dia said. "Baco, meet Samantha Bell. Sam, Baco Kastellanos."

"Baco, we get to meet face to face finally. D talks about you constantly."

"All good I hope." He leaned past Samantha to kiss Dia on her cheek.

"All good." Samantha winked at Dia as he delivered his smooch.

Dia spotted Baco's laptop. "What ya got there?"

"Work stuff. It won't take long. I had a deadline for a report but wanted to be here in time to see your friend."

"I am glad you did." She stepped around Sam to give her boyfriend a hug. "Do you want to use my room? We can go join the party if you want to."

"You don't mind? That'd be great, babe."

"Sure thing," Dia planted a quick peck on Baco's mouth and left the room with Sam to head downstairs.

"He's so chivalrous," Samantha whispered as they walked down the hall. "And sexy, too!"

"Hey, Sam. I appreciate you trying to make me feel better."

They stepped outside to the pool where Jackson and his friends played a game of Marco-Polo.

"Happy thirteenth birthday, JJ!" Sam said to him.

"Thanks, Sam!" He yelped before dunking back under the water.

"Hi, girls!" Dia's dad called from the deck.

"Hello, Dr. Remington. Hey, Susan," Sam said.

"Susan said a gentleman came to the front door for you. Will he be joining us outside?" He opened the lid to a gas grill and released billows of smoke.

"He'll be down in a little bit. He had some work stuff," Dia said.

"Is he a boyfriend? I guess Susan was confused as to what his status is."

"He's a friend, Dad. That's all." She would explain later when everyone had had a chance to get to know him.

"He's not the gentleman you mentioned over breakfast a few weeks back?" he asked.

He was paying attention after all! "I don't know what you're talking about." She smiled and gave him the most innocent expression she could muster.

"You're not fooling me, daughter, but okay. We'll play it your way for now. You two ladies can grab a burger if you're hungry. I just took the first tray in a little while ago, but we're hanging outside if you want to join us back out here."

"Thanks, Dad. Let's go back inside, Sam. You're starving right?"

"Duh!" she winked.

"Dia?" Baco popped his head over the balcony as she reentered the house.

"What's up, babe?"

"I left something at my house I need for work. I'll be back in a jiffy. Mind if I leave my stuff here?"

"Sure! See you back here in a bit."

"Pleasure meeting you, Baco," Samantha said as he descended the stairs.

"Are you leaving already?" Baco asked.

"Sam spends her Saturday nights studying," Dia said.

"Ha-ha." Samantha tapped Dia on the arm. "Not yet, but I'll head out in a bit. Going to grab one of Dr. Remington's famous Wagyu burgers first."

"Interesting, maybe we'll be able to hang out more next time," Baco said. "Dia, I won't be gone long."

"See you soon." Dia planted a peck on Baco's cheek, then turned to Sam as he walked out. "Let's make our burgers and head upstairs. How much time do you have?"

"Thirty minutes or so. What did Baco mean by 'interesting?'"

"When did he say that?"

"Just now, after I said I was going to eat one of your dad's Wagyu burgers."

"I think you're reading too much into things."

"If you say so."

When they returned to Dia's room, Baco's laptop beeped several times with notifications. "That's a bit loud," Samantha said. "Do you think we can adjust the volume on it?"

Dia hesitated. What would Baco think if he realized they'd fooled with his computer? She didn't want him to think they were nosey.

"D? Can I mute it?"

"I guess."

Samantha opened the computer up more fully and reduced its volume. The beeps lowered.

"Much better. Wait— What in the world?" She spun around to Dia with wide eyes.

"What? What's going on?" Dia peered over Samantha's shoulder into the screen. "Oh, that's messed up."

A series of cascading browsers were open on his device.

Each showed a woman posing nude. There was also a calendar and Word document.

"What Men Don't Want Women to Know," Samantha read out loud. "This sounds a bit provocative. Shall we see what it says it?"

Dia's stomach was in knots. "I don't feel right about this. If he comes back here..."

"Blame him for not password-protecting his computer… or muting it, for that matter. I almost think he *wanted* us to see this." Samantha pivoted back to his laptop screen. "It says, 'No man can be satisfied with only one woman.' Oh, good lord."

Dia sat down heavily on her bed. *Is this what he meant by "variety?"*

"He has something here with your name on it, D."

"Please! Turn it off. I don't want to see it."

"You don't want to read this? And who are all these women, anyway?"

"No! I don't care to hear or see another thing. We shouldn't even be looking at it!"

Confused by Sam's discovery, Dia struggled to reconcile events and conversations with Baco from the past several days. All along, he'd told her how special she was to him. *Was it all in my head? Did I hear what I wanted to hear? Or did he point-blank lie to me?*

She sat back on the edge of her bed in disbelief. What they'd shared in her room on Monday activated a deep reservoir of feelings. It may have not fully qualified as intercourse, but she'd felt attractive, sexy, desired...and loved. She'd trusted him. She was preparing to take the next step with him. *Am I just one in a long line of girls?* Was he really a player as Anita had suggested? Her thoughts were interrupted by a familiar baritone voice.

"Ladies, what's up?" Baco walked back in. "Hey, why is my laptop open?" He stared at Dia, and his eyes darkened.

EIGHT

SATURDAY, MARCH 27 – WEDNESDAY, MARCH 31, 2004

"WHAT THE FUCK ARE YOU DOING?" Baco asked. It was a question as much as it was an attack. Never in all their time together had he cursed. He glared at them from the doorway. "Wow! You bitches got a lot of nerve poking around my stuff. Do I poke through your computers or books? For fuck's sake!"

Dia sat paralyzed, unfamiliar with his rage. No one ever spoke to her like that, and she felt like a little child caught with their hand in the cookie jar, only worse. She was equally upset too, though. What *were* those pictures and files all about? Would she have found her photos if she and Sam had more time to explore? She stared at her feet, unsure how to respond.

"I can't believe you'd sneak through my computer like this," Baco said.

"And I can't believe you'd leave something so offensive on it for someone to discover," Samantha said.

"Sam, don't," Dia said.

"What?" Samantha grabbed her hand. "Look, he's acting all butthurt over something he *allowed* to happen." She turned to him. "Dude, an alarm was going off on your laptop when we came back upstairs and all I wanted to do was mute it. We weren't 'sneaking' or 'poking around your stuff.' It's like you left it here for us to find it."

"I guess I'm confused," Dia said. "What are all those photos about, anyway?"

"And what exactly is it 'men don't want women to know?'" Samantha asked.

"I don't have to listen to this. You're the ones who are wrong here. Not me." Baco yanked the power cord from the wall and snatched the device from Dia's desk.

"Wait! You're leaving?" Dia stood up.

"There's no relationship without trust. Sorry. I can't do this!" He turned and stormed down the hallway.

Dia stared through her open doorway as he disappeared down the stairs. *How is everything we shared gone in less than two minutes?* She considered chasing after him but hesitated with Jackson's party going on. This was not the impression she wanted her dad to have of her boyfriend. *We're still in a relationship, right?* Dia sat on the bed next to Sam, then fell back and peered at her ceiling in disbelief. Her thoughts shifted to Anita as the heat of anger and shame crawled past her collar.

"You okay, D? Listen. Screw him! You hear me? That's some major bullshit, not just the stuff on the computer, but his entire reaction. What the hell? Can you believe how he reacted? Defensive much? I mean, like…trust me, you're better off without that kind of behavior."

Dia blinked her tears away. "I'm so confused. What just happened?"

"Which part?"

"All of it. Everything was fine, then poof."

Samantha picked up Dia's right hand and held it gently. "Do you really want to be with someone who talks to you like that, let alone views women like that?"

Dia remained silent, slowly releasing her breath. "A lot of guys watch porn, Sam."

"That looks like something more than porn, but maybe that's just me." She brushed the hair away from Dia's face. "Squeeze my hand if you'll be okay."

Dia squeezed Samantha's hand. "I'll manage. You have more important things to worry about than this, so...go. I'll call you later."

"I can stay. You shouldn't be by yourself right now."

"It's fine. I'll be okay. Go, really. You've got bigger problems to deal with than my relationship drama."

"I don't know about that, but if you're sure. Maybe you can go hang out with your family."

That's the last thing I want. She sat up as Samantha rose from the bed, grabbing her backpack. "Do you want to take your burger home with you?"

"Um, yeah." Samantha followed Dia downstairs where she retrieved a plastic baggie.

"D, I'm gonna tell ya something that you probably don't want me to say. I have no clue what that stuff is on your boyfriend's computer, but if I'm honest with you, he's off somehow. I... I've never seen or heard any of my guy friends talk about women like that. Have you? Does Brogan think like that? I get some of them like porn, not that porn's okay, either. But this crap about no man being satisfied by one woman? Talk about some messed up shit...especially if the man thinking it is the one you think you're falling for."

Dia shrugged her shoulders.

"Hang in there. You're not wrong, so watch out with this dude. If you ask me, he's not everything he pretends to be."

"I'll call you tomorrow."

"Bye, honey."

And just like that, Dia was left alone with her thoughts and a house filled with Susan's relatives.

Dia didn't see Baco again until just before Tuesday's shift. She struggled to swallow her dinner from Panda Express as she observed her former boyfriend through the artificial ferns. He chatted it up with a female employee from Regal Cinema. The voluptuous redhead threw her head back in raucous laughter at one of his jokes as bile collected in Dia's throat. Jealousy coursed through her body. *Does he plan to use this girl as much as he used me?* Her work friend was right. Baco had played her for a fool.

It was almost time to get back to Macy's. She exited the food court hopeful to avoid being seen. Her face was flushed when she made it back to her department.

"Are you okay?" Gina asked.

"He's there at the food court, talking to some ginger."

"To a *what*?"

"A redhead!"

"Oh, sorry. I'll bet he's trying to make you jealous."

"I doubt it. I wonder if that's who Anita caught him flirting with last week."

"Does it matter?"

Dia released a loud exhale through her nose. "What's your point, Gina?"

"Look, I'm not going to sugarcoat it. This is most likely going to be the first in a series of disappointments in your life, but you're acting as if your world is ending over one guy."

"What's that supposed to mean? God! You both think you know everything."

"We're trying to help. Be thankful it ended before you got in over your head."

Dia wanted to cry, but she pulled herself together enough to finish her shift without making a scene.

Jackson rattled on and on about his seventh-grade science project and how his teacher wished for him to compete in an upcoming science fair. Uninterested, Dia stared at her plate, moving mashed potatoes through a thick puddle of chicken gravy. Yesterday's anger still clung to her, but a growing depression forced its way in as she sat at dinner in a cloud of despondent despair.

"Yeah, so Mr. Williams says my experiment has a strong chance of placing if not taking first," her little brother said. "How awesome is that?"

Dia pushed back from her food. "May I be excused, please?"

Susan opened her mouth to speak, but Kyle motioned from across the table intercepting what would have most certainly been a snarky response to an otherwise reasonable request.

"You haven't eaten very much, honey. Are you feeling okay?" Her dad gave her a look of sympathy she was unaccustomed to.

"She's still upset over her boyfriend," Jackson joked.

"Shut up, Jackson!" Dia said louder than she would have liked.

"All right, we don't need to talk like that," her dad said, blocking Susan from protecting her son with a snippy comment of her own.

Dia stood, grabbed her plate, and walked it to the sink. She had to exercise restraint to not throw it. She retreated to her room in silence.

A little while later, a gentle knock at her door cut her solitude short. Then her dad entered without an official welcome.

He found a place to sit next to her on the bed. She tried ignoring him by focusing on her ceiling, but he cleared his throat and she turned to meet his gaze.

"I'm sorry it didn't work out with your friend," he said.

Moments passed, silence punctuating the air between his thoughts. "Your mom would have handled this so much differently if she were here."

The mention of her mother triggered the release of a tear which trickled down her temple and disappeared in her hairline. *Lots of things would be better if she was still alive.*

"Kyle," Susan said from downstairs. "Is everything okay?" Dia resisted the urge to sigh. Was the woman completely unable to let her husband talk one on one with his daughter?

"Yes, dear. Down in a minute," he answered back. "You know, from what Susan could tell, your friend looked a bit too old for you. I didn't get to meet him, but…you're not serious, are you?"

"Does it matter now? Chances are I'll never see him again, so don't worry about it."

"Look, it probably doesn't seem like it right now, but this *will* pass, and you *will* be okay." Her dad rubbed his hands together, unable to look his daughter square in the eyes. "Come back down when you're ready, and we'll watch something mindless on the TV." He patted her leg before returning downstairs.

Dia rolled on her side and set her gaze upon Lucy occupying her perch on a bookshelf above Dia's desk. She stood and retrieved her doll as she had weeks earlier, desperate to derive direction, or comfort if nothing else. She spoke out loud to Lucy. "Was it only a giant misunderstanding?"

She ran her fingers down Lucy's braids and reflected on what she had seen on Baco's computer. She assumed his document referred to her and to their relationship, but in hindsight, Dia realized she'd never gotten the chance to ask him what any of it meant. *But what about all those naked women?*

An incoming call interrupted her thoughts. Her exboyfriend's number flashed across her cell phone screen. Anxious for any prospect of reconciliation, she answered.

"Hello," she said.

"Babe," Baco said. "I'm..."

She replaced Lucy on her shelf and returned to her bed.

"Listen. I just wondered if we could talk. I…I want to apologize first, but I thought, I mean… Can you forgive me? Please say you will. I can explain everything."

Dia sat up. This was exactly what she'd wanted—an opportunity for them both to discuss things to better understand what happened.

Sobs emanated softly through her phone. "I'm so sorry because I would never make you do something you weren't comfortable with. I meant it when I said you were what I'd been looking for in a relationship. All that stuff on my laptop? Just some of my dumb friends' ideas… Please believe me."

"I wasn't intentionally poking around on your computer. When Sam and I came upstairs, it was beeping. We only wanted to mute it when all those screens popped up. I would never spy on you," she said. "But what were those all about, anyway?"

"Porn one of my buddies shared with me. It's nothing, I promise."

"You could've said that. I'm young, but I'm not stupid, ya know?"

"I never said you were."

"True. You took off instead. You were really ugly to me."

"I'm so sorry I lost my cool. You deserve better than that," he said.

Dia relaxed as the weight of their argument lifted. She wanted to ask him if they were still boyfriend and girlfriend and whether they'd be going to the dance in three days. *If we do go, will we have sex afterward?* Images of Baco talking with the redhead popped into her mind, reigniting jealousy and self-doubt. She grimaced, wondering if Baco's apology was sincere or an effort to pacify her in order for him to pursue his sexual fantasies with her. She shifted her eyes up to Lucy, craving the doll's reassurance from where she sat.

Sounds of laughter made their way upstairs as her family cleaned up from dinner, cementing her loneliness. Her relationship had been ideal up to now. *But nothing is perfect. No one ever lives life or falls in love without some bumps in the road, right?* Dia felt accepted by Baco. Any affections her father had were trumped by his commitment to his wife and her son.

"Are you still there?" Baco asked.

"Yes, sorry. I'm thinking."

"About us, I hope," he said.

"Yeah."

Baco breathed heavily on his end of their call. Minutes passed as neither spoke. "I have an idea," he said, penetrating the silence.

"Tell me."

"Remember how we were discussing a trip to Port A or South Padre?"

"I do."

"What if we went right now? We can leave tonight."

"Right now?"

"Alone *together*. We can go away for a few days and talk things through. A long weekend away is all we need. We can get away from everyone and everything."

Dia contemplated Baco's suggestion. Getting away sounded intriguing, and she wanted to feel his arms around her more than anything. There was no way she would be able to secure her father's permission for something like this, though. She needed to leave without asking, but she worried how much trouble she would cause by doing that.

"What are you thinking?" Baco asked.

"I want to, I do, but I don't know. You don't have to worry about being missed or getting consent from anyone."

"Okay, we'll just go for a day then. Tell him you'll return tomorrow."

"Not sure that's much of an alternative."

"Babe, this might sound a little mean, but do you actually think they'll miss you while you're gone?"

His question cut to the core of everything. What difference would leaving for a night really make in the big scheme of things? "I don't know," she said.

"Dia, honey, leave a note. That way you're not asking, but you're not running away, either, or going without some sort of explanation. It'll be easier to beg forgiveness than to ask permission."

Dia's world had been ripped from under her four days earlier, and no one had been able to console her until Baco had reached out to her. She was convinced that he alone had her best interests in mind. Anita, Sam, and her dad all offered advice, but their words were empty platitudes at the end of the day. They had their own lives to lead with careers to cultivate, scholarships to strive for, and patients to attend to. Baco, on the other hand, wanted one thing: Dia.

"We'll be gone for one, two nights max. Then we will be back in time for your dance," Baco said.

"Okay, I'll do it. When? What should I bring?"

"What if I head over now? Can you get away?"

"Sure. They'll be watching TV, so I can meet you out front."

"Oh, I am so excited, babe. I can't wait to see you. Grab a sweatshirt and jeans. A swimsuit in case we're able to catch some rays between rainstorms, and a toothbrush. Whatever you'd take for overnight."

"Got it. See you soon."

"Bye."

She thought about calling Samantha to keep her in the loop that she and Baco had reconciled and were going away for a day or two, but she knew Sam would try and talk her out of it. Her best friend refused to understand what she shared with Baco. With complete confidence, she now knew Baco would take care of her in a way no one else ever had. She located her backpack and dumped its contents out onto her bed. She retrieved a spiral notebook and pen and sat down to compose her a short letter:

Dad, please don't worry. I would have asked permission, but you would have only said no. Baco called, and we've worked everything out. We're going to the beach just for a day—maybe two—and I'll be back. I love you, Dad. See you soon.

XOXO,

Dia

She placed her note on her desk and grabbed items for their trip, stuffing T-shirts, yoga pants, a UT sweatshirt, and bikini into her backpack on top of her Burt's Bees skincare products and toothbrush. Dia found it difficult to contain her enthusiasm over being back together with Baco and going on vacation with him. She knew she risked upsetting her family. *Will they care that much?* she asked herself, reflecting on Baco's comments about whether they'd really miss her. She caught her reflection in her dresser mirror. Her cheeks were flushed pink, and her eyes shined bright.

Dia snuck downstairs as quiet as a thief. She listened as her dad and stepmom laughed over a line from *King of Queens* while Jackson begged to understand what was so funny. She opened the front door without anyone noticing, stepped over the threshold, then pulled the door shut behind her. She jogged stealthily over to the live oak tree in their front yard and waited.

Headlights snaked around her street corner. Baco turned them off halfway up her block to avoid catching her family's attention when he drove up. Dia walked to the end of the driveway to meet him, her stomach turning in anticipation.

He reached across the passenger seat to unlatch her door for her. "Hey, baby. You look gorgeous. Hop inside, and hand me your bag."

Dia handed him her backpack, which he threw into the

back, and took a seat in Baco's car. She leaned over the gear shift and kissed him, wanting to devour him with her mouth and tongue. Now that they had reconciliation behind them, they would spend several hours happily driving toward Texas' Gulf Coast and their new future—one made bright by the promise of love. "I am so stoked right now. You have no idea," she said. "Thank you so much for calling. I thought I'd never see you again."

Baco grabbed her face in his hands. "You mean the world to me, babe. Let's get out of here before your dad or someone spots us." He gently pushed her back.

"Sorry, I'm excited, is all." Dia reached behind her to grab a seat belt. She turned to buckle herself in then met Baco's gaze. He wore a curious expression. "What? Is everything okay?"

"Everything is perfect, just like I planned," he said.

Dia chuckled, unsure what he meant but too distracted by her excitement of being back together to take pause. If they didn't leave, they may never get away to reclaim their chance at a relationship. "Let's go, then," she instructed.

Baco sat back and put his car in drive with his eyes locked firmly ahead on traffic.

Back in Dia's bedroom, Lucy toppled off the shelf and hit the floor with a thud.

In the Gila mountains, La Loba woke with a jolt. *It's starting.* She rose from bed and exited her cave into the crisp, evening air. The stars above shone with brighter-than-usual clarity while her mind remained clouded.

No part of her wished to see Dia suffer, but La Loba's mom had extracted a fierce commitment from her years ago. "Bad stuff happens, Onawa! You can't steer people from the path before them. Swear to me you'll never again interfere with someone's destiny."

"I promise," La Loba had said back then. She tightened her long-deceased father's serape around her shoulders in search of a solution she could live with moving forward. "I promise not to interfere...*too much*."

PART TWO

"Compliance causes a shocking realization that must be registered by all women. That is, to be ourselves causes us to be exiled by many others, and yet to comply with what others want causes us to be exiled from ourselves. It is a tormenting tension, and it must be borne, but the choice is clear."

—*Women Who Run with the Wolves*

"Nosing Out the Facts: The Retrieval of Intuition as Initiation" chapter

NINE

WEDNESDAY, MARCH 31 – THURSDAY, APRIL 1, 2004

DIA SAT NEXT to her man, smiling ear to ear in his company as music played through the Honda's speakers. She was proud of herself for taking this step toward her independence and for her relationship. He guided his car with caution out of her River Place suburban neighborhood and headed west to Ranch Road 620.

Baco reached for Dia's hand, and she turned to meet his gaze. His eyes appeared more open now, their gray color more vibrant than normal with specks of violet and azure. They struck Dia as wild-looking even. An undefinable pinch of alarm stirred somewhere deep inside. It soon gave way to other thoughts, though, and her unease retreated as he shifted his attention to traffic and curved right toward I-35.

"Hey, baby," she said. "I just want you to... I mean, we already said it earlier, but I apologize for...well, everything from last weekend. I hope you know I'd never intentionally do anything to get into your business or between you and your friends—or work, even. I promise you; I'll always respect you. Okay?"

"Thanks. I love ya, babe," he said, squeezing Dia's hand.

"I'll make it up to you. I'll prove you can count on me," she said, unsure what she was promising, exactly. Baco kept his eyes focused on the road. He acted differently now, but she couldn't put her finger on it. Maybe their disagreement lingered in his mind. It would take time to regain his trust, but they'd be better for it later—stronger even—she convinced herself.

"Listen, babe. I'm not blaming you in any way. You explained what happened, and I believe you," Baco said. "I'm sorry, too. I overreacted."

Dia relaxed as he spoke. His matching apology put her at ease and confirmed they'd move past this to experience a deeper connection.

"That being said, I can't stress how happy it makes me that you respect me. It means a lot to me *as a man*, and I hope you'll always remember that. I want...I need you to obey me and do what I say…always. Whatever I say goes because...well because I'm your man. Right?" He squeezed Dia's hand with more pressure than before. "Right, Dia?"

"Right," she said in a near whisper.

Interstate 35 stretched out ahead of them and Baco sped with increasing momentum through Round Rock and North Austin. They passed exit 239 for Highway 183, which could have returned Dia to her home in River Place if she'd asked. She turned to her right to catch a glimpse of 183, but an 18-wheeler blocked her view. Looking through the front windshield, she read the exit signs one by one as they drove: St. John's Ave., US 290, 51st Street, and Airport Blvd. She mused if their entire trip would go like this, ticking off mile markers of her old life until new ones appeared for unknown destinations and experiences.

Was it a good idea to leave to fix things with Baco? What about school and work? The reality of leaving sank into her mind, but only for a moment.

"I love you, Dia."

He always knew what to say. Like magic, her doubt evaporated. *We'll only be gone for a couple of days.* "I love you more."

"That's not even possible." Baco smiled.

Dia's excitement returned with her boyfriend's words of validation. "How long will it take to reach Port A? Or did we decide on South Padre? It's so late, it may be tomorrow before we get there, right?"

"Sure, I think so."

"Are you going to drive all night? I can help if you need to take a nap or something."

"Hey, are you thirsty or anything? I could use an iced tea. In fact, I can't even remember if I ate today."

"Seriously?"

"Yeah, well, things got really busy at work. Plus, I kept thinking back to Saturday and worried I'd never see you again. Are you hungry? I'm starving."

"Nah, I had dinner with my family. Wait, now that I think about it, I excused myself without eating much. I was thinking about us, too. Never mind what I said. A cheeseburger sounds great."

Baco pulled into a McDonald's drive-thru. "Iced tea to drink?"

"Dr Pepper, please."

Baco placed their order. Within a few minutes, they were greedily tearing through wrappers to satisfy their hunger.

"So, what's our plan?" Dia asked.

Baco took a long sip of tea through his straw before answering. "My thought is to put some miles between Austin and us. I probably won't drive *all* night. I'm tired, to tell you the truth, but I can go for another hour or so. Then we'll pull over for some rest. Sound good?"

"Sounds awesome," Dia leaned over to kiss him. "I'm serious about my offer to take the wheel, though, if it helps."

"I appreciate it, but you don't really drive anywhere besides your neighborhood. Am I right?"

"Technically, you are correct."

"Babe, you're cute and smart as a button, but it looks like I'll do the driving on this trip. I don't want you to get in trouble with the law," he said with a wink.

"I'm just trying to help," she said. "Hey, I wonder if I should check in with my dad…before it gets too late." Dia retrieved her backpack and reached inside the front zipper pocket for her phone.

"What are you doing?"

"I know what you said about my family not caring that much and all, but I'm sure he'll be worried if I'm not there when they wake up in the morning. I just want to call and tell him he doesn't have to be concerned."

Baco put his hand on her lap, facing his palm up. "Babe, you'll only worry your dad giving him a head's up at this hour. Let's wait and maybe ring him tomorrow, k?"

She held the phone in her hand, unsure what to do.

"May I have your cell, please?"

Dia hesitated.

"Hand it to me!"

She dropped the device into his hand as tears gathered at the edge of her lashes. "You don't have to yell at me."

"I'm sorry, babe."

"You said you wouldn't raise your voice at me again."

"Shit, I apologize. Listen, I'm just wound up from the last few days still and eager to get to the coast. If we call your dad, it'll only delay us. You get what I'm saying, don't you?"

A woman in double-platform heels walked down the sidewalk in front of their car as Dia wiped a lone tear from her cheek. "Sure, Baco. I understand." She returned her backpack to the rear. "I think I'll take a nap then. Is that okay?" *Or will that piss him off, too?*

Baco nodded and smiled at her. "Go right on ahead, babe. I'll wake you at the next stop."

She collected their trash, then laid her seat down as Baco merged back onto I-35 and snaked his car southbound through downtown Austin past the Texas Capitol.

Dia woke to sounds of gravel passing beneath the vehicle, and her head bounced lightly against her headrest. She opened her heavy eyelids. Two beams of light shone on what appeared to be a county road or a long, secluded driveway. She couldn't tell which. Oak and cedar trees stood in random clumps along either side, entwined by a barbed-wire fence overgrown with weeds and grass. If there was any beauty to be seen, it'd have to wait for the light of day. The Honda's headlights sliced through the darkness for another mile before a lit structure emerged from the shadows. *How long have I been asleep?* she wondered.

"Oh, hey, babe. You're awake," Baco said, patting Dia's leg as he pulled up to a singular ranch house. Even in the dark, she observed it needed a power wash and fresh coat of paint.

"Where are we?"

"My friend Danny's place. We're gonna stay here then head out tomorrow morning. Cool?"

Dia shrugged her shoulders. "I told you I could help drive. How far are we from the coast?" Her questions went unanswered as a lamp flickered on from inside, followed by a dim porch light. A man stood inside through the foyer window.

Baco parked the car and got out. "Grab your bag, D."

She reached for her backpack and trailed him to the front door, which didn't exactly square with the frame like it should. Scores of mosquitos and June bugs lay dead in the ceiling-mounted lamp overhead. Someone, presumably Danny, opened the door. He filled the doorjamb, and his head—covered with greasy brown hair—grazed the top. Pebbles of inflammation dotted a face already scarred by pockmarks. Dia tracked close behind her boyfriend.

"Thanks for letting us crash here tonight, bro," Baco said. He dropped his stuff and motioned for Dia to follow his lead. "This is Dia, my girlfriend I was telling you about."

"No problemo, man. Great to meet you, Dia," Danny said in a deep, bass voice. He smiled at Dia as she diverted her eyes.

"Hey, Dan, can you excuse us for a sec? I need to talk to my girl, here—alone, if you know what I mean."

"Sure thing, man. I'll be down in my room. Text me when you're ready. Oh, before I forget, there's some beer in my fridge."

"Thanks, bro."

Ready? Ready for what?

Danny lumbered out of sight down his hallway and Dia followed Baco to a refrigerator where he retrieved two Tecates. Drab yellow paint that matched the appliances coated the walls. The house screamed "ugly" and begged for a makeover. There was popcorn texture on the ceiling. Even Dia knew that was out of style, but then again, nothing about Danny's place felt right.

"Here, have a cerveza. We're on vacation now, babe!" Baco drew the tabs back on their cans and drank deeply for several seconds before stopping to catch his breath. Her Dr Pepper was long gone, and she was thirsty. Dia consumed more than half of her own can then burped.

"Atta girl," Baco said. "Drink up!" Dia emptied her can as Baco retrieved two more. "I want to make love with you, my little mamacita." He handed her a second beer. "Will you let me share this experience with you? Please? I want you so much, it hurts."

Here? she wondered. *With Baco's friend, Danny, less than thirty feet away?* "I don't know, Baco. I mean, I kinda wanted it to be more special my first time, *our* first time. You know? Like, can't we at least wait until we reach the condo?" She held her arms out wide. "I mean, look at this place." A trail of mouse feces caught her attention as she followed the length of her arm toward the kitchen sink.

"Don't you love me, Dia?"

She turned back to Baco's voice. "What? Of course!"

"Then what difference does it make what someone's house looks like if I'm looking at you?" He pulled her up against him and she recognized the now-familiar firmness of his penis behind his jeans. "See, babe? The thing is, I don't want to wait any longer. This is the longest I've dated someone without making love, and I'm about to explode, to be honest."

About to explode? She was starting to second-guess, if not triple-guess, her decision to join him on their trip. "Is it okay if I call my dad now that we're out of town? I just want to tell him I'm safe. I'm worried what he'll think if I'm not there tomorrow."

Dia walked toward her belongings in the front room, but Baco scrambled around her and blocked her path. "Hey, now, wait a minute. We're not making any calls to parents tonight, you understand? It's late, and you'll only end up raising a lot of alarms. Look, you'll be fine, babe. I get you're doing this for the first time, but look, losing your virginity is really not that big of a deal. Besides, you're going to enjoy it, I promise. You remember how good I made you feel last week, right?"

Memories of being touched down there produced an unfamiliar sensation in her panties. She took several gulps of beer, although the alcohol was already starting to take effect. Would finishing the second can on a near-empty stomach make the surroundings of Danny's home more palatable?

"Come here. You're thinking about it, aren't you?" Baco held Dia against him. They stood in Dan's kitchen, and the fluorescent lights buzzed overhead as he bent down to kiss her. She returned his kiss, melting into his embrace.

He broke away gently. "Let's get more comfortable on the couch." He grabbed Dia's hand and pulled her in front of him as he sat down. "You stand right here. I want you to undress for me so I can examine every inch of your beautiful, naked body."

"But Danny is down the hall…"

"Honey, you worry too much. Anyone ever told you that? Look, don't think about it. Here, drink your beer." He watched her as she drank the remaining Tecate and placed it on an end table. "Let me help you here." He untied Dia's sweatpants and shimmied them over her bottom toward her feet. "Go ahead. You take off everything else."

Dia stared into his eyes. Her concerns faded away as she planted both feet in front of him. She pulled her T-shirt over her head and stood in her bra and undies. Baco's mouth opened, and he licked his lips. He leaned deeper into the couch, adjusting himself into a more comfortable position as he took all of her in. Her heart raced in anticipation.

She reached behind her back to unfasten her bra. With only her panties remaining, Dia slid her fingers beneath her waistband to shimmy them past her feet. She stood naked in front of Baco, electrified and aroused for the first time in her entire life.

Baco took his own turn at undressing. He unbuttoned his jeans and slid them off from where he sat. She saw him naked for the first time, including what protruded from a dark mass of curls in his crotch. He leaned forward and brought his hands up between her legs. "I want you."

"I want you, too." She had zero clue about what to do next.

"Come here." He pulled her on top of him, so they were sitting face-to-face. "Put your feet underneath like you're squatting over me. You got it…perfect."

Dia positioned herself directly over Baco, grasping couch cushions for balance with him beneath her.

"Okay, go ahead…lower your body on mine," he said.

She hesitated, then squatted ever so slightly.

"Don't worry. You won't hurt me. That's it, babe. Oh, God, you are amazing. Do you like it?" he asked.

Dia nodded as she lowered herself completely over his shaft. He instructed her to move, and she rose up and down, Baco guiding her with his hands on her waist. He brought her breasts to his mouth and sucked at them.

"This feels so good, baby. Here, let's lay down on the floor." He lifted Dia from their couch position and knelt, supporting her weight effortlessly. Positioning himself on top, Baco spread her legs so he could enter her again. He moved rhythmically, bringing his lips down on hers.

They made love with their arms wrapped tightly around each other. She wanted to press her body up to his as close as possible. Dia turned to her left and opened her eyes as Baco kissed her neck. A large figure watched from the doorway to the kitchen. It took a moment for her to realize Danny had positioned himself there with a video camera, its recording light blinking red. Dia froze. *How long has he been there filming us?*

"What's wrong?" Baco spun his head in the direction of Dia's.

She waited for Baco to react and to yell at his friend to get lost. Those words never came.

"Dan, my man. How long have you been standing there?"

"From Dia's little striptease 'til now. Want me to stop?"

"Ah, hell no. We're just getting started."

Fear overrode every other emotion in her body. *Just getting started?* Baco withdrew and stood up, leaving Dia exposed as Danny walked over to capture her on tape. She scrambled for her clothes.

"No, babe. You won't be needing those." Baco retrieved her top and bottoms and tossed them behind the couch, prompting her to cover herself with her hands. "You see, Danny here, he's a good friend, one of my best friends, and he's been lonely for a super-long time."

What is he saying? Dia kept her eyes on Baco as he spoke.

"I want you to do for my friend here what you were doing for me...*exactly* like you were doing it for me."

"No, I'm not doing that."

"I don't think you understand. Fucking him is precisely what you're going to do." Danny walked over to Dia, who stood struggling to keep her private areas from his view.

"I like your titties, little girl," Danny said, reaching for Dia's breasts. She recoiled and backed up without giving him satisfaction, but Danny reached his long arm out to grab her. He yanked her toward him, thwarting her ability to shake free.

"I'm done playing cat and mouse here, Dia," Baco said. "I'm done pretending to be your boyfriend and acting like I give one fuck about your feelings. God, you exhaust me."

"What do you mean, 'pretending?'" Dia stood there as a dim picture of her future came into slow focus.

"You're going to do what I say without any goddamn resistance. Do you hear me?" He slipped into his jeans.

Danny's grip around her arm tightened while he continued filming her with his other hand. Dia stood mortified as she listened to Baco.

"And you're going to start by screwing my friend, here." Baco turned to face her with all traces of feigned affection gone from his eyes. "Hand me your camera, Dan!"

Danny handed off the video recorder, which Baco brought up to Dia's face. "Do you want to say 'hi' to your family? To your perfect, precious father?"

Dia bowed her head in shame as she now understood why they were filming her.

"Down on your back, girlfriend. Time to work."

She looked up, dumbfounded through the camera lens.

"Don't give me that look. Just do it."

Dia shook her head no.

"NOW!" Baco's booming voice drove an imaginary ice

pick through Dia's lower body, and urine trickled down her leg.

Terrified he might hit her, she lowered herself down to the floor as Danny released his grip to remove his belt and pants. She turned her head away as Danny pushed her legs apart and lowered himself. The video camera shifted back into record mode. She grimaced in pain as Danny lay on her. Tears ran down her face. "I can't breathe."

But no one heard her. Indifferent to her suffering, Baco zoomed in on her face to maximize her humility. "Fuck with me, and everyone will see a copy of this—your family, your coworkers...even your loser classmates."

Dia tried to see through the vertical blinds as sunlight slipped past the grime-coated front window. A vague dream of some woman calling her name still swirled around in her brain, but it faded into the ether as the sun rose. She lay exhausted on Dan's dust-covered couch, no longer her own person—a sophomore getting ready for her first dance or prepping for the PSAT. She one hundred percent belonged to a man she thought she once loved and who she thought cared for her, but he only viewed her as his property.

"You can rest once we're on the highway." Baco returned from the kitchen with coffee. He sat down beside her and patted her bottom. "You're good, babe. Hotter than I even imagined. Danny liked you, too. Didn't you, buddy?" Baco asked over his shoulder.

The man grunted in reply as he adjusted his pants.

"Boys will line up for this for miles! Put your clothes on, babe. We need to jump back on the road to show you off for your first night of work. You owe me for all the bullshit I've put up with all these weeks—more than most bitches, that's for damn sure."

Danny smirked at Baco's comment. Dia rose to retrieve her items from behind Dan's couch and found it hard to determine which was worse: the hours of sexual assault or Baco's hate-filled words. She struggled to make sense of his betrayal and feared how much nastier he would make things.

TEN

FRIDAY, APRIL 9, 2004

MINUTES FLIPPED MECHANICALLY on a radio alarm clock. Dia lay under her third "customer" as she watched the time advance from 2:03 to 2:04 to 2:05 to 2:06.

How long will this one take to finish? She remained focused on each minute's rotation to avoid making eye contact and to try and ignore everything possible about this situation she now found herself in.

Fast-food wrappers with partially eaten cheeseburgers and French fries laid strewn in a corner opposite her clock where a solitary lamp draped with a red bandana cast weak shadows. Within the reach of their darkness was a mattress where Dia lay beneath a man she guessed to be thirty years her senior and three times her weight.

He pumped away at her, his head up and eyes closed as he worked his way to some imaginary finish line. A solid one hundred pounds overweight, he slowed every few seconds to catch his breath, lowering his head to rest on Dia's shoulder.

Rivulets of perspiration rolled down from his greasy scalp to his forehead. One by one they dropped to her skin before cascading to her mattress where they collected in a growing puddle. Her whole body was wet from his sticky perspiration.

She could barely breathe beneath his rolls of fat. Then a wave of nausea lurched from her stomach to her throat.

Her sudden movement did not go unnoticed. Her guest raised his head and studied her. She turned her head and closed her eyes to avoid being seen, feeling ashamed. He grunted and resumed his pace. His head up, he lifted himself from his elbows to his hands. Sweat plashed on Dia's chest, and she grimaced in revulsion as his body clenched in spasm. A final thrust and he fell on top of her, blanketing her as she struggled for air.

"You're a quiet little thing," he told her. Dia strained her head left, but the man wrapped his meaty fingers around her jaw and made her turn toward him. "Look at me when I'm talking to you." She raised her eyes to meet his. "You're not the prettiest girl I've had, but you're tight. I'll be back for more of you." With her face still held in his hand like a vice, he pursed her lips together and kissed her.

A knock at her door prompted him to release his grip. Dia reached for a sheet to cover herself. "Stop. I want to look at you while I dress." He leaned against a wall as he climbed back into his slacks. "Yeah, I'm definitely coming back for more of you. Mm-mmm. Damn, you're fine." Another tap at the door reminded him his time was up.

Dia prayed the next customer would be less disgusting, maybe more like those boys from earlier that afternoon. Teenage brothers had arrived as she started her ninth day of work for Baco. Older sibling, Phil, had wanted to provide his thirteen-year-old baby brother an "educational experience." She could barely imagine her stepbrother having a girlfriend, let alone sex. Phil's younger brother felt pressured, from what Dia could tell. He took inventory of the fast-food packaging strewn across the room while his Phil took his turn.

"Come on, Frankie. See? All there is to it. Just put your little pecker in her like so," he ribbed. It took five minutes of coaching and cajoling, and little Frank accomplished his required task less than eight seconds later.

Beer cans fell in Dia's room, jolting her back to her present situation. She'd finished cleaning up from her last john, but now she turned and saw three men staring at her. Her next customer had brought a couple of friends. They were drunk and speaking English with heavy accents. Fear gripped her as she listened to them discuss what they had in mind. Something about "doubling up." It was hard to tell, she only had a year and a half of high school Spanish under her belt, and they spoke so fast.

They filled her room with the stink of perspiration. The third one fell against her door as he closed it. The first man approached her. His stench—a combination of body odor and Lone Star beer—grew with each step. Disgusted, she suppressed bile rising from her stomach by breathing through her mouth.

"Don't look so scared. We're not going to hurt you," he said.

"Much," the second guy snickered. Their buddy slid down the wall and lay slumped over five feet from her mattress.

"Come here," Number One told her. He grabbed her by her arm and pulled her in front of him. He moved his hands over her shoulders and brought them to rest at her breasts. "I like your chi-chis," he said. "Juan, her boobs look like her pic on Baco's website. You like them big, don't you, bro?"

Dia had learned that the phrase "making love" was a lie. Sex was a weapon, and she began to think that rape was worse than death. She struggled to see through her tears.

"Crying won't help you, little bitch," Number One spat. "You're a whore. We know this ain't your first rodeo, so let's go!" he smacked her face and forced her down on all fours.

Following his friend's lead, Juan spanked her behind.

She did what he told her to do in hopes it'd be over sooner. Minutes ticked by one after another and Dia focused on her clock while the two assaulted her with unnecessary roughness. Soon they'd be done, but she knew their friend would want his own opportunity to get his rocks off.

As if reading her thoughts, the third one spoke in a drunken slur, "Hurry ya two. I want my turn before we have to get back to work."

"Okay, she's all yours so come on over," Juan called. "I got her lubed up for ya, unless you're going for the backdoor like last time."

Number Three rose from the floor and tripped on his way to where she lay.

Dia lurched forward.

"Where do you think *you're* going?" Number Three asked. "Come over here!"

Resistance was futile, yet Dia scrambled off the bed to prevent him from penetrating her. If only Number Three's friends weren't there to assist him. She made it two feet off the mattress when they overpowered her and pinned her down back in the center of the bedding. Unable to retreat, she used one remaining tool in her arsenal and screamed in hopes Baco would care enough about his property to come in and save her. But no one came to help. The trio had their fun and left, making plans for more beer after work.

Dia fell exhausted onto her mattress—her prison. She searched for her sheet to cover herself and found it crumpled past her feet. With a few weak tugs, she placed it over her bruised and bloodied body. She closed her eyes, hoping to catch a nap. Instead, Baco stalked into the room.

"Did we have a problem here this afternoon?" he asked.

She opened her eyes to meet his steely gaze. He crouched next to her; his head bent to his left to look Dia square in her eyes. He'd started to grow an uneven beard. Strung out Baco was nothing at all like the person she'd met only a few months earlier.

"I asked you a question!"

"No, there's no problem."

Baco reached out, and Dia thought he might hit her. She flinched as he grabbed her by her ear. "You're never to resist a customer again. You understand me?"

Dia lay unresponsive.

"I said, do you understand me?" Baco yelled. "I *own you. I* say how it goes, and what my men want, they get. Got it?"

Dia nodded, her eyes filling with tears.

"Now go clean yourself. Your next customer will be here in an hour." He let go of her ear and flicked her on her head as he rose to leave. She uncurled from a fetal position to gingerly place her feet on the floor and walk to a shared Jack-and-Jill bathroom.

Petite roses dotted the faded wallpaper that covered portions of the small adjacent room. It peeled up from the baseboards and down from a ceiling, exposing concentric, asymmetrical green circles. Brown stains colored the sides of a toilet in need of cleaning. Dia yanked a plastic shower curtain back, and wafts of mildew further assaulted her senses, reinforcing her life's ugly turn of events. She pulled a valve to facilitate the arrival of water and remove any residue left by Baco's clients.

Grime coated a small window opposite her bathroom's vanity, removing any need for a privacy shade. A late afternoon sun hung heavy behind the tree line outside, and she guessed it must be getting close to four or five. Overgrown grass and empty beer bottles lay scattered. She had no idea where they were. *Austin? Corpus? Somewhere else?* Desolation crept over her as she waited for her shower to turn hot.

Squeals of laughter interrupted her thoughts. In the connecting room, another of Baco's prostitutes was hard at work. *How could anyone find this funny?* she wondered. Were there any girls who enjoyed getting fucked against their will ten to twelve times a day by as many different men? Dia heard a man encouraging the girl from behind their bathroom door.

There'd been no cheering for Dia from *her* customers. Only abuse—rape.

She couldn't fathom ever being in a place of acceptance over this new life she found herself in. She hoped someone from home would locate her soon so she could return to her ordinary life—a life she'd seriously taken for granted and naively scorned prior to leaving.

An airplane flew overhead, followed by a second and then another, leading her to believe they were near an airport. The regular rumble of jet engines served as Dia's sole anchor in assessing her possible location. Baco, or "Daddy" as he now preferred to be called, kept Dia away from all media. There was no TV, no radio, newspapers, or magazines. She was a slave—cut off from everything and everyone she'd ever known.

Dia caught her reflection in the mirror. Her hair appeared thinner and oilier, its drabness accentuating growing dark circles under her eyes. A loss of appetite was beginning to take its toll as she counted her ribs. She'd always aspired to be skinny, and she wallowed in the fact that being kidnapped and forced into prostitution got her there.

Shower steam clouded the mirror, making her disappear. A hard knock at her door returned Dia once more to her present situation, and she stepped into a stream of boiling water to prep for another long night of endless faces.

ELEVEN

FRIDAY, APRIL 9, 2004

CHEERS ERUPTED ONCE MORE from Dia's adjoining room as she dried off from her shower. Karyn's customer clapped vigorously for her, and Dia failed to comprehend what they found so damn entertaining. She wiped steam away with a sour-smelling towel, then retrieved a bag from beneath the sink in search of cosmetics to mask her emotions. As she applied her eye makeup, she questioned if perhaps Karyn's squeals of delight were *her* way of covering up her feelings.

Dia poked around her pouch of makeup for an ivory foundation. With Karyn's counsel, she'd learned to apply it perfectly, blending it with a reusable sponge. In fact, Karyn had taught her a number of things since her arrival.

"Home," as Baco called it, was a modest, nondescript single-story house, not unlike Danny's. Yellow-beige paint peeled from the siding on three of the four sides. Limestone was stacked in an asymmetrical, haphazard design across the front and reminded Dia of those early 1980s ranch-style neighborhoods that had at one point defined Austin's most northern boundary. Isolated from civilization, its tired facade mirrored Dia's when she'd been driven up that circular drive her first day.

A young woman had exited the house upon their arrival to greet both of them. Baco brushed her aside, which deflated the woman's mood immediately. She turned her attention to Dia. "Welcome, Dia. Baco told me a lot about you. My name is Karyn." She spoke with a European accent Dia couldn't place. *Is she German or Russian*?

"Karyn will show you how we do things here." Baco returned to his car for a bag. "She'll be like a sister to you...until you piss her off, anyway."

What's that supposed to mean? Dia scrutinized Karyn for insight. She stood tall, almost six feet, and stared indignantly after Baco as he walked away and turned the corner. Then she let out a heavy sigh and glanced down at Dia with green eyes and an apologetic smile revealing crooked, stained teeth. "Follow me. I'll show you your room."

Karyn led her down a long, dark hall, stopping at the first door on their left. It opened into a small room with two sets of twin bunk beds separated by a dressing table under a curtained window. "This is where you'll sleep," she said. "You won't take customers here, so make yourself comfortable. The top right one is mine, so take whatever you like from these other three. It's just two of us—for now, anyway."

Dia dropped her backpack on a bed to her left.

"Do you need help unpacking?" Karyn asked in a maternal fashion. It was the first kindness Dia had experienced since leaving Austin less than twenty-four hours earlier.

"Oh, I don't really have much here." She dumped her backpack's contents on to her bed. Her swimsuit fell out on top of jeans and sweatshirt and reminded her of Baco's broken promise to visit one of Texas' beaches. Tears filled her eyes and rolled one by one down her face.

"Hey, don't cry," Karyn said. "It's not so bad. Here, check

this out." She walked to a closet and opened its doors to reveal a selection of clothes. "These are for both of us."

Dia wiped her face with her hands. The closet was filled with a dozen different kimonos, short skirts, and camisoles.

"Try one on. I'll bet you look great, especially with your...uh." She hesitated, then finally said, "boobs." Dia blushed and reached for the black mini and red satin camisole that Karyn held out in front of her. She had never worn something so skimpy and revealing in all her life. She shook her head as she returned the outfit to her new roommate. *This has to be a mistake. I should be on a beach or in school, looking forward to Saturday's dance.*

"What's wrong?"

"This isn't right. I shouldn't be here. If I could just get my phone and call my dad."

"Look!" Karyn crossed her arms. "I'm not sure what you were expecting, but I'm trying real hard to treat you nice. Are you going to put this on, or what?"

"I don't want to."

"It's not really up to you, Dia. You can wear this or deal with the consequences."

What could be worse than what happened last night? Then Dia remembered something Baco said earlier about showing her off for her first night of work. He said so many things, something about men lining up for miles, about owing him for all the bullshit. *What does he want from me?* "Can I have some privacy at least?" she asked.

Karyn stared down at her with her green eyes narrowed into slits. "Princess, there ain't no such thing as privacy anymore, you hear me? Undress and put these clothes on —now!"

Dia stood with her mouth agape, trying to make sense of Karyn's sudden change in mood.

"Do it!" The energy of Karyn's words pierced through Dia, much like Baco's had the night before when she resisted

Danny. Seeing no way out, she undressed and slipped into the outfit as Karyn's eyes moved over her body. She blushed crimson under her gaze and suppressed every desire to cry. A knock at their bedroom door pulled Karyn's attention away from Dia.

Baco stood in their doorway. "How's it going?"

"Fine. Getting her ready for tonight."

Dia snuck a peek at Baco, searching for a sign of compassion.

He gave her a once-over, avoiding eye contact. "Be sure to help her with her makeup. I need her to be fresh...and to smile, if possible."

Dia stepped forward as her one-time boyfriend retreated, hoping to talk one on one and clear up this confusing new situation she found herself in, but Karyn shut the door on his heels.

"Baco's not interested in hearing you whine. From now on, anything you want to say goes through me. Chain of command, honey, chain of command. Baco, then me, our customers, and then you."

Like a dog being reprimanded for peeing on the carpet, Dia stepped back with her head hung low. She worried Karyn might explode if she resisted or released even a single breath.

"That's more like it," Karyn said. "Do as I say, and we will get along perfectly. Now, follow me, and I'll show you where you bathe. You smell disgusting, by the way, and we want you squeaky clean and pretty for tonight's big debut!"

Dia struggled to shake off the memory of her first day as she returned the foundation to a see-through vinyl cosmetic bag and fished around for lipstick. No amount of makeup disguised her distress, but she smudged her lips with candied-apple color.

Karyn's treatment of her was not much better than Baco's. Dia had learned she was a foreign-exchange student from Germany before meeting Baco under circumstances not unlike Dia's. The difference was this woman had somehow convinced herself she was their pimp's *actual* girlfriend. She fawned over him, going out of her way to accommodate and please him and to make him want her. His ever-dutiful lieutenant, Karyn had prepared Dia for her first night in the brothel and presented her to a trio of horny customers within a few hours of her arrival.

Dia stood there in a bedazzled thong, staring at the floor as an obnoxious, drunk student from UT claimed his prize. She tried pulling her arm back from his grasp, but all the resistance in the world wasn't a match to the man's thick-muscled arms and hands. He dragged her to the back, indifferent to her protests.

A buddy of his went next, followed by another. One by one, they took their turns, taking no interest in her as a human being, only as a doll they could have just as easily masturbated on in their frat house. It was 2:00 a.m. when they all left.

Baco knocked at her door just as she started to drift asleep. "Why don't you come join us out front." It was a command more than it was an invitation.

Dia wrapped herself in a robe then fumbled out to the receiving room where Karyn lay on one of three mismatched velour couches. The German's head was in Baco's lap, and her lean, svelte body lent her an air of beauty. She might have worked as a model had it been a real talent agent who'd approached her instead of Baco in Houston's Galleria Mall that fateful day.

He ran his fingers through her chestnut hair while she took a drag from a cigarette. Dia plopped down opposite them in an oversized chair, her bottom raw and sore as she sunk into its cushions.

"Not bad tonight, little sister," Baco said. "Daddy is proud of you."

She sat with clenched teeth, unable to make sense of her first night of work as a prostitute. The constant stream of alcohol dimmed her ability to remember with any clarity, but perhaps that was a good thing.

"We always like to celebrate the end of a long workday with a little breakfast," he continued. "Hungry? Sounded to me like you worked up quite an appetite in there." He flashed an ugly smile.

Less than twenty-four hours ago, I was a virgin, Dia thought. *Now I've been raped by more guys than some people sleep with in their whole lives.* She stared down at the floor as she adjusted her kimono around her bare body. The shame of sleeping with so many people made her blush. What would Sam or her family think if they knew? She wiped a drip of mucous away with her hand.

"I don't think our little princess here likes you anymore, Daddy," Karyn said with a snort.

"Families don't always like one another, Karyn. Don't worry if Dia hates me at this moment. She'll get over it eventually, especially when it sinks in how much she depends on me. Right, Dia?"

Dia sat motionless, raising only her eyes. Susan came to mind, and she imagined the woman's response to her stepdaughter's new reality, *I told you, you were too young to date!*

"Karyn, baby. I'm starving. Why don't you cook up some eggs?"

"Anything for you, Daddy."

"You're my mamacita." He grabbed her butt as she walked toward the kitchen.

"Stop, you." Karyn smiled, happy for any attention Baco gave. She cast a look over at Dia as if to say, *See, I am number one, and he prefers me.*

Money was fanned across a coffee table in front of Baco,

but Dia had zero clue to its value. *Do customers pay in twenties? Hundred-dollar bills? What's he charging for me?* she wondered. Her mind continued to race. *How much is Baco making? How could he do this? What is my dad doing? Does he even care that I'm gone? What about Anita, Gina, and Sam? Or Brogan or Todd? Are any of them worried about me right now?*

"I can tell you have questions," Baco said to Dia. "You're going to have to stop thinking so much. This is your life. Just forget everything you've known up to now. It'll be easier if you do."

She stared at him from her chair and shook her head. *Forget my life?* "Never," she mumbled.

His first lieutenant banged around in the kitchen, making loud sounds as if to keep Baco from engaging with his newest piece of property. He was not distracted by her antics. Instead, he rose, sauntered across the room, and delicately grabbed Dia's hands as he knelt in front her. "You *will* learn to accept your life here. The sooner you do, the happier you will be. Trust me," he said, glaring at her with cool, gray eyes. Those eyes had hypnotized her since their first encounter at Panda Express.

Karyn walked out of the kitchen, over to the radio, and flipped it on to a rock station, but Baco's attention remained fixed on his newest acquisition. His eyes conveyed his intent, and Dia's anger waned as a flicker of romance emerged and melted her resistance to him. She did not know a human being could have this kind of power over another. He helped her up from the chair, then turned to lead her back down the hall from where she'd come.

The German stared at them, her eyes wide as saucers and her face contorted with jealous rage as they passed by her. There'd be hell to pay later for giving in to Baco. If looks could kill, Karyn would dice her up into a million little pieces and stuff her down a garbage disposal.

Dia shook her head and hoped any retribution would not

be that dramatic, but a little inside voice told her it was coming, no matter what form it took. As she followed Baco into the master bedroom, she took one more look back at Karyn whose mouth twitched.

"Submission is your modus operandi from now on," Baco said to her as he closed his room door behind them. "My customers want it. My boss expects, and I demand it." He stared into her eyes and caressed her hair as he spoke. "Every hot-blooded heterosexual man wants the woman he is about to take to submit to him. Your new life with us will go much easier if you accept what I'm telling you."

He rested his hands on her breasts, circling them with his thumbs while standing toe-to-toe with her beside his bed. She swallowed a lump in her throat. She was too nervous to do or say anything to upset him.

"Remember, your old life is over. You're mine now. I own you, and there is no going home." He removed her kimono and eased her onto his bedspread. He retrieved unscented wipes and aloe from his nightstand.

"How well you do here—how *happy* you'll be—depends one hundred percent on your choice to *be* happy. Surrender, and you're more than halfway there. Submit to me like you did last night," he said as he cleaned her and applied healing gel to her privates. "That's what men are paying for here, babe, and that's what I want them to receive from *you.* Fail to do what I say, and frankly, well…I'll kill your whole family."

Dia stirred in her sleep. Across time and space, a familiar voice called to her. "Mom?" She raised a single eyelid to find herself lying behind Baco. Whoever it was calling to her, their despair matched her own. Dia stared at the back of her former boyfriend's head, a seed of resignation taking root as she realized how wrong she'd been about him.

TWELVE

THURSDAY, SEPTEMBER 16 – MONDAY, SEPTEMBER 20, 2004

HRUSKA'S CAME into view as Baco, Dia, and Karyn made their way toward Austin on Highway 71 in the lingering autumn heat. Dia's mouth watered as pangs of hunger ricocheted in her stomach. She'd last eaten in Houston hours earlier and was eagerly anticipating biting into a sausage, cheese, and jalapeño kolache from the Czech bakery. If they were lucky, their pimp would allow them to eat two. Maybe she'd ask for four in hopes he'd settle on two. *A girl can dream,* she thought.

Baco whipped his new Nissan 350Z into a space and put it in park before coming to a complete stop. He jumped out. "Let's go, ladies!" It was three o'clock, and they had less than two hours to make it into town, unpack at their motel, and start walking 6th Street to promote their unique brand of fun to attendees of the Austin City Limits Music Festival. Baco draped his arm over Dia as they approached the store. "Babe, we're gonna be in your hometown soon. I hope you're not getting too nostalgic."

After more than five months away, Dia welcomed her return to the Live Music Capital if only for the familiarity of its architectural surroundings. She doubted her biological family would even care. Surely her dad embraced the chance to concentrate on his second wife and stepson. *They're better off without me, anyway.* "How do you mean?" She turned her head to meet her pimp's stare.

"Well, you're closer to home than you've been in a while, but don't forget. You're one of us now. Kyle and Susan have moved on. Besides, what would they say about your new life if they had any idea what you'd been up to?"

Chickens pecked at seeds and crumbs around Hruska's entrance. Which was worse? Baco fulfilling his earlier threats to kill her dad, or him sharing the video of her first night at Danny's with him? *How could I have been so dumb?* "No problem, Daddy." Dia diverted her gaze as he held the door open. "I'd never do anything to break up our family."

"Good girl. I almost believe you. Let's go inside for a long-overdue snack. You girls have earned it!"

Snack? How about a meal? Dia had dropped fifteen pounds since joining Baco's "team." Hunger was her constant companion as Baco oversaw everything they ate to keep them thin for the clientele. On this day, however, he surprised her at the kolache counter and sprung for three for each of them. He paid for their food and pulled back onto Highway 71 less than five minutes later to continue their trip west.

An hour passed. Secondhand shops dotted an aging retail space along Riverside Drive in East Austin as they drove into Gigi's, a privately-owned adult bookstore. The signage had seen better days.

"Why are we stopping here?" Karyn asked.

"I'm tired of looking at you in those same, old outfits. I want to see you in some sexy new clothes for ACL." Baco escorted them to a back room where nighties, garter belts, and corsets in varying shades of purple, red, and pink occupied a wall.

Dia made her way to a corner display where she spotted a purple satin robe trimmed with gray faux fur on a store mannequin. She used to blush putting on skimpy miniskirts and camisoles. Now she entertained how good she might look in something luxurious, even if it was pre-owned. Besides, there was something about the ash-gray fur that struck her as familiar—almost like a distant memory from her childhood that she could not place.

Dressing rooms lined two sides of the adults-only store. Dia grabbed the furry smock from its hanger and reached for a complimentary nightie decorated with peacocks. Karyn noticed it as well and grabbed it simultaneously, pushing Dia into a trifold mirror in her efforts to wrestle it away.

"Oops, sorry about that," Karyn said. "Go find something else. This one has my name written all over it." Her eyes widened with greed.

"Stupid bitch," Dia said under her breath.

"Excuse me?"

"Fuck you."

Karyn forced Dia up against one of the mirrors. Odious waves of digesting sausage kolaches wafted up from her gut as she spoke. "Stop acting cocky with me, you little shit. In case you forgot, I will fuck you up."

Dia stopped resisting, a bruise on her forearm reminding her all too well of Karyn's propensity for retaliation.

"Shut up, Karyn, for Christ's sake." Baco walked up to both of them. "Grab something and let's go!"

Karyn gripped the peacock lingerie, and Dia went back to select three black teddies to wear beneath her fur-trimmed robe. Baco paid in cash for the frocks and led them to the car without another word about their fight. Forty-five minutes later, they checked in to a by-the-hour motel with a neon pink, flashing vacancy sign.

Karyn set up her makeup on the singular bathroom sink. Sitting at a dimly lit desk mirror, Dia painted her face with hand-me-down eye shadow from her roommate. She thought of Samantha. *What would she think of this?*

"You both need to wrap it up in here. We leave in ten!" Baco slammed the door to his adjoining room behind him. What point was there in dwelling on her best friend or anyone else from her past? She quelled her thoughts and self-pity and retrieved an eyeliner from her bag, then turned her attention to dolling up for her first night back in the Texas capitol.

Throngs of people filled the sidewalks up and down 6th Street, Austin's primary entertainment corridor. Dia was inspired to be in her hometown and found herself feeling less demoralized than usual as she trolled for business. Live music, which had put Austin on the map, poured onto the downtown street as ACL fans kicked off the multi-day festival weekend, which officially began Friday at Zilker Park.

Dia smiled at scores of horny men as she walked in front of the popular bar, Maggie Mae's, when a small group of boys caught her eye. Mortified they may have spotted her, she ducked behind a bouncer as some of her former classmates passed.

"What's your problem?" Karyn asked.

"I think I know those guys."

"Which ones?"

"Those three over there."

Karyn followed Dia's finger as she pointed. "Trust me. They have no clue who you are."

Dia had felt invisible inside the walls of Cedar Park High School even on her best days. Her nemesis was right for a change. Now that she was made up to look like she was twenty, the likelihood of someone from Dia's old life recognizing her was slim to none. She stepped out from behind the bouncer to resume her task.

Kinko's had served as Baco's interim office their last week in Houston. He'd printed off reams of multi-colored, eye-catching flyers promoting his "product." Now on 6th Street, Dia and Karyn had the job of distributing as many as possible to schedule three days' worth of bookings on the calendar.

They'd met their objective by 9:30 p.m. Baco texted them to hustle over to their room at the motel so they could start "earning their keep." A quick taxi ride returned them by ten, just as four guys pulled up in their truck.

Awakened by the urge to pee, Dia strained her neck to see what time it was. The bedside alarm clock read 5:47 a.m. She considered how best to move from beneath her customer who'd passed out on top of her an hour earlier. The toilet beckoned as her need grew. She wondered how much she'd had to drink as her full bladder pushed against her abdomen. Just then, her john's left leg drifted upward then came to rest over her waist as he half-straddled her in his sleep. She'd have to relieve herself in bed if she didn't wriggle out from under him soon.

She chanced waking him by running her fingernails lightly down his torso beneath his armpit. Her efforts were rewarded as he rolled over on his back, swatting at an invisible insect. Dia rolled off the bed and waded through beer cans, liquor bottles, and Solo cups in pursuit of a release. Memories of their previous night's debauchery flashed through her mind as she fumbled for a switch.

Fluorescent light flooded the tiny bathroom, which was still littered with Karyn's cosmetics. Dia relaxed onto the toilet's porcelain seat opposite the sample-size lipstick tubes and eyeshadow tubs. A flow of urine opened, bringing sweet initial relief, but vacating her bladder entirely eluded her. The longing to pee remained as Dia refocused her efforts with zero success, giving her fearful pause. What made her body disobey as the need to go persisted?

Karyn knocked at the door. “Everything okay?”

Shit. “Uh, yeah…I think so.”

“‘Think’ so?”

“I’m fine. I’ll be out in a minute.” She heard Karyn return to bed. Eager to thwart any attempt her colleague might make to tattle, Dia muscled through her discomfort to eliminate as much pee as possible.

The weekend ticked by with one john after another. Their efforts with flyer distribution Thursday paid off handsomely. They barely had a break as their pimp collected fistfuls of cash from insatiable men, young and old alike. Dia was more exhausted than normal by Sunday night, and her situation “down there” grew more dire.

She’d last tried peeing that morning. Twelve hours later, she panicked as her bathroom trip yielded a trickle at best. Wiping out of habit, Dia spotted blood on the toilet paper that she could not attribute to her period. She returned to bed and stared across her room at a pair of jeans belonging to the most recent customer sawing logs next to her.

ACL tickets poked out from his rear pocket. How wonderful it must be to spend three days eating, drinking, and listening to music. Dia imagined herself walking from stage to stage and checking out Franz Ferdinand, The Killers, and Modest Mouse as they belted out tunes she’d only ever heard on the radio. *The Austin Chronicle* lay open to ACL’s musical lineup page beneath her john’s pants. Dia saw one of Sunday’s featured acts was Wilco. *Samantha loves them,* Dia recalled. *Will she take a break from studying to make the concert?*

The burning pressure in her bladder reminded Dia of her current situation. A beaded line of perspiration formed across her forehead. *Am I dying?* Medical attention seemed warranted in light of her worsening condition, but a knock at her door indicated how many customers still waited for their turn with her.

Three hours later, she still strained to pee. Her chest had an unfamiliar tightness, and she struggled to catch a full breath. Her last customer of the weekend had left moments earlier, oblivious to her discomfort and intent on humiliating her with his final vulgar request. Dia peeked through the curtains. The morning sun dipped in and out of clouds, as if reconsidering its ascent and gave Austin's skyline a pinkish-purple hue. It was 6:25 a.m., and she was past any point of working through the pain. She feared bigger problems if she delayed getting help and longer.

Dia poked her head out of the bathroom and spotted Karyn's sleeping form under multiple blankets on her queen-sized bed. She was snoring softly and would, without a doubt, become annoyed if disturbed.

I'm going to end up in the hospital if I don't say something. She crept over and nudged Karyn's shoulder gently, hoping to wake her with minimal drama.

The German's eyes opened one at a time. "What?" she said hoarsely.

"I think I'm sick."

"Go away and stop whining. You Americans are so weak."

"I'm not *whining*. I can't pee. I've barely gone at all since Friday morning."

"What? Why didn't you say anything sooner?"

Dia stared down at her feet, but at this point, she was concerned more about her health than her colleague's wrath. "I thought it would go away, but it hasn't. I'm scared."

Her eyes filled with tears, and she lost her train of thought when Karyn's features transitioned from annoyance to empathy. She whipped off the blankets and sprang into action, the likes of which Dia had never seen. She sprinted to the door that separated Baco's room from theirs, moving stealthily into his room. Moments later, she returned with his keys.

"Let's go," she said.

"What? Where are we going? We can't leave without his permission!" *I can't believe she's helping me like this.*

"We can, and we are. Come on, grab your stuff." Karyn changed into street clothes. "If we're fast, we'll be back before Baco wakes up. You got everything?"

What was there to get? she wondered. She had no purse, no identification...only a jacket and her shoes.

"Never mind," Karyn said, as if realizing how ridiculous her question sounded. She closed the door behind them as they walked out and headed to the Nissan.

Though grateful for Karyn's assistance, Dia couldn't help but wonder, *If it was this easy to sneak away, why haven't we tried getting away for good?*

THIRTEEN

MONDAY, SEPTEMBER 20, 2004

DIA CHEWED ON HER THUMBNAIL. "Permanent damage?"

"No, nothing like that...at least, I don't think so. But it might move up to your kidneys and you'll have to go to the hospital then, which I'm sure would piss off Baco. At this point, you'll need antibiotics if it's a UTI."

Finding a clinic took longer than they anticipated, and each pothole deepened Dia's bladder discomfort as they traversed East Austin. Bus stops were packed with people who appeared as tired as Dia felt, although their reasons for lack of sleep likely paled next to hers. "What if we pull over for a Yellow Pages? Maybe we'll find a listing for Planned Parenthood or something like that."

Karyn slumped over the steering wheel. "Why didn't I think of that?"

Dia smiled weakly. In a weird way, this road trip might unite them. A 7-Eleven on their left had a phone booth that caught Dia's eye. "There, I see one."

Karyn followed her lead and took a quick turn, navigating around gas pumps, pedestrians, and stray dogs. She jumped out of their car and returned in less than two minutes with a page ripped from 7-Eleven's Yellow Pages.

"That was good thinking. We're only a few blocks away from this place." She pointed to a listing.

"Let's try it."

Karyn reversed, narrowly missing a dog. She drove to the woman's clinic located a few streets east of the 7-Eleven.

They parked in the nearly vacant lot and walked inside. "Should have worn my sweatshirt," Dia said. The AC worked overtime to combat Austin's outdoor temperatures. The lobby was empty, so maybe she'd be seen quickly.

Karyn grabbed Dia by the elbow. "No matter what they say, no exams. You just want medicine. I'm serious, Dia."

A woman whose name tag read "Angela" greeted them from behind the receptionist's desk. "How can I help you this morning?"

"My friend has a urinary tract infection. Well, at least I think she does." Karyn spoke before Dia had a chance to open her mouth.

"What are your symptoms, sweetie?" the receptionist asked.

"My bladder feels like it's going to explode. But when I pee, barely anything comes out, and it burns."

Angela's brown eyes crinkled as she offered a slight smile. "Hmm. Well, that's not good. Do you think you can eliminate enough for us to draw a sample? You need to try and go up to this line." The woman pointed to a spot on a cup.

Dia held back tears at the thought of possible relief. "I'll do what I can."

"Don't worry, you're going to be fine, all right?" Angela reached over the counter for Dia's hand. "Believe me. I've been in your shoes. It happens to all of us eventually. Come this way."

Angela pushed a button from below her desk to buzz Dia through to her side. Karyn started to follow, but Angela stopped her. "I got her, honey. I need you to fill out some paperwork, okay?"

"But I'm supposed to stay with her. She needs me." Karyn deployed a pout in her campaign to convince Angela.

"She's fine. Here, take this and start on the paperwork. We'll return in a bit," Angela squared her shoulders to Karyn and handed her a clipboard. Her short, sturdy frame rooted her like a tree.

Karyn backed up half a step as she accepted the clipboard but didn't hesitate to issue a warning stare straight at Dia when Angela turned back to her patient.

"Follow me," Angela said, directing Dia into a small bathroom with a changing closet. "You can go in here. There are a few packaged cups and wipes in our cabinet to your right. Follow these instructions here." She pointed to a laminated list. "Then place your specimen here on the other side of this little door in the wall when you've finished. You'll find medical gowns in this drawer. Change into one, and I'll come for you in a few minutes."

Angela left her alone and pulled the door closed behind her. Dia remembered Karyn's words, "No exam." Fear gripped her. *Who am I more worried about pissing off, Karyn or Angela?* she wondered. The latter didn't seem like the bullying type, but she was a force to be reckoned with, nonetheless, considering how she kept her German colleague at bay out front. Dia concluded it was in her best interest to follow Angela's instructions for now. She retrieved a gown, then proceeded in doing all she could to produce a specimen.

Angela returned and escorted Dia to an examination room.

"Jump up on the table and put your feet in these stirrups," a woman in scrubs said.

A pelvic exam struck her as unwarranted when her issue involved failing to pee, but Dia did not resist. She felt no more able to refuse the medical assessment than she could reject the ten-plus johns a night forced on her during ACL weekend. If there was a silver lining to this experience, perhaps she'd snag free samples of birth control, seeing how Baco's supply of pills made her face break out. She glanced around the draping to study the nurse's face. Her brow was furrowed. *Does she know? Can she tell how many men I've screwed over four days?*

"All right, you can dress," the woman said turning off her exam-table lights. "I'll be back in a few minutes and should have preliminary lab results on your urine specimen."

Dia dressed in under a minute and disposed of her paper gown in a biohazard waste bin. She took a seat on the patient bed to wait, and then her room door opened. Dia found Karyn glaring at her.

"You'd better not say a word to these people, D," she said. "I will tell Baco, and he will fuck you and your family up like you cannot imagine."

"What are you doing? Leave before they come back!"

"Tell me you understand."

"I get it. Now go or *you* will be the one who gives us away."

Karyn left and shut the door. Did she overhear something? *Why is she so paranoid all of a sudden?* Karyn was the one who suggested they come to the clinic to begin with. What if someone suspected what was going on? *What should I do if they ask?*

The thought of Baco's recording flashed through her mind as her exam-room door opened again. The woman in scrubs had returned, but this time, she was accompanied by a woman dressed in a suit. The second woman took a seat opposite Dia as the nurse retrieved paperwork from a folder.

"Honey, I want to introduce you to Linda," the nurse said. "She'll speak with you in a moment, but first, the results of your labs do show proof of a urinary tract infection. So, here. I want to give you some samples to get you started along with a prescription." She handed Dia two small vials of pills with a sheet of paper listing two medications. "The first pill will relieve your symptoms within the hour so you can urinate. This second is an antibiotic. *Please*—I cannot emphasize it enough—you must follow my instructions and take one every day, twice a day until they're gone. Otherwise, your UTI will return with a vengeance. Does what I'm saying make sense?"

"Yes, ma'am."

"Good, we should have the results back on whether you have any STDs in a few days too. You can call us back at the number on your prescription. Any questions?"

Dia shook her head.

"All right, then. I'll turn it over to Linda. She's a caseworker here, and I thought you two might want to visit for a little bit."

Taking her cue, Linda rose and walked over to them. "Hello, Janey." She reached out to shake hands.

Janey? "That's me," Dia said, assuming Karyn had supplied them with a fake name. She sensed all of Linda's strength and confidence in her grip, a grip she herself was too weak to reciprocate. She had met a woman named Linda when she was a little girl, but the details of their encounter eluded her beyond a head of curly hair and the gifting of her doll, Lucy. Dia studied the woman's face in front of her and guessed she was in her mid-forties. Her short, dark brown hair complemented her tan skin.

Linda's smile and brown eyes put Dia at ease, but then she remembered Karyn's warning. "Where do you live, Dia? I'm looking at your paperwork your friend filled out but your address...she left it blank. Do you reside nearby or go to UT?"

"No, I'm from Houston. We came to town for ACL." Dia turned her gaze to a poster of female anatomy on the wall opposite her.

"Really? Me too. Well, I have a home here now, but I attended ACL all weekend with my friends."

She's lying. She looks too old to be hip, Dia thought.

"Who did you catch for last night's final show?"

"Wilco." Dia lied, remembering the lineup from *The Austin Chronicle.*

"Yeah, they were great. They're a fan favorite without a doubt." Linda dipped her head to the left while maintaining eye contact. She smiled slightly, helping Dia feel less nervous.

"So, you're on your way home to go to class then?"

"I'm out of school."

"Ah, okay. You don't seem old enough to have graduated already. You'll have to hook me up with your skincare regimen."

"Sure." Dia looked back to the poster, positive Linda's friendliness was a ploy to extract honesty from her. Saying anything else about school or Houston or ACL was the last thing she should do. Basic questions had been asked, and she was concerned Linda would drop her pleasant façade and begin asking tougher ones. Her mouth grew dry at the thought. It was better to remain noncommittal than to keep lying, she decided. Nothing good would come from talking or being candid about her new life. She didn't want anyone to ever discover how foolish she'd been to trust Baco that night back at Danny's. The memory of it made her blush. Even worse, she didn't want anything to happen to her family.

"Can I go now?" She didn't see why or how they could detain her any longer.

Linda shifted her attention from the nurse practitioner to Dia. "Are you sure you want to go? You're welcome to stay."

"I'm good. Thanks, though. I appreciate your help with my pills here." She hopped down from her exam table.

"Dia, there are people who can assist if you're in trouble."

"Thank you, but I'm fine...really." She moved toward the door with her medications, eager to find a water fountain or anything to expedite relief of her symptoms.

Linda's mouth turned downward as she reached in her

purse to retrieve a business card. "Keep this and call me if you ever want to talk or something. Will you do that?"

Dia peered into the woman's eyes. *I don't want to lie to her.* "Sure…thanks."

Karyn jumped up from her chair when Dia exited into the lobby. They walked quickly to Baco's car. Once behind closed doors, she badgered her with questions. "Well? Tell me what you told them!"

"I didn't say anything, okay? Nothing!"

Karyn stared at her, surprised by the response. "No way! Seriously?"

"Mm-hm." Dia nodded. She retrieved Linda's business card as proof. "Here, take this. It's from a social worker." Karyn continued to stare in surprise as Dia tore the card in half. "We should go, but we'll need to find a Walgreens or something on the way back," Dia said as she reached for her seatbelt.

Separation from her old life seemed unequivocally complete now. Her one chance at escape diminished in the passenger mirror as they drove out of the parking lot and made their way back to the motel, but at least her father and friends would be safe and never see Baco's video.

Karyn blathered on for half a block before Dia started paying attention again. "Family is super important to Baco. Sure, he'll rage at us when we get back, but do you know how impressed he will be to know you didn't squeal? I promise he'll reward your loyalty, Dia, one way or another."

Dia smiled as they waited for their traffic light to turn, her medicine already starting to work. The pressure on her bladder diminished ever so slightly.

"I didn't thank you," Dia said.

"For what?"

"For taking me to find help. I don't think I could've taken much more."

Karyn reached for Dia's hand. "I'm glad you're okay."

“Light’s green,” she said with a smile.

Karyn took her foot off the brake. Within moments, they’d pull into the motel where they’d pack up and hit the road once more, leaving Austin and its faceless sea of customers in their wake.

FOURTEEN

SATURDAY, OCTOBER 23, 2004

CIGARETTE BUTTS PILED up in his ashtray. Baco stared at his open laptop, scanning internet sites in search of business, muttering to himself.

"Whatcha looking at, Daddy?" Karyn asked.

"Don't talk to me right now, okay?"

"Whatever," Karyn said as she turned her attention back to polishing her toenails.

ACL had been a boon, but Baco had grown aggravated over shrinking sales in the weeks since. Dia sensed that if things didn't change soon, he'd need to make changes.

What could he get for his pimpmobile? she wondered. She studied him from across the room, trying to fathom what she ever saw in him beyond his looks. To be low on cash so shortly after they'd come back from Austin indicated he knew as much about running a business as he did about maintaining a respectful relationship. At the same time, it struck her as strange that the demand for their services had fallen so drastically. If there was one thing Dia had gleaned over the past six and a half months, it was that man's need for sex was endless. They could satisfy all their cravings and still be ravenous for more. Not that she minded the break, but perhaps Baco needed to improve his marketing skills. *Or maybe he isn't cut out for business at all.*

Maps were laid out over the motel desk next to Baco's laptop. Someone he knew had suggested a website called Backpage a few days earlier, but he worried about taking the risk with an unknown service. He looked up over his screen at Dia, then shifted his gaze over to Karyn. "We're back in the game, ladies. With any luck, I'll have you working bachelor parties full time. From there, we can try out fraternities...you name it."

"Ew, bachelors? Thought they were more into strippers," Karyn said. She blew on her freshly coated toes.

"Guess you'll have to learn how to dance then." He shut the lid on his computer to retrieve a camera from his bag. "This service needs me to upload photos of the two of you, so get freshened up."

"I wanted to watch a movie," Karyn said with the remote in her hand.

Baco crossed the room and snatched the TV control from her hand. "Enough! Hurry and get ready! Goddamn, I can tell you two are getting super lazy, and that's gotta change, pronto!"

The girls scurried to the bathroom to clean up. "What's his problem?" Karyn's rhetorical question went unanswered. The nightly meals of canned refried beans and crackers reflected their situation. Dia was down five more pounds since ACL. Not an ounce of fat remained on her once curvy frame.

After ten minutes of hair and makeup, the two presented themselves to their pimp-turned-photographer for their close-ups.

Calls trickled in within moments of Baco pushing their profiles online. "Sounds great. Yep, I've got the two girls. So, you're hosting a party in Lufkin near Davy Crockett National Forest?"

Karyn nudged Dia. "Who's Davy Crockett?"

"Some famous guy who fought at the Alamo," Dia tilted her head to better hear Baco's phone conversation.

"The what?" Karyn asked.

Dia ignored her question.

"Yeah, it's a bit of a ride. No worries, though, we'll arrive by nine tonight," Baco said. "Sure thing. See you soon." He slipped his cell into his jeans pocket, turning to the two of them. "Pack your things. We're headed to East Texas."

Live oak trees lined a long drive through a sparsely populated neighborhood as Baco drove in search of the bachelor party. It took ten more minutes of searching before he found the address—an estate on three or four acres behind a golf course. Its well-edged driveway and sidewalks were accented by scores of outdoor lawn lights.

Karyn's mouth hung open as they approached a mansion-sized home. "Pretty."

Dia nodded in agreement. The property reflected a level of class she had not expected. The buildings were a combination of Spanish tile, stucco, and limestone. A wrought-iron gate gave the entrance a Tuscan touch, and there was no shortage of guests. More than fifteen cars filled the circular drive and side portico. They were all luxury vehicles, from BMWs and Mercedes to Porches and Range Rovers. Baco's face lit up as he calculated the money he'd walk away with, but Dia had an unsettling feeling growing in her stomach.

Twenty minutes later, she sat atop an extra-large king-sized bed. Its thick, wood corner posts drew her attention as her hands caressed the white cotton comforter beneath her. She was wearing the robe with gray fur that Baco had purchased in

Austin. She waited for her host who took his time getting ready in his master bath. He'd introduced himself as Paul earlier when he'd greeted them outside. Dia guessed he was somewhere in his late twenties or early thirties. He was more handsome than any man she had ever met—even Baco—with his chestnut hair, amber eyes, and olive complexion. She wondered if he owned the house.

Paul emerged from his bathroom still fully clothed. He took a seat beside her, drumming his fingers on his thigh. She waited for him to make his move, but he sat breathing for several moments more. Finally, he cleared his throat to speak. "So, Dia, was it?"

She nodded.

"We both know why we're here, but I need to tell you..." he turned to her. "This really isn't my thing. You won't be upset if we don't..."

She stared at him. *Is he kidding?*

Paul continued, "You seem great, and you're so pretty, but I'm very much in love with my fiancée. My buddies down below may drag their knuckles like Neanderthals, but my only vice is a quiet game of poker."

Dia sat dumbstruck. After several months of observing men at their worst, she'd caught a glimmer of hope that good guys existed after all.

"If it's okay, I'd prefer to keep this between me and you," he said.

"Okay. I won't say anything."

"Thanks."

"Sure."

"I'll still pay you, though," he added. "Your pimp downstairs...he is your boss, right? He acted kind of funny when I brought you up here, like he was jealous or something. I thought dudes like him had to maintain emotional distance from their *employees*."

Dia laughed quietly. "Is that how they're supposed to act?"

"That's how they are in the movies." Paul rose from the bed and held out his hand. "Shall we go out to join them?"

"Yeah, I think so."

She accepted her host's hand and accompanied him downstairs.

Heavy bass poured from unseen speakers as they descended into the kitchen. The track ended, and a person screamed from another room before the next song started. One look at Paul's face told her he'd heard it, too—shrieking cries for help. His jaw tightened as they reached the bottom of the stairs. He ran through a swinging door, and Dia followed him into the living room. A group of guys circled Karyn, who was kneeling and naked. Red handprints stood out on her buttocks where somebody—maybe several people—had spanked her.

Different men were tapping into the ring like wrestlers and violating her one by one. Tears streamed down her face. Dia had never observed such a scene nor seen her partner-in-crime so vulnerable. Sex toys of varying sizes and whips were scattered on a table outside the circle. Pink welts covered Karyn's back and legs. *How can they get away with this?* She scanned the room for Baco. Two guys blocked him like a caged animal by the butler pantry. *Did he try to help?* she wondered.

"Hey! There's Paul's special lady! About time you brought her down for all of us to enjoy. Let's bring her in on this action." Dia stood behind Paul, hopeful for protection.

"How did it go?" One of Paul's buddies ran his hand over Dia's arm, grazing her breast.

"Fine. What's going on here?"

"One last hoorah, buddy."

Dia made eye contact with Karyn. Her fear and humiliation were palpable as the man in back of her continued his assault. *Why do they have to hurt her?* She grappled to understand. Paul's moment of humanity had sparked a flame of hope in her moments earlier, but it faded as his wealthy associates grew rowdier and raunchier. Two of them broke from the group to come and grab her.

"Your turn," one slurred between gulps of Scotch. Dia stood terrified. She turned to see Baco straining to escape from his captors to no avail. They landed numerous punches in Baco's face and stomach before he fell into a wall of wine bottles. Some toppled and shattered around him.

"You've gone too far. Shut it down," Paul said.

The pair of men grabbing at Dia tugged at her shirt and bottoms. "You're joking, right?"

"No, I'm not, Jesse," Paul said, raising his voice over the intense music. "This is not what I signed up for. Leave her alone and let her friends go." He motioned toward Karyn and Baco. "For Christ's sake! What the *hell* is wrong with you guys?"

Jesse and his buddy backed away from Dia. Paul moved over to the stereo and flipped a switch. The loud music abruptly ended capturing everyone's attention. "Party's over, folks!"

"Shut the fuck up, bro!" someone shouted back.

"No, *you* shut the fuck up! This was supposed to be a bachelor party, not a gang rape! Jesus!"

Dia remained close to her host, unsure of how her hero might fare against two dozen or more drunk and horny men. His friends stared at him, trying to focus their eyes and digest what he was saying. Those circling around Karyn backed away as she crumpled into a ball on the Turkish rug. Paul appeared to have a significant influence on the group. Baco slumped as his captors released him and slipped away. He looked the worse for wear. Unable to stand alone, Paul and Dia helped him to his car as Karyn followed them in silence.

"Your friend here looks like he needs to see a doctor," Paul said as they guided him into the back seat. "But..."

"But what?" Dia asked.

"I'd prefer you not to tell anyone where you spent your evening. It'd be bad for me, as you can probably imagine."

"I think we're just lucky to get out of here alive," Dia said.

Karyn glared at the two of them, shivering in October's crisp autumn air. "Well at least *someone* is lucky."

Paul moved forward to assist her.

"Get your paws off me. I don't need your fake charity." Her colleague's German accent was thicker than normal. She slid down into the passenger seat and pulled the door shut on the Nissan.

"You don't belong with these people," Paul said, turning back to Dia and grabbing her hands in his. "Do you know what I mean?"

"You don't belong with those people inside, either."

"Touché."

"Goodbye...and thanks again." Dia climbed behind the steering wheel of Baco's car, wishful for someone else to drive. She squealed down the driveway without looking back.

Miles past Lufkin, Dia glanced in the rearview mirror at Baco, crumpled over the center armrest. She guessed he was unconscious but had no clue what to do about it.

Karyn sat next to her, chewing her fingernails to the nub. "We have to do something for him."

"Like what?"

"There was this other girl, Lea, before you. Anyway, she got really messed up and threatened to go to the police. He said that Uncle Dominic would take care of her."

"Who?"

"Baco's boss, I think. He said how he was his mentor."

"Oh, yeah. I remember him mentioning an uncle," Dia said, recalling their man-woman talks in the weeks leading up to the ill-fated beach trip.

Karyn rummaged through the glove box. She took out a piece of paper. "Here. The car is registered to Dominic Kastellanos. Here is the address and a telephone number. Let's call him."

"I don't know." Dia drummed her fingers on the steering wheel. "What do you think Baco meant when he said Dominic would take care of that Lea person?"

"All I know is that one day she was here, and the next she was gone." Karyn turned to Baco as he moaned from the back seat. "Look! I know you could not care less about Baco, but he's everything to me. Can you do what I ask just this once? Please!"

Good grief. Dia suppressed an eye roll and glanced at the car's fuel gauge. They had less than a quarter tank and would need to refuel soon. "Fine. Looks like we're coming up on a town if you feel that's the right thing to do."

Dia found a service station with a telephone booth and drove up to a pump. "How are we supposed to pay for gas?"

"Do I have to do everything around here?" Karyn rifled through Baco's pockets and located his credit card. "Here!" She jumped out to make a call with loose change from the car's console, leaving Dia to fill the tank.

She took the card inside and paid for the gas. When she came out, Karyn ran over to her. "Dominic said to meet him in Livingston. As we pull into town, we'll see a Whataburger, so stay on 59 South. He's driving up from Houston."

What if I just toss the keys and run back into the store begging for help?

"Come on!" Karyn said, pulling her by the arm. "We need to get going."

Dia's desire to avoid a scene overrode her instinct to run as she moved in step with Karyn back to the car. They drove in silence.

"I saw the sign for Livingston," she said ten minutes later.

"I don't care," Karyn said. "Just get us there."

"Why are you so upset with me? I didn't ask for any of this to happen!"

"I'm *pissed* because you're a phony. You don't give a shit about us. You were up in Paul's house getting treated like his girlfriend while the others abused me as if I were some..."

"If it hadn't been for me, y'all would be a lot worse off. What happened is not my fault."

"Whatever, Princess. Dominic will take care of you and this situation once we meet up. I'm taking a nap."

"What's that supposed to mean?"

Karyn ignored her and rested her head against the cool window, leaving Dia alone with her thoughts as she continued the drive south.

Why am I doing this? she asked herself. Dia felt a sudden urge to take off for New Mexico or anywhere but some stupid small town in East Texas. *I could if I was by myself,* she thought. She glanced at her companions then kept the Nissan on its course.

Xenon BMW headlights flooded the Whataburger parking lot with eye-squinting brightness. Baco and Karyn were still sleeping as the vehicle approached. Dia knew it had to be Dominic. His 740iL pulled up next to them, and a man with a round, authoritative face rolled his driver's side window down.

"You must be Dia," he said.

She nodded in acknowledgment.

"I'm Dominic," he told her with a subtle smile and direct eye contact, as if he somehow knew her and could read her mind. The man unnerved her. "Where is this house you visited tonight?"

"North Lufkin, by a lake."

"Here, hand him this." Now awake, Karyn handed her the

piece of paper Baco had scribbled Paul's information on earlier.

"Why do you need the location?" Dia passed the paper to Baco's uncle.

"Because I'm going to burn it down."

Dia leaned her head out her window. "What?"

"You heard me," he said with a slight accent that Dia couldn't place. His face darkened as he spoke. "How bad is Baco?"

"I don't know. He's out cold."

Dominic retrieved a notepad and pen from his glove compartment. He jotted a few lines down then handed her the piece of paper, brushing his fingers against hers.

"Take him here. They'll give him everything he needs."

She read the note which had a Houston address then peered up into Dominic's eyes. She blushed under his penetrating stare. "Then what do we do?"

"Wait for my call." A gust of wind blew up between their two cars, sending a chill down Dia's back.

"I've never driven in Houston," she said. "How do I find this place?"

Dominic blinked his eyes, as if irritated by her question, and took a deep breath before answering. "Dia, darling. Something you're going to learn pretty quickly is I am extremely impatient with people who come to me with problems. You seem like a smart girl. Figure it out. I have other things that require my attention right now. Understand?"

She nodded, but she didn't like this man one bit. He scared her more than any man she'd ever met, and she wanted to make sure to stay out of his crosshairs. Without a moment's hesitation, she put the Z in drive to continue their journey south and hoped that anyone still at Paul's house—particularly Paul—would manage to escape alive.

FIFTEEN

MONDAY, NOVEMBER 15 – TUESDAY, NOVEMBER 16, 2004

BACO SHIFTED in his chair and raised an eyelid. "Everything okay, uncle?"

Dominic drew in a long breath as he stared at his nephew convalescing in a La-Z-Boy. With a clenched jaw and hands balled into fists at his side, he struck Dia as a caged animal waiting for any opportunity to spring into an attack. "How are you feeling? Do you need another pain pill?"

Dislocated fingers and a broken wrist had been the least of his injuries. He also had a missing tooth, a shattered eye socket —which by best estimates reduced his vision thirty percent— and a crushed sinus cavity. Dia almost felt sorry for him. According to a physician friend of Uncle Dominic's, his nephew needed six more weeks to heal and required additional help the senior Kastellanos seemed impatient to deliver.

"Not at the moment. I'm a little hungry, though," Baco said.

"Karyn! Come make a grilled cheese or something!" Mattress springs creaked from a bedroom up front, but no one emerged in response to his demand.

"You didn't answer my question," Baco said. "You okay? It's like you're angry at me or something."

"I keep asking myself when you're going to man up, is all."

Baco closed his eyes and drifted back to sleep.

In the days since their arrival in Houston, Dia had learned only fourteen years separated Dominic from his nephew. The only child of Dominic's long-deceased brother, Georgios, he had taken Baco under his wing seventeen years earlier to relieve his widowed sister-in-law's anxiety. He had coached him to pursue any number of business interests and kicked his ass when he got into scrapes with local law enforcement over shoplifting or selling weed. Unfortunately, all the coaxing, counseling, and threatening fell on deaf ears. The younger Kastellanos had been stubborn and hell-bent to forge his own path. He wanted to "be his own man," Dia overhead Dominic lament two nights prior on a phone call.

"He *can't* go back to Dallas," he had said to the person on the other end of the line. The firing, or whatever it was, had resulted in Baco coming back to work with Dominic in late fall of 2003. "Look, I know you tried to raise him after Georgios, but he works for me now, and, frankly, the kid lacks skills and all respect for authority. The only thing working for him is that Hollywood image he struts around with. Disagree with me all you like."

Dia suspected Baco's physical looks had been a magnet for women even as a child. His jet-black curls and gray eyes likely solicited comments from young and old alike. Now in his late twenties, Baco's handsomeness had been the perfect weapon for luring girls into his uncle's most profitable side hustle.

With a cell phone glued to his ear, Dominic paced the floor between the kitchen and family room. "The issue I see is he's gotta figure this shit out and soon! Go to school? You're kidding, right? You know there aren't any schools teaching what I do for a living, Sonja. Men want sex and lots of it. Baco has to work out how to market it. He's a pimp, for Christ's sake! How hard can it be?"

"Dominic!" The woman's voice was audible through the phone.

"What? Seriously? Nope, it's not my problem if they have wives, fiancées, and girlfriends. Sonja, look, you're going to have to get over it because I'm not Georgios. I didn't ask to be your kid's dad, but as it is, he's going to have to get in line if you want my help."

Dia saw for herself how men navigated around roadblocks like commitment. They wanted sex and paid to acquire all the experiences their minds craved, especially those their significant others refused to give at home. But Baco's mom clearly disapproved.

"I'm telling you, he has a computer, cash, and two somewhat attractive bitches to do his bidding. I'm going to figure out where the disconnect is and mold him into someone you'll be proud to call son, I promise."

Tinkling glass roused Dia's attention to the present. *What the hell was that?* She stood frozen in her tracks, temporarily forgetting what she had wanted from the kitchen.

Dominic glanced in her direction. "What just happened? Did you break something?"

"I, I don't know," she said. "All of a sudden, there was a whizzing noise then a clinking sound."

A hole no larger in diameter than a pencil eraser presented itself above the mantel. *Has that always been there?*

Dominic ran his finger over it, then passed Dia going to the dining room where he discovered a cut in the curtains as high as the one over the fireplace at about the same height as Dia's temple.

He pulled the curtain back, revealing tiny specs of silicon dusted across his windowsill. "What the fuck is this shit?"

Dia remained rooted in her spot as he examined the smattering of glass particles. She raised her gaze and found a break in the windowpane. "Is that from a bullet?"

"Looks like it barely missed you before lodging into the

wall," Dominic said. He brushed the broken shards into his hand and tossed them in the trash. "A split second later, the slug would've passed through your head."

Who is shooting? "I almost died!" Dia trembled, unable to move from where she stood when the round tore through the room.

"I'm calling the police." Dominic relayed details of the gunfire to the 911 operator who promised to send a black and white to investigate.

"They'll be here soon." His face softened for the first time since their arrival three weeks earlier. He held a gaze with her for what felt like an eternity before crossing the four feet of carpet to stand in front of her.

What does he want from me? Her heartbeat raced, but whether it was due to her near-death experience or Baco's uncle standing within inches of her was unclear. She avoided eye contact, focusing on a wood-framed painting of the Texas hill country in the dining room on the opposite wall.

Dominic raised his arms. Without permission, he pulled Dia up to his body and hugged her. Unsure how to respond, she stood there, rigid, and unyielding. Was he trying to hit on her or make some play? No one in this new world of hers ever offered up sympathy or compassion. *He must want something.*

"What are you doing?" she asked.

"Shh." Dominic's hands laid flat and open against her back.

Dia relaxed within his embrace as heat spread across her back. The sensation reminded her of a heating pad, except that the warmth extended beyond the span of his limbs now. It was spreading around her ribs and down past her waist. She rested her head upon his chest as warm, pulsing energy vibrations stretched to the crown of her head and the tips of her fingers and toes. Her breathing slowed while her heartbeat settled into a gentle rhythm. How could someone have this effect on another? It felt as if he surrounded her with a protective, energetic shroud to make her impenetrable to future stray bullets —accidental or otherwise.

The heat receded, and Dominic loosened his grip. "I learned that from a mentor down in New Orleans a few decades ago," he said. "Back when I was a very different person than the one I am now."

Dia stepped back. "Louisiana?"

"My uncle went there to study with a voodoo priestess back in the eighties," Baco said from his chair.

"Mind your own business, Baco."

"It's true. Careful, Dia. Piss him off, and he'll curse you. That is, if he doesn't kill you first."

"What's wrong with Princess?" Karyn emerged from one of the bedrooms.

Dia backed away from Dominic, irritation robbing her of the brief calm she'd felt only a moment earlier.

"Too bad you were in the other room just now."

"For fuck's sake, what are you talking about?" Karyn revealed crooked, stained teeth as she spoke.

"A stray bullet came through our dining room window a few minutes ago. It missed Dia by a hair," Dominic said, nodding to his left.

Karyn walked to the fireplace mantel and ran her finger across freshly exposed sheetrock. "How unfortunate...and a shame your wall got messed up like this. Easier to mop up blood than to patch a hole."

"We *didn't* ask you," Dia said.

"Knock it off, you two! For Christ's sake, for three weeks I've listened to nonstop bickering like you're in some competition. Guess what?" Dominic shot a glance toward Baco and rolled his eyes. "There's no prize here!"

"What's that supposed to mean?" Baco asked.

"You're the reason they act like this! How can you be so blind? Jesus, their constant fights? It reflects your complete inability to lead, plain and simple. If you were even *half* as business minded as me, you would have beat them into submission already. For example, Karyn doesn't need any help being a bitch. She comes by that easily enough on her own, so make her your second in command. Delegate! Like I said, 'man up.'"

Dominic stomped into the kitchen where he mumbled to himself, but not so quietly that Dia couldn't hear him say something about pecking order and profit center from where she stood. What happened to the man who'd calmed her down with his voodoo energy?

He slammed the refrigerator shut after retrieving a beer. "What are *you* staring at?"

"Nothing," Dia said.

"Go get ready for work. I need to speak with my nephew before customers show up."

She scuttled to the front of the house, eager to create some distance from her enslaver, but the bathroom door did little to shield her from the ugly conversation.

"Uncle Dominic, I'm too tired for whatever lecture you're about to give."

"Look. You gotta pull your head out of your ass! I keep telling you it's not that hard, that women are emotionally needy. Baco! What part of this don't you understand? Leverage their emotions against them. It's clear as day Karyn is jealous of Dia. Use that to motivate her because if she perceives herself as winning, then any self-pity she's internalized will fade. She'll make more money for you, and so will Dia if you stop treating her like some goddamn girlfriend!"

Girlfriend?

"Give me a break. She means nothing to me."

"Right," Dominic said. "That's why you look at her with those soft puppy dog eyes of yours."

"I do not!"

"Do you think I was born yesterday? You act tough and

indifferent when you think I'm paying attention, but I see how you look at her when you think I'm not."

"Like when? How?"

"You grow despondent every time she takes a customer to the back."

"Translation please."

"Gloomy. Dejected. It's like you think she's cheating on you or something. Newsflash! She's not!"

"I don't think so. I took her virginity and watched as Danny fucked her. You really think I'd be in love with someone and let another man do that?"

Dia studied her reflection in the vanity mirror. She needed to get in the bath if she was going to get ready in time for her first john, but the question nagged. Did Baco care about her after all?

"You need to remove any lingering sense of identity or autonomy she still has to gain compliance," Dominic said.

"How do you propose I do that?"

"You won't. I'll tend to it, starting tonight." Footsteps approached the bathroom, followed by a heavy triple tap on the door. "Why isn't the shower water running?"

"I was brushing my teeth," Dia said.

"Pick up the pace. You're beginning to cost me more money than you make!"

Dia thrust the tub faucet handle up and to the far left, drowning out any remaining dialogue between her captors. Listening to the older Kastellanos talk about her the way he did made her not only see her former boyfriend in a different light, but Karyn too. No wonder the girl had so much animosity for her. But was it true Baco had feelings for her after all this time? Love had no place in their line of work. It weakened girls and their pimp, as well, to hear Dominic tell it. Where it existed in a sex-for-profit business, other detrimental emotions followed. It led to jealousy, insecurity, anger, resentment, and depression. From Dominic's perspective, the drama resulted in violence at best and lower productivity and profitability at worst.

Water rained over Dia's head. What had the man meant by *removing any lingering sense of identity or autonomy to gain compliance?* He seemed intent on wedging himself between her and Baco starting tonight. The prospect of what he might do sent a shiver down her spine that all the steamy showers in the world couldn't squelch.

The cops were long gone. Some idiot neighbor across the alley had been cleaning his rifle when the gun "accidentally fired," sending the stray bullet through Dominic's house. The guy offered to come over and apologize but Dominic declined, saying it was unnecessary.

"1994," Dia answered. After a short night of work, Dominic and Dia were on their second beer. Baco continued to convalesce in his recliner as Karyn slept in her room. Dominic leaned into Dia as she described her mother's death and the ensuing funeral where a woman whose ostensible sympathy concealed her bigger agenda to turn a grieving man into her next husband.

"Sounds like you had a pretty joyful childhood while your mom was still alive," he said. "I'm sorry your dad couldn't have been stronger to resist your stepmom's obvious advances."

"Thanks." Dia took a swig from her bottle. She resented Susan like any child whose deceased, perfect parent was replaced by a money-seeking twit concerned more with her financial status than her responsibility as a stepparent. Familiar rage bubbled inside her, yet Dia restrained herself from expressing too much anger in front of the man sitting across from her. Why did he suddenly care about her as a person? He'd almost reached out to hold her hand a moment earlier, then withdrew it as if reminding himself she was less than human.

"I can see what Baco likes about you."

"What do you mean?"

"You have a vulnerable side. It makes you very appealing."

Does he think I'm weak? Dia finished her beer.

"Ready for another one?" Dominic asked.

"Sure."

"Or would you like to try something better? I think you'll like this...it causes you to experience happiness in a way you never have before."

She hesitated to say anything as she scratched at her Shiner Bock label. Sticky white scraps of paper collected beside her empty brown bottle as he reached into his pocket.

He shook a few pills onto the table from a small, unlabeled vial. "This is Ecstasy, X, or Molly, some call it. It's a drug to make you ecstatic about everything and everyone, thus its name."

Dia picked one up and rolled it between her fingers. "I can use all the happiness I can get."

"We'll need orange juice." Dominic walked to the fridge and returned with a carton and a glass.

"Will it kill me?"

"No. It works a bit like a stimulant and might keep you up all night...leave you with an achy jaw come tomorrow from smiling so much, but nothing more."

"Smiling? Is it addictive?"

"Not like coke or heroin...you may feel euphoric in a way you want to repeat, but you won't become dependent."

She studied the pill.

The older man stared at her, making her uncomfortable. "You have curiosity written all over your face," he said. "I've never seen your eyes so open and bright. Your cheeks are flushed, even."

"Okay. I'll try one," she said.

"Great, I'll join you." He poured juice into a shared glass, and they took their respective pills. Then Dominic set a microwave timer.

"What's that for?"

"Takes twenty-five minutes, maybe half an hour for the drug to kick in. It may take less time since we haven't eaten in several hours."

"Ah."

"Now tell me, what's your last memory of your mother?"

Thirty minutes later, Dia still talked about her mom as the buzzer went off above the stove. "We'd been on one of our camping trips in Big Bend. At a gas station outside the park, I got separated from my parents, and some old Indian witch woman found me. It's kind of a blur now. All I remember is her hair to be honest. She had tons of long, black spirals…What?" Dia stopped talking and looked at Dominic.

"Nothing," Dominic said.

Dia spoke at a fast clip. "So, this woman, she came from nowhere and helped me find my mom. She struck me as really weird with her wild hair shooting out from her head in all directions. Super sweet, though, not like anyone I've met since. She even gave me a doll. What was her name? Hmm... Lucy! Yeah, that's it." *God, I am talking wayyyyy too much.* Dia's skin tingled. "I feel so warm all of a sudden."

"You're taking off," Dominic said. "I'm feeling it too, now, for the past five minutes or so."

"How is it possible to be this happy? Wow, your eyes! Your pupils are huge!"

"So are yours, sweetheart. Giant black orbs have replaced those beautiful, hazel-colored irises."

"You think I'm pretty?"

"Of course, I do. I see why he likes you."

"Hmm. You know? You're not so bad now, not like that night I first met you." Dia wiped a bead of sweat from her upper lip. "Do you mind if I get naked? It's really hot in here suddenly." She didn't wait for him to reply, and he sat there with his mouth open as she peeled off her clothes.

Dominic reached for her hand with zero hesitation this time, inviting her to join him in his room without uttering a word. She followed him obsequiously, tiptoeing around Baco who slept unaware of the interaction between her and his uncle.

"I'm going to make love to you," Dominic said as he closed his bedroom door. "I'm going to train you in the art of being a woman." He lit candles on the nightstands and bookshelves before turning off his overhead light. "Come, sit."

Dia crawled past him to the middle of his bed and glanced up into his face as he ignited one final candle. In all of her months of servicing men, she'd never experienced feeling sexy or in charge like she did now. Dominic's clothes lay in a heap by his feet, and he stiffened in anticipation. He joined her on top of the comforter, moving his hands over her torso to pull her closer when, without provocation or warning, candlelight blazed up several inches from the four corners of his room.

"Linda?" he asked, cradling Dia's face between his palms.

"Who's Linda?" Dia's eyelids fluttered, and for a moment she felt disconnected from her body and from reality. It was as if the laws of physics no longer applied as she moved with the grace of smoke. Gravity, meanwhile, rooted Dominic like a tree. Any perceived sexual tension faded into the ether as she stared at him with an enormous, Ecstasy-induced smile. The energy of a wild animal coursed through her veins, filling her with a desire to pounce.

Images of blood and torn flesh passed through her mind as Dominic's erection withered. Did he also see the visions dancing in her head? He withdrew to the side of his bed as Dia rolled around. She was consumed by other thoughts now and oblivious to his earlier advances and attempt to break her down. At the moment, she could have cared less about Dominic.

He redressed as she lay there running her hands over her body, getting to know it as if for the very first time. She had no doubt he would have normally stayed for the show, but he retreated as if something in his gut beckoned him to leave. Dia couldn't understand how she knew this, but it was an instinct that—even in her drug-induced state—she couldn't shake.

SIXTEEN

THURSDAY, DECEMBER 30, 2004

HUSHED VOICES CREPT into Dia's bedroom beneath the door. She listened as Dominic chastised Baco once again for his lack of leadership and his failure as a pimp. She heard words like "idiot" and "grow your business" as she struggled to open her eyelids.

Grow the business? *How?* she wondered. *Does that mean screwing more men a night, or richer clients? Or will they trick another girl into this stupid, fucked-up world?*

Dia rolled over and saw that it said 10:45 a.m. on the alarm clock. She'd had more than seven hours of sleep, but she remained exhausted. Ragged and run down, Dia rose to go pee. She grabbed a robe to avoid losing body heat as she waited for hot water to pump its way to the shower head. She contemplated her image in the mirror, searching for evidence of her former self in its reflection.

Nothing about her appeared healthy or normal anymore. She had dark roots in her garishly highlighted hair, and she hadn't washed off the smudged makeup from the previous night's shift. She was down another ten pounds since ACL, and her frame looked emaciated like those concentration camp victims she'd seen pictures of in world history class. Even her once double-D breasts had gone down in considerable size. She wanted to gain weight, but despite feeling hunger pangs, she lost her appetite every time she sat down to eat. Karyn's cooking was subpar, not only because she lacked any culinary talent, but because the ingredients Baco shopped for were inferior. Dia's last good meal had been more than a week ago.

Dominic had taken all of them out for dinner at Denny's on Christmas Eve as a sort of celebration. The parking lot had been surprisingly busy, considering they made it to the restaurant within minutes of it closing. Dia gorged herself on a three-egg Denver omelet accompanied by pancakes, hash browns, and an extra side of toast. She'd washed it down with a large orange juice and four cups of coffee. The protein and caffeine chased away the cobwebs and the zombie-like state of mind she'd wandered around in since her first introduction to X. Karyn ate with similar gusto.

Satiated from the meal and without customers for a change, Dia slept for the first time in months that night. However, life returned to normal on Christmas Day as dissatisfied husbands, fathers, and their descendants sought refuge between her legs.

Snowbirds who'd made their way south scoured illicit internet sites also in search of relief. Minnesota's retired boomers and pedophiles packed RVs for their winter migration to Texas' Rio Grande Valley, where she and Karyn now found themselves working.

Was it weird to look at their situation as "unfortunate" when there were fewer college boys than there were perverted sixty-five-year-olds? Half of the older men couldn't complete screwing with their miserable limp dicks, while the other fifty percent went on endlessly with Viagra-induced erections that lasted well past their allotted appointment time. Prior to this life, Dia had never given any thought to male pubic hair. With the geriatric johns, she discovered how old age grayed their pubes as much as it did their thinning strands on top. Gravity pulled a number on the grandpas. Their ball sacks hung to mid-thigh on some.

Hell had to be better than this. Baco's long absences from their rental house made matters worse. It wasn't that she missed him, but it left her alone with Karyn and Dominic. Her former boyfriend disappeared around 2:00 p.m. each day, often not returning until after midnight.

She had no idea where he went or what he was doing, and she wondered if it had anything to do with the lecture his uncle gave nearly daily. For reasons that were unclear to Dia, tensions ran high between the two of them. Now that Baco appeared ninety-five percent healed from November's injuries, would the senior Kastellanos maintain his authority or depart?

Cracks in the floorboard outside her bathroom door sent a line of tension creeping up her spine and shoulders. She stepped into the shower, hopeful that Dominic would go away if he found her preoccupied. Her hope faded as he made his way inside her heated sanctuary, introducing the cool outdoor air and giving her goosebumps.

"Dia?" he asked.

She hesitated, hoping he'd take her silence as an invitation to leave.

"I have something for you."

She already knew what he was referring to. Since their first night together, Dominic had presented her with X almost daily. Not that she minded too terribly. Her chemical-enhanced trips provided passage to places of joyful memories, growing self-awareness and consciousness of a mystical world around her, even in circumstances such as this.

He interpreted her reticence as a sign to join her and pulled the shower curtain back to reveal himself naked and at full staff.

She retrieved her pill as Dominic produced a glass of orange juice. She swallowed it without hesitation.

"Good girl." He gestured for her to pleasure him with her

mouth. His body writhed and clinched in an ecstasy all its own as she gave him what he wanted. Her own anatomy felt warm, and she adjusted the water temperature.

"Turn around," he said. Ever submissive, Dia turned to give him access from the back. Her first trip on X remained fuzzy, but she vaguely recalled that the man couldn't perform that night. He'd made up for it plenty of times since, always taking her from behind as if to avoid looking in her eyes. That worked for her. The lack of emotional intimacy made dealing with him more palatable for her. Increasing quantities of drugs and alcohol further anesthetized her and helped her accept the growing realization she'd never leave this life.

"Let's go to the bed," he said. She welcomed winter's cool air now that X coursed through her veins. She resumed Dominic's preferred position, but he spanked her violently this time as he came up behind her, taking her breath away. She fell flat against the comforter.

"Rise up!"

Dia obeyed as tears stung her eyes. She might be high, but his sudden assault shocked her senses, nevertheless.

"I'm going to be leaving soon," he said, caressing her buttocks. "Baco has clear instructions on what to do, and I don't want you fucking it all up."

What the hell does he mean by that?

"You need to forget any lingering thoughts or romantic notions you have hanging around in your head. You're a whore, a piece of shit, a slut, and nothing more. You're a number, Dia, and *you* as a person no longer exist."

He worked his way in between her legs, then pulled her up into a sphinx-like position and entered her once again. Karyn whined from another room about Baco leaving again, then there was a knock on the door.

"Come in," Dominic said.

"I'm heading out. I'll be back late." Dia didn't see his face but imagined Baco feeling hurt to find his uncle doing this to her. At a minimum, she hoped he was stunned. Whatever his facial expression, his voice gave no indication of betrayal or dismay.

"Very good, and remember our talk, Baco. Everything's going to improve from here on out," Dominic said.

"Sure thing." Baco left and pulled the door behind him without uttering another word.

Dia rested on her forearms as Dominic fucked her. In her altered state, his words found permanent residence, *I am a whore and nothing more. I am a whore and nothing more.*

He spanked her hard again and would have continued the beating but for a ring on his cell phone. He jumped off the bed to take the call.

"Patrick, my man! How you doing, buddy? It's been a while." He gave a wicked laugh. "I'm sampling the merchandise for you, bro. Hey, let me put her on speaker for you."

He walked over to the bed. "Say 'hi,' Dia."

"Hello," she said.

Patrick spoke with a deep baritone voice, "Hello, darling. Hope you like beaches."

"I've never been to one."

"You're going to like it, and it sounds as if I'm going to like you. We're going to have some fun."

She knew what "fun" meant. She stared blankly into space, and Dominic pinched her butt to prompt a response. "Great, I'm looking forward to it."

"Me, too, sexy. Me, too," Patrick said.

Dominic returned the phone to his ear but continued to hover.

"Dom, how long before I see all of you?" she heard Patrick ask.

"Not sure I'll make it, but you'll be meeting my nephew and his girls in time for your big party."

"Sweet! Sorry you won't make it, but I can't wait to meet this newest lady and her friends."

"You got it, buddy. I'll call you in a few days to iron out the details."

"Sounds good. Later."

He threw the cell on the floor. "Florida's going to be fantastic for you, Dia. We'll pack up here by week's end, and Baco will take you east to one of our best clients. Pat's a huge football fan. You like football?"

"I've never paid much attention to it."

"Why not? Is your dad a homo or something? He didn't follow a team?"

"My dad's not gay. He's into golf."

"I see. Golf's cool. Football is a real man's sport, though. You'll like Patrick. He's as alpha as they get." Dominic scooped up his clothes, dressed quickly, and left the room without another word.

Dia lay there depleted and amazed that she could be subjected to new depths of demoralization even after all these months. She rose after a few minutes, then returned to her bathroom sanctuary to cry and finish showering.

When Dia came out of her room for her normal post-shift breakfast, she found a girl no older than twelve sitting at their kitchen table. She had an innocence like most kids do at her age. *Why is she here?* Surely Baco did not mean to use someone so youthful in his organization. *Is this what he and Dominic had been arguing over earlier?* she wondered. Karyn stood at the stove, humming some song. *Is she happy for a change?* Reality appeared more topsy-turvy than usual as Dia took it all in.

Karyn brought a bowl of scrambled eggs over and placed it in front of their guest. The girl had dark skin and curly, long hair that was black as oil. "Oh, Dia. I didn't hear you come in," Karyn said. "Meet Christina. Christina, this is Dia. She'll be your other big sister now."

Big sister?

It was a mystery how someone as young as Christina fit into their family. No customers had expressed an interest in children, at least not to Dia's knowledge. She gazed up as Dominic walked into the kitchen. He wore a lustful, greedy expression on his face, setting her nerves on edge. His vile words still rang in her ears: *a whore and nothing more.* Dia believed little in an afterlife, but she hoped there was an exceptional place in hell for both Kastellanos men. She studied the older one as he made overtures at the newest addition to their group.

"Hi there, I'm Dominic. Baco's told me so much about you," he said.

Christina lit up like a Christmas tree, as if flattered by the thought that someone had spoken highly of her. Dia rolled her eyes.

"I see you've met our girls here," he continued. "Dia will show you the ropes, but Karyn? Well, she's bottom bitch, and what she tells you is law. She reports to Baco. Baco, Karyn, Dia, then you. Sound good?"

Christina nodded, clueless as to what Dominic meant.

"Baco says you were living on your own more or less, yes?"

She moved her head up and down again.

"Well, welcome," Dominic said, and the girl smiled.

Runaways had to be some of the most vulnerable prey for pimps and other predators. Dia guessed Christina had come from parents or maybe even a foster home where she'd been abused. If so, her transition into her new family would be seamless. And if Dia's assumptions were accurate, then the youngster had been groomed for the moment when someone like Baco could swoop in as the savior and "rescue her" from a life of torment and neglect. Of course, the middle schooler—if she was that old—had no idea how bad it was about to get.

Dominic leered at her with lecherous desire. "You are absolutely beautiful. Anyone ever tell you that, Christina?"

She shook her head.

"Are you black? Or Mexican?"

"I'm mixed. My mom's bi-racial. My dad's from Colombia."

"Your skin has an amazing color, almost like cinnamon. Do people sometimes call you that?"

"No, sir."

"I think that's my new nickname for you, Cinnamon. Mm, I can taste it now."

Karyn smirked from the stove as Dia cringed.

"It's been a pleasure meeting you, Cinnamon." Dominic rose to leave, and Dia noticed his suitcase sitting by the front door. Relief washed over her in a wave as she let out a long, deep breath. He was finally leaving them, but her feelings were complicated by young Christina. Dominic's presence over the past few months had messed with their usual group dynamic, and Christina's would change it again.

Dominic turned his attention to Dia. "I hope we'll see each other again. I've enjoyed your company." He winked and walked over to the door, where he retrieved his bag. "Karyn! Have fun here. You're in charge, girl. Don't fuck it up." He poked his head back into the kitchen. "Give Baco my best."

With that, he exited, leaving them alone to consider where they'd go next.

SEVENTEEN

WEDNESDAY, FEBRUARY 2 – SUNDAY, FEBRUARY 6, 2005

BUSINESS SLOWED as January drew to a close, and Christina—or Cinnamon as they now called her—settled into her new life in Baco's "family." Older than Dia's stepbrother, Jackson, by two weeks, the thirteen-year-old looked ten or eleven due to her petite size, making it easy to promote her to higher-paying pedophiles. Viler than their regular johns, their ceaseless demand for the perverted made Baco more money than he knew what to do with.

An even greater payout sounded imminent back east. Dominic's buddy, Patrick, locked in his plans to host them at his Super Bowl party, and Baco traded in his Z for an SUV. Dominic had signed off on a black pre-owned BMW X5 to better match his protege's reputation as a professional pimp with the logic that if he appeared upper class, he'd be more successful at *attracting* elite clients.

High-class or no class, their customers were all demented predators in Dia's mind. "If you ask me, the only upside to this car is that we can stretch out some," she said.

Cinnamon lay in the optional back row. "It's way more comfortable than that other thing he was driving."

"It's almost like we're normal teenagers," Dia said.

"Hmm..."

Dia popped her head up over the seat. "Everything okay?"

"I don't want to talk about it."

"Yeah, I don't either." Dia lay back down. "I wonder what's taking them so long?"

"Who cares? Every minute Karyn's not around is a chance I can just chill."

"Sorry she's such a raging bitch to you."

"It's not your fault. She's like that to you, too."

"True." Dia studied the roof of Baco's X5. The cloth liner separating the inside of the SUV from the sunroof had a tear in it with a string hanging down. She pulled at it, and the hole grew larger.

"Better knock that off. Your boyfriend will lose his shit if he sees that."

"Gotta keep it classy, right?"

Cinnamon laughed. "Yeah, we're all soooo classy around here."

How does she laugh in this place? Dia pondered whether Cinnamon's behavior was somewhat normal for her—if years of grooming had made it easier for her to fall in step with their pimp. As suspected, she'd run away after enduring molestation from her foster brother and his father for more than a year. Her biological parents were incarcerated for drug trafficking, and after one sinister night at her foster home, Cinnamon, an only child, had nowhere else to turn but to Harlingen's streets. She'd wound up at a local mall where she hung out with other homeless kids, and like Dia, met Baco at the food court. Cinnamon fell right into Baco's open arms, hopeful for charity from a stranger.

It had been a different story for Dia. Or was it? Hadn't she, too, been desperate? Maybe she wasn't trying to escape an abusive situation back at her father's place, but she was desperately craving attention, affection, and love. A tear rolled down to her hairline. "I wonder where our boss stashed the X."

"Girl, you're like, getting addicted to those things."

"Don't be a hater." Despite Dominic's claim that Ecstasy was not addictive, it was Dia's preferred method for numbing out. She sat up between the driver's and front passenger seat, hopeful to find a random pill.

"Here they come," Cinnamon said.

Baco walked with a swagger as he returned from the store, his one arm carrying a sack of food, the other extended and holding on to Karyn's hand. Though the beating that night at the bachelor party resulted in permanent damage to his vision, he acted stronger now than Dia had ever seen him. Under Dominic's wing, he'd gleaned some new lessons in pimping. He stood taller and only spoke to her on rare occasions. He ignored the youngest member of their troop completely.

He channeled any necessary communication through their German colleague, who glowed with authority from the man's attention. In turn, she ran the other two ragged with johns. Karyn still worked as a prostitute, too, but as a bottom bitch, she received the first right of refusal and selected the better and less-disgusting customers. That left the more degraded and violent clients for Dia.

They were two days into their road trip back east and Dia felt grateful for the break from hooking. Cinnamon had endured a UTI, much like Dia had during ACL. Antibiotics cleared the infection, but D-mannose powder was a staple in their diets now, thanks to Karyn's role as a cook, business manager, and healer. Regardless of the medical attention, Cinnamon still cowered around the German drill sergeant. Karyn barked orders at their young ward to clean or help with meals every second she wasn't servicing customers. As a result, she had become quite thin. She was frailer and acted needier than she had upon her arrival, which made her even more appealing to the growing list of pedophiles.

With a waif-like appearance, her online profile pulled in a record high amount of clients during their final days in Texas, filling Baco's pockets with enough cash for them to eat three times a day as they drove east on I-10. Their stomachs were full for a change, but Dia had taken note of Cinnamon's diminished spirit as she gulped down a milkshake somewhere between New Orleans and Gulfport. She, like Dia, had begun to fade like a photograph exposed to daily sunlight. No amount of horrible early childhood experiences made what men did to her okay, and Cinnamon knew it, although she never said anything.

Karyn, on the other hand, appeared impervious to Baco's and Dominic's hellish scheme. "Hey, babe. How much longer?" She settled back into the front passenger seat and grabbed the bag of food from Baco as he slid in behind the wheel.

"I don't know…an hour and a half. Two tops. Pass the snacks back to the others."

"Is there nothing to drink?" Dia kept a sub sandwich and passed the other back.

"Grab a water from the cooler," Karyn said.

"Fine." Dia rolled her eyes and sat back to take in the remaining few hours of freedom she'd enjoy before the long weekend.

Luxury greeted them upon their arrival on Amelia Island. Last in a chain of Atlantic Sea islands on Florida's east coast, the barrier isle was home to wealth unlike any Dia had ever seen. She remembered her dad's friends with their oversized cabin-cruisers on Lake Travis. They paled in comparison to the magnificent lifestyles she now witnessed northeast of Jacksonville.

Dia adjusted her tube top as they pulled into one of Amelia's extravagant high-rise resorts. While the X5 might make a statement, she wondered, *What will everyone think once the doors open, and we come out?*

A uniformed valet came to her door. "Any luggage?" He

scanned the length of Dia's body, his expression revealing a familiar mix of lust and mild dismay.

Her entire night-time wardrobe fit loosely in a backpack alongside her non-working clothes—a pair of form-fitting yoga pants and three baby tees. Dia smiled weakly. "Nope, this is it."

Fashion had never been a priority in her previous life, even with her retail job, but she had learned how brand names were essential to anyone invested in looking their best. Resort guests projected their wealth via Christian Louboutin, Manolo Blahnik, and Louis Vuitton. Women walked by in sexy, slinky dresses while their men wore complementary suits or slacks. Dia wondered if one of these gentlemen was Patrick.

A seed of hope took root. Could this guy rescue her? Could he decide to take her out of this life? If he had enough money to stay here, then maybe he could afford to buy her from Baco. And if he was super decent, perhaps he'd return her home. She thought back to Paul and the bachelor party, then pushed the idea out of her head. *Don't be stupid. This isn't the movies.*

Stares from the rich and glamorous made Dia self-conscious, but something else tugged at her attention. Several of the guests had pets with them, and it didn't escape her attention how they were treated better than most people. A woman approached the hotel's front, revolving door leading a black and white Siberian Husky on a bejeweled leash. The canine turned and stared at Dia, causing her to gasp. Something about the animal's features were familiar to her as it held her in a gaze. Baco broke the trance by thrusting a fistful of cash and a credit card at Karyn. He whispered something and left the three of them alone with the vehicle.

"We're going shopping!" Karyn smiled from ear to ear. Baco had handed her his BMW keys as well.

"Where?" Cinnamon asked.

"Centre Street...wherever that is."

"Let's ask the concierge," Dia said.

"Con-see what?" Cinnamon asked.

"Con-cie-erge," Karyn said patronizingly. "Do you see one, Dia?"

Dia surveyed the lobby and saw two well-dressed men near a bellman's station. "Follow me."

Cinnamon lit up like a child in a candy store when they visited the stores on Centre Street. They browsed through Harbor Wear of Amelia Island, Pineapple Patch, The Gauzeway and Twisted Sister. The oldest and newest members of their so-called family seemed oblivious to curious and hateful stares, but the judgmental gawking didn't escape Dia's attention. She couldn't wait to slip into decent attire and become invisible.

Less than two hours later, her goal was accomplished. Fitting into a size two, she checked out her image in one store's three-way mirror. Her bosom, though smaller than a year ago, appeared ample enough to give the impression of a resort tourist. By the time they finished their shopping spree, they'd found plenty of shorts, capris, and sundresses to meet the wardrobe requirements of a Caribbean cruise. Dia couldn't wait to walk into their hotel lobby now.

"One more stop. Highlights are a must-have! I say we go in for a little extra pampering. Who's with me?" Karyn asked.

It seemed money made a difference in everybody's mood. "If you're okay with it, then it works for us," Dia said, exchanging looks with Cinnamon.

"Good! Let's find a place. There has to be a salon somewhere around here," she said.

They consulted the Yellow Pages and two strangers for directions. Ninety minutes later, all three looked like shiny new pennies.

"I reckon we'll look really good for our guys tonight. Don't you think?" Cinnamon stared at her reflection in a mirror, half smiling.

"Yeah…I guess we will," Dia answered with a twinge of melancholy.

"All right. We've spent all of Baco's money. Let's head back," Karyn said.

"Time, Karyn! Time!" Baco barked from his side of the door that connected their suites. He paced the floor. He was like a pressure cooker about to explode. It wasn't even 6:00 p.m. yet. Things rarely started before nine when it came to parties.

Dia shot an inquiring expression at Karyn who revealed nothing and dutifully escorted Dia and Cinnamon to one of the bedrooms. "I'll be back. Put your clothes away, and start getting ready for tonight," she said.

"What took you so long? For fuck's sake!" Baco yelled from his room.

"Jeez. What crawled up his butt?" Cinnamon whispered to Dia.

"Who knows?"

Cinnamon gathered her toiletries and headed for the bathroom.

Karyn returned moments later. "Where's your little shadow?"

"In the other shower. Is everything okay?"

Karyn paced the floor. "Yeah, he's…nervous is all. Patrick is a big customer and a very good friend of Dominic's. He wants it to go perfectly and is working really hard to establish himself, you know. This is a huge move for him…for all of us."

"All right, well, we got this. Cinnamon's almost done. It won't take me long, either, since we had our hair fixed.

Go...get cleaned up and we'll be ready to go in thirty minutes."

"Thanks," Karyn said with a sigh. "See you in a bit. And remember to shave!"

Patrick Simpson greeted them at the door to his penthouse suite, full of enthusiastic charm and a bigger-than-life personality. At first glance, he appeared gorgeous—blond, athletic, charismatic. He was a surfer-turned-businessman who now worked as a successful orthopedic distributor for one of the world's largest medical device companies. However, behind this highly manufactured veneer lay something vacant. Dia couldn't put her finger on it, but something was off.

"Ladies, it is a pleasure to meet all of you," their host said. "Please. Come in. I want to introduce you to my team."

Team? Dia wondered. He escorted them through his foyer to a giant living room adorned with multiple sofas, glass tables, and a view stretching endlessly into the darkness of the Atlantic Ocean. Since it was now dark outside, the floor-to-ceiling windows reflected dimly lit recessed lighting along the suite's perimeter walls.

Patrick jumped up on a limestone coffee table, threw up his arms, and commanded everyone's attention with dramatic flair. He beckoned more than a dozen guys to take their seats on one of three white leather couches circling him. Dia had not seen them until now, having been so taken with the beautiful surroundings. She watched as men ranging in age from their 30s to 40s filed in from the kitchen and bar.

"My friends," Patrick began. "Welcome to our annual get-together where we meet to celebrate another incredible year of sales. Once more, you've done it! You've not only hit your targets and grown the territory by double digits, but you've made us number one for four years in a row!"

"Hear, hear!" Several of them clinked their drinks.

"No celebration is complete without hot and sexy mamas by our side. Let me present tonight's entertainment!"

Patrick's men catcalled and whistled at them. Karyn beamed as Patrick took her hand.

"Follow me, ladies." Patrick paraded all three of them around coffee tables filled with endless vodka bottles, mixers, and ice buckets. The scene reminded Dia of Paul's bachelor party, and she felt like a heifer going to slaughter.

"Maestro Patrick!" someone shouted. Patrick dropped Karyn off in front of a group of four guys by the bar. He returned for Dia and led her to a throng of men hungry for a show in an ever-increasing circus environment. "Who wants to bid on this blonde beauty?"

The spectacle morphed into an auction with a chorus of responses. "Twenty bucks!"

"Fifty," said another.

"Gentlemen, look at her. She's gorgeous, and according to her manager, she clamps on you like a vise."

He leaned in and whispered, "I'd pay fifty dollars for your fine, little ass."

"One hundred!" a slick-looking man in his fifties said.

"SOLD! To my right-hand man and best friend, Larry," Patrick said. He handed Dia off to the middle-aged man.

Belittled by their bidding, Dia followed Larry to a white couch in a corner. The double dose of Molly she'd taken started kicking in, helping her suppress the animosity and humiliation that had begun to bubble up once more inside her, but all the X in the world couldn't completely chase her feelings away.

Dia stifled a grimace as Larry caressed her from where he sat and removed her clothes. She was standing naked before him and everyone else as he produced his cock for others to enjoy the show. "Come here, my queen. I'm going to fuck you like you've never been fucked in your life."

"Like she's never heard that before," one guy said.

"You say that to all the girls," another said.

"Yeah, but I always mean it," Larry guided Dia down onto his lap.

"Larry! Larry! Larry!" Patrick's men chanted.

Dia stared into Larry's beady, dark brown eyes and manufactured a smile. The clock behind him read 10:05. Her night was only beginning.

"Let's go, baby girl," he said, bringing Dia's attention back to him.

"Anything you want, lover. Anything you want."

EIGHTEEN

SUNDAY, FEBRUARY 6 – WEDNESDAY, FEBRUARY 9, 2005

BACO YELLED at his mentor over his phone speaker. "Record-breaking revenue doesn't mean shit to me if your favorite customer's going to leave marks all over my merchandise." He drove like a madman, desperate to put as much distance as possible between them and Patrick.

Dia fell in and out of consciousness in Baco's third-row seat as he snaked his X5 westbound on I-10. Bruises covered her forearms, inner thighs, buttocks, and back. Welts from a two-inch wide leather belt made her too uncomfortable to lay flat. She ached everywhere except her feet. Patrick had managed not to batter those.

Align Medical's "King of Orthopedics" and his cronies had been excessively physical with the three of them during their orgy, but the one-time-surfer-turned-sales leader had reserved special treatment for her. He got off on inflicting pain in a messed-up kind of way. He liked it doggy style, not unlike a lot of his guys, but at the end of the night, after innumerable rounds of sadistic humiliation, he'd asked her to look back and into his face while fucking her from behind. Always obedient, she did as instructed, only to be clocked with his fist in her jaw when she did.

She was stunned and scared, and her left-side molars were knocked loose. Dia had bowed her head into a pillow to hide her tears. She awoke hours later to Cinnamon and Karyn's urgent cries. Now she listened as Baco slowly acquiesced to whatever Dominic told him over the phone.

Karyn withdrew an assortment of vials, creams, and gels from a bag. She removed the cap from a tube of arnica, and along with Cinnamon, worked to massage the gel along Dia's legs and arms. Sleep beckoned. With a mouthful of arnica tablets under her tongue, Dia slipped into a shallow pool of dreams.

Death has to be better than this. I could easily find some way to kill myself. Aren't I dying anyway? Her soul diminished fraction by fraction with each new john and corresponding assault upon her fragile body. She weighed the existence of the video that Baco kept somewhere in his meager possessions. She now considered whether she served anyone by allowing it to hold power over her. *Death by embarrassment or by prostitution?* she wondered.

Dying by the latter struck her as more likely because escape was for the brave and courageous, words no one would ever attribute to her. She drifted off to sleep. Distant drumbeats pulled Dia's dreams in an unfamiliar direction. The moon rose and shown over a flower—red, tall, and singular.

Baco honked the horn as they lurched through traffic, waking Dia from her dream. She poked her head up over the back seat and saw pedestrians standing along narrow avenues as he struggled to navigate his way into a hotel parking lot. The cheering, beads, and music meant they had arrived in New Orleans. They'd made the drive to the Crescent City in under a day. She hoped it was too late to go to work.

Without attracting too much attention, Baco ushered the

three girls into their two-bedroom suite. Less ornate than where they stayed in Florida, the building's interior still provided a sense of luxury with plush gray carpeting, cheetah-print benches, lavender walls, and eggshell crown molding. Baco dropped their bags in the suite's living room. He scratched his head before breaking his silence. "Dia, come with me."

She followed him to a room with two queen-size beds adorned by brilliant, white cotton duvets and lace throw pillows. He stood at their window inspecting the crowds below through the sheer curtains, then he jerked the heavier black drapes closed to block out New Orleans' blinking lights.

"You can sleep here," he told her, still avoiding looking at her. "Don't worry...I'm not going to try anything with you. No one's going to touch you at all tonight, maybe not for several nights." He walked toward the door. "I'm going to order room service for all of us," he said. "Do you think you can eat something?"

She stared at him, unsure what to say. A single word floated its way up to her mouth. "Yes."

He shrugged and shuffled away, leaving her alone in silence.

Baco made good on his promise of ordering food, and Dia was soon looking at a giant tray of chicken soup and French baguette. Even after a long, hot soak in the room's porcelain tub, Dia's body still ached, but she managed to tear the bread into chunks before drowning them in the creamy broth. The salty goodness of the soup-soaked bread slid down her throat and filled her belly. She chased it with gulps of the liquid, vegetables, and homemade noodles. When she removed the aluminum cover on another dish, she was pleasantly surprised to discover a bowl of ice cream topped with berries. There were also pralines on the plate, but she pushed them aside, fearing more damage to her aching jaw and loose teeth.

When she was done eating, she nestled into the pillow-top

bed and pulled the down comforter up to her chin. Feathery solitude embraced her like a glove. Funny how it took getting beat up to get a reprieve from Baco. *But at least he's giving me a break*, she thought.

Dia had slept more than eighteen hours a day since their Sunday arrival. Her former boyfriend had followed through on giving her a few nights off, which paid dividends for her. Her bruises were already fading from deep purple to a yellowish-green, and she could walk without grimacing in pain. On Tuesday, she stood at the window and parted its weighted black curtains to watch Mardi Gras revelers.

Fat Tuesday extended the weekend into a four-day trip of booze, beads, and debauchery. She watched as the crowd's intensifying enthusiasm waxed and waned with each passing float and wondered how many people below were kids close in age to her, just with different lives.

Her eyes hurt from the glare of outside light, so she closed the heavy drapes. Curiosity turned to sadness as she retreated from watching the celebration and headed back to bed. After nestling beneath goose-feather-filled covers, she worked her way into a deep breathing cycle that would soon carry her to sleep.

"Knock, knock," a voice said.

Dia opened her eyelids with the speed of a sloth to find her fellow prostitutes standing at the door with a tray. "Go away," she said with feigned annoyance.

"No, you have to eat," Karyn said. "Besides, you're going to really like this one—crème brûlée French toast."

"What?"

"Seriously, it's amazing," Karyn said.

Her cohorts walked in with the food still wearing last

night's miniskirts and halter tops. Baco was nowhere to be seen, and she figured he was out drumming up business.

Cinnamon sat on Baco's bed as Karyn set Dia's food down. Her eyes were wide with a wild excitement. She acted high on something—sugar from the maple syrup or something more nefarious?

Dia checked them out as she chewed each bite, noticing how both girls could barely sit still. Karyn, while attentive as a nurse, paced the length of the dresser. Cinnamon struck her as nervous and more compliant than usual, fidgeting with the hem of her skirt with one hand and chewing her nails on the other. Together, they waited in silence as Dia ate her breakfast. She wanted to ask where they'd been but thought it best to not discuss work, considering how they might view her predicament unfair compared to theirs.

Then, as if hearing her thoughts, Karyn asked, "Do you think you'll be getting back to things tonight?"

The French toast formed into a ball of dough in her mouth. She was unsure what to say and unable to swallow. If their pimp needed her to meet with clients, she would, but she hoped for at least another night's reprieve. She cringed to think about servicing anyone strung out on hurricanes, daiquiris, and God knows what else in New Orleans' sin-filled French Quarter.

"What are you two doing in here?" Baco barged in making Cinnamon jump a foot from the bed. She lost her balance and dropped to the floor.

Karyn turned more gracefully to meet Baco's gaze. "Nothing. We were just delivering breakfast."

He stared at her suspiciously. "You need to go get ready. I have customers dialed in from 1:00 p.m. until after midnight. Go! NOW! These rooms don't pay for themselves, you know." Baco chased them out of the room.

Dia's appetite departed with them. Alone once more, she slipped beneath the 1,000-count sheets and fell fast asleep. She dreamt of the silver German Shepherd she'd seen at the Amelia Island resort. It shape-shifted into a wolf and then into a woman. The woman sat in a dark cave with her eyes closed, chanting as she rocked back and forth.

Bells chimed in the distance, waking Dia from her slumber and a dream that had given her a strange sense of comfort. She turned her head to the nightstand alarm clock which read 6:00 a.m. She rested her head against the headboard. *I wonder where the church is.* Muted waves of music and drunken laughter had dissipated hours ago as partiers and tourists left to prepare for Lent or their long trips home with magnificent hangovers.

Though not a Catholic, Dia knew what today meant for the pious. It was Ash Wednesday, and back in Austin, her best friend, Samantha, had probably already received an ashen cross on her forehead to celebrate the Lenten season with her parents.

Dia's current "family" slept next to her in a matching queen bed. She glanced over at Baco, hopeful he would sleep for several hours considering he'd gone to bed only thirty minutes earlier. A pile of cash on their shared nightstand gave her an idea. Wide awake and hungry, Dia got up, dressed, and quietly slipped out the door of their suite. She took the elevator to the lobby and stopped to ask the sole doorman for directions. She made her way out to litter-strewn Poydras and Peter Streets in search of café au lait and beignets, then headed north past Canal and eventually found where North Peters Street merged into Decatur as the concierge had indicated. She caught a whiff of Cafe Du Monde above intertwining smells of urine, vomit, and rotting food.

Good and evil walked hand in hand in this place. Heavy, wet darkness seeped over levies retaining Mark Twain's

Mississippi and engulfed her, but she was indifferent to any potential dangers surrounding her. Besides, what could hurt her after everything she'd gone through up to this point? If someone were to attack from the shadowed alleys of New Orleans, it would certainly be a lesser hell than what awaited her once she returned to work with Baco. She crossed St. Peter Street and caught her first glimpse of Cafe Du Monde catty-corner to Jackson Square. She hastened her pace to grab a place in line along with scores of blurry-eyed tourists.

Twenty-five minutes later, she stopped herself from licking her plate clean. She peered out to the road that just the night before was inundated with artists, street vendors, and fortune-tellers. All had packed their wares, except for one middle-aged woman—a gypsy medium. *How do they do it?* she wondered. The lady glanced over at her as she drank the last few sips of café au lait. When Dia realized she was being stared at, she decided it was time to leave.

The woman called from across St. Ann Street, "Would you like a reading?"

Dia shook her head quickly as she exited the restaurant.

"Transformation can be yours. Come, sweetie, I won't charge you. You look like you could use a little direction."

Dia approached the long-haired, wrinkled-face fortune-teller with caution.

"A pleasure to meet you. I'm Martha. And you are?"

"Dia."

"Take a seat, dear." Martha shuffled a deck of tarot cards on the table and lay out three of them in front of her.

"Okay, Hanged Man Reversed is your present card," Martha said.

Dia stared with her eyes wide open.

"Don't worry, my child. It means you're becoming more focused on yourself and less self-sacrificing. Next, Knight of Pentacles...when the card's reversed like this, it suggests you're in a bit of a rut and you may be unwilling to change. Your world view might also be a bit pessimistic right now."

Dia studied the table as Martha took a breath, preparing to describe her third and final card. Karyn approached them before its meaning could be revealed.

"What are you doing?" Karyn grabbed Dia by her elbow.

"Nothing. I was about to head back."

"We thought you'd run away," Karyn said, trying to be vague in front of a stranger.

"Well, I didn't," Dia said between clenched teeth, wrangling her arm free.

Dia caught a glimpse of an upside-down card with what looked like five boys brandishing sticks.

"Should I go on?" Martha asked. "This is your future card."

Karyn's pursed mouth and threatening stare told Dia how to respond. "You've been great, but I need to go," she said.

"It means you're avoiding conflict," the gypsy said.

"What does?" Dia asked.

"Your card...it represents inner struggle. Now go...and take care of yourself, child."

Dia followed Karyn down Decatur. Her three-day holiday was now officially over.

NINETEEN

TUESDAY, MARCH 1 – WEDNESDAY, MARCH 2, 2005

BACO'S CREW returned to Texas as February flipped to March. Karyn and Cinnamon had been tasked with filling Dia's quota as she healed, but her diminishing bruises meant fully returning back to work two days into the Lenten season. Baco pushed all three girls to take on extra customers during their final week in Louisiana, earning them a well-deserved twenty-four-hour break before kicking off their next engagement.

Venison purveyors surrounded them as Baco parked the X5 outside Reliant Stadium. An overhead sign advertised Houston Rodeo's Giant Chili Cook-off, and the smell of outdoor barbecue hung heavy in Houston's humid, late winter air. As they walked past a large, sectioned-off part of Reliant's parking lot, Dia glimpsed the hundreds of smokestacks releasing the aroma of barbecue. The added layers of cooked deer meat, burning oak, and free-flowing beer made Dia's mouth water. People needed wristbands to enter the cooking tents. She wished that her reason for being there was to partake in the festivities.

Some years earlier, her dad scored tickets to judge a cook-off. He'd described with great enthusiasm his need to "cleanse his palate" with copious cans of Miller Lite and saltine crackers before tasting offerings that bore no resemblance to Susan's recipe. The chili at a cook-off rarely contained beans and, in most cases, consisted of venison, assorted chili powders, fresh jalapeños, and large doses of cumin or cayenne.

Throngs of people mingled around judging tents in starched, pressed shirts and cowboy boots. Thankfully, Baco had insisted they dress normally for a change and not like hookers. Their evening wear would be waiting for them later at their motel, assuming he could line up johns. He'd departed to do just that, entrusting Karyn to keep a tight leash on the girls as they wandered through the cook-off grounds.

Karyn's breathing relaxed in Baco's absence. "Do you guys want to check out the farm animals?" Although she was still a bitch on her best day, she was a bit less of one when their pimp was preoccupied with other matters.

"You mean like cows and stuff?" Cinnamon asked.

"Yep, steers, goats, sheep. You name it, you'll find it here," Karyn replied.

"Sure, why not?" Dia said.

They strolled through large crowds of kids, parents, and pedestrians, stopping now and then to look into livestock pens. Children who were not much younger than Cinnamon prepared their animals for competition. Some contestants used hair dryers to fluff the fur.

"No way!" Cinnamon exclaimed when she saw the grooming techniques.

"Seems like a lot of work for an animal that's going to slaughter once this show's over," Karyn said.

"You don't know that," Dia said. "It's weird, though, isn't it?"

"How do you mean?" Karyn asked.

"These animals are treated better than we are."

Karyn rolled her eyes and avoided agreeing.

"In a way, we're kind of like meat," Cinnamon said. "Don't you think?"

"Exactly my point," Dia said.

Oblivious to anything other than their competition, children and teens moved with a determined focus to prep their critters. Doting moms and dads stood on the sidelines, helping where needed but mostly staying out of their children's way. All were dressed in traditional rodeo attire—Levi's or Wranglers. *Everyone seems so normal*, Dia thought.

Dia hated admitting it, but she envied them with their perfect upbringing, involved parents, and sense of community. She'd judged kids like this as "hicks" or "kickers" back in Athens, but what she wouldn't give to brush the hide of a Lowline Angus cow now. She caught Cinnamon staring into a pen with twin goats. She peered past her and saw Karyn speaking on a flip phone. *When did Baco give that to her?* Dia wondered. Her earlier enthusiasm faded as Karyn's facial expression changed.

What's wrong? Dia mouthed.

Karyn shook her head but motioned for her to collect Cinnamon.

"Hey, we gotta go," Dia told Cinnamon.

"But I want to see the rodeo."

"Yeah, I know, but we can't. Looks like our boss has work for us."

Karyn put the phone in her pocket. "That was Baco."

"I figured as much. Do we have to leave right now?" Dia asked.

Karyn let out a long breath. "He says cowboys from all over are in Houston for two or three weeks, and he's found a group from Montana or somewhere who'd like to meet after their competitions this evening."

"If we're meeting later tonight, can we hang out just a little while longer?" Cinnamon pleaded.

The youngest member of their trio was so cute, even Karyn

had a hard time saying no. She smiled somewhat, acquiescing like a mom giving in to a child whose solicitations were sweet, well-meaning, and worthy of satisfying. "Fine. We can stay for a little bit, but I don't want any back talk when I say it's time to leave."

"Yay! Let's go see if we can catch part of the rodeo, then!" Cinnamon said excitedly. She pulled at Dia and Karyn's hands, and they yielded to the youngster's request to take in bull riding.

Patrons filed in and out of a dingy hole-in-the-wall restaurant as their waiter delivered plates of sizzling-hot rib eyes, potatoes, and corn on the cob. Baco—mindful of how late they'd be working—had ordered a large enough caloric meal to sustain them over their upcoming shift. Dia looked at her plate. The Ray's Steakhouse ambiance left a lot to be desired, but the food smelled amazing. She hadn't eaten a steak in ages and was delighted to find it pink on the inside when she cut into it. Cinnamon and Karyn attacked their meals with equal abandon. The cotton candy, hot dogs, and snow cones they'd consumed at the rodeo had long since burned off from the hours of walking.

Baco sat quietly watching them. He'd been annoyed at their delayed arrival and promised to punish them after their shifts, but Karyn placated him, promising that an afternoon of play would pay dividends to their customers and his bank account later.

"Let's go!" he said. "We can't be late."

All three picked up the pace.

Dia washed down her meal with a goblet of cabernet that their waiter had delivered, no questions asked. She was about to return her glass when the drink coaster caught her attention.

Mud flaps on eighteen-wheeler trucks normally provided the canvas for such tacky artwork. On the cardboard paper was a silhouette of a large-breasted female, sitting in a coquettish manner with a local Houston number. The restaurant may not have been five-star, but even this seemed out of place for the dimly lit, oak-paneled dining room. Dia glanced around; no other table had coasters. She turned it over, curious about the message.

She read from the meager light of a candle: "My name is Alexis, and I'm 15, being held against my will, and forced to have sex with a dozen men a day." A single statement underneath the quote said:

The truth isn't pretty.

Dia flipped the wine coaster, afraid Baco had seen it, but the Houston local news occupied his attention from a TV above the bar. She took the opportunity to turn it back over to study it more closely. On the bottom, it said:

Your call is anonymous.

Baco rose to chase the waiter down for their check, giving Dia space to make her move. She removed the coaster and placed it in her pants for safekeeping.

He returned to their table. "Let's go."

"I'm not finished!" Karyn pushed a heaping pile of potatoes into her mouth.

"Pack it in your napkin and eat it in the car. I want to go so you can shower."

Karyn rolled her eyes and wrapped her remaining steak. Like sheep, they followed him to the SUV.

Crimson filled Dia's entire visual frame as she dreamt. She stepped back some distance, and a cardinal-colored flower came into focus. It rose singularly upon a stalk covered in hairy green leaves with an outcropping of grass at its base. She checked around her and saw nothing but desert in every direction for 500 miles. It was nighttime, and the moonlight illuminated the earth below, casting the flower's long shadow westward.

A full moon, Dia recognized it must still be early. Something told her to move, to keep going somewhere...anywhere, but her body wouldn't obey, making her tremble. She woke suddenly to an unrecognizable voice.

"Hey, you." A West Texas drawl brought her back to reality. Puppy-dog eyes loomed innocent and large a few inches away from her own. She had to think for a moment. *Accent, sweet brown eyes, and a crew cut.* She spun through the Rolodex of names men provided over the course of eight hours. *Ben!*

"Hi, Ben. I'm sorry, did I fall asleep?"

"You did. You was cute to watch," he said sheepishly. "I hope you don't mind."

Why is he acting so tender? she wondered. "Did we...you know?"

"Do it?"

"Yes."

"We started to make out, but then you kind of dozed off." He smiled, running a finger first along her jawline and then down her nose.

She panicked. Baco would rip her a new one if this guy didn't get what he paid for. She moved to correct their situation.

"No, you're okay," Ben said, grabbing her hands. "You seem sweet, and besides, I was a bit tired." He studied her in the dim light of the motel room's nightstand lamp. "Your name's Dia, right?"

She nodded. They were alone, and she could hear the sounds of traffic passing by on the wet city streets outside their door. "How old are you?"

"Twenty-two."

"You're sure you're that old?"

"Of course."

He continued to stare, waiting for her to say more. "I like you."

Seriously? "I like you, too."

"I bet you say that to all the guys," he said with a wink.

"Hey, that's not nice!" she said with a slight smack to his shoulder.

"I'm teasing. I joke with people I like," he laughed, trying to duck a second blow. "I have to take a whiz. I'll be back in a minute."

Ben walked naked to the bathroom. Under other circumstances, he could be her boyfriend. Nothing felt normal, unfortunately. When he closed the door, she retrieved the coaster from her pants. His cell phone lay on her nightstand with his other personal belongings, including condoms and Chapstick.

She grabbed the device, flipped it open, and dialed quickly. She worked to calm her nerves and find her voice when someone answered.

"Hello, this is Adrian. Are you safe? Do you need help?"

"I'm okay. I saw your coaster at dinner last night."

"Are you free from danger? Can you chat right now?"

"Yes, no…I don't know."

Ben flushed the toilet. He'd be out any second. Yes, he'd been sweet to her considering the lack of sex, but he'd want what he came for before leaving and there'd be hell to pay if she refused or got caught trying to run away. If there was one thing Dia knew by now, it was that johns—along with pimps—could flip from gentle to hostile in a heartbeat.

"I gotta go."

"No wait!" Adrian said.

Dia ended the call and replaced Ben's phone on the nightstand just as he opened the bathroom door.

"Don't you look like the cat who ate the canary," he said. She eyed the coaster on the floor. It must have fallen during her phone conversation. She prayed he didn't see it as he approached. A quick glance below his waist revealed where his attention was focused.

"You know, I'm not so tired now." Ben leaned over to kiss her on the mouth.

This one isn't so bad, she thought. "I can tell." She pulled back the sheet to welcome him.

"What the hell is this?" Baco loomed over Dia, holding up the coaster.

Damnit. Ben was long gone, and retrieving the coaster from the floor had slipped her mind as heavy tiredness pulled her into a deep sleep. The moon, the flower, and a gray wolf filled her dream, and a moment before Baco woke her, a voice whispered, "Walk."

"It's just something I picked up from the restaurant last night," Dia said. *Please don't hit me.*

"You and I have been doing just fine, Dia. Don't you even give one second to leaving me or you know what will happen!"

"How could I forget?"

"Excuse me?"

Suddenly, Karyn's yelling pulled Baco's attention away from her. Dia covered her head with a pillow to drown them out, to little avail. She popped an eye open in the direction of the bedside clock. It read 11:30.

"Look, you little brat. This is *my* stuff. Mine! You get it? If you want to use quality makeup, then buy it with your own money!" Karyn spat.

"But I don't *have* any money," the youngster cried.

"That's right. Do you know *why*? Because I'm boss around here."

"Must we start this early with the fucking arguing?" Baco

asked. He threw up his hands and left the room. Dia had a brief moment of relief.

Karyn rarely received cash from Baco unless they needed supplies. Every dollar they earned went straight to their pimp and stayed there. She managed to snag a few dollars here and there, though, and socked it away to periodically procure nice things for only her to enjoy.

Cinnamon looked around Karyn and with her eyes implored Dia for protection from the woman's wrath. Karyn knew her young colleague had nothing to call her own, but Baco had started to talk more with Cinnamon in recent weeks, to joke around even. *Maybe Karyn's jealous.* Dia stared on in horror as the bottom bitch chased the youngest member of their family around, trying to hit her with a hairbrush. Dia jumped up and interceded on Cinnamon's behalf, taking a whack across her temple while Cinnamon trembled behind her.

Any hope of escape had vanished. She hated every prospect of her future stuck with these people. Baco's continued threat of violence kept her tethered to them, but something else nagged at her. *What would happen to Cinnamon if I left?* "Karyn, I'll take care of it. Just calm down, okay? She has nothing, not that she doesn't work hard to earn it. Hell, she puts up with more crap than the two of us combined from all those perverted creeps."

"Done lecturing me?" Karyn rolled her eyes and turned away. "Like I really care what you think."

Dia glared at the back of her head and gave her the finger.

Cinnamon rose from her crouching position for a hug. Their conflict appeared to be over for now as Dia comforted her, but a growing bitterness nudged its way in. *I'll never be able to leave as long as she can't fend for herself.*

TWENTY

SATURDAY, APRIL 2, 2005

"HEY, Cinn. Up for a milkshake today? They got chocolate or vanilla," Baco said as he led his team into McDonald's.

"Do they have strawberry?"

"Possibly. They have 'em with cookies, too, I think. Are Oreos okay?"

"Strawberry, please!"

"What about me? I want ice cream," Karyn said.

"I wasn't talking to you," Baco replied.

Karyn scowled at him. Her jaw tightened into a fierce clench to hold back the torrent of angry words that were surely building up inside of her. Their pimp tilted his head, daring her to make another comment. Challenging him had resulted in a violent slap across her face back in South Padre over spring break. She inhaled deeply before softening, then turned and skulked off to the ladies' room.

"All of you go use the toilet while I get the food," Baco said. "And don't take too long. We'll need to get back on the road pronto!"

Cinnamon grabbed Dia's hand, and together they followed after Karyn. Someone's stomach grumbled.

"Was that you or me?" Cinnamon asked.

"Hmm, pretty sure that was me," Dia said. "I could go for a Big Mac and super-sized order of fries."

"Yeah, me too."

"At least you're getting a milkshake, though," Dia said.

Cinnamon shrugged her shoulders.

Dia sensed that her younger colleague appreciated their pimp's occasional kindness, but did she know how much they bothered his second-in-command? Up ahead of them, Karyn had pushed the bathroom door open so aggressively that it banged against the wall, causing people to turn and stare.

"Don't mind her," Dia said to one of the diners. "She's a little upset we missed the breakfast cutoff."

Inside the bathroom, Karyn lunged at Cinnamon from the stalls and pinned her beside the hand dryer. "I want half that milkshake, you little shit, and you're going to give it to me!"

"You're hurting me!"

"Stop whining, you little baby!"

"Jesus! Knock it off, will you?" Dia asked, trying to pull them apart. "Do you want people to call the police?"

"Shut up. Both of you act so fucking chummy," Karyn spat. "I'm tired of it. You hear me? Sick and tired of it!" She stomped into one of the stalls, yanked toilet paper from the dispenser, and blew her nose.

After a few tense minutes using the bathroom, all three returned to Baco's vehicle, where he greeted them with bags of burgers and fries plus one frozen strawberry milkshake. Across the parking lot, a gardener operated an industrial-sized lawn mower, cutting down grass and Texas wildflowers. A mutilated bluebonnet landed at Dia's feet, reminding her it was late March. *Has it been a year already?* She slipped into the backseat with Cinnamon and waited for Baco to distribute their meals.

"Where to now?" Karyn asked as he passed the pink milkshake to the back row. She made eye contact with Dia, then rolled her eyes and turned to the front.

"I'm thinking New Orleans," he said.

"Don't they have hurricanes during the summer?" she asked.

"Let me worry about the weather. Here. I've got a single burger—no cheese—for you."

"No fries? First, no shake, and now no fries?" Karyn crossed her arms, and her eyes fixed firmly on their pimp. "You know, I'm hungry, too, in case you haven't noticed."

Baco took a long sip through his straw as he squinted out the windshield. "Dominic thinks it best if you avoid eating so much for a while."

She stared at him, her mouth agape. "Your uncle said that, or *you* did?"

What in the world is he talking about? Dia studied Karyn, looking for signs of impending obesity from her fellow prostitute. So what if her belly stuck out beneath her shirt a little more than it used to? Surely, a few extra pounds weren't enough to dry up the sex-buying pipeline. The other question Dia had was *how?* Weren't they all eating the same, measly amount of food? Or had Karyn been hoarding away snacks like she had been hiding the premium makeup?

"Dominic thinks part of the reason we're pulling in less business is because of you," Baco said. "I don't know how you're doing it, but you're putting on some LBs, so it's time to go on a diet."

She smirked and shook her head, placed her feet on the dash, and gazed out the passenger window. Dia supposed Karyn knew the pointlessness of debating it further. How could she or any of them ever win an argument when all the man in charge had to do was threaten to beat them or to kill their loved ones back home?

"Pass your trash up to me if you're done eating," Baco said.

Cinnamon slurped the final drops of her shake and burped, a guilty expression on her face as she passed her stuff over. Dia shook her head in mock annoyance and handed their wrappers and empty cup up to Baco.

Interstate 10 stretched before them as they drove east, with silence and the smell of fast food onions hanging heavily inside the X5. Dia churned Baco's comments over in her mind. Did he really believe Karyn's weight gain was to blame for fewer appointments? She laughed a little to herself. Baco heard and made brief eye contact with her in the rearview mirror. Cinnamon had heard it, too, and raised an eyebrow. Dia quietly smiled, then gazed at the passing mile markers outside.

South Padre Island—the scene of their most recent adventure—didn't fill Baco's pockets like previous city stops. It didn't take a rocket scientist to figure out why. Tens of thousands of high school and college kids poured onto the Texas beach every year for six weeks straight beginning in March. Why would dudes pay for sex when they could get it for free from an eager coed? Or *take* it?

Days earlier, Dia lay on a lounge chair under an eight-foot umbrella abandoned by a gaggle of sorority girls from the Midwest. Her T-shirt and flip-flops sat on top of the neighboring chair, along with Karyn's and Cinnamon's towels and shorts. Without any of their normal tension, her coworkers stood waist-deep in the Gulf of Mexico's clear emerald waters, taking turns with a discarded scuba mask and snorkel. That was due in part to Baco's temporary absence. He'd not meant for their trip to become a holiday, but the lack of business had left them with no other choice. They were dropped off at the beach to form "new connections" so he could work the phones back in their one-bedroom condo.

Partiers, vendors, and music stages blanketed the coast from as far north as Dia could see down to where the Rio Grande emptied into the Gulf. Everyone swayed, stumbled, or slept in their own little worlds that hazy Tuesday afternoon, giving the astute observer plenty to gawk at. Perhaps it was the bustling energy of the crowd that made the guy with reddish-blond hair think no one noticed him, or possibly it was his arrogance.

Earlier in the day, Dia heard him bragging to a friend who benched 300 pounds. “Bro, that’s nothing. I gotcha beat at 410!” Then, he’d stood on a closed Igloo cooler doling out ratings on bikini-clad females as they strode past him. “Five! Okay, maybe you're a six,” he’d shouted. Then, to a girl walking solo, he’d said, “And you, my dear…you’re a seven… wait. Nope, you're an eight and a half.” She stopped to chat with him. Thirty minutes later, the guy was partly carrying her away from the beach. *Did she drink too much?* Dia wondered.

Now he was back, deploying near-identical tactics to get girls to stop and talk with him in exchange for free beer. As the latest coed approached the turquoise water, Dia peeked out from under her baseball cap. “I’ll be right back, Jonathan!” she called over her shoulder before wading in, probably to use the ocean as a toilet.

Past her, Dia saw Karyn and Cinnamon taking turns diving into the Gulf and standing on their hands. She then looked back over at Jonathan just in time to see the strawberry-blond with biceps as thick as some men’s legs placing a Bud Light into a koozie and popping the top. He turned left and right, oblivious to Dia watching him. After a quick check of the shore to confirm his newest conquest was still in the water, he dropped a pill into the beer.

What the hell was that? Dia stiffened.

Warnings to always watch one’s drink had been disseminated throughout Cedar Park High School freshman year following a national story on date rape from a college out west. Dia flashed back to the girl from earlier. She could barely walk. Jonathan most definitely had not escorted her to safety. Now he swirled the can, squinting his eyes narrow with his lips pursed.

He’s totally going to drug her. Oh my god! Dia’s heart raced as she fully realized Jonathan's spring break pastime. Why would someone with decent looks resort to using roofies for sex? And how many girls had already been raped by this prick? One question after another played out in her head. Now that she understood, she couldn't just sit there and watch him do it again.

Get up, Dia! She rose from her lounge chair and made her way to where the ocean met the sand. "Hi, there. Care if I sit?" she asked the girl.

"Nope. Not as long as you don't mind the water being a little warm," the girl giggled.

"Listen, I don't have a lot of time, but I think you should know the guy you're flirting with—"

"Jonathan? Isn't he a stud?"

God. "Uh, sure." Dia leaned over. "But I think he put something in your drink."

"No way!" The girl scoffed. "He's sweet. You're just jealous. Maybe you need to work out or something, you know, or wear more makeup."

"No, that's not it," Dia said. "I'm trying to help you! I saw him with a girl earlier. She couldn't even walk. And just now, he dropped a pill in your beer can. He's probably going to wait until *you* can't walk and," she made air quotes, "*help* you back to his room."

"Is that so wrong? I didn't drive from the Upper Peninsula to play board games this week, girlfriend…." Her words trailed off with a laugh, followed by a hiccup.

Dia's head fell forward in defeat. A moment passed between them before she lifted it and looked the girl straight in the eyes. "It's bad if he forces you."

The coed stared back at Dia.

"I promise, you won't like how you feel afterward. Tomorrow, he won't even remember your face, let alone your name. Or what if he kidnaps you and forces you to have sex with hundreds of men a month?" Dia looked at the girl pointedly then, trying to communicate her own terrible existence. *Please tell me you understand.*

Instead, Jonathan's intended victim stood and walked away. When she didn't join him, Jonathan called after her and even pursued her for several feet until the young woman flagged down a police officer on the beach. Jonathan walked back and tried to quickly pack up his Igloo and leave, but the officer was already on his heels. A few minutes later, after an animated conversation, Jonathan the creep was being led away by the officer.

"What's all the commotion?" Karyn asked as she walked over dripping with water.

"Just another guy being a 'dude,'" Dia said.

"Funny," Cinnamon said. "'A guy 'being a dude.' Gonna have to remember that one."

Dia drifted to sleep in the X5, thinking about that day in South Padre. Pushing the memory of Jonathan aside, she remembered the sounds of the ocean and how it felt to float in the water, weightless for just a short while. Before long, she found herself in a world of familiar dreams where darkness stretched across a desert sky, and the moon ascended over lizards, tarantulas, and sand dunes. The celestial body rose bright enough that the rocks and shrubs cast shadows. She spun around in all directions seeking the flower from her previous dreams—red, tall, and singular.

"Walk," someone said.

She turned to find its source but was disappointed. No one was there. Then, she heard it again.

"Take the first step."

Trusting the voice, she put one foot in front of the other and began her long march toward freedom.

TWENTY-ONE

THURSDAY, NOVEMBER 10 – SATURDAY, NOVEMBER 12, 2005

ACCORDING TO KDFW METEOROLOGIST, Hannah Gray, dropping temperatures were headed their way. "Be sure and cover your outdoor faucets, pull out old sheets to place over your plants, and keep your pets inside," she said, staring into the camera lens at her audience with a beauty-queen smile.

"Or leave them outside to die," Dia said for no one's benefit but her own.

"This will be a dry cold front," Hannah continued.

Dia hoped the woman was right. Lower temps were a welcome reprieve following a sticky summer in Southern Louisiana and a hotter-than-usual fall in Dallas, but not if it rained. The thought of another Christmas with Baco depressed her. She didn't need sleet and snow to bring her down further.

Wrapping up her segment, the weathergirl shifted to the topic of the Coats for Kids drive. "And remember, anyone can make a difference this holiday season. If you have winter jackets your children have outgrown at home, then please donate them at any of our seventeen drop-off pantries."

"Thanks, Hannah." Her male co-anchor resumed control of the news program. "And you can find a list of those locations on our website. Coming up, we talk with Dallas police detective, Matthew Bennett, about human trafficking and its proximity to DFW suburbs."

Cinnamon pushed lumps of wilted romaine around her plate. They were meeting customers any moment, and Dia felt a sense of urgency in Hotel ZaZa's lobby restaurant as her colleagues poked at their dinner. She'd finished her steak and side salad during Hannah's dramatic weather report and hoped to catch Detective Bennett's interview in the remaining minutes before their shift started.

"How long do we have to work tonight?" Cinnamon put her head on the table.

"I guess it depends. Why? Are you sick?" Dia placed a hand up to her forehead. "No fever from what I can tell."

Cinnamon shrugged her shoulders in response. Dia had not noticed until now how peaky she looked. Blueish-green circles puffed under her eyes, but another examination of her forehead confirmed her temperature was normal. Maybe their last two months of nonstop hooking were starting to take their toll on the youngster.

"You going to eat your bread?" Karyn asked Cinnamon.

She needs a breadstick like she needs a punch in the head, Dia thought but didn't say.

Seven months of badgering from their pimp had had the opposite effect on Karyn. She now struggled to fit into her clothes more than ever. Karyn's gut protruded over her miniskirt. Dimpled skin revealed itself below her skirt in front and behind her thighs. The last thing she needed was for Dia to pile on after being forced back to work two nights earlier.

Bar patrons filled ZaZa's lounge now, reducing Dia's capacity to hear the TV over the crowd, but Dia could still read the captions that rolled across the bottom of the screen as the KDFW investigative report began.

"We're seeing a rise in prostitution around the entire Metroplex," Detective Bennett explained. "Because of human trafficking, this is no longer limited to just the urban parts of Dallas or Fort Worth. These criminals bring young women and children to work in the sex trade throughout North Texas suburbs against their will. This takes place under our noses, and people need to know the signs to help us stop it."

Dia studied the KDFW infographic as the reporter read aloud. "Two hundred thousand U.S. citizens are at risk of being trafficked within the United States each year."

Two hundred thousand? Dia struggled to wrap her mind around how people in their own country wrote off 200,000 of their own. Did she and her peers factor into Detective Bennett's math? To her knowledge, no one back home was aware of her location or what Baco required of her. Someone in her peripheral vision caught her attention, and she turned as three dudes approached them. They ranged in age from forty to mid-fifties.

"Ladies," one of them said. "Are you our company for the evening?"

The two older men ogled Cinnamon and Dia up and down, devouring them with their eyes, while the third man stood off to the side, eyeing Karyn with an increasingly red face.

"My name's Hal and this here is Alan." Hal had a East Texas drawl. "Behind Alan, here, is our young buddy, Tim." Tim scowled.

"Hi, Hal. I'm Dia, and these are my friends Cinnamon and Karyn."

"Karyn looks *nothing* like her picture," Tim said. "Sorry, guys. I'm not fucking some fat ass. Hell, I'll go to my room and rub it out myself if I have to." Karyn picked at the hem of her skirt as she recoiled from Tim's stinging insult.

"Good grief, Tim. Lighten up," Hal said. "She may be carrying a few extra pounds, but what do people say? 'More cushion for pushin'?'" Tim rolled his eyes as Alan laughed out loud.

Dia smiled nervously.

"Fuck off, Hal." Tim cast a hateful look at the girls, revealing his annoyance with each passing second and putting everyone on edge.

Dia knew there'd be backlash from Baco if Tim walked out, but she didn't want to know what would happen if Tim influenced his two friends to join him. Her stomach tightened at the possibility of a violent response from their boss. "Maybe we can all just have a cocktail." Dia waved toward the patio bar.

"You know what?" Tim said. "Fuck this bullshit. I ain't buying you no drink, no dinner, no nothing, and I sure as hell ain't paying for fatty here to get laid. Let's go, fellas. We can find prettier bitches than these three anywhere. Hell, probably won't even have to pay for it, either."

Dia took a deep breath. "I don't know why you have to be such an ass. We have an arrangement for tonight, and you can't back out. What's your fucking problem, anyway? You sound like a hick, and look at *you.* You're whining that my friend has put on some weight. Did *you* have to add extra holes to your belt to hold up your pants under your huge beer gut?"

Tim eyed Dia with contempt. "No one talks to me like that, you little fuckin' bitch. You're a whore who isn't even worth the hundred dollars you're asking for to open your legs." He peered over to Alan and Hal. "Are we going, or what?"

Dia tightened her grip around a glass she'd depleted of gin and tonic. *A whore, huh?* Her glass went flying out of her hand and knocked Tim in the head before she could stop herself.

"You fuckin' little cunt!" Tim reached for Dia's throat. She darted left and escaped his grasp. He fell into their table then crashed to the floor. ZaZa's lounge went silent as patrons waited for the man to regain his footing.

"All right, you're coming with me," said a man standing

behind Dia. She turned as police officer, Carlos Loba, grabbed her arm.

"Wait a minute! I didn't do anything. This asshole started it."

"Watch your mouth, young lady," the officer told her.

"I want her arrested for assault and battery!" Tim said. Officer Loba ignored him and pulled her out of Tim's reach.

A second officer named Rodriguez stood beside Loba. "You're both under arrest, actually. I'm arresting you for disorderly conduct, sir." Rodriguez cuffed Tim.

"Oh, come on!" Tim said.

Cinnamon and Karyn followed after Dia as she was escorted to a black and white.

"What should we do?" Dia heard Cinnamon ask Karyn, but her reply disappeared in the noise of the crowd as Officer Loba covered Dia's head and ducked her into his patrol car.

What will they try to do? she wondered. *Question me?* She thought about the news report and whether she would finally tell someone about her eighteen-month captivity. *What happens to Cinnamon if I tell them?* The squad car turned on McKinney toward downtown, giving Dia time to contemplate her next move.

"For fuck's sake!" Baco yelled through the phone loud enough to turn heads on her end.

Dia listened to him berate her as she sat inside a Dallas Precinct Police Station. Her pimp had been her one call.

"I should let you sit in jail for a couple of days. It would teach you a few things and make you realize how lucky you have it when you get out. Did you even think for a second about me when you got into this mess? Fuck, no!"

Baco's tirade exhausted her. She zoned out as she watched the arresting cop speak with a man in street clothes. She recognized him as Detective Bennett from the news interview earlier. He looked in her direction as Officer Loba spoke to him.

"I'll do whatever you want, but right now there's a serious-looking policeman coming my way. Unless you want all of your business out there to dry up, stop your bitching and come post bail."

"You little—" Baco's voice cut off as she hung up on him.

Loba and Bennet walked over to her. Detective Bennett was an imposing six foot five. He loomed over Dia, carrying a Dr Pepper in each hand.

"Ma'am, I want to introduce you to Detective Bennett. He'd like to ask you some questions."

"Thank you, Officer Loba." Detective Bennett put one of the sodas down and stuck out his hand to greet her. "Evening. Do you mind if I visit with you for a bit?"

Dia found herself unable to talk. *A few questions. Why?* What made Dallas' human-trafficking expert want to visit with her? *Baco'd better hurry*, Dia thought. As Detective Bennett steered her toward an empty room, Dia decided her best defense strategy was to say as little as possible.

Officer Loba left and shut the door behind him. Detective Bennett eyed her, one eyebrow higher than the other by a slight smidge. He slid one of the Dr Peppers across the desk. "Thirsty?"

"Sure," she replied. *Is he gonna bribe me with a soda?*

"Let's chat for a moment." He pulled a chair up next to her. "Are you from Dallas?"

Dia shook her head.

"Close by, then? Fort Worth?"

She shrugged her shoulders, neither confirming nor denying her hometown location.

"Is this how we're going to do it?"

She stared at her can of Dr Pepper, watching condensation roll down and collect in a ring-shaped puddle.

"You're not in trouble here. We're talking a 500 dollar fine, tops, but I have to ask, is there something else going on I can help you with?"

Dia raised her eyes up to Detective Bennett's. She saw kindness she didn't normally see in the face of men. *But what can this one guy do? Be a superhero? Rescue me from Baco and send me home to my Dad and Susan? How could I go back now, especially with those recent videos he forced us all to make? What happens to Cinnamon if I say anything? Who would take care of her if I spilled my guts?*

"Listen, my girlfriends and I went out for a night of fun. We're fine. I'm fine. End of story."

"You're a little young to be hanging out in a hotel bar, don't you think?" He studied Dia's face, looking for an in to start asking deeper questions, she was sure. Dia held her emotional cards tight, though, and refused to budge.

They sat there for an uncomfortable eternity before Detective Bennett broke his silence. "I guess that's all I have, then, but I tell you what. If for any reason you change your mind and want to talk someday, call me at this number here." He fished a business card out of his pocket, circled his cell phone number with a blue pen, and slid it across the table to her. "Sound good?"

Another business card being slipped into her hand by a well-meaning adult. "Sure," she said, certain freedom would never come. There were more reasons to stay with Baco than to leave at this point. Detective Bennett got up from his seat. He seemed disappointed, but it wasn't her responsibility to feed him information.

"Have a good night," he said before walking out.

A young officer came in a moment later. "You're free to go." Dia rose and followed him through the station and a secured door. They ended up in a small lobby where Baco stood waiting. He was putting his wallet back in his pocket.

"You owe me big time," he said with a sneer.

Dia strode past, ignoring him as she made her way outside. He caught up with her and led her toward his X5 where Karyn and Cinnamon waited anxiously.

"Everything okay?" Karyn asked when she climbed into the SUV.

"Yeah, it's fine," she said.

"Did you have to talk to Tim? Did they take his side?" Cinnamon asked.

"He was a real jerk, Dia. I appreciate you sticking up for me," Karyn said, casting her eyes down.

"It's not a problem."

"You bitches need to finish patting each other on the back. Thanks to Dia, we have to leave town."

Dia flipped Baco off behind his back. It made no difference if they stayed in Dallas or left for Houston or South Padre. Prostitution was prostitution, no matter where they pitched their proverbial tent. The work was nasty and routine —not unlike a lot of dirty jobs—but there was a rhythm to it on some level. *Or maybe I'm just numb by now.*

When they returned back to the hotel, Baco packed in record time. Dia heard him on a call as he moved frantically around, stuffing bags. Dominic must have been on the other end of the line. He grunted his responses in agreement to whatever his uncle told him. When he finally spoke, his hushed tone did not disguise his anger and disappointment.

"I'm not justifying anything!" Baco slumped into a chair, leaned forward, and cradled his head in his free hand as he pressed the phone in his right hand against his ear. Dia recognized the posture of a whipped dog taking a verbal lashing but did not feel sorry for him. *He should do the right thing and shut this all down...let us go.*

"Fine, I'll do what I can," he sighed and ended the call. "Let's go!"

Moments later they were on the road to San Antonio.

Dia woke up in the seedy motel. Baco had left the three of them alone. He'd taken to leaving them for long stretches of time in recent weeks. Karyn had shared how the drives helped him sort through his thoughts, but he might also be out searching and stalking new, young girls to join their so-called family. With an hour or two of privacy before he returned, Dia decided to conduct a little research on Baco's laptop. She booted up the computer and plugged the modem into the phone jack. She was more self-assured since being taken to the Dallas police station. Her mind kept circling back to Detective Bennett. *Why did he think I needed his help?* she wondered. *What tipped him off?*

She pulled up a browser and entered, *Detective Bennett,* into the search bar. She retrieved his business card and typed in his phone number to improve her query. The first result was for "Matthew Bennett, Dallas Police." Several links appeared underneath from various North Texas news outlets. She checked out some of the articles. It seemed the man was determined to end human trafficking in the DFW area. The stories basically made him out to be Dallas' expert on sex slavery. That was a term unknown to Dia until watching that newscast in the Hotel ZaZa bar. One news feature was a profile piece that gave her more information about his background:

Born and raised in Austin, 30-year-old Bennett began his career in Round Rock, Texas. From there, he transferred to Austin and earned a quick promotion to detective. An opportunity to lead a newly formed vice unit in Dallas lured him away from Austin. Now, two years into his new role, he has devoted his life to saving children from pedophiles and other sex predators.

Dia wondered how he fought a crime that lived in the shadows. Pimps and traffickers were like roaches. They were chased out of one place only to resurface in other cities along the U.S. interstate highways. She sighed, curious if she'd missed her best opportunity for escape since her clinic visit a year earlier.

She stared at Detective Bennett's picture a little longer. He was handsome. A swath of lights washed over the room. Suspecting Baco's return, Dia erased her internet search history before powering down, unplugging the modem, and returning to bed.

TWENTY-TWO

THURSDAY, MARCH 16, 2006

KARL PUMPED AWAY AT DIA. It was his fifth visit in as many days, and Cinnamon had teased earlier that the forty-ish john wanted to marry her. Dia now suppressed an urge to smirk over Cinnamon's comment as she lay on her back under the married, middle-aged musician from Lago Vista who had two young children. He had positioned her in such a way that he knelt on his knees before her with her thighs up over his. This was his second-favorite position, and he reminded her of an alpha gorilla with his furry muscular chest and shoulders. *Don't laugh out loud,* she thought.

He'd insisted on candles and olive oil for ambience and "natural" lubrication, and he requested she keep her eyes open for "romance," too. He seemed hellbent on standing apart from every other man she'd ever had, clueless to the fact that she screwed people for a living. The end of the month would mark two years with Baco. Surely the johns she'd serviced outnumbered the bumps in the popcorn texture overhead. It exhausted her to try and even calculate those from the past week. Due to repeat clients, the annual music and film festival, South by Southwest, was proving to be their most profitable event yet.

Transitioning to part two of his appointment, Karl turned her over to assume what he referred to as "rabbit position." Small guttural grunts escaped from him as he worked himself up to his inevitable climatic moment. Dia was grateful for the olive oil he used as the time ticked by on the bedside clock: one minute, two, three... At seven minutes in, she recognized the hastening in his rhythm.

Thirty seconds later, his body blanketed hers. The six-foot-four bassist fell to Dia's mattress and pulled her up beside him as he dropped into a deep sleep. Heat radiated out from him, and Dia waited several seconds before slipping out from his heavy embrace for the bathroom.

Dia chewed her fingernails, sitting on her toilet as the shower water warmed up. Karl's clothes were draped across a small vanity, and she spotted his laminated festival credentials hanging from a lanyard with SXSW printed on it. He played both standing bass and bass guitar with a band called Eddie and the Skyliners, but that meant nothing to her. She'd never heard of them, and Karl seemed more like the office cubicle type—hairy, chubby, and completely ordinary.

After she'd showered inside and out, Dia found Karyn making breakfast in a robustly equipped kitchen. The dining table featured a porcelain cup placed in the center with bluebonnets peeking over the rim. Baco sat in the corner counting cash while Cinnamon sipped coffee laced with heavy whipping cream and sugar.

"How's your boyfriend?" Cinnamon asked.

"Ha-ha," Dia shot her the middle finger and poured herself a mug of dark roast.

"Is he still here?" Baco pulled a .45 Glock from his pants and sat it between piles of grubby, green-colored bills. "You'll need to stir him if he doesn't wake up soon." His gun had become a fixture in their lives since Dallas. Dominic, who still coached his nephew from time to time, had suggested it.

"He's sleeping," Dia answered.

Baco had lined up a house rental in Austin's hippest zip code, 78704, for South by Southwest. It was a vast improvement over their accommodations from previous Austin visits, facilitating easy access for customers and lending credibility to Baco's operation as he worked to position himself as more of an upscale sex service. No more seedy hotels or rural cabins.

Dia reflected on the first house where she'd met Karyn and endured her first night of johns. Her innocence had long vanished, and her life revolved around her pimp and fellow prostitutes. She'd squandered every opportunity to escape to avoid the shame of her secret being discovered by family and friends but to also protect Cinnamon. She was stuck.

Contemplating her old life never made her feel better. It always led her down a road of regret and melancholy only Ecstasy or alcohol could assuage, but still she went there. If she'd never left that fateful night, she and Samantha would be shopping for prom dresses. They'd be preparing for graduation and making plans for college. Samantha. How long had it been since she'd even thought about her one-time best friend? Three months? Six? Two years?

At fifteen, she'd imagined Baco as her one and only. He'd doted on her with flowers, walks along the creek, and make-out sessions. She wanted him as her first and last lover at that point. He was handsome, and he seemed legitimate with his stories of a software sales job.

Baco was edgy and irritable most days now and bore zero resemblance to the guy who he had portrayed himself to be two years ago. His criminal enterprise had even exacted a toll on him: his once boyish features were now hard-chiseled lines. He appeared gaunt and emaciated and cinched his black jeans around his waist with a belt Karyn used to wear. He smoked 24/7 and chased his own demons with bourbon. But what worried Dia more than anything was how Baco, who was becoming increasingly violent, now carried that pistol everywhere.

"Four thousand dollars, ladies. Not bad for two days of work," he said as Karyn set a plate of French toast in front of him. Dia looked up at her quiet German friend who rolled her eyes at Baco's enthusiasm. Softer and fuller than ever, she had to weigh more than she did before Christmas. They didn't own a scale among their scant possessions, but Dia figured her to weigh a solid fifty pounds more than a year ago. If it was her strategy to get out of servicing johns, then it worked. Baco, wanting to avoid customer dissatisfaction and any ensuing conflicts, seldom put her to work these days beyond running errands and cooking for them. Only the occasional request for a curvy Lolita brought her off the bench.

Dia stared at the piles of green bills wondering, *Where does the money go?* Her trance was broken as Karyn set breakfast before her.

"Thanks," Dia offered quietly. She sensed Baco watching her and stole a quick glance at her pimp to catch him staring. She returned her gaze down to her food to avoid engaging with him.

He pulled a handful of Benjamins off one of the stacks and slid them to Dia. "You know what? I think you two deserve a treat for all of your hard work."

"Really?" Cinnamon jumped up out of her seat.

"Yeah, I do." His eyes remained fixed on Dia as if expecting a reaction from her as well.

"What about me?" Karyn asked.

"Shopping? Can we go shopping? Please, please, pretty please?" Cinnamon implored him with her eyes wide open. He turned to his youngest girl with a smile. Browsing for clothes would be a welcome reprieve from the monotony of staying inside.

"Yes. Shopping it is," Baco said.

"Yay! Thank you, thank you, thank you!"

"Can I go too?" Karyn asked again. "I want to go."

"Sorry, K. These girls have worked double-time to make up your volume. It wouldn't be fair."

"Fair?" She threw a plate of eggs intended for Baco who ducked in time for his breakfast to hit the wall. "What's fair about any of this fucking shit?"

Baco placed his hand over his pistol, a gesture not lost on any of them.

"Whatever!" Karyn left them in a flurry, punctuating her exit by slamming her bedroom door.

Lakeline Mall came into view as Dia rounded Pecan Avenue. Baco had given explicit instructions to stay south, but a gnawing curiosity to head north outweighed Dia's fear of repercussions. *Besides, how would he know?* she convinced herself. She turned into the mall's perimeter lane and circled around until she spotted familiar signage for Macy's. She debated if she should go inside. *Would anyone I once knew still work there? Would they remember me—or even recognize me?* She bore little resemblance to her fifteen-year-old self from two years ago.

Cinnamon piped up beside her. "Where are we?"

"The mall where I used to work."

"I thought we were supposed to go to some place called Baron Creek?"

"*Barton*, you forgot the T," Dia corrected.

"Whatever. You know what I mean."

Dia ignored her and looped back to an entrance nearest Regal Cinema. Victoria's Secret and Frederick's of Hollywood both had stores inside. *Do we have to get work clothes, or can we buy teen stuff like jeans or shorts?* she wondered. Baco's X5 dashboard clock read 10:02 AM, and she pondered whether her dad would be at the hospital and Jackson at school. Then she remembered it was spring break.

"Are we going in or not?" Cinnamon asked.

Dia knew she might not secure this opportunity again and put the SUV in reverse. She opted to drive to her father's home and pointed the Bimmer toward Ranch Road 620.

"Wait. Aren't we going shopping?" Cinnamon asked. "Baco's not going to be happy if we come back without anything. Where are we going now?"

"Chill, will ya? You're stressing me out. It's just that I'm gonna head by my dad's house first."

"I hope you know what you're doing." Cinnamon shook her head and looked out the passenger window.

Ten minutes later, Dia studied her house from the community pool parking lot. It appeared vacant. The grass looked dead. *Did they move away or just go away for spring break?* She turned the radio off to focus.

"This is where you grew up? It's beautiful," Cinnamon said.

"Since the middle of eighth grade…I spent my first thirteen years in a different town."

"Are we going inside?"

What if they're home? What if they're not and someone caught us snooping? She opened the driver's side door, pushing all of her considerations aside. "Follow me."

She retrieved a key from above a side entrance to the garage, relieved it was still in its hiding place. They walked through the garage void of vehicles and into the kitchen. Dust coated every surface. The two girls tiptoed their way through the house, poking their heads around corners with caution. After a few minutes, Dia determined not only were they alone, but her family's home had been deserted for some time. Blinds were askew and her former residence reflected an unfamiliar level of dishevelment. At the same time, the living room furniture, all chosen by Susan—modern with grays and turquoises woven through the cushions—sat in position as she remembered it. *Where is everyone?*

Dia made her way to her father's den. Paths of fingerprints interrupted layers of dust across his desk long since covered by additional coats of grime. Half-empty coffee cups displayed spots of diverse levels of mold growing on the surface. What captured Dia's attention most, however, were reams of paper piled in haphazard fashion on the bookcase behind his chair. Dia retrieved one and saw her sophomore class photo when she looked like any other normal fifteen-year-old.

Scores of flyers dotted his office with varying rewards if a tip led to her safe return home. She tried to imagine what her dad must have gone through when he discovered her missing the next day; and if she were considered kidnapped or if her note had provided weak evidence that she was a runaway. His flyer asked only for people to call with information leading to her homecoming. Nothing else on it gave insight into what might have happened to her or whether she was in danger. *How did I miss how much he loved me?* She choked down her emotions not wanting to openly show anything to Cinnamon.

"Wow, you were so different!" she said as she picked up a flyer. "Were you chunky back then?"

"Seriously? You think I was fat?"

Cinnamon shrugged her shoulders. "Maybe not fat, but your cheeks were so round...like little apples. I could just bite into them!"

"Yeah, I suppose I was a little husky compared to what I am now." Dia replaced the paper in her hand to the top of the stack. "Let's go upstairs."

They made their way to Dia's bedroom. Was Cinnamon wondering how someone with a seemingly supportive family got roped into Baco's circle? Nothing in her dad's home suggested a common background to Cinnamon's, not that she deserved to be a prostitute any more than Dia.

Her young friend's upbringing didn't make her an automatic mark for becoming a pimp's property, but drug-addicted parents who couldn't be bothered to raise their own child primed her to become a candidate for the broken-down foster system. Were kids who were unwanted and unloved more susceptible to pimps and traffickers?

If so, then what made me fall for him? Dia wondered. *Being lonely? Needing attention? Sexual curiosity?*

Dia looked around her room. Little had changed; her bed was still made up with its dusty-rose duvet and throw pillows. School books remained stacked on her desk where she'd left them. Her stereo, covered in dust, sat silently in her bedroom corner. She concluded that her father had kept everything in place in hopes of her return. *He isn't so upset that he didn't go away with Susan and Jackson. Or have they gone looking for me?*

A vibration in her pocket indicated an incoming call. She retrieved the flip phone and found Baco's familiar number on its screen. Tension pulled her shoulders together and up toward her neck as she braced for a torrent of yelling. "Hello."

"Hey, Dia, checking in," Baco said.

He never acts this laid back, she thought.

"We've got customers lining up for this afternoon. Are you close to being done?"

Thankful to not be in trouble, Dia recognized she had to leverage this small opportunity with Baco's generosity. "Oh, hey. No problem. We haven't had any luck finding anything, though. Do we have time for one more stop?" She glanced across her room at Cinnamon who stared at her with raised eyebrows.

"Yeah, that's fine. See you in a bit," he said.

She closed her phone shut and returned it to her pocket. "He sounded strange."

"Karyn probably slipped him a nice pill, or maybe he's high on all the money we're making him."

"Funny, I'm sure his mood will change if we don't get moving." Dia took a final look around her room. Lucy sat perched on a shelf where Dia had sat her two years earlier prior to her meetup with Baco. She walked to the doll's perch, took her down, and caressed its braids.

"What is that?"

"A doll someone gave my mom and me before she died." Dia gazed into its painted eyes but did not find comfort as she had so many times growing up. Another image entered her mind—blood, dirt, and darkness.

"What's wrong?" Cinnamon shook Dia out of her trance.

"Nothing, let's get out of here." They made their way of out of her house with Lucy in tow, exiting the same way they had come. As she climbed into the SUV, Dia couldn't shake a heavy feeling of dread inching into her consciousness. It was as if Lucy were trying to tell her something. She stuffed the doll under the front passenger seat and turned her attention to finding a retail shop.

TWENTY-THREE

SUNDAY, JULY 16, 2006

AFTER-CHURCH DINERS PACKED Denny's on I-10 in El Paso. Dia, Karyn, and Cinnamon sat on a bench just inside the exterior doors as Baco checked on their wait time. Over eight hours of driving from Austin had left them cranky and tired, and everyone hoped one solid meal at their favorite diner would recharge them for whatever event brought them to Texas' furthermost western point. Someone had placed a folded *El Paso Times* on a nearby stool, and one headline caught Dia's attention. "Three Girls from Juarez Missing, Another Found Dead." Curious, she picked up the paper and unfolded it to learn more.

The article stated that hundreds of females had disappeared from the Mexico side of El Paso. They were disappearing while at work, shopping, or on their way to school. Authorities had spent years investigating, but no one would say with any certainty why they vanished or who was responsible. Family members demanded answers from police and local government who they believed knew more than they were letting on.

Depleted from three months of nonstop hooking in Austin, Dia contemplated Juarez's lost young women and whether death was the only exit she could hope for from her life. She failed to see any alternative, but she lacked the courage to take any action to end it herself. Even if she *was* brave, she possessed zero means to inflict self-destruction. Baco conservatively parceled out any drugs she took to thwart possibility of an overdose, and his gun rarely if ever left his backside. The barrel rested snuggly above his buttocks.

Their pimp returned from Denny's hostess stand with a scowl on his face. He'd just resumed his spot on their bench between Cinnamon and Dia when his phone rang. "*Bueno,*" he answered.

He proceeded to conduct the discussion as if Spanish were his native tongue. Dia had zero clue of Baco's ability to speak a foreign language and had forgotten most of what she herself had learned. She peered over at Karyn whose own face reflected Dia's surprise.

Only Cinnamon seemed to comprehend what he said. Her face drained of color and her eyes grew into saucers. *What is he saying?* Dia wondered.

"*No problemo.*" He ended his conversation and returned his phone to his pocket.

"Who was that?" Dia asked.

"No one," he said.

"Why does Cinnamon look upset? Were you talking about her on your call?" Dia pressed.

"I said it's not about you. Now fuck off!"

Cinnamon rose from her seat next to Baco and sat on Dia's other side. She glared out at I-10 through the front door glass.

"Hey, come back. There's nothing to worry about," he said, but she remained in her spot.

"What are you doing?" Dia demanded. Clearly, something had been discussed relevant to their youngest family member, and it was bad, gauging from her facial expression. Dia turned back to Baco, tossing her hands up with a shrug as she waited for an answer.

"Networking, if you must know, Dia. It's something businesspeople do, which you're not," he said.

"Is that what we're calling it now? '*Networking*?'" Karyn mimicked from her side of their bench using air quotes.

Baco bristled, but otherwise ignored her. "As I said, businessmen and women network. You have to recognize when it's time to mix things up to grow revenue. We're making some changes. Cinnamon's just overreacting."

Cinnamon turned around abruptly and looked directly into Baco's face. "You're trading me for two skank-ass Mexican girls. I thought you cared about me! I thought you loved me, but you don't. You tell me whatever it takes to keep me working for your sick, perverted, nasty customers, but I'm nothing more than an animal to you."

Baco's business plans explained their proximity to Texas' shared border with Mexico. He had made arrangements to sell off Cinnamon, but why? She was the most sought-after girl in their group. *Why is he trying to break up our family now?* Dia wondered.

Tears dropped onto Cinnamon's legs. Dia choked down her own emotions, stunned by news of her friend's imminent departure. She held her hand. The headline from Sunday's *El Paso Times* ran through Dia's mind: *Will Cinnamon end up like one of those girls?*

Baco continued his efforts to calm Cinnamon, but she knew better. She stood and bolted out the door to escape.

"Cinnamon, stop! Everything's okay," he said, his words trailing after her. She didn't run far before Karyn darted out after her in hot pursuit. She was down at least ten pounds since spring break, and her authoritarianism had reemerged bit by bit with every pound she shed. Dia chased after Karyn to thwart any attempt to bully the girl into submission, knowing hate-filled threats would serve to only further distance her from them.

"You're going to be okay," Karyn said, catching up to Cinnamon and running her hand up and down the girl's back.

"No, I'm not. Nothing good comes out of girls like us going to Mexico."

Dia stepped forward to intervene, but Karyn gave her a face like she had everything under control. Dia sat down next to them on the parking lot curb, a growing tension pulling her shoulders up around her neck.

"None of us like this," Karyn said. "You think I'm thrilled to see you go in exchange for a couple of little brats?" Her attempts at humor were not particularly empathetic, but at least she wasn't being ugly. "Come inside. We'll eat some breakfast, then find a motel and get some sleep. We can ask more about what he's planning then. Okay?"

Dia peeked around to see if Cinnamon was encouraged. She'd wiped tears away from her face and turned to rest her head on the older girl's shoulder. "I want to stay here with you two," she cried softly. Karyn nudged Dia, imploring her to contribute something.

"Honey, we want you to, too," Dia said. "Karyn's right, though. For now, we need to head back. We'll talk more after we eat and sleep. Maybe Baco will change his mind."

Cinnamon lit up slightly. "You think so?"

"We'll have to wait and see," Karyn said. "I don't think we can promise anything, but let's go inside and see how it goes."

What makes Karyn think we can change him now? Nothing they ever said or did influenced him to do something in their interest, but Dia wanted to have faith in Karyn's words. She rose up and followed the two girls into the restaurant's cool, air-conditioned lobby.

Alone in bed, Dia turned restlessly from her stomach to her back between threadbare motel bedsheets that felt as if they were last cleaned at the turn of the century. Light crept in through an interior door that adjoined her room to Baco's. Sleep eluded her as she replayed the morning's events in a repetitive loop in her head. Baco had been somber over breakfast, and Dia struggled to read his emotions. Questions bombarded her mind: *Does he really not care? How could giving Cinnamon away be "just business?"*

Baco wore a blank expression through their morning meal. Tensions ran high as the four of them picked at pancakes, omelets, and hash browns, trying to summon the courage to broach the topic of Cinnamon's imminent departure. No one said a word, though. Baco paid the check, and the three left with him in silence. Cinnamon was now in Baco's adjoining room, and Dia listened as her friend spoke up after a day filled with anxious silence.

Karyn lay in the bed next to Dia's tossing and turning, unable to sleep while Baco and Cinnamon's words filtered through the connecting door. Dia slipped out from between the sheets, positioned the desk chair at the opening, and leaned her head against its cool metal frame to better decipher their mumbling.

"Please," she said. "I haven't done anything wrong. I've done everything you asked. I thought...I thought I was important to you."

Dia ached to console the girl who was like family to her. Yes, their lives were horrible, and there was zero doubt they endured unrelenting humiliation every night, but they had each other. *How will we do without Cinnamon?* she wondered. More importantly, what would life look like for the fifteen-year-old as property of a Mexican gang leader?

"Why don't you push that door open a little bit so we can *both* hear?" Karyn whispered. Dia nudged it slowly, creating a gap wide enough to eavesdrop and catch a glimpse in the other room.

Digital blue light shone on the wall from Baco's laptop,

and his fingers clicked away at the keys. He was trying to placate her, but his sighs increased with the girl's pleading.

"What can I do different?" Cinnamon stood with her hands on her hips. "Do you want me to dress younger? I, I can work harder." She pulled his hand up between her legs. "Do you want more of this?"

Dia shook her head at Cinnamon's suggestions as Karyn squeezed in closer, her facial expression imploring Dia to describe what she saw.

Baco closed his laptop and took a deep breath, "Come here," he told their youngest member. She complied, dutifully sitting next to her *daddy* on his bed. Dia watched him pull his ingénue in a side-arm embrace, patting her head as she laid it on his shoulder.

"Cinn, I'm sorry. My clients—*our clients*—don't want a girl on the verge of being a woman to *dress* like she's twelve. They actually want a middle-school-aged child—younger if possible. Lucky for you, you're extremely pretty…exotic even. These Mexicans appreciate that quality of yours, and they're not only willing to pay me for you, but they're going to throw in a couple of eleven-year-olds as part of our deal. You're taking this way too personally, which disappoints me, and you're honestly starting to irritate me. It's business—plain and simple."

He spoke without a hint of compassion or empathy in his voice. Dia sat dismayed, grieving for Cinnamon...Christina. "Now, if you will excuse me, I need to take a piss," he said.

Karyn reached for Dia's hand. "Should we go in to help?"

Dia wanted to support her, but she didn't want Baco to know they'd been there listening. She hoped their younger colleague would join them back in their room instead. If nothing else, then maybe they could assist her to escape as a sort of last resort.

Cinnamon had moved out of view, sniffling as the bed springs creaked beneath her. Dia listened as she rifled through clothes. Cinnamon's suitcase was in the room with Dia and Karyn, which meant she was going through Baco's luggage. *What is she digging around for in there?* Then Dia caught it, the unmistakable sound of Baco's pistol landing on the table with a loud metallic thud.

"What do you think you're doing?" Baco said when he exited the bathroom. There was a hint of panic in his voice. He seemed to remember the gun was always loaded, and he moved slowly toward Cinnamon.

"Don't get any closer, Baco. I'm not leaving here. You call it *business?* I call it hell." Cinnamon clicked off the safety. "Tell Dominic and your Mexican friends they can all fuck off."

Dia leapt from her chair and barged into Baco's room. "No, Cinnamon, don't!"

Time slowed. Cinnamon pointed her pimp's pistol at her head with tears streaming down her cheeks. She looked at Dia. "Bye, Sister." Without hesitation, she squeezed the trigger and fell into Baco's arms just as he reached her, her blood and brains splattering the walls, headboard, and lampshade.

Cinnamon's body lay half sprawled over Baco. Rivers of red ran down her limbs and collected in a pool on the worn, stained carpet beneath her. Karyn, who'd run in after Dia just as Cinnamon ended her life, started screaming incoherently. Baco knelt under the weight of his favorite prize pony. Time slowed further. Dia's own heartbeat drowned out Karyn's voice. Dia cupped her mouth with her right hand, muffling her own screams as her left hand searched wildly for a wall behind her. Dia narrowly avoided a floor lamp as she fell backward, and a wave of nausea overcame her. She vomited and slipped out of consciousness.

Dia woke to sounds of Karyn yelling in her ear. "Wake up! We have to leave now."

She sat up slowly. Vomit clung to her hair, and the taste lingered on her tongue. Life had not made sense for a long time, but Cinnamon's violent end added a layer of confusion too surreal for her to comprehend. *Did she really just kill herself?* Dia raised her eyes for proof—the blood splatter confirmed what she'd refused to accept.

"We're leaving," Karyn told her. "Get your stuff."

"Where's Cinnamon?"

"The X5."

"But how?"

"I don't have time for questions right now. You have to trust me, Dia. Just get your crap, and let's go."

"And Baco?"

"Waiting for us in the Bimmer," she said.

Karyn marched around the room, giving orders. "Listen, I'll explain when we get in the car. Grab your shit! This place will be crawling with cops soon. GO!"

Dia jumped at her command, and although she wished the police would show up, she followed the bottom bitch's instructions, nevertheless. She packed and was ready to go in less than three minutes. She headed outside. Baco sat unresponsive in the passenger seat, not moving, which explained Karyn's state of hyperactivity. In absence of a leader, she'd stepped up to lead their diminishing ranks.

Karyn walked up alongside Dia and grabbed her duffle bag and backpack. "Cinnamon is laid out in back. Sit behind Baco and keep your eyes forward. You'll only be upset if you look."

Dia climbed into the rear as instructed.

The West Texas night air was dry and hot. Sparsely populated streetlights lent an eerie, dull orange glow as they departed unnoticed from the rundown motel. Dia had no idea where they were going next and struggled to understand what they were to do with Cinnamon's remains as Karyn drove.

"Juarez is west of us," Karyn said.

Juarez? Dia thought, alarmed. That was where gangs disposed of girls and young women like trash.

"I think we can drive there without too much trouble from anyone, least of all El Paso police," Karyn handed a map over her shoulder to Dia.

"What am I supposed to do with this?"

"Hold on to it," Karyn said.

Baco sat comatose and did not protest when Karyn took the cell phone out of his hand. She shook it at his head. "You need to call your contact and tell him we've hit a snag. There won't be a swap."

He reached for the device but dropped it in front of his feet. He bent over robotically to retrieve it. Dia caught her breath. She remembered Lucy was stuffed under the seat and hoped he wouldn't notice the doll. Baco's translucent skin appeared paler than usual. He sat sullenly, hesitant to make the call.

"What will we do with her?" he asked finally.

Karyn stared through the windshield at the road ahead of them. Dia assumed she was considering a thousand different possibilities, including how they were going to return stateside without documentation. She braked at a stoplight and looked back to Dia with an expressionless, calm face. A switch had gone off as if Karyn had waited for this moment all her life.

Dia wished she could summon Karyn's strength, but she only wanted to cry. She turned her attention out her side window where a coyote poked its nose in an overturned trash bin. *He doesn't know how lucky he has it*, she thought.

The light changed to green, and Karyn moved forward. She placed a hand on Baco's arm. "Call your people."

He pressed the necessary buttons. After one or two rings, their day ended much like it had started.

"*Bueno.*"

TWENTY-FOUR

MONDAY, JULY 17, 2006

IMAGES OF CINNAMON'S suicide looped through Dia's head. She remembered the sound of Baco's gun making a metallic thud on the table when she'd barged into the room where Cinnamon uttered her goodbyes. Dia had witnessed all of it but still sat in disbelief as they navigated Mexico's twisted dirt roads in search of a crossing back to their home country.

Their pimp's disregard toward their coworker's mortal remains clouded her mind further. Sometime after 3:00 a.m., Dia had woken up to hear Karyn driving the X5 over gravel. They came to a slow stop outside a gate. She observed a sign written in Spanish overhead and discerned they were entering a ranch of some sort based on the barbed wire and cows standing near a water tank. Moonlight cast a glow bright enough to reveal tumbleweed imprisoned between fences and a house half a mile up. Maybe it was where Baco's contact lived. She looked out the window at the full moon from her dream.

"Stay here," Karyn told her, breaking her reverie as she and Baco exited the SUV.

Dia's two remaining companions approached the house. Someone met them before they had a chance to knock, their faces were shadowed as light poured out from brightly lit rooms inside. She recognized the person as a man only because of his height and square shoulders. He towered over the couple as they stood there talking. Several minutes passed, and they returned to the vehicle followed by a pair of slender-looking boys.

"We need to go. Grab your things!" Karyn opened Dia's passenger door.

"Where are we going?"

The two young strangers jumped into the front seats. They made quick eye contact with her, which sent a chill down her spine. Dia exited quickly and helped get their bags out of the back. Cinnamon's body was all that remained, wrapped in a sheet with a dark patch of color at one end—presumably her head.

She turned to Karyn. "How are we getting back into the States? What's going to happen to Cinnamon?" Tendrils of panic pinched inside Dia's chest, making breathing difficult. *Are they going to leave me here in her place?*

Karyn grabbed her by the arm. "Listen, you've gotta calm down. We're lucky to be leaving here with our lives at this point. Grab your stuff and keep your mouth shut."

Dia heeded her words and followed her to a Toyota Camry with chipped paint that had allowed for the formation of rust. She placed her bags in the trunk and took her spot in the back seat. Exhaustion overcame her, and as the car moved forward, she slumped over and fell asleep.

Familiar sounds of the highway passed beneath them hours later—a contrast to Mexico's rough and pitted gravel roads. Bright and cloudless sunshine poured over her, suggesting late morning. Her legs were cramped from lying in fetal position, and she made an effort to sit up. She stared at the back of the heads in front of her—Karyn was driving. Then she brought her eyes down between the headrests and was surprised to find Baco holding her hand.

Karyn glanced in the rearview mirror. "Hey, sleepyhead," she said with affection. "We're coming up on a town where we might grab some lunch. Hungry?"

Hungry? Sleepyhead? Why is she being so nice? Dia questioned. "Where are we?"

"We just passed Tucson a little while ago, but you were sleeping. We'll stop east of Phoenix."

Dia tried to piece together the last twenty-four hours. A day earlier, she'd attempted to comfort Cinnamon about Baco's plan to trade her for younger girls. The day ended with her friend getting a final say about how her life story would conclude. Her remains were probably distributed among patches of rock and dirt never to be visited by loved ones while her pimp and fellow prostitutes navigated their way through Arizona. *How did we end up here so far from home?*

Exhausted, she lay back down in her seat and turned over to avoid facing the other two. She wanted to die herself, but for now, sleeping and dreaming provided her with her only escape. She was close to drifting off when Baco mentioned Dominic. Too tired and too sad to care, Dia slipped into an abyss of unconsciousness where she temporarily broke free from her grim circumstances.

In her dream, she walked across the desert for miles until her feet blistered. Her bones throbbed from her ankles to her hips. "Focus," someone said. "Keep moving." Dia recognized something familiar in the feminine voice but strained her memory to place it and associate it with a name. She knew it wasn't her mother's, but it belonged to some type of maternal force. A woman draped in fur looked down on her as if from heaven. The figure clutched something against her chest—a doll. Dia abided by her instructions and moved forward, pushing her pain aside.

She woke up as the Camry pulled into a diner parking lot. Her first thought was of Lucy, who she had stuffed under the front seat of Baco's X5 back in Austin during South by Southwest. She hoped she was resting with Cinnamon now, giving her comfort in death.

Eighteen months had passed since Dia had last seen Dominic. Countless men had raped her in that time, and thinking about his lustful gaze creeped her out. She suppressed her feelings and forced a smile in an attempt to hide her apprehension. She didn't want the senior Kastellanos in her head any more than she wanted him between her legs.

They had arrived at his condo after lunch. Baco sat stoically on his uncle's couch with Karyn by his side. Dominic studied them, and his attention narrowed in on Baco who shrunk under the older man's scrutiny.

"You're a worthless piece of shit!" Dominic lunged at his nephew, grabbed him by his hair, and yanked him up to stand face to face.

Baco howled but did nothing to fight his uncle off.

"Cinnamon was the greatest thing you ever had, you stupid dumbass! How fucking incompetent can you be?" Dominic roared into Baco's face, throwing him to the ground. "I've done everything I can to make you successful, and you fuck it up by getting your highest-earning girl to kill herself. For fuck's sake!" The man landed multiple kicks in Baco's stomach, groin, and legs.

"Stop!" Karyn tried to pull Dominic away from another potentially fatal scene.

He threw her down next to Baco and delivered three kicks in her back before backing away. He loomed over them both but restrained from any further assault. He walked away slowly, breathing hard as he wiped beads of sweat from his brow. "Leave," he said. "Get out of my sight!" He dropped onto the couch.

The pair rose cautiously. Karyn reached over to the end table and grabbed the car keys and her purse. They moved quickly to the door and left without another word.

Dia stared after them. *Should I follow?*

"Guess it's just us. Thirsty?"

Shit. "Sure." She hated being alone with Dominic.

He went to the kitchen and returned with a carton of orange juice, two glasses, and a fifth of Absolut. "You've been through a lot, young lady. How are you holding up?"

"It is what it is." She knew he didn't care one way or another about Cinnamon. She'd been nothing but a commodity to him—just like Dia. *And how many more?* She assumed his nephew wasn't his only pimp.

Dominic mixed the vodka and OJ at the dining table. "'It is what it is.' You speak sage words of wisdom." He offered her the cocktail, and she took it. "Cheers," he said. He held his tumbler up to hers and clinked it. Something about how he looked at her made her think the blows he inflicted on the other two would not happen to her. *Right? I mean, I haven't done anything to piss him off.*

Dia gulped her drink down, somewhat out of thirst, but more to anesthetize herself against whatever might come next. She returned her glass to the table.

"Another? Or would you like something else?" He withdrew a small plastic baggie from his shirt pocket. She stared at the Ecstasy tablets, doubtful of their ability to improve her mood. She raised her eyes and tried to determine his age. He struck her as too young to be someone's uncle, yet that's who he was to Baco. He appeared younger than forty, but she had a vague recollection of him being older than that. A thick patch of jet-black hair—almost blue like his nephew's—topped his crown, but any resemblance ended there. He lacked symmetrical beauty. His face bore roundish, uneven features, and his left eye sat higher and more pronounced than his right. A day's stubble covered his jaw.

"Here, take one. Take two, actually," he said, smiling. "You'll feel better; I promise." He tapped two pills into his hand and poured a splash of orange juice over her alcohol-infused ice. Dia popped both tablets in her mouth and returned her empty glass once more. "Good girl." Without asking, Dominic refilled it with vodka. "You're not very talkative."

"It's been a rough couple of days. What do you expect?" The booze quickly absorbed into her bloodstream. Its chemical magic washed over her brain, reducing her inhibitions, and gave her courage to engage in conversation. She studied her captor's face which was puffy from too much partying or unhealthy food. "Is this what you do?"

"Is *what,* what I do?"

"Travel around, stealing girls from their families and making them be prostitutes."

Dominic stared at her from across his table. "I don't steal young women from their people. They come willingly, just like you."

"Is that what you think?"

"You're upset, girl. You've lost one of your own, but attacking me won't bring her back."

Dia rolled her eyes as she sat in her seat. "Fuck you."

Dominic rose from his seat and squatted beside her. He turned her chair until she faced him.

"What?" she asked.

"I don't give two fucks about your feelings, little girl. I give even less fucks about your friend's death. You girls are a dime a dozen, as replaceable as shoes or jeans. You're shit—a whore and nothing more—so let me make it perfectly clear. You *do not* talk to me like that. Understand?"

Dia stared straight at him. He wanted to scare her, but she

resisted his intimidation. She was tired of feeling afraid. A knock at the front door interrupted his speech.

"You have company," he said softly. "They'll remind you of your place."

He left to greet his guests and yelled back. "Mix some drinks. Your customers will want to hydrate before they take their turns with you."

She cringed but followed his orders, mixing a third drink for herself as her X started kicking in. If he required her to work, then she would do what she had to do to numb out.

Three men walked in past Dominic and gathered in the kitchen on either side of her. "Dia, meet my friends, Jack, Raymond, and Calvin."

Calvin was uglier than any man she'd ever met. Half of his face appeared melted, and his scalp was bald above his left ear. Calvin and his buddies leered at her. Soon, her molly-induced fog would take over, and she would have no memory of entertaining this ensemble of middle-aged losers. They stood there, evaluating her like cattle.

"Dom, where'd you find this one? Her tits are amazing." Calvin grazed his hands down from her neck to her breasts and waist until they rested at her T-shirt hem. "Let me help you out of this."

Calvin pulled Dia's shirt up over her head and tossed it behind his head. Braless, she stood there as he ogled her chest.

"Don't stop there. Let's see what's going on below," Jack coached.

"Oh! My bad," Calvin said. He proceeded to pull her shorts down, exposing her fully. "Spread your legs, darling."

She moved her feet out and turned her eyes up toward the ceiling.

"Now, Dia," Dominic said. "You need to look our friends in their faces. Be professional like I taught you and show these gentlemen a good time."

She adjusted her gaze obsequiously to stare into Calvin's

ugly, burnt face as he drove his fingers inside her. The gesture made her squirm in discomfort, but none of them noticed anything about her other than her anatomy.

"Take them to the master bedroom. I'll bring everyone's drinks," Dominic said.

Accepting her reality, she led all three back for what would most certainly be a long night of work.

TWENTY-FIVE

TUESDAY, JULY 18–SUNDAY, JULY 23, 2006

KARYN AND BACO sat on Dominic's couch fondling and kissing each other as Dia made her way past them to a recliner. She had no memory of them returning to the condo. Their interaction was not as pimp and prostitute. It was as if a romance bubble had enveloped them. Meanwhile, Dia ached all over. Her head throbbed where the aspirin had not yet managed to penetrate.

"Rough night?" Dominic glared at her with a sardonic grin from his kitchen archway. He had a cigar in one hand and a cell in his other. His question disrupted the lovebirds, who paused for a moment to consider their peer. Something had shifted between them over the past twenty-four hours. Baco didn't look like the man who'd skulked out of his uncle's condo. In fact, he bore a close resemblance to the man Dia thought she'd fallen in love with more than two years earlier. His face appeared softer and kinder. If only she could return to her former self, too.

Desolation engulfed her. Her colleagues-turned-lovers resumed flirting as Dominic took a call on his cell. She closed her eyes, desperate for sleep, when she caught a familiar tone in Dominic's voice as he spoke. His forced laughter filled the room and grated her nerves.

"You bet she is, my friend, and I'm sure she'd welcome your company." He glanced over to where Dia sat as she lifted her gaze to his. *What did I ever do to him?* she wondered, fearing her potential fate was tied to the person at the other end of the line.

"Patrick, you're my best customer. There is nothing I wouldn't do for you. Of course, we'll be there Saturday night. I'll contact you tomorrow to lock in details." He placed the phone in his pocket, and turned his head toward Baco and Karyn, who remained in each other's arms oblivious to what had just transpired.

"Baco!"

"Yes, Uncle." Gray sullenness returned to his face and dulled his eyes.

"Your chance at redemption is here."

"What do you mean?" Baco gave Karyn's hand a slight squeeze as Dominic shook his head in exasperation.

"How can you be so fucking dumb?" Dominic charged across the living room and grabbed his nephew by the throat. "Get off my couch! You need to pull your head out of your ass before I cut you up into a million pieces and ship you to your mom in a box. Oh! And this cunt next to you? She isn't your girlfriend, and you're not allowed to fuck her for free anymore. Pick yourself up and return to doing your goddamn job! Don't let what's happened be some excuse to fall apart. You've got an appointment tomorrow with Patrick. He's with his team at some mid-year sales meeting and looking for company. Line it up. I'm warning you...do not screw this up."

Dia closed her eyes, glad Dominic directed his attention to someone other than her. Then she thought about Align Orthopedics' number-one guy and the pain he might inflict on her again. She tried to remember what had set him off last time in hopes of doing something to avoid it this time but failed to recall with any certainty what she'd said or done to trigger his attack. Her headache subsided as she eased into the recliner, turning herself over to sleep and a familiar dream.

"Focus," a woman's voice encouraged. "Keep walking."

On Saturday, Baco chauffeured Dia and Karyn to a Phoenix resort and spa. Black flags with white lettering competed for attention among royal palm trees draped in Christmas lights. The pennants were evenly spaced every fifty feet and corporate signage grew more concentrated as they approached the resort portico. The professional branding of Patrick's company in this upscale hotel belied what awaited the two women.

"Good afternoon, sir. Checking in?" a valet asked Baco.

"No, thank you. Just here for lunch."

"Very well. Here's your parking ticket."

Baco took the paper receipt in exchange for a twenty and handed it to Karyn. "Let's split up. I'll investigate things out poolside. You two go check out their lounge."

Curious stares followed Dia and Karyn as they descended a tall marble staircase into a crowded bar where throngs of guests sported lanyards promoting Patrick's company.

The Align Orthopedics workforce consisted mostly of men —many of them casting familiar looks of inquiry their way. The few female employees, however, glared at them. Karyn remained oblivious to their judgement.

Unlike their visit to Jacksonville, events surrounding and including Cinnamon's death precluded a shopping spree that might have allowed them to dress more appropriately. Dia was in cutoff jeans and Karyn in a miniskirt. They took their seats at the bar and stuck out like sore thumbs next to the business-women dressed in Ann Taylor power suits and J. Crew slacks with color-coordinated blouses.

Four such women stood in proximity to Dia and Karyn.

Louis Vuitton, Hermes, and Christian La Boutin adorned their shoulders, ankles, and feet. Two middle-aged men accompanied them as they gossiped about their day at the meeting. One asked for drink orders as the others bellyached over how unappreciated they were.

"Rum and Coke," a guy with salt-and-pepper hair said.

"Vodka martinis for us ladies," said a petite brunette with masses of curls held away from her face with a barrette. Her female colleagues laughed out loud. It was only a little past noon, and already their crew seemed half lit.

"Make those extra dirty," one of them added in a heavy Southern accent.

"Well, all I'm saying is it would be a pleasant surprise if just once they could recognize our team and what we do to help them," the salt-and-pepper gentleman said. "How many of these guys hit their quota because of me meeting them in their territory every week?"

"Now, Lorenzo, be nice," one of the ladies said. "We work for one of the best companies out there." Her Southern accent varied slightly from her dirty martini peer's.

Their colleague returned with a round of drinks, including gin and tonic for himself with extra lime. "Carol Ann," a man with a pronounced New Jersey accent said, "Lorenzo is right. The reps only use us."

"Hey, at least our CEO is doing what he can to make our company more inclusive of women." A tall blonde from the back of their group rolled her eyes. Her name tag said "Jessika."

"Take your complaints to that guy!" The curly brunette tipped her head toward the glass doors opening from outside. Everyone turned to watch Patrick walking in. The words, "Hooray for Boobies" were printed across the chest of his T-shirt. Men surrounded him in assorted tanks and golf shirts, and laughter erupted from one of Patrick's more senior team members. Dia remembered the guy as Larry.

“What a tool.” Jessika drank from her refreshed martini.

Dia pivoted away from the action, not yet ready to face someone who craved her with stalker-like zeal.

“Lorenzo, how do you stand working with that jerk?” Lorenzo’s New Jersey pal asked.

“Fortunately, I don’t, really. He’s never in my territory when I’m there with his salespeople, and his reps—despite some of the rumors we’ve heard—are fairly decent to work with,” Lorenzo said.

“Even Larry?” Carol Ann asked.

Lorenzo nodded as he nursed his rum and Coke. Discussion of Patrick had brought the group’s lamenting about their jobs to a halt.

Dia was wondering how long they’d have to hang out when Karyn nudged her.

“Looks like we may have competition,” she said. Two Asian women sauntered up to order drinks. They eyed Dia and Karyn as they approached. One wore a tight, eggplant-colored satin dress that clung to her ribs and hip bones, accentuating her extreme thinness. Her friend—taller by six inches and thicker in her middle—donned a bright yellow kimono. The hem stopped just south of her buttocks. Dueling emerald and scarlet dragons encircled the torso of the garment. A mane of ebony hair hung over her left shoulder. The shorter, anorexic woman, who couldn’t have been much older than Karyn, asked for a Woodford Reserve bourbon and French 75. They glared at Dia and Karyn with palpable hostility as they waited for their specialty cocktails.

“What are you staring at, bitch?” Karyn finally asked.

“My name’s not ‘bitch,’ it’s Angie, and I see two girls here who don’t belong,” the petite woman said. “You think you can come to our territory without permission? We *own* this place and don’t need white-trash sluts like you bringing your low-class taste here. When did you last shower? You smell like oyster sauce.”

The audacity of these two women to bully them for being prostitutes left Dia dumbstruck.

"Who are you calling 'slut,' you whore? Besides, we're not here to take 'your business.'" Karyn made air quotes. "We're meeting up with friends, fuck you very much."

"Honey," Angie's twin-dragon friend chimed in. "We got this. Run along before you hurt yourselves. I'd hate if something happened to you." She advanced on both of them, close enough for Dia to see amber-colored jewels were sewn in as dragon eyes on her kimono. She towered in stilettos over her German counterpart, but Karyn outweighed her by at least thirty-five pounds.

Does she really think she can take Karyn? Dia feared that no advantage in girth would matter if they got into a street fight at this fancy resort.

Karyn must have read her mind; she grabbed Dia's hand protectively. "Let's go."

"What's your rate?" Someone asked once they reached the valet stand.

Dia spun around and saw a man who looked fresh out of college, but she chose not to respond to him.

The twenty-something male sneered at her. "I'm talking to you. What do you charge, ho?"

Karyn took Dia's hand one more time and led her to a parking attendant. The young man followed them. "Tell me what you charge, bitch."

"Two hundred dollars," Karyn said.

"You're kidding, right? Shit! She should pay me two hundred."

Karyn was losing patience and asked a valet to hail a cab instead of waiting for Baco.

The guy continued to pester them. "What are you gonna do for those two Benjamins? Huh? Think I can get the two of you for that—for the *night*?"

Dia rolled her eyes. She was finding it difficult to hold her tongue and was about to respond when a lumbering middle-aged man stepped forward and yelled, "Daniel, knock it off! Let's go. Time for golf."

"Your loss, ladies. But, hey, maybe I'll touch base with you later." He left with a wink.

"*Gute Trauer,*" Karyn muttered under her breath as Daniel walked away and joined his friend.

Dia raised her eyebrows.

"That means 'good grief.'"

Disco music poured onto east High Street from Blue Martini Lounge. It was too soon for a crowd to form or for dancing. But it wasn't too early to grab a drink before their evening with Patrick got underway. Though still dressed in a miniskirt and cutoffs, Karyn and Dia were now dolled up with fresh makeup and salon-styled hair. Their adult appearance—along with Karyn's flirty demeanor—netted them two cosmopolitans as they waited for Baco. Dia stared at her cranberry vodka elixir for a moment then slammed it down.

"Ready for another?" The bartender smiled at Dia. She nodded and adjusted her shorts as she crossed and recrossed her legs on the barstool.

"It's going to be okay," Karyn said.

"Yeah? What makes you so positive?"

Karyn sipped at her first cocktail as Dia received her second. "I guess I don't know for certain, but I can't believe he'll hurt you. It may have been just a heat-of-the-moment accident that time. I'm sure he didn't mean it."

Dia thought back to their night in Jacksonville and stretched her jaw wide, remembering the velocity of Patrick's fist as it smashed into her. Everything blurred after that. Doubtful the successful businessman had calmed down in the eighteen months since their last meeting, she grabbed her drink and drank it as quickly as her first, hoping being numb would provide her with a strategy for managing the narcissist and his malicious demands.

The man of the hour swung the double doors wide to his suite. He still wore his "Hooray for Boobies" T-shirt, as did most of his guys. Dia reflected on what the woman named Jessika had said earlier about how inclusionary the Align company was. *How can he wear something like that?*

"Ladies, welcome to Phoenix. Come on in." Her biggest fan gestured with his arms to steer them to his living room. Karyn flashed her best smile, grabbed Dia's hand, and strutted her stuff in front of the whole team. Dia prayed a silent mantra to herself: *Let it all be over soon.*

"My favorite private dancer!" Larry tripped over a coffee table as he stumbled on his way to Dia. "I've got a gift for you," he laughed.

"No one wants to see you naked, Larry," one guy said.

"No really, I do have a present. Here!" He squelched a burp as he placed Dia's hand between his legs. It smelled as if he was already drunk on whiskey and Coke.

"You shouldn't have," she said.

The man didn't notice her sarcasm. He plopped into an oversized chair and pulled her with him.

One by one, members of Patrick's team took a turn with Karyn and Dia. Patrick watched his party festivities from a barstool as he nursed his scotch. The two women put up award-worthy performances, acting like willing participants in the scores of poses his guys positioned them in—on their knees being suggested more than any other.

Dia choked down what they gave her along with her pride, avoiding eye contact with the man who'd lay down her most punishing treatment whenever his turn came around. Sound waves reverberated in Dia's ears from a clock hidden somewhere in the suite. She counted as the chimes ticked to twelve.

"Gentlemen, I hope you'll excuse me, but it's time I got a shot now." Patrick retrieved Dia on the twelfth and final chime. A cry of disappointment ran out among his team.

"Let's track down those Asian bitches we saw poolside today," Larry said.

"You can do whatever you like. Karyn's here to keep you company. You," Patrick said, pointing at Dia. "Come with me."

"Boss man likes the blonde," some dude next to Larry said.

"I think he has a crush," someone else said.

Patrick ignored them as Dia rose and followed him to a room down a long corridor with wallpaper that had a snake-skin print. "Let's take a shower."

She thought about how johns expected unadulterated enthusiasm and receptivity from their escorts when it came to their sexual desires. Most wanted to have straight sex, but there were occasional requests for something more—for romance. Either way, the amorous encounters always ended with identical results to the straightforward, sex-for-money appointments.

"Take those clothes off," he said. Steam filled the bathroom. Through the lens of her brief history as a prostitute, she perceived his bathing request more like a build up to one of his spiteful games than the fulfillment of some fantasy.

Dominic's number-one customer undressed, revealing defined muscles and a golden tan. Naked, he reached for Dia's hand once more and led her into the terrazzo-tiled shower with its dual rain sprinkler heads. He placed her under a stream of gently flowing water and washed off all traces of the other men who'd been inside her that night. "I want to shave you," he said.

"Excuse me?" Fear filled her stomach.

"Come, sit. I want to shave your pussy." He escorted her to

a stone bench and retrieved a razor from an overhead rack. "Spread your legs."

She yielded to his request, afraid to deny him as he lathered up lavender and eucalyptus soap.

"I really like you, you know? You're different from other girls, and I can't quite put my finger on it," he said as he navigated the blade around her genitals. "It's like you have this depth. You don't say much, which I like, but I can sense it."

Dia listened to him, waiting for him to flip a switch like last time, but still hopeful this time would be different.

"Bend over so I can shave your butthole. Here, stand up with your hands against this wall here and spread your legs. Now, stick your ass out to me a bit."

He slathered soap up her bum and continued his task of shaving. She did not know what he was up to other than wanting to further humiliate her and reinforce her lack of will. Dia heard him replace the razor overhead and return with more bath wash. He used it all over her body, paying particular attention on her bottom. It didn't take long to figure out why as his penis brushed up against her legs. Patrick penetrated her anally, causing her to jolt.

"No, no... You're fine. Stay right there."

Please let this be over soon, she thought. She closed her eyes as he pumped away at her. He started to spank her, making her jump with every strike.Patrick grew excited with each smack he landed on her wet skin. *Is he working himself up to more?* she feared. Tears rolled down her face, washed away by the shower.

"To my sink," he said aggressively. "I want you to look at me as I'm fucking you." He walked her past the glass door of the shower and then yanked her across to the above-counter sinks that were installed in front of six-foot framed mirrors. Dia braced herself against his vanity and Patrick reinserted himself as water gathered in a puddle at their feet.

"Open your eyes!"

She hesitated, and he spanked her hard.

"Now!" His boyish, handsome features mutated with rage into a face now etched with harsh lines. His eyes bored into hers. "Come, you little slut. Come all over me and I'll know you like me."

She couldn't do that, though. She'd never been able to enjoy sex under these circumstances, not since her first time with Baco.

"What's your problem?" he asked.

Dia narrowed her eyes. Dominic's ugly refrain of *you're a whore and nothing more* flitted through her mind, but she was more than what he defined her as. A vision into a different identity took root as she stood there watching Patrick. *I'm not a whore*, she thought to herself.

"What did you say?"

"Go to hell," she said.

He smacked Dia's head, and his palm landed on her ear. She tried to cover it to blunt more blows. Her momentary flash of defiance vanished. *Why does he do this? I did everything he asked me to do. Why does he want to break me?*

Patrick hit her again, which titillated him even more. He pressed her down to the vanity countertop, thwarting her ability to catch a full breath.

This is how I'm going to die. "Please," she cried quietly, but he ignored her. She wasn't human to him. He rained a cascade of slaps and punches at her head, her back, and her bottom. When she thought it couldn't get worse, Patrick's hands encircled her neck.

"Look at me!" he said through clenched teeth.

Dia raised her gaze up into a mirror to make eye contact. Tears rolled down her cheeks.

"I fucking hate you. I resent all of you worthless pieces of shit, but I despise you most of all! You don't know me, so take that judgmental expression off your face!" He pressed his fingers tightly around her throat as he arched toward his climax.

Breathing became impossible as her vision narrowed in on her rapist-turned-murderer's face. He faded away into a dot at the end of a long tunnel until everything went dark.

TWENTY-SIX

SUNDAY, JULY 23, 2006

"COME GET YOUR BITCH," Patrick said.

Those were the last words Dia had heard as she lay on the floor. She drifted in and out as her pimp and fellow prostitute dressed and wrapped her in a blanket and carried her from Patrick's suite. After what seemed an eternity, they scurried under a hotel exit sign into cool desert air. An unknown amount of time passed before she came to again, and she caught a glimpse of road signs.

"For Christ's sake!" Karyn said. "You have to say something. He can't get away with this. He's practically killed her."

"What do you suggest I do, exactly? Call Phoenix police? Tell them some rich, punk-ass john murdered my hooker? Then what? Tell them, 'Oh, by the way, you might find her in some database for missing children?'"

So, he admits it? Dia slipped in and out of consciousness as the Camry jostled her in the back. Breathing proved difficult and pinpointing why eluded her. She ached over every square inch of her body from her eyes to her toes. She had no way of knowing how much additional damage Patrick had inflicted on her while she lay on his floor unconscious. Pain penetrated her from each angle and sleep provided her only escape.

Though less than two feet away in the front seat, their voices reached her from miles away as snippets of anxious dialogue flew back and forth between Baco and Karyn.

"What if we go to a nearby hospital?"

"How is that different from calling the police?" Karyn asked.

"We'll just drop her off. Look at her, for Christ's sake. What if she's dying?" he asked.

"Someone will see us."

"This car's from Mexico. They can't trace it."

"Don't be naïve," Karyn said. "If we dump her off, and she dies, all they have to do is go to surveillance footage to see who brought her in. Then they'll put out an APB or whatever they call it."

Interstate lights whizzed by as Baco drove the Camry. Eastbound I-10 signs, blurry through Dia's swollen eyes, revealed prospects of a return trip to Texas. She hoped she'd make it that long. The two upfront seemed paralyzed by fear and indecision, unable or unmotivated to assist her.

She found it difficult to reconcile that this was how she was going to die—anonymously—a result of one fateful decision to escape with her boyfriend for a beach vacation more than two years ago. Dia began playing her what-if game for the umpteenth time, but only for a second. Something leaked from her body and spread from between her legs. She peed involuntarily; warm fluid turned cold in the car's air-conditioned interior.

"What's that smell?" Baco asked.

Karyn checked back on her. "What's wrong with you?"

Dia cracked one eye open, unable to speak.

"Oh, good lord."

"What?"

"I think she pissed herself," Karyn said.

Panic returned to Baco's voice. "We need to *do* something...this isn't right."

Karyn pivoted back in her seat and sat silently as Dia closed her eyes. Discomfort radiated from within her in ways she didn't know possible. Sharp pain pierced intermittently like a stabbing knife while low rumbling aches throbbed nonstop up and down her spine and abdomen. She could not determine which was worse because the swelling around her neck and throat distracted her more. Purple bruises emerged like patchwork across her arms and legs, but she feared something ailed her internally, which had caused her to uncontrollably wet herself. Karyn acted disgusted, but Dia didn't care at that point. She ached when moving, and she hurt lying still. She labored to breathe. Finally, she yielded to sleep's heavy lure as it pulled her beneath reality's surface.

Gravel crunched under the Camry's weight as Baco slowed to a halt. She struggled to open her eyes. *How long have I been asleep?* Her heartbeat raced as she tried to reposition her body. Unable to command it, she gave up and fell deeper into her seat. Her companions seemed oddly quiet, then she realized only one of them was still with her. She recognized Karyn's outline through the slits of swollen eyes. Outside and leaning against the passenger window, Baco stood with his cell phone next to his ear.

Music played from the radio, making it difficult to discern what he was saying. *Is he talking to Dominic?* she wondered. The younger Kastellanos so completely lacked the ability to decide anything for himself. He would never be a leader.

Karyn turned back to look at her. "Still alive?"

Dia struggled to speak; her voice caught in her throat.

"I'm gonna tell you something," Karyn continued. "I've prayed for this so many times. I've wished for you to just *disappear*. I've hated you from your very first moment with us because you've always been his favorite, even over Cinnamon, and I didn't understand why. There is absolutely nothing extraordinary about you, but I can tell by what he *doesn't say* or *do* that he loves you, and I *resent* you for that. I am supposed to be his special girl—not you."

Any compassion her fellow prostitute had exhibited earlier had vanished as she spoke. Karyn adjusted in her seat and Dia strained to keep her eyes on Baco's first girl who she'd thought had become her friend.

"You may think you're unique, but from what I can tell, you're also close to being dead. I hope you *do* die because then I'll have what I've wanted more than anything all along. I'll have Baco. I will win, and you will lose." She whipped back around to face forward.

Dia wanted to respond, to argue back and maybe punch the bitch's face. She yearned to have the last word and to tell the woman to go fuck herself, but her words sat pinched in her throat, unable to escape. She turned in her seat to relieve pressure on her back, her hand landed upon an open bag she recognized as Baco's computer satchel. *What if?* Dia lowered her hand inside in search of aid—a solution not unlike the one Cinnamon had deployed. But instead of a gun, her hand settled upon something familiar—her doll, Lucy. He must have discovered it, but it was a mystery why he kept it rather than throwing it away.

As Baco opened the driver door and slipped behind the wheel, Karyn gave him an insincere smile. "So, what did he say?"

"Mountains."

"Sorry?"

"He said to keep on I-10 'til we reach signs for the Gila Mountain range near Silver City. We're to find a spot to bury her somewhere away from traffic, up past a tree line."

"She's not dead yet," Karyn said.

"She will be before long," Baco said as he turned the key in the ignition and pulled the car onto I-10 heading east.

Dead? Just like that? She'd wanted death to take her so many times, but its imminent arrival now frightened her. She brought Lucy up to her face, desperate for answers, eager to live. In all her time with him, Dia had done nothing but try to obey and be nice in exchange for a chance to go home one day, to be free. As she lay there, it began to dawn on her that her deference to others had only led to greater and viler mistreatment by her captors.

Dia looked into Lucy's eyes and remembered how she'd once believed the doll had special powers, how she thought it spoke to her. "Tell me what to do, my little friend." She closed her eyes as images of desert flowers, lizards, and caves—memories from long-forgotten dreams—filled her mind. She grappled to make sense of them as a voice whispered a familiar word to her: *Walk*.

Baco drove the Camry past mileage signs for Silver City until they reached the final mile marker that informed him to turn left off I-10. The only sound from inside the vehicle came from Dia as she struggled to breathe. She pulled herself out of unconsciousness as Baco wound the Toyota up mountainous roads. She forced her eyes open to take in their surroundings, but her efforts were futile. Darkness engulfed the car from both sides. She closed her eyes and stuck her hand back into Baco's satchel...an act of defiance forming in her once subservient mind as cold metal warmed to her touch.

Where are we now? she mused, trying to determine how much time had passed since exiting off I-10, but she was too tired to engage her body, let alone her brain, as the car slowed for one hairpin turn after another.

A change in temperature stirred Dia awake and she realized Baco and Karyn were removing her from the rear seat. Baco carried her torso and head while Karyn held her legs at the knees. They moved in sync, using the dim headlights to guide them. Dia attempted to speak. She tried to move and resist their efforts, but the only energy she was capable of exerting was peeking at her environment through swollen eyes.

She slipped back into darkness, then came to again as cold earth penetrated her from below. She focused her remaining life force on raising her eyelids and determined they'd placed her in a hole of some sort, long enough and sufficiently deep to bury her, she realized, but not so deep as to preclude her from seeing her surroundings. She observed forest growth beyond the hole's edge and connected with a set of glowing orbs at a tree line separating mountain from road some thirty feet away. She stared into yellow circles, immobilized by her condition, and paralyzed with fear—fear of dying—fear of her remains being torn apart by whatever wildlife lurked at this forest's perimeter. Then she felt it—a sprinkling of dirt as Baco and Karyn began to shovel earth onto Dia's final resting spot.

"Is she dead? Check her pulse."

Baco laid two fingers on her neck and withdrew them slowly. "No, not yet."

"We can't bury her alive."

He knelt there next to Dia seemingly unsure how to respond. Moments passed and Baco ran his hand over her hair, lingering alongside her cheek. Then he placed a hand over the bottom half of her face. She wanted to resist and yield simultaneously. She lifted her right eyelid and inspected his face.

"What's that in her hands?" Karyn asked, standing behind him.

"What are you talking about?" He scanned Dia's body and his eyes returned to meet her gaze. With a final thrust of will she pulled the trigger on the gun she'd found in his bag and hid in the waistband of her cutoffs. The recoil lent brief light as he tried covering her nose and mouth with more force until only silence and darkness remained.

Dia, unable to exhale her last breath, chased a lingering thought into eternity.

"One more mile," a voice stated calmly.

Is this real? A flash of red obscured her path, then vanished. *Where to go, where to turn?* From the rim of a desert valley, she spotted a hut. She moved toward it and knocked.

"What are you waiting for?" someone asked. *"You've come so far. It's time."* Arms opened wide to embrace her at the hut's threshold.

"*Mom?*" A long-forgotten caress went down her head, smoothing her hair. *"You're home now,"* the person said.

This isn't Mom's voice, but it's familiar.... Darkness closed in once more, followed by complete and total nothingness.

Paws covered in ash-gray fur emerged from forest brush. With mild trepidation, a wolf lowered its muzzle to a shallow grave and contemplated its next move. The girl's companions were gone and unlikely to return since they'd driven away, distancing themselves from their final act of violence. Affirming its solitude, the animal stared down an empty mountain road.

Dirt stirred amid her paws, eventually gaining momentum, and growing into a dust devil that swirled around her canine form. Then, as quickly as it started, the sediment settled back to the earth. Aged boots replaced the creature's feet. Frayed leather covered the tops of her toes and heels atop dirty wooden soles. Perhaps black at one time, her now-faded gray boots moved toward the shallow grave and stopped by its side. Kneeling, La Loba inhaled deeply before mightily blowing away the loose dirt and exposing Dia's mortal remains.

PART THREE

"A woman's psyche may have found its way to the desert out of resonance, or because of past cruelties or because she was not allowed a larger life above ground. So often a woman feels then that she lives in an empty place where there is maybe just one cactus with one brilliant red flower on it, and then in every direction, 500 miles of nothing. But for the woman who will go 501 miles, there is something more. A small brave house. An old one. She has been waiting for you."

——*Women Who Run with the Wolves*

"The Howl: Resurrection of the Wild Woman" chapter

TWENTY-SEVEN

SUNDAY, JULY 23, 2006

TO THE UNINFORMED, cessation of respiration and heartbeat signaled death. Dia lay at rest in a hole less than twenty-four inches deep after more than two years of forced violence, rape for profit, emotional abuse, and misogyny. The subhuman people who'd left her for dead were long gone. Their final attempt to dissolve her identity forever would have been complete except for two small facts: one, there had been a witness, and two, Dia was still very much alive. Her breath and pulse were merely suspended.

La Loba stood over Dia's body, grateful the bullet she'd directed through Dominic's home nearly two years earlier had invoked its intended protective charm. The girl's spirit now hovered overhead by a tendril, tentative yet eager to return to its physical host.

Mountains rose from all sides, engulfing the pair in silent darkness. Pursuit of the would-be killers filled La Loba with a thirst for violence all her own, but she turned to Dia instead. *Am I ready to follow through on this?* Should she fulfill the promise she'd made to herself long ago when she first met Dia? La Loba retrieved Lucy, who had been tossed into the burial site beside its host. The doll triggered a memory of the girl's mother, who'd sought help on her own journey to the afterlife soon after their one-and-only meeting.

La Loba bent over and placed her arms beneath Dia's lifeless yet still-warm body. Mindful of her head, she lifted the girl up out of her earthly resting spot and readied her to make the long trek home deep in Gila's mountains. La Loba's hair was a mass of black, white, and gray wild curls that spiraled in dizzying directions down her back. It whipped around her face as she trudged through alpine foliage. Her nomadic existence prepared her legs for tonight's journey, but sixty-one years of living and the weight in her arms caused La Loba's lungs to tighten in the cool, dry Gila air.

Time and sunlight had pecked away at her femininity, leaving behind a face adorned with handsome features. Her crêpe-like face made her look like a woman twenty years her senior, with deep vertical lines running down her cheeks. Her brown right eye scoured trails of earth ahead of her as she sought her cave, while her blue left one—milky in color and blind—looked toward a future she'd been anticipating for more than a decade.

Mescalero Apache and Tarahumara ancestors had endowed her with certain healing abilities, but her restorative talents—coupled with a newer knack for prognosticating—surpassed those of her mentors and peers, triggering envy and fear and eventually resulting in her expulsion from her mother's family. La Loba withdrew deep into Gila's mountains before her forty-sixth year and left the forest sanctuary only on rare occasions. She'd be roaming the grounds of her abode tonight if not for this chance to interfere with fate. Mother Earth had left her unable to birth a baby of her own, but tonight's interception of Dia's soul granted her the ability to fulfill the maternal instinct that still stirred inside her.

Thirteen years had passed since La Loba's first encounter with Dia. A rare visit with old friends in Terlingua brought La Loba to a gas station on old Indian Head Road that day. She had been on a hunt for CornNuts when she rounded a corner and bowled over a child who appeared no older than five. Alone and startled in an aisle lined with confections, chips, and cookies, the youngster attempted to right herself.

"Oh, honey! I'm so sorry," La Loba said. Dia, then an innocent little girl with blonde hair and bluish-green eyes, hesitated, then turned her gaze upward. "You okay?"

Dia nodded, then lost her footing again as she peered around the woman in front of her. La Loba grabbed her by both arms to thwart a crash into the rack. Contact with Dia's skin that day precipitated a cascade of images La Loba could not unsee, the final one being a glimpse of the girl's shallow grave.

La Loba realized then what she'd do tonight. Her revivification and resurrection abilities had drawn fear from her family several years earlier in the face of mounting consternation from tribe elders. Seeing into the future and healing with natural herbs and flowers was one thing. Bringing the dead or near-dead back to life was another. La Loba understood she differed from everyone else, but she could not resist her desire nor her ability to save those whose time was not yet due. She was an anomaly among her own, but for others, she was a blessing and a gift.

She knew in 1993 that this day would come to pass. If La Loba got it right, Dia, who was now cradled in her arms, would be the answer for all lost girls. Evil took many forms, always eager to snuff out the light. La Loba saw it, from the reservations to the cities and back again. People were exponentially kind to one another on one hand yet turned on a dime to dole out cruel punishment if slighted or threatened on the other. Then there were those who were dark for no reason at all. They were born wicked. Her early teachers had tried warning her to be wary of people's motives until she was more familiar with them, but sometimes even those she thought she knew suppressed their darkness to draw her in. On more than one occasion, she had been clueless about the danger lurking below the surface of certain people and who they presented themselves to be.

Evil's omnipresence weighed heavily on La Loba as she carried Dia to her home. Once innocent and seeking tenderness, this child was an empty shell of who she'd been, depleted not just of goodness but of spirit itself. Baco took Dia's deep craving for connection and twisted it into something reprehensible. He mirrored many men La Loba had come in contact with over the years, guys who—consciously or not—believed women were naïve and victims of their emotions. At the same time, men seemed to resent the feminine for their emotional intelligence, and they searched for ways to exploit and squash it.

Strength and determination emanated from Dia as a child. La Loba had seen those traits in her at almost five years of age, but a person's qualities waxed or waned depending on which paths people took. Dia was no different, which explained why she met her end at the hands of Patrick. It was revealed to La Loba that day in Terlingua everything the girl would endure—from her mother's death to meeting Baco. Nothing La Loba might have done years ago would have altered her course. And despite all of her supernatural competencies, it wasn't La Loba's job to intervene in someone's destiny. She could affect it after the fact, though.

With the powers she *did* possess, La Loba could potentially reset a person toward a different destination once they were brought back to life. Dia's path would now be programmed to enhance the natural strength she'd displayed thirteen years earlier. La Loba hoped to instill qualities of trust and belief as well. However, there were some feats even La Loba couldn't accomplish. Learning to count on others while believing in herself would fall squarely on Dia's shoulders and would not come easily if it came at all. Getting to a place of hope and faith required forgiveness, but how could she forgive years of vile, evil acts inflicted on her by unknown numbers of faceless men?

Bitterness seemed a more probable result once she healed. Bringing a soul back from eternity's edge wasn't impossible, but controlling how reanimated souls perceived and responded to their world afterward was. Everything in this universe had a price, and while La Loba feared the prospect that Dia's rage might one day manifest itself as revenge, she suspected—hoped—the payoff for this transformation would outweigh the cost. The outcome of tonight's efforts would not be realized for months, if not years, after tonight.

La Loba rounded a granite façade that served as a natural fence. A gust of wind rustled coniferous trees and gave the full moon occasion to light her final steps as she approached her cave. Careful not to hit her head, she ducked, turned sideways, and crossed the threshold of her home with Dia in her arms. She laid her down on a mat across from the softly glowing embers she'd abandoned hours earlier in a fireplace large enough for someone to stand in. The gravity of what the girl had experienced now rooted La Loba to the floor, and she struggled to free herself from its grasp. She stared down at the inert teenager. Dirt clung to her clothes and hair; her eyes and mouth were shut, revealing a tranquility that brought La Loba out of her fog and to her task at hand. La Loba's dream for this lost creature was peace, and her road to serenity began tonight.

TWENTY-EIGHT

WEDNESDAY, MARCH 17, 1993 – SATURDAY, JUNE 25, 1994

SUNSHINE WARMED the Texas Hill Country as winter slipped away with the speed of a quick-moving thunderstorm. Afternoon highs hovering around sixty-three were replaced by temperatures in the mid-eighties. Meanwhile, Big Bend National Park's Basin still held winter's chill, warranting coats at night and light jackets during the daytime. Desert air lent a crispness that invigorated tent campers those March days and nights. Almost five years of age, Dia stood at the firepit on Site 24 as her parents made breakfast. Her blonde hair blew in a gentle breeze, and she warmed her hands over glowing briquettes.

The basin sat on top of the Chisos Mountains. The park's southern boundary was defined by the Rio Grande, which one could cross without incident to trade with or make purchases from Mexican citizens in Boquillas. Canyon walls secured Big Bend's eastern and western borders in partnership with the river, and hundreds of thousands of acres of desert grassland stretched between mountain ranges.

Dia's folks traveled every spring break to Site 24 to tent camp, so even as a child, Dia was well-accustomed to the camping lifestyle. She delighted in staring into their campfire each morning as her parents cooked. Her father, Kyle, a self-described grill master, fried eggs in bacon grease in an iron skillet and baked scratch biscuits in the Dutch oven. Meanwhile, her mom poured coffee, mixing in what her dad considered "a perfect ratio" of Kahlua and half-and-half. According to Kyle, breakfast in Big Bend tasted a hundred times better than at home, even if the core ingredients were identical. Something about being outdoors made food taste more yummy.

Kyle had proposed to her mother, Natalie, in Alpine, Texas, a two-hour drive away from their campsite. Today's pilgrimage included an annual return to the little house-turned-restaurant, where the owners called them by name and would likely help them celebrate their sixth wedding anniversary.

"Hi, honey. How's my little girl doing today?" Natalie joined her daughter by the firepit.

"Good," Dia said with a smile as the flames danced.

"Staying warm?"

Dia nodded.

"Good. You know how much I love you?"

"To the moon and back?"

"Yep, and then to the edge of our universe, which is always what?"

"Expanding?"

"Exactly. Constantly growing, just like my love for you." Dia's mom kissed the top of her daughter's head then took her hand and met Kyle at the picnic table.

"How long 'til we get there?" Dia asked.

"We just passed a sign saying two more miles," Natalie said.

"Which takes how many hours?"

"Only two minutes, I promise. Are you able to hold it?"

Just like eggs and bacon, orange juice went down the hatch far more easily outdoors. Dia had drunk more than twice what she normally would during breakfast at home. "Yeah, I guess."

"You're doing so great, honey. We'll be there soon."

Back at camp, their cooler and food were secured away in bear-proof storage bins. They had tidied their site up, zipped the tent shut, and loaded up in their F150 to go for gas west of Big Bend. Their drive to Alpine almost always included visiting Terlingua, where they picked up essentials and grabbed snacks for the road after a toilet break. The first stop out of the national park gave everyone a chance to use a decent bathroom and provided warm water for washing hands.

Terlingua was a hamlet where all types of people came to live—retirees, hippies, artists, motorcyclists, and survivalists. Every single person there had a story, and whether it was from a life lived hard or a life in the dry climate and isolation of West Texas, Terlingua residents aged faster than in other parts of the Lone Star State. Border-town men presented themselves as a bit scratchy and raw, while long days of sun and wind blunted the women's girlish attributes.

Dia's family pulled into the Alon gas station in Terlingua off Texas 118. Dia took care of business and rejoined her dad as her mom took her turn in the single-toilet facility in desperate need of a cleaning attendant. Relieved in more ways than one to be out of the fly-infested restroom, Dia scanned shelves of candy in search of her family's favorite confection: Goodart's Peanut Patties.

She felt her dad's absence as her eyes roamed past sugary treats and gum varieties. She peeked around a corner for his tall, slender frame but couldn't see him. Separated, Dia started to worry they'd left her when an older woman swept into the aisle and knocked her off her feet.

"Oh, honey, I'm so sorry," she said. "You okay?" Black and

silver curls poked in a thousand directions from the strange woman's head, and warmth beamed from her bright eyes.

Thinking a witch had landed on her, Dia pulled herself up and tried to move around the mysterious woman in search of her parents. Her clunky hiking shoes, effective when walking trails, now slowed her efforts to sidestep the weird lady in front of her. Her left foot tripped over her right, she lost her balance, and almost tumbled into a display of candy bars and gummy bears. The woman caught Dia before she fell a second time.

The lady's face shifted, morphing from one expression to another like a character in some cartoon, as she righted Dia on her feet. The woman's hands, enclosed around her upper arms, radiated heat unlike anything Dia had ever experienced up to that point, prompting her to try to wriggle. She saw the witch-woman's face return to normal.

"Where are your folks?" the witch-woman asked her.

"Dia?" Her dad's voice called from somewhere in the store. "Oh, there you are," Kyle said as he and Natalie came up to them. "Did you find our peanut patties?" Her parents shifted their eyes from Dia to the woman next to her.

"Everything all right?" Natalie asked.

The witch-woman spoke first, "Hi, yes. Sorry, I didn't see your daughter when I turned the corner, and I knocked her over, poor dear."

"You okay, Dia?" her mom asked.

Dia nodded.

"I'm sure she's fine," her dad said. "Found 'em!" He reached for a Texas-shaped, red-nut patty wrapped in cellophane on the top shelf. "I'm going to go pay for all this stuff."

"Looks like you made a friend, sweetie," her mom said with a wink. Then she raised her eyes up to the woman. "Are you from Terlingua?"

"Silver City, New Mexico," the witch-woman said. "I'm visiting friends here. You?"

"Athens, Texas. My husband proposed when we were out here six years ago, and we make it an annual family vacation now."

"How charming. Well, I suppose I should let you get to it then." The witch-woman fished around in her pockets. "Here, um, before I go, I want to give your little one a memento."

"That's not necessary," Dia's mother said, draping an arm over her daughter.

"It's not a big deal; a friend of mine puts these together back home, and I bring them to Terlingua when I travel sometimes." She retrieved a homemade-looking doll from her jacket. Bright woven reds and fuchsias covered its four-inch frame. Ebony braids hung down over each side of her face. The witch-woman held the toy out. "This is for you, dear."

Dia eyed it for a second, checked her mom's expression for approval, then reached for it with both hands.

"What do you say, honey?" her mom asked.

"Thank you."

"You're welcome, sweetie. You can use Lucy, here, as a sort of good-luck charm."

"Lucy," Dia repeated.

"You're very kind. Thanks," Natalie said, catching her husband's attention. "Okay, time for us to get going. Come, baby girl. Ma'am, it's been really nice running into you."

"Literally," the witch-woman said with a smile.

"Right… Well, enjoy your holiday. Maybe we'll run into you again before we head home to Athens."

"I'd relish such an opportunity. Travel safe, now."

Dia left the gas station holding her mother's hand. Feeling someone's eyes on her, she turned to find the frizzy-haired witch staring after them.

Dia snuggled with her parents in their tent later that night. They'd celebrated her parent's anniversary over steaks, followed by a visit to McDonald Observatory in the Davis Mountains. Vast darkness stretched across the West Texas skies, making the stars and planets appear brighter than at home. Their long day left her too tired for conversation as she clutched her new doll close to her chest and began drifting to sleep. "I love you, Mommy and Daddy," she said.

"We love you too," her mom said.

"Love you more."

"Love you most." Her dad gave her a final good night kiss.

The holidays crept up on their family a quick nine months later. Dia joined her fellow kindergartners on stage at their annual holiday pageant as they attempted to harmonize on "Silent Night." Families large and small squeezed into an auditorium with hundreds of HD video recorders and 35mm cameras, attempting to freeze their child's age in time. Lucy was nestled in her mother's purse. Dia's doll had become her favorite companion since the encounter last spring with the witch-woman whose wild black hair remained stuck in her mind.

She never told anyone, but Dia swore her doll's face changed its expression sometimes. Logically, she realized dolls didn't actually move, yet something made her think it had magical powers that allowed her to communicate.

Christmas came and went, then New Year's Eve, Valentine's Day, and another trip to Big Bend. It wasn't long before spring slipped seamlessly into summer. School marked the passage of time, and release from Mrs. Reeve's classroom meant freedom to swim as often as her mother would let her. Lucy kept an eye out from her perch on a bookshelf as six-year-old Dia shimmied into her one-piece swimsuit.

She'd just pulled the second strap over her shoulder when a loud thump followed by the sound of breaking glass came from downstairs. She looked up at Lucy, whose subtle smile had suddenly looked like a frown. Something was wrong. "Mommy?" she called out. Seconds passed as she waited for a reply but heard only traffic passing behind her house.

What made that sound? Dia grabbed her doll and scurried down the long hallway. She glimpsed her mother's feet as she peered over the floor banister. "Momma? Mommy!" She ran down the stairs, halfway tripping herself. Her mom's body lay twisted in a pile of broken coffee table glass. Scared and fearing the worst, Dia raced to the kitchen to call 911 like she'd learned in class last fall.

"9-1-1, what's your emergency?"

"Something's wrong with my mommy!" Dia said.

"Do you need an ambulance?" an operator asked.

"I think so," Dia said, volunteering her address.

"Is your mother breathing?" Dia peeked around a corner. "I...I don't know. Hurry!"

"We're sending one right now. Are you able to unlock your front door to let paramedics in?"

"Yes, ma'am."

"Can you stay on the phone with me?"

"It won't reach, and I want to be with my mommy." Dia didn't wait for additional instructions. She unlocked the entrance door and ran to her mom to kneel beside her. Blood trickled down one side of her face and into her hairline; otherwise, her mother lay completely still as the growing whines of sirens surged closer to their house.

"Please wake up!" Dia ran her hand across her mother's head, smoothing out disheveled hair. She laid her head on her mom's chest, hopeful to hear a heartbeat, but the ambulance kept her from hearing any sound as it came to a screeching halt in her driveway. Within moments, their living room transformed into an emergency room overrun by EMTs, machines, and noise.

Tears dropped to Dia's lap as cemetery workers turned crank pulleys to lower her mother's casket into its final resting spot. A blue tent shielded them from the summer sun as she played her death over and over in her mind. *What should I have done?* she wondered, sitting there next to her dad. They held hands in a sweaty, stiff grasp, caught between disbelief and moments of sorrow so profound Dia thought she'd suffocate.

Streams of people solemnly walked by, offering their condolences. Some followed them to their house, where Dia's paternal grandmother attempted to mother her. She chased Dia around as if hoping to thwart a fall or other potential accident. Dia yielded to the woman, unsure what to do or how to act as her father struggled with his own grief. He could barely speak with his daughter, let alone chat with friends and relatives who'd come to pay their last respects. Her mother's death had flipped a switch that turned off his life force.

By dinner, her father had softened somewhat, and a woman Dia recognized from family reunions sat next to him, making small talk. Dia's young mind strained to place her. *Are we related?* She tried to withhold judgment when the woman laughed softly and placed her hand on her dad's arm.

Dia followed her grandmother's instructions to dress for bed by herself in her room at night's end. A week ago, she was six and changing into pajamas with her mother's company. Now she was on her own. She removed her clothes and laid them on a shelf in her closet. When she was ready to climb under the blankets, Dia scanned her room in search of Lucy. She'd been moved by someone, and her doll now sat in a box as if intended for garbage or Goodwill. Again, Dia thought she saw vague frown lines form as she gazed into her little doll's face. *Are you sad, too?* she wondered, knowing she wasn't seeing things.

The doll's expression matched her own—sadness mixed with a lot of confusion. She retrieved Lucy and crawled under the blanket. She was eager to forget the events of the past week and desperate to pretend her mom was still alive. She wished with all her heart she could go back to the life she'd lived up to a few days ago.

TWENTY-NINE

SUNDAY, JULY 23 – SATURDAY, JULY 29, 2006

DIA'S SPIRIT hovered overhead in the frigid air near the apex of La Loba's cave. Enclosed in a sphere, vapors of violet, indigo, and fuchsia swirled together in a slow-moving dance. If one inspected it closely enough, they could discern slight appearances of constellations in a miniature cosmos with billions of specks of starlight shimmering from inside. Below, La Loba tended to a fire in her oversized hearth. Heat expanded from its coals and stretched upward, inviting Dia's essence down from its perch.

Mule deer, black bear, silver fox, and gray wolf furs lined the cave walls flanking the fireplace. Bones of these same forest and mountain animals hung clean and dry from a wire in front of their furry counterparts, clicking and clacking against one another as warmth radiated from the growing inferno. Tapestry rugs crisscrossed over her den floor, layered upon each other at various intersections, protecting one's bare feet from penetrating cold. La Loba sat atop her most ornately woven rug as she stared into a roaring fire. Dia's body lay behind her in shadow.

Purple and black bruises circled the girl's neck where Patrick's hands had choked her. Lacerations highlighted her cheekbones, chin, and shoulders. He'd barely left a patch of skin untouched from his blows and strangulation. Dia—still clothed in apparel from the night before—lay stretched out upon a six-foot-long bamboo mat. La Loba added more wood to the flames. Each log propelled the mercury higher, raising the room temperature and drawing Dia's soul nearer to its host. "I see you," La Loba said as she pivoted from the fireside.

She shifted her eyes up to the ceiling to confirm what her intuition told her. Dia's spirit floated two feet lower from where it had been an hour ago when it followed La Loba into her home. La Loba kneeled next to her young ward's side, placing her hands inches above Dia's thoracic region. "I see you," she repeated, keeping her arms stretched out over Dia for several more minutes. Then she moved them over the length of her body numerous times before bringing them to rest on the head. "I see you." She stared into the girl's face as if willing it awake, then resumed her examination. She poked, grasped, and prodded Dia's ribs and extremities, focusing on each spot that had absorbed Patrick's vicious blows while searching for broken limbs.

A steady wall of heat radiated from coals as one log after another caught flame. Hotness also emanated from La Loba's hands as she summoned her energy into Dia's still form. She directed it like a laser beneath the epidermis and through her peritoneum. La Loba channeled life force to Dia's organs and shattered bones, mending her wounds as if in possession of an invisible needle and thread.

Dia glowed, and her soul edged closer toward La Loba as she worked. It was hesitant yet curious. Several minutes passed before La Loba withdrew her palms from her healing efforts, and the girl's skin went blue again.

Guttural sounds emerged from La Loba as she backed away from Dia's body. She directed her focus to a collection of hanging skeletons. Dia's spirit—now a gaseous ball of swirling navy and lavender hues held together by extreme gravitational force—receded ever so slightly as La Loba alternated her attention between the animal bones and Dia's lifeless form. Wolves howled from miles away. Their penetrating melody echoed through the cave and signaled her next move.

As she arose from the hearth, she struck up an ancient Athabaskan chant and then paused in front of a fur that once belonged to a gray alpha wolf. Her tune segued from melancholy to hope as she ran her hands over the same wolf's skeleton. The bones clacked against one another percussively as La Loba's eyes narrowed in on its rib cage. Suddenly, La Loba snapped a rib from the donor spine and marched to Dia's corpse.

From outside the cave, wolves joined her in song. Holding the rib in her left hand, she knelt down and relocated her previous surgical site. Dia's skin began to glow once more as La Loba generated heat from her free hand, and her crooning reached a steady, forceful cadence. Finally, at its crescendo, she plunged the gray wolf's rib laterally into Dia, grafting canine bone to Dia's own broken ribs.

La Loba withdrew her hand and shook with exhaustion as she summoned another round of energy to complete her work. Repositioning herself, she peered up into Dia's essence. "You're coming home, my child." She moved her hands over Dia's heart and resumed singing. Dia's soul dropped within a foot of its previous host, and as La Loba thumped her upper trunk, sparks of orange flickered from inside. "Yes! That's it!"

Dia's celestial body drew near, inching closer as La Loba came up on her knees. She layered her fingers and palms above Dia's chest as if to administer CPR. Gravitational force, which held Dia's spirit in its tightly bound sphere, obediently loosened and released swirling tendrils of twinkling specks of light into a cirrostratus over the teenager's body.

La Loba gathered up her remaining strength and—with both arms—drove a bolt of energy through Dia's heart that lit her up from head to toe. The might of her gesture ignited Dia's cardiovascular and pulmonary systems, and La Loba fell away from her body. "It's okay," she said as she regained her balance. "It's safe to come back now. I've got you."

Dia's spirit paused momentarily and then dissipated over her prone frame. The girl inhaled suddenly, and her skin color returned to normal as blood began to pump through her veins.

Breath escaped Dia's lungs. She opened her eyes and turned to her left where heat radiated from roaring flames. She scanned the space in search of walls or other architectural boundaries, but not even the glow of fire could overpower the darkness of the room. Something cast a shadow, and she strained to distinguish it more clearly. *Are those animal bones?* Dia shook her head, the light not quite strong enough to reveal what hung on either side of a ginormous fireplace.

A log tumbled from the hearth without warning and rolled out toward Dia. She bolted up to escape it, and her head exploded with pain, immobilizing her. Her head throbbed from the back of her skull to her frontal lobe. She brought her hands up to her temple to massage away the spiking tension to no avail, the discomfort squeezing memories from her mind like a vise.

"Welcome back," a female said.

She turned to the source of the voice, unable to assign it to anyone in the room with her. Had she made it up? Where had it come from? She scanned left to right in search of its origin, the anxiety of not knowing distracting her from the throbbing in her head until a figure emerged from behind some animal furs. *What in the world?* The familiarity of the woman slowly assuaged her fear.

Somehow, she knew this woman. *Where do I know her from? How long has it been?* The woman in front of her looked old enough to be someone's grandmother. She stood in a flannel shirt, faded jeans, and bare feet. Her soles were dry and cracked, and a shawl was draped over her shoulders. Her curly, wild hairdo appeared gray now, but Dia remembered when it was black with spiraling streaks of silver. *Witch-woman!*

The woman smiled and approached tentatively. "My sweet, dear child, oh, how this world has missed you." Witch-woman crossed the room, clasped her hands around Dia's, and then reached to brush the hair away from her face.

"I don't understand. Where am I?"

"Answers are coming. For now, rest." Witch-woman assisted her to her mat and covered her with a wool blanket.

"My head... It hurts worse than I've ever felt. Can you..."

"You're dehydrated. I'll get you something to drink," witch-woman said. She walked to a small end table beside an overstuffed chair near the fireplace. She poured a glass of water from a ceramic vase painted with red flowers.

I've seen those flowers before, Dia thought.

The old woman turned with a smile and took the water over to Dia. "Here, drink," she said.

The cool liquid made its way down her throat in five gulps. It chipped away at the pain gripping her head. Witch-woman brought her a second glass, which she greedily consumed. Satiated for the moment, Dia readjusted herself on the mat, wincing.

"You've been badly hurt."

Dia searched witch-woman's face for an explanation as to why her body ached or why she was so far away from home without friends, family, or anyone who knew her. The woman stared back at her. *Why is she being so quiet?* She wanted desperately to understand the circumstances leading to her arrival in what appeared to be a remote cave. Were they in the mountains?

"Stay here. Try not to move too much," witch-woman said. She scrounged around a rickety cabinet and returned to Dia's mat with a mortar, pestle, herbs, and a tin of salve.

"What do you mean, I'm 'hurt?' What happened?" Water had relieved her headache, but her memory still failed her. "Was I in an accident?" An uneasiness crept over her. She stopped asking questions, unsure if she really wanted to hear what the lady might say. She watched as witch-woman soothed her limbs with a veneer of fresh-ground ointment before covering them with gauze.

"Rest. I promise answers are coming," witch-woman said.

Dia fell asleep within moments of closing her eye lids.

Days passed, and Dia woke intermittently when encouraged to sip fluids or swallow spoons of applesauce. Sleep pulled her into a state of such profound dormancy, that one might have thought her deceased. La Loba tended to her—changed her bandages and applied balm to her scrapes and cuts until they faded. Other changes were noticeable too. Dia would have blown over in a stiff wind on her first night in La Loba's cave, but her body had thickened with dense muscle as she healed—quadriceps, biceps, and triceps grew around her once fragile skeletal frame. She had more than made up for what she'd lost in her time with Baco. Dia became stronger as she slept. The deep rest—combined with La Loba's resurrection efforts—restored her physique, but her mind remained troubled as she tossed and turned in her sleep.

Dia had a dream where she was behind the wheel of a car as it drove over a cliff. Death was certain as the vegetation below her drew closer. Boulder and pine trees increased in size as she propelled toward a mountain base. A second before impact, Dia shot straight up, fully awake with rivulets of sweat flowing down her temple and neck.

Wood crackled in a fire next to her as briquettes fell through a grate one by one and landed with soft thuds against coals nested in a bed of hot ash. She turned to the sound and found two rabbits turning on a spit. Dia still had no idea where she was, but she was thankful to be alive. Images passed through her mind. *Did I die, or was that just a dream?* A memory of camping at Big Bend and stopping for gas pushed its way up to her consciousness. *I was in a store—a woman bumped into me and almost knocked me over. She gave me a doll....*

"Lucy." Witch-woman stood a few feet away, her arms heavy with twigs and logs. "Hi, Dia."

"You're that witch-woman from Terlingua, aren't you? But how did I get here?" She opened her eyes fully, now certain the cave was real—not a dream. She gazed toward the opening and saw the sun shining from a dazzling blue sky. Energy coursed through her veins. As much as she wanted answers to her questions, she felt an unsurmountable urge to bound through the door and run a million miles away as fast as she humanly could.

Humanly? She looked over to the woman who'd nursed her back to life. "What did you do?"

THIRTY

SATURDAY, JULY 29, 2006

THE SUDDEN URGE TO vomit distracted Dia as she prepared to question witch-woman on what she'd done in her efforts to revive her. Just as suddenly, her body began to morph into something inhuman. Fur covered Dia's frame as she rose on four feet. She struggled to reconcile wild scents and an insatiable craving to pursue large game. *What is happening?* she was desperate to know. She sought out the witch-woman's figure against her cave wall, unable to speak. A deep growl emitted from her throat instead.

"It's okay. Stay calm," witch-woman said to her.

Dia's ears twitched and turned to better hear hooves that trod over fallen pine needles half a mile away. A mule deer's scent wafted more fully in her nostrils, triggering her appetite, and motivating her to give chase. Dia charged from the mountain den into the sunlight, bolting through trees and underbrush wanting not only the prey but to distance herself from witch-woman's home. She vacillated between her desire to eat and her wish to escape what had happened. Locked in momentary indecision, she stopped for a moment to glean her target's location.

Canine ears funneled sound from her intended victim

down her canal and into her inner ear. She localized it and turned her head to lock it in her sight. She pivoted right. There it stood, less than 200 yards away, staring at her as it evaluated its next move. Dia didn't hesitate. Subtle twitches along the creature's muscles caused a rippling in its skin, triggering an ensuing strategy and well-choreographed chase through the woods. Five hundred… 250 feet... Dia pounced on the majestic animal's hindquarters as it mewed and bucked.

The deer swung around 180 degrees and threw Dia to the ground, but she refused to quit. Driven by hunger and rage, she pursued the animal and nipped at its heels. With fierce determination, she brought it down and clamped her jaws upon its neck.

Ravenous, Dia devoured her kill. She gulped chunks of meat down her throat and licked at the blood surrounding her muzzle. After she had satiated her craving, she dragged the wild game's carcass into a ravine and kicked leaves, dirt, and pine needles over it. She'd enjoy its remains for another meal tomorrow or the day after next. Content with her work, she stared into the shallow grave as an odd thought tugged at her memory.

Dia walked back and forth, hopeful her meditative efforts would clue her into what nagged at her. A twig snapped nearby. She remained still, daring to move only her ears. Images of lying in an earthly hole of her own overwhelmed her, and she felt a seismic pull across her flesh as fur withdrew into her limbs and torso. Her bones cracked, and her hips moved beneath her, forcing her into an erect stance. She watched as feet replaced where her back paws stood, and hands supplanted the ones up front. Dia's humanness returned as a memory of dirt falling on her face came into focus.

She'd been not unlike this deer once, attacked and left for dead. Something had saved her, though. No, not something... *someone*. Standing naked, Dia cowered behind a conifer as another twig snapped—this one closer in proximity. She turned her head precisely to the sound's source and found witch-woman eyeing her.

A name bubbled up to consciousness. She rolled it over in her mind. *Baco.* A man who'd professed his affection for her at one time had covered her with dirt in a shallow grave not far from here. He had been her boyfriend for a while, then he became something else altogether. In her mind's eye, she saw mattresses strewn across dirty floors with guys waiting their turn. Fleeting pictures of men having their way with her filled her head, and fur began to reemerge with her ascending rage.

"Dia." Witch-woman withdrew from behind a tree. "Come on out. I brought something to cover you with until I can find some clothes for you."

Breathing slowly, Dia noticed the fur dissipate as she emerged into full view. "Who are you? *What* are you?" A low-lying branch scratched the flesh beneath her knees, causing her to wince.

"I think you know who I am," witch-woman said. She approached tentatively, opening a blanket up as an invitation. "Did you get enough to eat?"

Blood splatter stained the front of Dia's body. She tried to wipe it away while nodding sheepishly. "You're the woman from the gas station…by Big Bend. I couldn't find my dad and thought they'd left me when you and I ran into each other."

"Here we are thirteen years later," witch-woman said, wrapping Dia's shoulders with the cover.

"Death would have been better than this." Dia's voice rose, triggering an uptick in blood pressure. "What did you do?" She pointed at the deer's remains lying in its grave. "I've gone from one prison to another. What am I supposed to do now?"

Dia stomped off ahead of witch-woman, grasping her blanket around her frame as she made her way to the cave using her olfactory senses. She'd never be normal again and never be able to undo the damage inflicted on her by Baco, Patrick, or any of the johns who'd abused her.

An image of Cinnamon flashed through her mind, and Dia stopped in her tracks. Sorrow found its way to her heart, and it broke into a million pieces like glass thrown upon a rock. Her young friend had been smarter than all of them, rejecting Baco and Dominic's plan to determine her fate in El Paso. Dia wished she'd had that kind of courage. Fear, and nothing more, had allowed those people to hijack her life, to intimidate and humiliate her, to remove any trace of dignity she'd once had.

She cried for Cinnamon and for herself, thinking of the hundreds if not thousands of men who'd taken something she'd never be able to get back. Every single one of them played a role in her death. Dia's body was wracked by uncontrollable sobs, and she fell to her knees. Her life had been over for more than two years. She'd existed as a ghost, invisible to the world, to her folks, to herself. *Why keep living now?* she wondered.

Dia sensed witch-woman watching her and looked back. "What do I call you?"

"My name is Linda, but some...they refer to me as La Loba."

Big Bend and her annual trip with her parents came to mind. Their second-to-last visit there as a family had taken place before Dia's fifth birthday, and she clearly recalled running into this woman. She appeared much older now and had an odd-looking left eye. Flat with a milky-blue color, it lacked the vibrancy of her right, which remained brown with shades of amber.

"I remember you catching me." A question popped into her head. Did she want it answered?

"Go ahead, ask me."

Dia spotted a hawk sitting atop a conifer as if eavesdropping on their conversation. "Did you know?"

"Did I know *what*?"

"I may have been a kid, but I saw how your face looked

that day. You knew what would happen to me...to all of us... right? I'm sure you did because your eyes got so big when you caught me. It was like you were touching a crystal ball or something. It was weird to me then, but it makes sense now."

"Nothing I could have said or done would have helped, Dia."

"You can bring people back to life, but you can't change their future if you see how fucking bad it's going to be? Sorry, but that's pretty messed up, if you ask me."

"What would you have had me do? Explain to your mom how I can predict how someone's life will unfold with a simple act of touching them—her child, no less? Should I have told her that her little girl would be left alone to fend for herself a little more than a year later when she died? Maybe I could've warned her about Baco. Would she have believed that from a stranger on the basis of a single meeting, and a quasi-metaphysical one at that?

"I can't tell you why I'm able to do what I do because, after all these years, I still struggle to understand it myself. All I can tell you is how it happens and what I can do with it. I sensed your mom would die and that you'd more or less be on your own afterward. I caught a glimpse of Baco...and his uncle. I had a sense of what you might endure. I tried to mitigate it where possible. I am so profoundly sorry for what you've gone through. I'd have stopped it if I could, but my abilities only involve healing or fixing what has already come to pass. I suspected they'd dispose of you here in these mountains, so I waited. I've intervened now because I've always believed something which would..."

"Something which would...what?"

"I've always been able to foresee all of your future, Dia—a life beyond your fate at the hands of Baco. There was no way I could *not* be there when you were left in your grave. You're here for a reason, and I believe I am, too."

"You talk as if I'm special or something." Dia waited for

the woman to laugh and deny it, but she didn't. Her benefactor stared back at her, imploring her with an earnest expression on her face. "Seriously?"

La Loba cast her gaze at the forest floor, then raised her head and took a deep breath. "I'm trying to tell you that when you're ready, no girl in this world will need to suffer under people like Baco, Dominic, or Patrick ever again."

Dia shook her head, "Really? And how am I supposed to keep girls from getting hurt? By turning into a wolf or whatever the hell it is you've changed me into?" Anger bubbled close to the surface of her mind, and if Dia had gleaned anything since coming back to life, it was how her emotions triggered a cascade of events far beyond making her skin goose-pimple. She needed to remain human for now and thwart any unconscious transformations that might preclude her from digesting what La Loba was telling her. "I meant what I said earlier. You should have left me for dead because it would have been better than this. Do you understand? I'm ordinary. If I wasn't, I would have left Baco a long time ago."

"That's not true. You're not weak, and you know it," La Loba said as she stepped closer.

"Stop it! I could have run away a thousand times, and I didn't!"

"Fight or flight is not always available to someone under attack," La Loba said. "Freezing—appeasing even—is as common a response, and it doesn't indicate consent, Dia. You were...you *are* a trauma victim. Stop blaming yourself." La Loba took a deep breath and lowered her voice. "You've been through enough, don't you think?"

Refusing to discuss it further, Dia turned her back on La Loba. In a week, she'd gone from being a pawn in Baco's pathetic prostitution scheme, to a corpse, to a wolf, and all because some witch thought she was destined to save womankind. Overwhelmed by all that had transpired, she wanted to do nothing more than sleep—for 100 years, if possible. With her heightened senses of sight and sound, she continued along the path to La Loba's cave, aware at all times of the woman as she followed. Mental exhaustion accompanied physical fatigue as she passed the cave threshold. Dia dropped to her floor mat.

Emotions she had refused to allow herself to feel for more than two years ached for release as she curled into a fetal position in front of the fire. She listened for La Loba to walk in behind her, but after several minutes, she realized the witch-woman had opted to leave her alone. She remembered when she last felt happiness—pure happiness, not the artificial joy of capturing some boy's attention. It was long ago during her life in Athens with her mom and dad. Her mother loved her so much. Dia's happiness ended when her mom died. She'd been left feeling void of bliss until she met the version of Baco he'd wanted her to see. She had been so spectacularly naïve. In his mind, she'd been nothing more than an object to manipulate. Tears rolled down her cheeks.

Childhood shriveled into a speck in her memory as she lay there. It had been over for a long time, but she couldn't identify with being an adult just yet, either. She reflected on her mom and what she might say had she lived. Dia probably never would have encountered Baco. *Would we be at the mall right now, picking out clothes, sheets, and dorm-room stuff for college? Did Sam shop for college with her mother? Did Sam ever stop to think of me after I disappeared?*

She wondered if anyone from her family missed her, especially since she'd grown apart from her dad in the wake of her mom's death. *Did he do anything with all those flyers? Does he miss me, or has he moved on with Susan and Jackson*? Her mind churned.

Dia turned the memories of her parents over in her brain until she grew tired. She slipped beneath her blanket and lay her head down, where the weight of introspection and self-pity pulled her into a fitful sleep.

THIRTY-ONE

FRIDAY, AUGUST 18, 2006

HANDS WITH FINGERS thick as sausages and skin cracked from freezing temperatures reached around Dia's throat from the hatchback's rear seat. She struggled to loosen them or fight the culprit off without losing control of her car. The vehicle swerved right and bumped a curb before skidding back into traffic. Dia freed a hand from her steering wheel to pull at the digits closing in on her windpipe. Frantically, she struggled for a view of her assailant in her rearview mirror. A knitted ski cap covered his features except for two light-colored eyes that made contact with her own. She failed to identify him.

Dia leaned forward, desperate to escape his grasp. Nothing she did worked, then her location shifted without warning. Instead of a car, she found herself sleeping on her stomach on a mattress in the middle of nowhere. Someone sat on top of her, closing thick, meaty fingers around her neck once more. She woke abruptly, gasping for air with her heart beating in her ears. She scanned her earthly dwelling but did not see her mountain host. Pots and pans clanked from beyond the cave, beckoning her to rise from the mat, so she slipped into a pair of secondhand jeans, a sweatshirt, and sneakers and stepped outside.

La Loba cooked over an open fire, stirring a brown stew with chunks of carrots, sprigs of rosemary, and cuts of unidentifiable meat. "Hope you're hungry." She stood up and studied Dia's face with her milky eye. "You were dreaming, yes?"

Is she psychic?

The witch-woman smiled as if to answer her unspoken question. "Maybe more often than not, people interpret a nightmare as a harbinger of bad things to come."

"Aren't they?" Dia asked.

"Not always. Sometimes, dreams of shadowy figures dressed in dark clothing can symbolize change or an initiation into a new level of awareness and knowledge for the dreamer. Frequently, they represent a malignancy in our culture that the dreamer is being called to stand up against."

Dia turned her mouth up and shook her head. "I've gone through enough already."

"You need time to heal from everything you've experienced, Dia, and trust me, you *will recover*. But look, it doesn't matter how old you grow or how many horrible experiences one does or doesn't have—you will find initiation around every corner in your life, which will present you with opportunities for higher levels of knowing. Dark-man dreams symbolize imminent psychic change, that's all. The scarier they are, the more they suggest you're hesitating to take the next step in life." La Loba bent down to stir her stew. "By the way, I thought I'd use some of that mule deer you hunted and make us a few sit-down meals from it. It's aged well over the past two or three weeks."

Dia's cheeks flushed a deep red, conflicted over whether to be embarrassed or sad over her killing. "Sorry I killed it. I…I don't know what got into me."

"You don't have to apologize. You were doing what comes naturally. Besides, plenty of animals populate these woods.

You did Mother Nature a favor." La Loba motioned to a spot next to her on a log. "Please, have a seat," she said, ladling a heaping portion of stew into a dented copper mug.

"Aren't you going to have some?"

"I will in a bit."

Dia took a bite, at first unsure whether meat from a kill nearly three weeks earlier was safe. Savory juices activated her saliva, though, and she suddenly realized how hungry she was. She ate with quiet gusto, barely slowing down to chew.

Several moments passed, and La Loba cleared her throat. "Predators can be real. For some—like you—they show up as these well-defined tangible captors. Most of the time, however, predators manifest more as emotional forces in opposition to one's instincts and dreams. Failure to reconcile their existence leaves people vulnerable and incapable of navigating their lives without falling prey—physically *and* psychically." La Loba poked around at the coals simmering beneath her cauldron of stew.

Sweeping her index finger along the inside of the mug, Dia salvaged the last bit of gravy and minuscule strands of meat. "I'm confused," she said, licking her finger clean. "What do you mean by 'predators are emotional forces?'"

"Say somebody wishes to start a new fitness routine to lose weight. She broadcasts to anyone who will listen how much she wants to work out and take better care of herself, but never takes action toward it. She makes excuses versus going for a run after work or consistently goes to bed too late to get up early to hit the gym. Or say someone wants to go back to grad school or write a book, but she never carves out the time to make it happen because she feels inadequate—not *good enough* or *smart enough*. Her entire creative life grinds to a halt because something deep inside her silently screams she's unworthy. And instead of taking command over that little voice, she gives power to it by telling herself she's not important, not educated, or—worse yet—that she doesn't have time.

I want to shake women to wake up and stop filling their heads with such lies, but it's not necessary. That's the purpose behind the dark-man dreams. The shadowy figure can be interpreted in a myriad of ways: as an awakening to higher consciousness, as a hateful attitude the dreamer has about oneself, or as a call to fight or flee some situation she is in. He might also symbolize that the dreamer's life needs to change because she's caught in suspended restlessness and is anxious to step forward and play full out." Without asking, La Loba refilled Dia's mug with more stew. "You looked like you could eat some more."

"It's like you read my mind." Dia took the cup back in her hands. "Thanks."

La Loba winked. "In literature and mythology, you learn about characters who have this type of internal energy of aggression, strength, and action. Some view these qualities as masculine, and that's not an inaccurate label. In so many women, those traits are bred out. I'm sure you've observed on more than one occasion where women are told to calm down, to be nicer, to be less aggressive."

Dia nodded.

"The thing is, as women, we *need* this opposite-gender nature because it helps us defeat the voice which tries to tell us we're not good enough or smart enough, that we never finish anything. Without it, a woman has lots of creative ideas and notions, but she lacks the ability to bring them into existence. She's incapable of following through, and she never realizes her dreams. In other instances, the lack of masculine energy leaves women unable to recognize and steer clear of hazards.

"Your mom's passing interrupted your development and kept you from acquiring these traits. Your father's spiritual and emotional absence didn't help, but your mom wasn't there to initiate you in our world's customs or to instruct you on what it takes to be female. She wasn't there to *snap and snarl* at you like a wolf bitch to her pups when they get too close to danger. Maybe she could have intervened somehow. Perhaps her mere presence would have helped you avoid him altogether. Who knows for sure? Now, though? Now you can cultivate your inner energy to balance the feminine and masculine, to find the strength to move forward."

Dia was overwhelmed by La Loba's feedback. She choked up at the mention of her parents and hung her head.

"Child, look at me."

She met La Loba's gaze.

"Listen. What you went through doesn't have to define you. *You* get to say who you are and what you stand for. Do you understand? You've been injured beyond what most people dare to comprehend; traumatized into submission by a dark and sinister group of people who extracted your strict compliance. This isn't your end. It's the beginning of *their* end. You hold the psychic energy you need to reclaim your life and defeat your captors if you like. Do you hear what I'm saying?"

"No, I don't!" Dia cried. You're telling me I have to save this screwed-up world! I don't *care*! Don't you get it? No one came to help me. No one! How the hell am I supposed to help others when I wasn't able to help myself?"

"Dia, your dream from earlier...what do you think it means?"

"That I'm scared? That I hate being so naive?"

La Loba shook her head.

"What I went through will happen again?" Dia shuddered at the thought of ever seeing Baco, Dominic and Patrick again. "What if they find me and get rid of me for good?"

"At a basic level, it indicates you need to cleanse your life of Baco, his uncle, and all those other men. They perpetrated cruel, hateful acts upon you, and I am sorry I wasn't there to stop it. They made your life a living hell, but you fought back—twice! And you escaped."

"Is that what you call being left for dead?" Dia asked.

"If you're willing, let me help you use this experience to uncover how you survived and take back what they took from you." La Loba paused before continuing. "Introject yourself with qualities that will inoculate you from ever becoming a victim again. You need time, is all. Well, that and an environment conducive to healing your intuition so you can practice listening to it. Once you hear your inner voice, you can act on it. Don't fear your nightmares, Dia. Allow them to propel you into higher consciousness. Your dreams affirm necessary life changes."

"'Introject?'"

"It's a psychoanalysis term used to describe an unconscious process where you incorporate the characteristics of another or an object into your own psychic apparatus."

Dia sat quietly for several minutes, remembering the mule deer and how its muscles twitched right before she gave final chase. At some point in those initial weeks of dating, she must have twitched or submitted subconsciously to Baco in his pursuit of her.

"There are times to shiver and run, and there are times to take your stand," La Loba said. "You'll never grovel again, Dia. I promise, *never again* will you fall prey to the predator. You will evolve into the hunter. You will become the wolf if you allow it."

Dia was done listening. She was exhausted from processing it all. *How could I have been so dumb?*

"You're only making yourself feel worse. You have to quit thinking that way," La Loba said.

"Please stop reading my mind! Seriously! Just stop it! I need to think about all of this without you looking in on my private thoughts, goddamn it!" Dia transformed and bared her teeth. At that moment, she knew how easily she would be able to tear the old witch-woman apart. Even though La Loba was not her captor, she'd been instrumental in creating this new situation Dia now found herself in. She didn't want any more anecdotes about how to leverage the past two years into answering some higher call of duty.

Dia growled at La Loba, daring her to say another word, but the woman refrained. Leaves flattened beneath the paws of some undefined forest animal miles from where she stood. She barked in warning, then bounded into the woods to gnash her teeth at anything standing in her way. She darted around boulders, pines, and underbrush as she raced up and over Gila's Mountain range. Rocks and woodland growth eventually gave way to an open, clear plain for her to charge full throttle. She sped toward an alpine peak with momentum unlike any she'd ever known, covering great expanses of ground with each forward surge. She came to a crevasse in Gila's granite and leaped across it without hesitation. Dia stopped and looked back at the gap in Earth's surface, which was at least twenty feet wide. *I can't believe I just made that jump.*

She turned around and resumed her ascent. Grass and flowers blurred beneath her as she ran, and she pointed her muzzle down to glimpse the path she cut with her own four feet. Her paws faded in and out of her view. Glancing down again, Dia realized that while her paws were invisible to her eye, they nevertheless propelled her over Gila's terrain.

Another quick examination revealed her legs to be fully indiscernible. Each uptick in speed hastened the disappearance of her remaining physique as her senses of sight, hearing, and smell remained. Dirt, grass, and rocks flew beneath her as powerful muscles fueled her every move. Dia lacked a reflective surface to confirm it, yet she believed with 100 percent certainty she was imperceptible to anyone who might glance her way. She closed in on the last quarter mile to Gila's Mountain summit and jolted to a halt once she reached her goal. The fur on her new canine body came back into view as her heartbeat and breath slowed. Dia scanned to her left, looking westward as the sun dipped below a magenta and orange skyline. Her future—bleak and unknown to her an hour ago—looked less terrifying as she took inventory of her skills.

Besides an unnatural ability to transform into a wolf, Dia possessed strength, speed, and now invisibility. She sat on her hind legs to muse over her life-changing circumstances. She'd invited none of this but knew there was nothing she could do now that it had come to pass. The vibrations of mountain goats reached her beneath her paws, and she turned her ears. Hungry from her exertions, she rose to track dinner.

THIRTY-TWO

WEDNESDAY, MARCH 19, 2014

SNOW WEIGHED AS heavy as sandbags upon Gila's highland vegetation, causing conifer needles to fall across a blanketed forest floor. Dia bore witness to her eighth season of winter from atop her favorite mountain peak as spring teased closer. The frosty weather system promised to be the season's last as subtle shifts in temperatures drew Dia nearer to her twenty-sixth birthday. For eight years, she'd witnessed seasons transition and mark time's silent passage in New Mexico's southwest corner.

In her human form, Dia had filled out into an adult female who stood five feet, nine inches tall. She was athletically built with strong, firm quadriceps, broad shoulders, and arms carved from stone. She moved with fierce determination through the forest. In her canine state, she towered over every other wolf in the Gila Mountain range with a thick skeletal system one and a half times longer than any other New Mexico wolf. Her fur coat was not unlike her human hair. It was ash blonde underneath but highlighted with streaks of white and wisps of wheat on top. With perseverance, she had learned to turn invisible at will and to sustain her invisibility for extended periods of time in both her human and wolf forms. Her hearing and smelling senses had matured also, making it easy to track down more than dinner.

Dia stood behind a warehouse in Silver City, observing Syd's Convenience Store across Market Street. It was less developed than her disappearing skills, but Dia had an emerging talent to intuit people's behavior. From the shadows of Silver City's industrial park, a young woman around sixteen years of age named Anna unsuccessfully pumped air into her car tires. The girl rolled her eyes and blew her bangs out of her face in exasperation after a dozen attempts to place a hose on the front passenger-side tire valve.

"Everything okay, miss?" A slender man inquired from his F150 bumper. He stood in Levi's and a wool-lined sheepskin coat with a collar that came within an inch of his cowboy hat. The same system dumping mountainous snow unleashed a chilly, steady mist over the small university town.

"Looks like you could use a hand," another man said as he exited the store and handed his friend a fountain drink. They both wore pointy leather boots in need of new soles and several coats of polish.

"Oh, hi," Anna said, flipping her hair out of her face. "Y'all are so sweet to offer to help."

The girl's friendly alacrity reminded Dia of herself as a teen and how disconnected she'd once been from her fighting instinct. Anna's cheerful receptiveness attracted the men's attention as she tinkered with the air hose, balancing being nice with a sense of self-protection. She needed assistance. Dia wished she could make the guys leave. They'd exchanged a look between themselves that had escaped Anna's notice, indicating a nonverbal agreement to "aid" her in more ways than one.

Harming her would be easy enough. No one was around to witness it. Wet and bitter winds kept customers from the grimy little convenience store with its overpriced gas. Dia began to wonder why Anna chose Syd's to inflate her tire, then caught herself. Predators never needed an excuse to justify attacking someone. *They do it because they can.*

The slender man in the sheepskin coat bent over to lend unsolicited help with the tire hose. He glanced over his shoulder at his buddy, gave him a wink, and then turned back to their targeted victim. Dia studied him with laser focus from across the street and picked up on the shared dark intentions the two had for their young prey.

"I don't think so." Dia muttered under her breath as she emerged from the shadows and onto the lit road. "Hi, there," she said. "Need some help?"

The skinny guy's jaw stiffened, his lips withdrawing into a tight grin while his buddy dug his free hand deep into his jeans pocket. Dia judged from their expressions that the men did not want her there as they stepped back. *Are they disappointed to find their chance slipping away?*

Anna greeted her would-be savior with a smile and opened her mouth to speak when the slender man's truck's rear cab doors popped open.

Two towheaded kids stretched out their necks. "Daddy? Can we go now?" one of them asked.

The women exchanged looks with one another, the younger one visibly releasing a breath as the children emerged. "I wondered if you needed any help," Dia said.

"Oh, how super nice of you to ask, but I think I've got it. These gentlemen offered to lend a hand, too, if their kiddos don't care to wait a bit longer."

Dia glanced over to the slender man and his sidekick to find them smiling at her. "No problem," she said. "Good luck." She turned and began her trek up the mountain.

"La Loba, what if I'd done something to those guys? Christ! I felt so certain listening to them, hearing what they were thinking. Then those kids popped out!" Dia ran the hypothetical scenario through her mind in a continuous loop. If she overreacted every time some guys spoke to a woman, she'd soon earn a reputation for crying wolf instead of being the wolf hunter she aspired to be. She paced back and forth in front of the giant fireplace. "I came really close to making a total fool of myself out there. I'll bet that teenager thought so, too. She probably wondered why I was poking my nose into her business."

"Be gentle with yourself," La Loba said. In eight years, the witch-woman had never raised her voice, despite all of Dia's protestations, challenges, and resistance to change. She moved over to Dia to stop her from pacing, grabbing her face between weathered hands with bluish-green veins rippling across their tops. Dia knew she could trust whatever was about to come from her mentor's mouth. "Look again. Take a deep breath, like I've shown you. In your mind's eye, go back and look harder."

Exhaling, she allowed the tension in her muscles to cease.

"Close your eyes. Now, tell me what you see."

Dia quieted her thoughts as her breathing deepened and her mind grew blank. An infinitesimal speck of light appeared from the infinite darkness of her consciousness. It grew until it spanned across Dia's internal field of focus, and in a meditative state of profound concentration, she gleaned what happened after her awkward departure.

The men's names were Lee and Shane. The latter had coaxed Lee's youngsters back into his truck as the former charmed Anna into letting him air her tires. Bruises covered the children's legs. Dia saw Shane return to his buddy, where he grabbed Anna from behind, putting a cloth over her mouth and nose until she fainted. A series of images crystallized as she remotely viewed where they held the teen captive. A video camera sat on a tripod in a rundown house a few blocks from the convenience store. The last mental picture was of Anna lying on a mattress in Lee's dilapidated house, her hands and feet bound as she started to wake from her chloroform-induced nap.

Several moments passed before she popped her eyes wide open. "I have to go!" Dia transfigured into her canine self and ran from the cave with lightning velocity. She turned invisible at the perimeter of La Loba's front yard. In her altered form, she raced down snow-covered trails toward Silver City, determined to intercede in Anna's life after leaving her with those two men.

Dia bounded down Gila's mountains purposefully, her speed and strength imbuing her with invincibility. She dodged obstacles in her path, jumping over and around trees, creek beds, and alpine roads. Still in the shape of her wolf when she arrived at Syd's, she summoned the exterior image of Lee's house from earlier. On a rickety metal mailbox affixed to the left of a broken screen door, she read the number 3742. She shifted her attention to her right and saw a corner street sign —Trail of the Mountain Spirits. Within moments, she stood invisibly on human feet at Lee's front door.

Over the years, she'd acquired every skill available for her to fight those who forced themselves on innocent victims, yet she felt paralyzed at crossing Lee's threshold. A thought raced through her mind. She recalled a recent memory where La Loba cautioned her not to project her experiences onto all naïve girls. "This world isn't all bad," she remembered the old witch-woman saying. "And not all men are like Baco and Dominic."

But what if I'm wrong? Dia questioned whether the images she'd seen of Lee's kids' bruises and the chloroform were real or imaginary. Then a car approached from the south. It slowed and came to a stop in front of the long sidewalk leading up to the porch. A short man exited with a six-pack of Coors and made his way up to knock on Lee's door.

"They're not all bad." La Loba's words circled through Dia's thoughts. "But the ones who are will keep you busy for all your remaining days if hunting them is what you choose to do."

They're not all evil, Dia contemplated as she played judge and jury to this latest addition to Lee and Shane's party. He stood hunched over, his spine crooked, and his body wizened from decades of hard living. Strawberry blond whiskers poked out of his chin. He tapped on the glass door, and a porch light flipped in response. "Let me in, Lee. I'm freezing my balls off out here," the man said.

"Dwayne! Buddy! You're here," Lee said, jarring his front door loose to open it. Dia required more evidence before issuing a judgment that could potentially result in a death sentence for all three men. She followed Dwayne inside; the slow spring action of Lee's door provided ample opening for her to enter. Shabby wood paneling wrapped his living room walls. Faded gold-colored shag carpet covered his floor except for a patchy bald path that had been worn down to the concrete foundation.

Dwayne finished his first Coors and set his empty can on an end table next to a two-person couch where Shane sat. Dwayne withdrew his second beer from its plastic rings. "So, where's our little princess? I'm ready to get this party started," he said.

"Our new friend is in the master bedroom," Shane said. "We haven't touched her yet. We thought with it being your birthday and all, you might want first dibs."

"Aw, shucks, really? I appreciate that." Dwayne wiped a drip of alcohol from his pointy chin and took another giant gulp.

Dia stood motionless, assessing the pending confrontation. It was her first opportunity to save someone, and she wouldn't have minded the benefit of some liquid courage herself. *Focus.* She snuck a peek down Lee's hallway into a room with a pale-blue glow. If she crept down it silently, perhaps she'd persuade

Anna to sneak out a window while Lee and his friends consumed more and more beer up front.

"Where are those kids you mentioned?" Dwayne asked.

"Shit, Dwayne. You want it all," Shane said.

Kids? She had forgotten about them momentarily. *He's farming out his own children?*

"Let's go," Shane said. The other two men fell in line behind him, passing an invisible Dia on their right. "Oh, baby girl! I hope you're ready for us. We have a surprise for you!" He paused to look back. "Lee, pop in on your young-ins to see what they're up to."

Lee peeled off to a side room as Shane and Dwayne entered Anna's room two doors down. "Hello, doll face," Dwayne said. "Daddy's here to make you feel better and keep you company. Let me get those ties off you."

She must have had tape over her mouth. Dia heard a muffled scream as Anna took her first glimpse at a man whose fantasies were about to become her living nightmare.

"Aww, she's got spirit, this one. Gonna be like breakin' a wild horse!" Dwayne disappeared from view, presumably around to where Anna lay.

Dia listened as the girl pushed herself up against a headboard, and memories of Dia's own rapes flooded her consciousness, causing her to lose concentration. Her ability to remain invisible flickered.

Lee emerged with two kids in the hallway halfway between Dia and Anna. "What the fuck ya' doin' here? How'd you get in here?"

"Lee?" Shane popped his head from the doorway to Anna's room. "What the hell?"

Everyone stood motionless, calculating their next move.

Rage coursed through Dia's veins as she snapped into her canine form, her ears filled with the sounds of children and adults screaming for their lives. Dia charged down the hall, baring her fangs down first on Lee and then Shane. Blood splattered the walls and flooded the carpet as she ripped both of them apart. Their yells and cries for help were futile as they flailed at her, vainly attempting to punch, kick, and wrestle away from a monster they never knew existed until now. Reduced to piles of warm, crimson flesh and bones, Lee and Shane no longer posed a threat. Dia ignored the sobs of the children and made her way toward the one remaining male adult in the house. She viewed Anna through her wolf eyes, trying to communicate that the girl had nothing to fear. Dia conveyed a different sentiment when she pivoted to the crooked-spined man with blond hair.

"Please don't hurt me!" He stood in a corner next to the video camera on its tripod. A red light glowed steadily near its lens. Dia leaped across the bed without hesitation and wrapped her jaw around Dwayne's scrawny throat. She ripped it out, leaving him to crumble down toward the carpet. She turned her attention to Anna to offer her as sympathetic a look as possible before dashing back through the house and out into Silver City's chilly night air.

She charged up to La Loba's mountain cave. Tears fell onto the Gila Forest floor as she ran, though she didn't know who she was crying for—Lee and his friends or Anna and those children? Herself maybe? Every year since her death at the hands of Patrick and Baco reminded her she'd never be normal, but tonight's violent act of justice cemented her transcendence from an ordinary human into something otherworldly. She had crossed a boundary from which she felt certain she could never retreat.

THIRTY-THREE

MONDAY, JUNE 20 – TUESDAY, JUNE 21, 2016

IT HAD RAINED for an unusual number of days in Gila's mountains. Sunshine poked its way through the remaining clouds, granting permission for spring flowers to open their blooms. Unfortunately, rivulets of rainwater had eroded the north-western wall of La Loba's perimeter hut used for drying and storing her various herbs and plants. Dispatched mud and stones lay in small heaps at the structure's base, and Dia found La Loba performing repairs after her morning hunt.

Witch-woman maneuvered her trowel across the hut's surface. She moved fluidly between wall and wheelbarrow, retrieving displaced rocks and working them into a thick mixture of straw and sludge. She applied the earthy goop to the cottage's exterior to bake beneath the sun as it ascended toward its zenith.

The woman knew so much about healing, nature, and people. It was hard to not admire her as she worked to rebuild an adobe outbuilding like a master carpenter. The hut, which Dia had passed untold times with little notice, appeared different today as La Loba worked her way around it. Dia struggled to unravel its mystery as she stared at its thatched roof. It looked somewhat out of place against the backdrop of the mountains. Dia drew closer to study it and recognized something familiar from a long time ago. In a moment of déjà vu, a cactus flower flashed across her mind's eye. *Nothing but desert in every direction for what seems like 500 miles...* Loose tendrils of a repetitive dream came into focus. A wolf, a red bloom, and images of this hut had come to her while she was in captivity. Standing beside it, she remembered the voice asking, *What are you waiting for?*

La Loba paused between applications of mud slurry. She looked at Dia with a knowing smile, confirming the young woman's suspicion that she'd dreamed of this place. Ten years had passed since her rebirth, yet at times it felt as if it were yesterday when she had lived her life in a fog of prostitution and abuse no human should ever endure.

Those years were long behind her, but the gravity of pain lingered even in this spot of immense beauty. Dia stared back at La Loba, receiving her acknowledgment, and returning appreciation for being saved. They exchanged a knowing look —each recognized how their time together was drawing to a close.

With her trowel in hand, La Loba returned to her repair work and left Dia alone with her thoughts. *How long will it be before I recover 100 percent from my past?* She was physically healed beyond her wildest expectations, but emotionally, not so much. She couldn't imagine how she could ever come to terms with Baco's and Karyn's betrayal or Dominic and Patrick's murderous hostility. *What happened to all of them?* Had the former found their happily-ever-after? Had the latter ensnared countless other innocent girls in pursuit of more and more riches? Would extracting revenge on any of them mend the sorrow?

Her thoughts flitted between self-pity and curiosity. Dia wanted to move on with her life and simultaneously craved a return to her life before Baco. Without internet service in the mountains, questions lingered about her family, too. *Where does my dad live? Have they forgotten me by now? Would they welcome me home if they knew what I went through?*

What had kept her tethered to a loser, ignorant pimp with zero awareness and even less self-esteem? How had she missed those signs from him in their initial weeks of dating? Was she so desperate for attention and love that she'd ignored them, or had Baco been so charming he'd fooled her?

Regret morphed into anger as she rolled Baco's deception repeatedly in her mind. It waxed into a seething rage as she remembered all of Dominic's venomous and verbal assaults. *A whore and nothing more.* It was as if women brought nothing of value to life but what men took from between their legs. Healing completely from her past might take an eternity but pursuing justice would surely hasten its arrival.

La Loba smoothed a final patch of mud near the hut's entrance. She turned to Dia and silently communicated what she'd said years earlier. *The ones who are bad will keep you busy for all your remaining days if hunting them is what you choose to do.*

"I understand," Dia said in a whisper.

"It won't be easy," La Loba said out loud.

"I know."

The seventy-one-year-old returned her trowel to a muddy spot in her wheelbarrow. "Let's get started, then."

Dia and La Loba faced each other in front of the fireplace. "You know your strengths," La Loba said. "I don't need to list them, but you are by far faster and more adept at shapeshifting and disappearing than any I have ever known. However, my child, I cannot emphasize enough how you need to guard these skills. You must never let others know who you are or where you come from." She paused for several moments, her eyes searching the ceiling above as if in search of something perfect to impart to her adoptive daughter. "If you had to guess, what do you suppose is one quality your enemies might have over you?"

Is this a trick question?

"I'm not playing around." La Loba gripped Dia's hands with rigid firmness. "What would someone whose intentions run counter to yours have over you if they learned *who* and *what* you are?"

Dia wracked her brain, but nothing came to mind.

"The element of surprise," La Loba said. "You're incredible, and there won't be much an adversary can do to thwart you. A smart criminal hell-bent on winning, however, can always find a way to outsmart his opponent, even if that person is you. Incorporate aspects of your wolf into your human self to remain vigilant and ahead of your enemy."

Should I ask?

"Go on."

"Are there others like me?" Dia asked.

La Loba cupped Dia's face in her hands. "Child, you embrace the full scope of powers derived from shapeshifting into your wolf self. Not even I possess all the skills you've been imbued with and now master, but it doesn't mean people won't cross your path with talents of their own. There aren't many, but you'll recognize them if you run into them. Never let your guard down, Dia. Stay present, remain curious. I don't have much more I can say other than you will win…eventually."

"Win what exactly?"

"Only you can say."

She studied her mentor's face. "You've not aged at all, La Loba, but something tells me the planet has changed a lot since I last lived in it. I don't suppose you have any tips on how to manage this crazy, modern world?"

La Loba pursed her lips. "I think all you need to accept about life off this mountain range is that you are never alone.

No matter how dire your circumstances, regardless how dismal things become at times, you are not completely on your own. Believe me when I say this. Trust these words I impart to you, and you will have everything you require in pursuing a life where you save others."

Dia lay in bed, restless as she considered her task. La Loba's coaching cycled through her brain. *Busy for all your remaining days if hunting is what you choose to do.* There were others out there once like Dia—lost, scared, and lonely, forced to perform the vilest acts in existence to avoid being killed by a pimp or some john. They dotted America's landscape, from rural desert towns to middle-class suburbs to urban centers everywhere. She suspected some of them truly wanted to be prostitutes, and perhaps because some chose it, everyone believed it to be a victimless crime.

That wasn't true for Dia, though, nor for Cinnamon. Not even Karyn, despite all her desire to please and be loved by Baco. Dia strained to get her mind around how many women and children were forced to have sex with the basest of human beings. She struggled to understand what entitled people to act so abhorrently, or to believe buying or owning another person was somehow an unalienable right. She would not have chosen this path, but having made it through her ordeal, Dia now needed to participate in something bigger than herself and defend those unable to protect themselves.

She fell asleep, and memories of her mom merged with those of Patrick's torture. Dia woke hours later, wanting to reconcile her emerging desire to help others with a burgeoning impulse to extract vengeance. Was Patrick still beating up prostitutes, or was he inflicting more heinous pain on people than in his younger days? She suspected hunting down the world's predators—a momentous task La Loba described as unending—might become her life's work, but first she had to administer justice to one of the three men instrumental in making her who she was now.

Patrick's name topped her list, but Dominic and Baco weren't far behind. Remembering the sales leader's employment with Align Medical would make flushing him out exponentially easier in this digital age. She also had a vague memory of him living off the Central California coast. Dia hoped La Loba's insistence to trust she'd have everything she needed included cash and an internet connection.

"No reason to hope, child, I meant what I said," La Loba said out loud as she reentered her cave. She approached bearing gifts and placed them on the mat beside Dia. "All that you've experienced in your twenty-eight years has brought you to this moment. You might not have imagined arriving here at this point when you and I first encountered each other all those years ago in Terlingua, let alone when you met and fell in love with Baco. Yet, here you are, uniquely qualified and more than capable of saving current and future generations of children.

"Tonight, I am honored to see you leave as a warrior. You came to me as a shadow. Your rebirth was uncertain. You came to me as a wounded child, and I brought you back to life. You have become like a daughter to me, not that I would ever try and replace your mom. But I have built upon her strong foundation of love and fortified you with qualities I believed you needed, not just to live again, but to begin anew. All good and decent parents yearn to see their children grow up and find fulfillment. I wish this for you as well, but your journey adds complexity to what I want for you. You possess a profound need to help others, and you seek justice. I support you in this mission and see value in starting with those who put you on this path. Hear me, though. I want your happiness, too. I believe in you. I love you. I want what's best for you. Pursue this work but trust it won't always define you. Someday, Dia,

Rieka, my child, you will be reborn yet again, and you will leave this world for good to become your truest self." La Loba extracted a necklace from her pocket and held it out to her.

"*Rieka*?" Dia asked as she rose. Standing toe to toe in front of La Loba, she bowed as the witch-woman placed the jewelry over her head. A round silver locket hung from braided twine; one side bore the image of a wolf while the flip side displayed an etching of the cactus flower from her dreams.

"It's Old German for a woman who has the power of the wolf. Diana, from which Dia is derived, has its origins in Roman mythology and translates into 'goddess of the hunt.' Not that you won't be hunting, but I thought you'd draw more strength from Rieka. It gives you a fresh start. This change in your designation cements your transition from child into woman and into someone who will continue evolving for years to come."

"*Rieka*." It sounded strange, and yet it resonated as authentic and true. She opened her locket and found it void of any image other than her own reflection.

"Look in here when you're lost. It will guide you to where you need to be." La Loba enclosed her hands around Rieka's and closed the item shut. "It's time."

Suddenly, Rieka had a million questions, but La Loba's countenance told her any and all answers would come. Without hesitation, she transfigured into the wolf. She took one last glimpse of La Loba and licked the witch-woman's face with affection.

"Go," La Loba said.

Rieka turned to the cave door, a gust of wind escorting her over its threshold as she leaped out of her home and into the light of day.

THIRTY-FOUR

WEDNESDAY, JUNE 22 – SATURDAY, JUNE 25, 2016

FOREST HUES OF EMERALD, moss, and olive lost their vibrancy as Rieka migrated westward from her mountain home of ten years. Southwest New Mexico's sky changed also. A deep azure from the vantage point of La Loba's cave, the heavens appeared scorched now, the air thin and parched. She wondered if it had always been this stark or if Earth had been bumped off its orbital path in the last decade. It was as if the atmosphere around it was cinched by a belt pulled too tightly. Everything seemed muted, heavy, and constricted. People—their spirit, their energy—felt oppressive compared to how she remembered it.

Rieka's return to reality had brought her through Arizona, the Mojave Desert, and across rugged terrain in the Santa Lucia Range. She now sat in the Carnegie Library in San Luis Obispo, reviewing LinkedIn profiles of Patrick and his Align Medical colleagues. They'd aged in their faces as she had, but they had grown fat and soft without the benefit of rebirth and animal transformation. Rieka studied Patrick's profile picture closely. His blond hair was highlighted by giant swaths of white, but his vicious gaze remained unchanged.

How smug can one person be? She shifted her attention to

his cover photo. A landscape shot captured a front entrance to his single-story business office in San Luis Obispo's warehouse district. It had floor-to-ceiling windows with tears in the tint covering misshapen mini-blinds. *He chose this picture to represent the company?* she wondered. It made her wonder if Patrick mismanaged Align or if he'd struggled in the recession some years back. Determined to find out, she slipped away into California's late afternoon sun, stealthy as a leopard.

Her earlier internet activity had confirmed Patrick's and Align Medical's location. She located the office off Industrial Way and Sacramento Drive with little effort. Standing in the shadows of a parking lot filled with domestic trucks and foreign sports cars, she surveyed her attacker and his team as they demonstrated the safe and effective uses of orthopedic products for their surgeon customers. From more than seventy-five feet away outside, she stood and discerned their presentation was drawing to an end as people closed laptops and zipped up backpacks and satchels. Beer bottles sat five rows deep at a sink for the cleaning crew to recycle later. Sales reps in scrubs handed their surgeons product literature while lower-level associates broke down lab stations.

Beneath the hum of their activity, Rieka picked up on the gregarious banter between Patrick and Larry, his sidekick—someone she'd once been forced to have sex with in front of half a dozen other men. She grimaced at the memory, then pushed it out of her mind to figure out Patrick's next move.

"Dr. Christopher," Patrick said. "Larry and I were thinking about heading over to Ciopinot. Care to join us? We could continue our discussion about tonight's lab."

"I'd do anything to avoid getting home in time for bath night," the young surgeon said.

"Right? Can't say I blame you," Patrick said. "Want to meet there, or can Larry and I give you a lift?"

"I'll catch up with you there, unless you think it'll be a long night."

"It won't be too late," Larry said. "We have a hunting trip planned this weekend, and I still need to pack."

Patrick shook his head, imploring Larry to keep quiet with wide eyes.

"Come again?" The doctor looked up from his phone.

"Larry said it'd be an early night," Patrick said. "Ready to go?"

"Yep, let's do it." All three men grabbed their jackets, bags, and car keys and departed for their individual vehicles, leaving Rieka alone to go inside and conduct her work.

Photographs of Larry, Patrick, and other sales team members adorned Align's office walls. Snapshots of them holding a Stanley Cup-sized trophy on a brightly lit stage lined a hallway near the front entrance. The plaque underneath the largest photo was engraved "2002." She traced her fingers over adjacent plaques hanging below the pictures, coming to a stop in 2005—the year their national sales meeting took place in Jacksonville, Florida. She studied their faces for glimpses of their depravity. That marked her first encounter with Patrick and his crew, but no photos or commemorative signs acknowledged their second one in 2006. She guessed nothing significant came from their last night together, though it had certainly sparked a whole new life for her.

Her quest for information led her down two more hallways until she reached the boss' office. A massive table-desk jutted out like a peninsula over a pedestal stand, presumably to foster intimate face-to-face discussions, and there was a small conference table meant for more formal meetings opposite the hefty oak furniture. Photos of Patrick's family were displayed on his desk situated under a book cabinet aglow with soft recessed lighting. She bent over with caution to avoid touching any surfaces and studied his children's cherub faces. His son was a miniature Patrick with bleach-blond hair and a California surfer tan. He looked to be eleven or twelve with a toothy, dimpled smile. His daughter did not have the same vitality. The girl and her mother had dark circles beneath their eyes and weak smiles, which struck Rieka as more than curious.

She struggled to make sense of the images in front of her. Either his collection of photos exhibited a man committed to his wife and kids, or it portrayed a façade. *So, which is it?* She thought back to all those copious customers she'd serviced. So many of them had "monogamous" marriages, also. She'd lost track of the number of wedding rings she'd seen, let alone the excuses johns dished up to justify their actions.

A line from some daytime talk show rang in her ears, "Past behavior best predicts future behavior." From what she could gauge in his pictures, personal development and an interest in self-awareness eluded her former tormentor. She studied the man in his family photo. He may have grown older on the outside, but Rieka would bet that Patrick treated women with as much disregard as he'd demonstrated in 2006. His only *growth* was in his waist size.

The photographs of Patrick's wife nagged at her. She would have guessed he was married to a blond like himself. Staring into the face of a stunning brunette, the woman reminded Rieka of Sam for a brief moment. His spouse could have been a model at one time, considering her facial symmetry and limb angularity, but her beauty could not mask something dark under the surface. *Does Patrick beat her, too?* she wondered. Rieka's heart went out to the woman who gave the impression of being as much a victim as she once was. She was uncertain about how best to fight for justice as she lingered over the photos.

"Stop it," she said out loud. Psychoanalyzing her former tormentor was pulling her off task. She tried refocusing her energy on uncovering more logistical information. Abandoning what she'd planned for several years was not an option. She turned from the man's desk and made her way into San Luis Obispo's crisp night air.

Rieka immersed herself in a tree line that separated Patrick's home from a golf course as he kissed his family goodbye twelve hours later. His son paced back and forth behind his father as he loaded his vehicle.

"Please, Dad? I'll do everything just like you showed me, I promise."

"I don't doubt that you would," Patrick said, placing two rifle cases next to a duffle bag.

"Then why?" the kid asked.

"Buddy, ya gotta cool it down a notch. This is an adult trip. I'll take you some other time." He closed the tailgate and suppressed an eye roll as he turned to his wife and children.

"Come on, Jake. Leave your father alone. He's in a hurry," his mother said.

"Whatever, Mom." He lunged forward to hug his dad one more time. "Bring me back something cool, promise?"

"You got it, son." He climbed behind the wheel of his black Lincoln Navigator and backed out of the driveway. His family waved after him as he drove off.

Eventually, Rieka tracked him to a Starbucks less than a mile from his home. He was about to get out of the car when a call came in over the speaker. "What, Jake?"

"I know, Dad, but I had to phone one more time before you head up to tell you I love you."

"Okay, son, me too," Patrick said, a smile pulling up the corners of his mouth.

His patience with his kid churned up second thoughts in Rieka once more. *Has he changed from the monster I knew ten years ago?*

"I'll see you in a few days," Jake answered.

"You sure will, buddy," Patrick said. "All right, I have to go. Take care of your mom and sister."

"I will, Dad. Have fun...and good luck!"

"Thanks." Patrick ended the conversation in his vehicle then opened the door. One foot was on the ground when his cell rang again. Rieka felt ready to ditch her plans if she had to endure hearing one more heart-tugging exchange with the man's son.

"Chuck!" Patrick checked over his left shoulder as if confirming no one else stood nearby.

Paranoid much? she wondered. Who would pay attention enough to eavesdrop on some middle-aged man in his SUV taking a phone call? Impatient to see what generated all his wariness, she snapped into her invisible self and crept up to the SUV. Patrick swung into the driver's seat, switched to speaker phone, and closed the door. His attempt at privacy had no effect on Rieka. With her canine hearing and proximity, she could listen to their conversation as well as if she were sitting in the backseat.

"Did you get my pics?" Chuck asked.

"No, where did you send them?"

"Check WhatsApp. They're in there."

Patrick tapped, swiped, and scrolled through his device to open Chuck's attachments. His long pause suggested that whatever Chuck had sent was engaging.

"Well? What do you think?" Chuck asked. "I think you're going to have one of your best hunts ever, my friend."

"Dude, you get me like nobody on the planet!"

Had Chuck forwarded pictures of 12-point-bucks or grizzly bears? *What type of game do Patrick and his buddies hunt, anyway?* The man seemed different from the person she'd obsessed over all those years with La Loba in her mountain cave. It stirred an internal argument. *Yes, he beat me and left me for dead, but what if he feels remorse all these years later?*

She peered through the driver's side window over her former attacker's shoulder to catch a glimpse at what captivated his attention. *Oh my god!* Her stomach turned and remaining invisible became a struggle as she discerned what the pair had meant when they said "hunting." Patrick flipped through image after image of some woman dressed only in panties chained to a tree. Dirt and leaves covered her head and body while blood coated her otherwise bare feet.

Rieka stumbled backward, then regained her balance to observe Patrick with his phone in one hand and the other in his lap. He tugged at his crotch outside his pants, growing aroused by images of this girl being held hostage. He'd not changed, after all. If anything, he'd grown worse, if such a thing was possible among psychopaths.

"Chuck, these are great!" Patrick turned her way as if sensing her seething judgment. "Hey, I gotta collect Larry here, but I'll catch up with you later. Sound good?"

"No problem, man. Listen, I've just sent you a pin drop on our exact location. Shoot me a text when you get close. I'll make sure this little hottie is ready for you."

Still on his phone, Patrick pulled up the site. He planned to drive four to five hours northeast through the Santa Lucia Range to his friend's hunting lease. Deep in the woods, she saw the girl, Emily, as Chuck unchained her from a Coulter pine tree and walked her toward a cabin.

Rieka turned her attention to Patrick as he emerged from his vehicle. Seven minutes later, with his keys in one hand and a Frappuccino in the other, he was headed back to the car with his loyal sidekick in tow for their boy's weekend. With any luck, she would be waiting for them when they arrived.

Darkness enveloped the lodge, which was secluded in a valley of chaparral and evergreens. Its isolation from civilization also precluded vehicular access, and visitors were required to travel by foot. Rieka paced around the building exterior in her lycanthrope form as she waited for Chuck's guests. Her patience paid off. At 8:30 p.m., she recognized the familiar banter between Larry and Patrick as they trekked in with their gear. They sounded obnoxious and drunk as they laughed out loud at their own jokes. She identified the clanging, mechanical sounds of bullets entering a rifle chamber. *Loading guns already?* They were miles away from any people and protected from being seen or overheard as they fired their weapons, but Rieka would also be safe from anyone hearing or seeing her when she chose to make her move.

The drunken duo loudly discussed their plans for Emily, starting with each "taking their turn with her." They'd assault her all night long and keep her from sleeping.

"She won't be able to run straight after we're done with her!" Larry said.

Patrick laughed as they dumped their bags and weaponry on the lodge's front porch. He searched for his flashlight and made his way inside, still laughing out loud at Larry's last comment, ignorant to one little glitch in their plan. Emily had been unbound and moved to a safe location neither would find without sobriety or intuition.

"What the fuck!" Patrick paced through their weekend getaway room by room a second time, colliding into furniture and overturning baskets and shelves. "Where the hell is she?"

Larry followed him, lighting votive candles along their journey.

The salesman's outrage grew with each candle until he returned to the front room, bumping into something he could not discern nor imagine. "Goddammit, Larry. Watch where you're fucking going."

"What are you talking about?"

She studied Patrick's face as he stretched out his arms to feel what impeded him. Invisible, she crouched low, then crept behind them both, blowing candles out one by one from where they'd just come, using breath from her snout.

"Larry, I swear to fucking God. Stop playing games with me or else I'll kill *you* instead."

"Brother, I'm not doing a damn thing."

Patrick turned 180 degrees as something brushed past him, ready to confront possible danger in the darkness as he reached for his recently chambered rifle. He looked confused about where to aim, though. Rieka could detect his blood pressure rising and his heartbeat racing as he struggled to make sense of his environment. This was the man she remembered, a person unable to temper his propensity for violence as his rage grew. "Something's in here with us, bro."

"Give me a sec—" Larry started.

Rieka took Larry down by his neck, rendering him incapable of finishing his sentence. Blood pulsated out his artery and filled his throat as he tried to scream, a bubbling gurgle escaping in its place. She knocked Patrick's rifle out of his hands with her paws next. She wanted as much space as possible between him and his weapon before revealing herself.

"I don't know who you are, but you need to fucking show yourself right now! What do you want from us?"

With fierce speed, Rieka transformed into her human form and secured the weapons. She relit one of Larry's candles and returned to stand in front of Align's number-one salesman who'd celebrated his success by breaking her all those years ago, pilfering a sizable amount of her soul. Dominic and Baco would be held accountable for extracting the rest of it.

"Hello, Patrick. Remember me?"

He strained his eyes as Rieka positioned the candle within their shared breathing space; whiffs of liquor and beef jerky emanated from him as he breathed through his mouth. "Where's Emily? What did you do to Larry?"

"That's not what I asked you," she said. "I asked if you recognize me. Here, let me get closer." She looked him in his eyes, and he stared straight back into hers. She waited as the light of familiarity grew with each passing second.

"You? But you died. They told me you were dead."

"Sorry to disappoint you," she said. "Speaking of disappointment, it seems your proclivities to hurt women has only grown since our last meeting. You're a real shit, you know that?"

"Screw you." He took a swipe at her.

"Too slow."

"I'll kill you again, but not before I get another taste of your fine ass!" He lurched forward but tripped and fell as Rieka side stepped beyond his grasp.

She extinguished her candle in a funnel of whirling wind and shed her human form once more. From a corner of Chuck's small lodge, she growled deep and low. She'd waited for this moment for ten years. She sat back, watching Patrick fumble from one dark section of room to another.

"You can't do this to me!" he cried.

Rieka crept forward, forcing him up against a wall where he slunk into a squatting position before extending his legs out in front of him. She pressed her muzzle into his face, now covered in beads of sweat, to breathe on him. Their shared space in Chuck's small lodge grew quiet except for the perspiration as it dripped down Patrick's chin onto this shirt.

"Please…I'm sorry."

Sure, you are. Rieka knew his words were empty. Nothing he'd ever said or done in his life had been selfless or sincere. She growled louder from the pit of her stomach. A decade's worth of anguish, betrayal, and anger gained momentum as it moved up through her throat. Standing there studying and taunting him was reaching its satisfying end. With a short but violent array of canine crying and howling, Rieka nipped, snapped, and bit at Patrick's extremities, leaving him incapacitated. For her final act of revenge, part of Rieka desired to remove his face from his skull while another part toyed with dismembering him. She changed back to her human self instead and retrieved an item from the corner of Chuck's lodge. Patrick followed her every move as she returned to kneeling in front of him. She removed a black rubber plunger no wider than a centimeter from inside an acrylic vial as she sat cross-legged opposite him on the floor.

"What are you doing?" Patrick asked. She ignored him and emptied powder onto a two-by-three-inch piece of glass. "If you think cocaine is going to hurt me, then you should guess again, doll face."

"You've spent ten years since our last meeting terrorizing women," Rieka said. "Your years of terror end tonight. This is poison, a little something a friend made for me. You work in the medical field. Tell me. What do you know about bufotenine or tetrodotoxin?" She blew the vial's powdery contents over Patrick's open wounds and into his face.

Patrick stared at her in horror.

Satisfaction pulled Rieka's mouth upward. "Yeah, from your expression, it looks like you might know a thing or two about this. You can expect your fingers and toes to start tingling in a bit as paresthesia sets in, which may lead to feelings of floating outside your body before respiratory distress becomes pronounced. Your lips, extremities, and body will turn blue in the process. What do you all call it? Cyanosis? You will enter a state of such profound paralysis and reduced metabolic rate that discerning whether you're alive or dead will be impossible to even the most well-trained physicians. By the way, police and paramedics will arrive shortly after I leave. They'll find you and poor Larry here, as well as Emily."

Patrick sat immobile, but he raised an eyebrow at the mention of Emily's name.

"Yep, she's safe. I got here first. 'Hunting?' Really? You truly are a sick piece of shit. Women are just here for your gratification and your objectification, right? Do you have any idea how easily I could tear you apart limb by limb? I gave it serious consideration but changed my mind. You don't deserve an ending like that. It's too clean, too...short. Nope, knowing you will be buried alive is so deeply appropriate for someone like you, and I must admit, it satisfies me in a way dismembering and chewing you up never could."

He whimpered as she stood back, but Rieka ignored him. She turned to collect her few belongings, and then left Patrick to reflect on whatever people like him contemplate when they realize death is imminent. Dewy, cool temperatures greeted her as she opened the cabin door. With the pain in her soul assuaged ever so slightly, she shifted her attention to finding Baco.

EPILOGUE

SUNDAY, JULY 3, 2016

SEA BASS BUBBLED in a shallow pool of extra virgin olive oil and capers as Karyn stirred her homemade marinara sauce in a separate skillet. Since discovering celebrity chef Lidia Bastianich on PBS, Karyn strove to try a new Italian recipe at least once a week. Tonight's dinner would also include a mushroom risotto—another first in her culinary adventures.

Cooking had always been a chore until recently. Now the aromas of roasting garlic and stewing Roma tomatoes instilled inspiration in the mundane and necessary act of providing food for family and friends. If she'd known how much she'd enjoy Italian peasant food, she would have tried making it years ago. Her life these days provided her with time and energy to discover what she wanted most in life, and not a moment too soon now that she was expecting her first child. She placed the bamboo spoon on the polished granite countertop while she patted her blossoming belly with her left hand.

Karyn shifted her gaze from Lidia's cookbook to an ultrasound image of her baby on the refrigerator. She knew now that she'd bear her husband a son. *I hope he'll be born with beautiful gray eyes and black curls like his father.* She smiled, thinking about her man. Her life with Baco looked vastly different from the one they'd shared more than a decade prior.

Their success had allowed them to make several luxurious changes to their lifestyle in recent years. They made regular trips to Europe and Asia and rode around in German and Swedish SUVs when they were back in Austin. Karyn worked out multiple times a week, including hot yoga, where she showed off the hourglass physique Baco had happily paid for a few years earlier. With a long, honey-wheat mane, she projected the confident, sexy image of the model she once aspired to be before traveling to Texas as a foreign exchange student. She stunned Baco with her transformation, and he catered to her every whim. He was more dutiful and loyal than she could have ever hoped.

Thunder boomed overhead, and lightning lit up their backyard, revealing a well-manicured lawn and scores of live oak trees and cedars beyond their swimming pool. Coyotes howled, which put her nerves on edge as she checked the sea bass. From his home office up front, Karyn heard Baco as he took a call on his smartphone. His tone had turned as dreadful as Mother Nature, and she felt her stomach tighten as she tried to eavesdrop.

"Everything okay?" she asked as he ambled into their kitchen a minute later with his decade-old limp.

"Patrick...remember him? From California?"

"Of course, how could I forget him?"

"He's dead."

"Passed away how? When?"

"Last weekend, I guess," Baco told her. "He was hunting with one of his buddies who was attacked by an animal of some sort. Patrick had superficial bites, but it's unclear what caused him to die. Maybe fright?"

"Like heart failure?"

"Not sure...maybe. They held a private service for him

yesterday in San Luis Obispo."

"We should go visit his wife and kids...his gravesite even."

Baco shook his head.

"What?"

"His family had him cremated."

"Oh." Karyn turned to lower the flame on her sea bass. "Wait, if they both died, who found the bodies?"

Baco opened his mouth to speak just as a door opened somewhere in their home, triggering their alarm system. Karyn studied her husband's face, and he motioned for her to stay put. He glanced back to his office trying to see the video monitors that would tell him what or who had entered their living quarters.

"What is it?" she asked.

Baco only shook his head. "The door coming in from the garage is open," he said. "I'll go close it."

"Take your gu—" Karyn started to say just as a figure appeared in their kitchen.

Confusion usurped Karyn's coyote and thunderstorm-induced anxiety from earlier as she struggled to make sense of what she saw. She would have remembered this woman's face for all her remaining days as a frozen-in-time eighteen-year-old left to rot in a shallow New Mexico grave. Karyn observed her nemesis standing across from them, very much alive, revealing a countenance void of exchanging pleasantries and hellbent on unraveling every shred of life she had devoted to weaving with her partner. Dia stared at them silently, but Karyn read her body language loud and clear: everything she and Baco held dear was about to come crashing down.

Karyn made a move to retrieve her ultrasound picture but stopped short when Dia, without ever saying a word, spontaneously transformed into something more monstrous than any coyote Karyn had ever seen. The wild creature cocked its head slowly, observing the dumfounded couple. Then it pounced upon Baco, indifferent to Karyn's screams.

A NOTE FROM THE AUTHOR

Thank you for reading *Unearthing Day,* Book One in The Lonely Hunter Series. I would love to hear what you thought about it. If you have a few moments, please consider leaving a review on Amazon.

Thank you in advance,

S.K.

CHASING DUSK SAMPLE

BOOK TWO IN THE LONELY HUNTERS SERIES

SUNDAY, JUNE 26, 2016

Scenes of Rieka's first revenge killing looped through her mind. The dusting powder she blew in Patrick's face had delivered the paralyzing effect she'd hoped for less than twenty-four hours earlier. *But did it last?* she wondered.

Sticking around to hear medics declare him dead had not been an option; she'd distanced herself from the scene of her first official crime. Rieka had to put her trust in the strength of La Loba's botany skills when imagining her murderer's final moments on Earth.

Would he suffocate slowly as gravediggers covered his coffin with dirt? Or would death come more quickly with cremation?

A smirk worked its way to the corners of her mouth, and she caught her reflection in the passenger-seat window of Kevin Howard's eighteen-wheeler as George Strait sang on the rig's radio:

Ya ever feel like you're standing in glue?
Going nowhere, yeah, man, me too
Busting your butt just trying to get ahead
Wind up tasting a little dust instead

The fifty-something-year-old truck driver shifted into second gear to turn into a truck stop off Interstate 40.

"Where are we?" Rieka asked.

"Welcome to Bellemont, Arizona, just west of Flagstaff," Kevin said, pulling into an elongated parking spot.

She glanced at the dashboard where the digital clock read 7:46 p.m. "Why is it getting dark here so early?"

"They don't observe Daylight Savings in this state. North of here, in Utah, it's closer to nine." He reached behind his seat and retrieved a black leather travel kit with frayed corners. "I'm gonna take a quick shower and grab a bite to eat before catching some shut-eye. You need anything before I head inside? If you ask me, you could use a double cheeseburger."

I could use a bath, too. "Go on ahead. I'll grab something to eat in a bit."

Kevin gave her an easy smile. "You sure? It's no problem."

Rieka shook her head.

"Okay, then." He placed a ten-dollar bill on the console. "In case you need the cash."

"You don't—"

"Please, I insist." He glanced at a polaroid clipped to his sun visor of a girl standing between two boys. "I'd want someone doing it if my daughter was hitchhiking out here." He jumped down from the cabin to the gravel-coated parking lot and shut the door quietly.

Why does kindness from random strangers always surprise me? Rieka reached for the money and pocketed it in her black leather jacket. Leaning back in her seat, she closed her eyes. Her thoughts shifted quickly to the previous night's events and the memory of Emily, who she discovered bound and gagged in Chuck's cabin. Dirt and sweat ran down the girl's arms and legs in streaks. Her tears exposed the fairness of her skin through a thick layer of grime. She'd tried to scream, her eyes bulging out of her head as Rieka broke in through a rear window.

"I'm here to help you," Rieka said, grabbing a knife from the kitchen. "Listen to me. They're coming—the men who kidnapped you. You have to go now!" She cut Emily's bindings away from her wrists and ankles.

Emily pulled the gag out of her mouth. "Where are we going?"

"Not *'we.'* Just *you.*"

"But you can't come here and just like...*half* rescue me. Don't you get it? That man took me in broad daylight from a Target two days ago! Threw me in the trunk of a car. How am I supposed to know where to go?"

Rieka scratched her head and scanned the room. The young woman made a good point. They were miles from the nearest town, but a vague memory of a building on stilts emerged as they sat there. *The deer blind.* It was less than half a mile away. "Emily, I'm going to need you to trust me. Can you do that?" Rieka asked, grabbing an Afghan off the couch and a pair of galoshes from a closet filled with board games.

"What happens if I don't?"

Rieka screwed her mouth as she draped Emily's shoulders with the blanket and escorted her outside.

"I know you're scared, believe me I do, but listen...you're going home tonight. The people who've done this to you won't be so lucky. I promise," Rieka said, leading her away from the cabin. They walked in silence for several minutes before they reached the deer blind. "Hide up here until you hear sirens and see lights. Okay?"

"Wait! You're seriously leaving me up here alone? Where are *you* going?" Emily asked.

"I'm going back to take care of the people who did this to you. I thought that was obvious."

"All by yourself? What if something goes wrong and those guys find me? Then what?"

"Again, trust me. If nothing else, hide up here until it's light enough to see where you're going."

Rieka urged Emily up the ladder and then walked off in silence. She'd hoped Emily would listen and wait until the police came before coming down from that blind. If the police had helped her, Rieka hoped Emily hadn't revealed too much about the person who'd rescued her. The girl would be traumatized for months—if not years—to come, but at least she'd go home in one piece without worse violence being inflicted upon her.

Rieka's stomach gurgled, and she opened her eyes as the sun slipped beneath the horizon. *When did I last eat?* The ten dollars in her breast pocket would come in handy after all.

She reached her arms overhead and stretched left to right, releasing a giant yawn. She'd finally had a good night's sleep. Rieka opened the passenger door and hopped down. Pebbles of gravel crunched under her feet.

Rows of sweet and salty snacks were displayed under the fluorescent lights of the Route 66 Truck Stop. Rieka would have to fight like hell to resist the temptation of packaged processed treats and seek fresh food. Shelves of freshly stocked M&Ms, granola bars, and bags of peanuts competed for her attention. *There's no way a truck driver can live long eating all this stuff.*

She scanned the top ledge for something sweet yet nutritious and spotted a box of Goodart's Peanut Patties. Rieka gasped. Her dad had loved them when she was a child. They reminded her of her family's1993 trip to Big Bend—the day everything changed for Rieka and La Loba.

The pinkish candy begged to be eaten, but its association with that fateful day left a sour taste in Rieka's mouth. She ran a finger over the bumps inside the cellophane wrapper, then walked away to the counter where a short-order cook grilled hamburgers and onions.

"I'll be right with you, ma'am," he said over the heads of two teenage girls.

They stood with their hips jutted opposite each other in double-platform sandals with red-painted toenails. One fidgeted with the hem of her cutoff shorts. The other chewed her thumbnail.

"You young ladies ready yet?" The cook stared at them with raised eyebrows and a slight frown.

The brunette on the left turned and glanced at Rieka before whispering in her friend's ear, "Do you think we could get help if we told someone?"

With her canine hearing, Rieka tuned into the girls' conversation in a way she wouldn't generally out of respect for their privacy. Something about them made her suspect, and she compared them to a younger version of herself.

"You think anyone would believe *us*? Or care, for that matter?" the girl with long black hair on the right whispered back. She had an indiscernible accent. She turned, took note of Rieka, and made brief eye contact before snapping her head back around. "Like this chick behind us…you think she can do anything? Girl, please."

"Janine!" A skinny man with two days of growth on his face and dandruff approached the girls from nowhere. He grabbed the brunette by her left elbow. "Jesus, is your mobile on silent? I've called you ten times and went straight to voicemail," he said between clenched teeth. He had a vaguely British accent. "What's taking you two so long?"

Janine wrestled her limb out of his grasp. "We'll be there *in a minute*, Lenny."

"Pick up your pace, or you won't get anything to eat until tomorrow. You understand me?" Lenny's eyes shifted right and refocused on Rieka's. "What are *you* looking at, you stupid twat? Ain't you ever seen a couple get into a row?" He pivoted on the heels of his cowboy boots to retreat as quickly as he'd appeared.

Rieka raised an eyebrow and stepped in the man's direction, then hesitated. He moved with such quick, long strides that pursuing him risked catching unwanted attention. *And I don't know if I'm up for a chase yet.*

"What's it going to be?" the cook asked.

"Two cheeseburgers with ketchup," the girl with black hair said.

"What about Darcy?" Janine asked.

"If she can't be here when it's time to order, then she's on her own."

"Jeez, Yumi. You want us to talk that way about you when you're not around?"

Yumi rolled her eyes. "I wouldn't want you gossiping behind my back. But after last month, it's every girl for herself." She reached up for their burgers and led the way out back. Both girls' heels clicked and clacked across the stone tile floor.

Rieka's appetite was gone. Dressed the way they were, the two girls had to be working as prostitutes. And Lenny reminded her of Baco, so was he their pimp? His agitation over taking so long to order food struck her as odd. It was as if he had customers waiting for them in line outside. *In a truck stop parking lot?* "Surely, johns aren't getting serviced in their trucks," she muttered.

"What's that?" Kevin asked from behind her.

"Oh, there you are."

"Came in for that burger after all, I see," he said. "Keep the ten dollars. I got this."

"Seriously, you don't have to—"

"Like I told ya, if you were my daughter—"

"Yeah, I know, but…." She hated being mean to the one person who'd helped her. "Fine. Double meat and cheese, please. You mind if I go clean up in the ladies room first?"

Kevin shrugged. When she came out five minutes later, Rieka stood at the counter and searched for her benefactor. *Where in the world did he go?* She walked past aisles of processed food, poking her head around promotional displays of Miller Lite, Doritos, and Pepsi products.

She was about to give up when the short-order cook yelled at her from the kitchen. "He took y'all's food back to the rig."

"Thank you!" Rieka called back and walked out to the parking lot.

Outside, a minuscule trace of orange light cleaved to the horizon while the rest of the heavens submitted to darkness. *I'll never find my way back to his truck,* Rieka thought. Semis filled more than three-fourths of the parking lot, making it impossible to discern Kevin's rig. Lights flickered on two of the four poles, further hampering her efforts.

"Hi, darlin'. You look a little lost. Need some help?" A man with a creepy smile asked as he studied her head to toe from his truck.

Ew. "No thanks." Rieka picked up her pace with each trailer she passed. *Where did all these trucks come from?* They were parked in tight lines of orderliness that obscured her view, and each trailer resembled the last. *Where did Kevin say he was from again? Illinois? Iowa?* She examined each license plate as she walked.

Wait. What was that?

Rieka stopped in her tracks as a woman wearing sandals and lingerie climbed into one of the cabs and pulled its door shut.

Was that the girl, Darcy, who Janine and Yumi had been talking about? Were they all in Bellemont willingly, or did Lenny serve as both pimp *and* captor to them? Part of her wanted to help if the girls were being held against their will. Really, how many people would *choose* to make a living selling their bodies at a truck stop?

No one deserved that life if they were forced into performing it. But saving every would-be prostitute wasn't exactly realistic, either. Rieka was conflicted. How would she finally get her revenge on Baco, Dominic, and Karyn if she stopped to save every person who she thought might be in trouble along the way?

Maybe Janine and Yumi were in distress, and maybe they weren't. If they were in trouble, it had to be easier to reach out for help these days. Posters about the seriousness of human trafficking now hung in public restrooms everywhere, including those at the Route 66 Truck Stop. Folks were surely more aware of an issue the media barely reported on when Rieka was a victim.

"SOMEBODY HELP ME!"

The female's voice pierced Rieka's ears, and she was immediately shaken from her thoughts. *What in the world?* Instinct told her it was the girl dressed in the equivalent of underwear. She stepped behind a set of wheels and transformed into her wolf.

Within thirty seconds, Rieka sat hunched beneath the driver's side door of the truck where the scantily clad woman had entered moments earlier. Steam coated the rig's interior windows and blocked her view. The cab lights were out too, but the door stood ajar an inch or less. *She's still up there, and you know it. Stop wasting time and make sure she's okay.*

Rieka looked left and right, then under the trucks searching for would-be witnesses. The yelling should have triggered a dozen or more truckers to check out the commotion. Were they really so indifferent?

Using her snout, Rieka nudged the door open to climb

into the truck's cabin. In the sleeper section, a middle-aged man with thinning hair and a paunch straddled the woman with a knife over his head. Rieka leaned in to release a slow, hot breath to the back of the man's neck. He swatted at his head as if shooing a bug away but didn't register the threat from behind.

His victim stared past him from the bed with eyes as wide as saucers.

"What are you looking at you stupid—" The last word caught in his throat as Rieka clamped it with her jaw. Stunned, he swung his arms in self-defense and tried to stab his attacker, but she matched his efforts by tightening her grasp up high on the man's neck. She crushed his windpipe in seconds, then retreated, leaving the man to asphyxiate.

Coming 2024

ALSO BY S.K. KARLSSON

Weaving Fate: The Lonely Hunter Series Prequel

Download free here: https://BookHip.com/ZDCGMSK

Unloading Zone

Chasing Dusk Coming 2024

ABOUT THE AUTHOR

S.K. Karlsson has been crafting stories for friends and family since elementary school. In recent years, her writing has turned professional with essays on **Medium** and episodes of the *Unloading Zone* on **Amazon Kindle's Vella platform**.

In the early 2000s, the idea for her first novel came to her in a nightmare. She dreamt of a young woman who avenged the murder of her mother. Inspired by the dark side of humanity, S.K. spent the better part of a decade researching the book you hold in your hands today, *Unearthing Day*.

Born in the Midwest, S.K. has called Texas home for nearly three decades. She is the mother to twin teenagers and returned to school in 2017 for an MBA in Healthcare Management. She splits her time between writing *The Lonely Hunter Series*, traveling, working out, and taking care of her family.

Follow her on online:
https://skkarlsson.com

www.ingramcontent.com/pod-product-compliance
Lightning Source LLC
LaVergne TN
LVHW100512110826
845146LV00002B/614

* 9 7 9 8 9 8 8 4 6 1 9 0 6 *